By Earl Thompson:

A Garden of Sand
Tattoo
Caldo Largo

THE DEVIL TO PAY

A NOVEL BY

Earl Thompson

NAL BOOKS
NEW AMERICAN LIBRARY
TIMES MIRROR
NEW YORK AND SCARBOROUGH, ONTARIO

Published simultaneously in Canada by
The New American Library of Canada Limited

NAL BOOKS TRADEMARK REG. U.S. PAT. OFF. AND FOREIGN COUNTRIES
REGISTERED TRADEMARK—MARCA REGISTRADA
HECHO EN HARRISONBURG, VA., U.S.A.

Designed by Alan Steele

SIGNET, SIGNET CLASSICS, MENTOR, PLUME, MERIDIAN
AND NAL BOOKS are published *in the United States* by the
The New American Library, Inc., 1633 Broadway, New
York, New York 10019, *in Canada* by The New American
Library of Canada Limited, 81 Mack Avenue, Scarborough,
Ontario MIL 1M8

Library of Congress Cataloging in Publication Data

Thompson, Earl.
The devil to pay.

I. Title.
PS3570.H598D4   813'.54   81-38418
ISBN 0-453-00404-0   AACR2

First Printing, October, 1981

1 2 3 4 5 6 7 8 9

PRINTED IN THE UNITED STATES OF AMERICA

Hell, I'm not going to launch this book upon the teeming literary seas without some
kind of special figurehead of passionate
personal acknowledgement to see it on its
way. It just would not be at all like me.

Let me then dedicate this to three beautiful
American graces:
   Linda Ronstadt, Emmylou Harris, and
   Dolly Parton, with the greatest pleasure
   and fondest regard.

October 8, 1978

Much Madness is divinest Sense
To a discerning Eye—
Much Sense—the starkest Madness—
'Tis the Majority
In this, as All, prevail—
Assent—and you are sane—
Demur—you're straightway dangerous—
And handled with a Chain—

—EMILY DICKINSON

Book I

One

THE OLD MAN was dying.

Dying in a homemade trailer house parked up a name-
less niggertown alley in Wichita; a white man; a pretty good
man at the end of his rope, dying as anonymously as he
had lived. He could have been any poor man dying naturally anywhere on the face of the earth. Anonymous though
his life had been, his poverty somehow made his essential
qualities universal, timeless.

Buds of snow intermittently swirled up the frozen alley,
forming little whirlwinds in the drafts between the ram-
shackle houses that fronted the streets divided by the alley.
There was hardly a house that hadn't at least a window or
two glazed with corrugated cardboard in lieu of glass. Two
wars had not ended the great depression for the people who
lived there. A poor-ass place to live and die. To *ever* have
to be. A billet in any army was preferable. The waste of an
interminable war was preferable to such poverty.

Wasn't it?

Carlson had been certain. Now he wondered.

For he perceived in the old man, his grandfather, an
integrity he had never seen so clearly in another, nor ever
felt so surely in himself.

Never mind that nothing the old man had ever said was
absolutely factual; everything he said was somehow true.

He possessed an integrity that transcended fantasy, doc-
trine, vanity (oh, yes, though bottom-of-the-bucket poor,
the old man was as vain as an exiled laird). His integrity
transcended frustration, failure upon failure, every bank-
rupt dream, rage, old age, and now death. His head could

3

have been minted on hard money—when nickels were Indian heads and nickelsilver through and through.

But step back, and objectively the old man could be mistaken for a fool, a stingy, uncaring, profane, perhaps parasitic, malcontented fool at that; one perfectly willing to let his long-suffering wife get up the necessary for as long as Carlson could remember. And he was a man not above pissing in the only sink in the house if he was not in the mood to step outside.

What the hell was it then?

A sense of humor in spite of all. An intelligence. A stubborn refusal to just be used, even if it meant letting others with a less stubborn streak work their guts out to permit him his pride.

There *was* that kind of ruthlessness in the old man.

Once when he was a boy, Carlson had sketched a pencil portrait of the old man. He had looked amazingly like a cross between Thomas Jefferson and Andrew Jackson. Carlson's teacher had remarked upon the resemblance.

The old man's attitude, bearing, manner, and truest intent were ultimately generous, magnanimous, brave.

Now he was dying of stomach cancer in a tincan niggertown alley where hungry, shivering dogs slunk along the backs of unpainted garages breathing little clouds of steam, their tails tucked down tightly to keep the cold gusts of wind from kissing their assholes.

I've destroyed better neighborhoods than this, Carlson thought.

When the old man's daughter-in-law telephoned to inquire about him, his wife spoke softly into the receiver, thinking the old man was asleep, whispering in a way that made her false teeth suck and clack. Had her false teeth ever fit properly? Carlson could not remember when they had. He did know his grandmother had paid twenty-five dollars for the teeth, and that she had had to buy them on time.

I've killed healthier, happier old people than these, he thought.

"Well, the doctor can't say, Helen," the old woman whispered into the telephone. "It could be just any time, I don't know. He hurts so bad, I think it would be a blessing. I *do*! It's been so hard. I don't think I can stand much more neither. Somebody has to be up with him all night almost. He's like a baby now, you know. Can't control himself at all. Well, Jarl's here. Yes. Came in the other night. That lets me get out a little to take care of what I have to do. I've just let everything else slide. I did get out last night to go to prayer meeting. I think it did me good . . ." Then, seeing that the old man on the narrow couch, which had once been Carlson's bed in the trailer, was awake and staring at her, she lifted her voice cheerfully. "Daddy, it's Helen! She wants to know what you want for Christmas."

The old man's strong features were sharper for the skin being drawn more tightly over his big bones. "Tell her I won't be here Christmas," he barked, rolling fully upon his side, plunging his hands down between his wasted thighs beneath the covers and staring blankly at the fire in the gas heater next to which Carlson sat on a straight chair, looking at the local evening newspaper. He could see the fire flicker in the old man's eyes and wondered what memories the old man was choosing to see now that he was sure he would be dead within a few weeks or days.

"Oh, he drove here from Missouri," the old woman spoke into the phone. "He's got a fifty-one Ford car. Drove here straight from that Army job. It's so much easier since Jarl's here, oh yes. He really doesn't seem to mind sittin' with him all the time. He hasn't even called any of his old pals since he got here. Maybe he's growin' up. But I hoped when he got back from Korea he would settle down and *do* something. He says he maybe ain't even staying in the Army. I just can't make head nor tail of what he's after, if anything. But then, like I say, I don't hardly understand nothin' about nothin' no more . . . Okay. I'll tell him. Bye."

She put down the phone and stood puzzled a moment as if trying to remember something. Her fingers fussed at the neck of her housedress. Then she gave up and said, "Shoot."

"What's the matter?" Carlson asked.

"Oh, there's something I wanted to remember or do, and I can't think . . . Helen says 'hello.' But that ain't it.

5

They are lookin' forward to seeing you at Christmas. You'll be able to meet your cousin Sam's wife. They have a little boy now and another on the way. Real little scamp too. He's as hardheaded and stubborn as Sam, and Sam's getting more like his grandpa every day."

Carlson felt a familiar twinge of jealousy. No one had ever said *he* was like the old man. The old man was the measure of all men within the known family. He had once turned a stampeding herd of cattle on the old Chisholm Trail, and had been a deputy marshal in Dodge City when Dodge was a railhead for cattlemen, and had never had to shoot anyone. He had been captured and held a few days by the Doolin gang from Oklahoma. He beat them all at four-handed pitch, ate their bacon and beans and biscuits, and was let go free on his word to let them have a day's head start. They hadn't done anything around Dodge to be arrested for and the old man had decided they were a more decent bunch of men than most of the bankers, lawyers, and businessmen in the town. He rode back and resigned, and went out near Rocky Ford to homestead. That was the gist of how he told the tale.

"Sam might not have gotten along with teachers at school," the old woman rattled on, "but he's doing real good, you know. He's the best body-and-fender man Martin's got. And he's almost a year younger than you. He only works on Cadillacs," she added with great pride.

Carlson's cousin had left school at fifteen to marry a girl about fourteen. He remembered at the time the old woman had complained that the girl was a Catholic.

Hurrah for Sam! I would volunteer to go kill again to keep from being a body-and-fender mechanic, Carlson thought. And the words he wanted to say to the old woman filled his throat as other words had so many times before. *Don't you understand? Don't you care? How much have I learned that Sam will never know? Shit.* He said nothing.

"Well," the old woman sighed, "I reckon I ought to do something about supper." She looked without enthusiasm at the end of the trailer where the little hot plate sat beneath an end window with a battered kettle on it.

"I'm not hungry," Carlson said.

6

The stench in the trailer was terrible. After he had first arrived, Carlson had almost gagged from the smell of the old man. He had opened the window and his grandmother had protested, "Daddy always complains he's cold. I got to keep the gas on all day and all night. I got the electric blanket on him too, but it's old and only heats a little. I think some of the little wires are broke in it. I washed it in Helen's machine. The man who sold it to me at Sears *said* you could wash it."

Carlson had put another blanket on the old man and left the window open a crack.

"Fresh air will do him good," he'd told the old woman.

When the old man looked at him, it was as if he were trying to place the young man in his memory. A small light of seemingly angry fear in the old man's pale gray eyes indicated that he thought Carlson might hurt him. The look sponsored such a rush of tenderness that Carlson lay his hand on the old man's grizzled cheek and offered: "In a day or so, when you feel better, Granddad, I'll give you a shave."

"I ain't never gonna feel no better and I know it," the old man said, looking the young man levelly in the eyes. "Nobody's fooling me for a minute."

"I'll give you a good shave anyway," Carlson insisted. "That will make you feel a little better."

"You still in the Army?" the old man husked.

"I am, Granddad. I just came for a visit with you."

"Visit." The old man coughed painfully, feebly thumping himself on the chest, and cleared his throat of phlegm.

"Now, Daddy, don't rile yourself," the old woman warned.

"You sure you don't want no supper?" she asked Carlson. "I'll be happy to fix something."

"No, thanks, Grandma. Maybe I'll go out after a while and get a hamburger. You ought to go out yourself for a little while. Why don't you go down to the corner and have something at the White Castle? It would do you good."

"I don't like to spend good money to eat in restaurants. Everything's so blamed high nowadays. Anyway, it's snowin'."

7

"It's about stopped. Just little wisps anyway."

"Aw . . . there's always a bunch of smartalecky colored boys in there now."

"Do they bother you?"

"No . . . But I just don't feel comfortable."

"Go on. I'll give you the money."

"Well, I 'spect you *need* your money. And I don't *like* eatin' alone," the old woman whined childishly. "And it's *cold* out. I might slip down. I *did* last winter. I was crippling around for two weeks. I could break my hip. Pearl Raskin's mother slipped and broke her hip, you know. On the way to church. Right on her front steps. She died. Mrs. Marsh—you remember, at church—she used to teach your Sunday school class, she slipped and broke her hip when you was in Korea, and they put in a metal one as good as new. She said it cured her rheumatism too. Oh, they can do miracles nowadays, if you got the money . . ." She was lost in a reverie of unlimited spare parts.

"Go on, Grandma," Carlson persisted. "Don't try to cook tonight. Here." He hauled out a couple of dollars and gave them to the old woman.

She was reluctant to take the money, and she was a bit flustered at being made to go out when she really did not want to. "That's too much! I could never eat that much. I'll just take a dollar and I'll probably bring back change."

"Okay."

"You were never any better at managing money than the rest of this family. You always did have a hole in your pocket."

He held her old coat with a fox collar so worn he could see the dead doggie hide through the fur. Someone she had worked for had given it to her. She had shortened it once to make it more fashionable.

He tucked the old woman's ratty collar up close beneath her stubborn little chin and peered through her bifocals into her small frosty blue eyes. There was nothing to say to her. There never had been.

"Take a flashlight," he reminded her, and got one for her.

He went out to hand her down the rickety steps. "Take your time," he advised.

"I'll probably slip and break my hip. Then won't we be in a fix, with nobody to do nothin'?"

Carlson sat there with the gas fire for light, watching the old man sleep, seeing the hump of his shadow on the cracked, buckled, ply-faced wall. There was ice on the small window above the old man's head. He had always looked so large to Carlson. Now he seemed an ordinary-sized old man who was dying. He groaned as a wave of deep, gut-ripping pain washed over his face. His lips trembled. A tear or two were squeezed from his eyes.

"Mama!" he called, panic gripping his voice.

"She went out for a bite to eat, Granddad. It's me, Jarl."

"*Mama!*" he called as if he hadn't heard.

Carlson touched him. "I'm here, Grandpa. It's me, Jarl. Can I help you?"

The old man rolled his head toward his grandson. His eyes found him and focused painfully. "Where's Mama?"

"She went to get something to eat up at the White Castle. She'll be right back. Do you want anything?"

His large, shaking hand reached out and Carlson took it. The old man's hand gripped fiercely—he was still re-markably strong—and he bore down as the crab's pincers bit painfully into his bowels.

"*Lord-Lord!*" he cried when the pain began to pass. Using breath that might be the last, he swore: "*Goddamn! Such a goddamn way of doin'!* I just got no control over myself, son. It's just as well I'm dyin'. I don't want to go on no more like this." He looked sheepishly apologetic, yet angry too. "I just messed all over myself," he con-fessed.

They came for the old man in the morning—two young men who operated the county's ambulance—to take Carl-son's grandfather to the hospital to die.

"Well, you won't be having to bring me back," the old man said, joshing the boys. When they made perfunctory sounds of protest at his contention, he said: "Hell, I know it. It's okay. You fellas don't have to feel responsible for anything on my behalf. At least I outlived that goddamned Roosevelt!" He chuckled at his victory. "But that Ike's another one. Truman was the only goddamned decent man we've had in the White House since Lincoln. And I ain't *all* that sure about Mr. Lincoln. But Harry was all right, by God."

The boys were not interested in the old man's politics.

At the door the old man reached up and touched his wife's hand. "Mama."

"What?"

"I can't go like this."

"What is it, John?"

He whispered shyly, "I don't have no britches on."

"It's okay, old-timer," one of the ambulance attendants said.

"No. Hold it," Carlson said. He got the old man's everyday pants—patched as a coolie's—and rolled them into a bundle. The cloth felt soft as velvet. He tucked them beneath the blanket where the old man could feel them.

"I love you, Grandpa," he said, touching the old man's face. He had never said that to the old man before. He wanted him to know it.

They buried the old man within the week. The laborers had to use jackhammers to break up the frozen surface of the ground. Old men and women, friends of his grandfather's Carlson had not seen since he was a boy, journeyed from the funeral home to the cemetery to stand around clasping their hands in the sunny cold while the old man's casket was put down. Their breaths were a collective steam in the old man's honor. It was the best funeral Carlson had ever attended. It really did seem all right. An old black man in overalls, a vintage corduroy sheepskin-lined coat, his nappy gray hair sticking out in tufts from a plaid cap with earflaps, stepped out of the crowd around the grave, tugged off a wool mitten, and gave Carlson his big, gnarled hand. He searched Carlson's eyes, his own

10

eyes still hard and deep though he was nearly as old as the old man.

"I was around when you was born," he said. "But likely you don't remember me. Used to shake you down ripe persimmons. You sure did like them 'simmons. Keep me from doin' my work goin' after persimmons for you. I'm Zeke. Me and your granddaddy built this cemetery with mules before you was born. I got me a plot over there too. They gave us plots instead of all our money. Lots of us worked here sold theirs off, but like Mr. Mac, I kept mine for me and my family. Your granddaddy was a pretty good man, boy. I hopes you always remember that."

"Yes, sir. I think I will."

Zeke had not been ashamed to show up in the clothes he had to wear, nor speak as if he was one of the family, which, of course, in a real way he was.

Touching. The ability to be truly touched, to touch truly, that was a big part of love, wasn't it? Not that Carlson had ever been certain what he meant by "love."

There was the sweet-sad, all-encompassing feeling he had for the whole world, all mankind, and in a heightened sense for some individuals. But he never could get sex and love absolutely straightened out. *Oh, I can sort it out intellectually,* he thought. *But in the doing of either or both, I get pretty mixed up. Maybe I do rather love everyone I fuck. . . .*

When the funeral was over and the old man's friends had finished whispering their soft words of comfort to his grandmother, Carlson put his arm around the old woman and led her to his car for the ride home.

The radio was tuned to something called the "Bible School of the Air." A divinity-candy-voiced woman wanted to know:

"And what is the shortest verse in the Bible, children?"

"Jesus wept!" Carlson was right there.

"That right. John Eleven-Thirty-Five. Jesus wept!"

"I don't blame him," Carlson told the lady.

Two

THREE TRAINING COMPANY first sergeants were having breakfast at a table in the club bar when Carlson walked in. It was his first morning back at the base since his grandfather died. The club was warm, clean, and inviting; the first sergeants were not. One of them said loudly, "Now there's one sonofabitch who has it made in this mothering Army."

Many of the older noncommissioned officers resented Carlson's boyish resemblance to a clerical corporal walking around wearing his first sergeant's jacket. In town or on leave, if the military police did not know him, he was often stopped and challenged to justify the six stripes and diamond on each sleeve of his blouse.

"You should be a fucking officer, Carlson," an old sergeant major confided over his breakfast at the club bar; the man had been a reserve major during World War II and had remained in the Army at his permanent rank. "You look like a fucking officer," the sergeant major said, "except there ain't that spoiled innocence and arrogance in your eyes. You think like a pretty damned good officer. And worst of all, you walk like a fucking officer. If I don't have my glasses on and see you coming, with that tension in your right shoulder, my body tightens up and I get ready to salute. If I'm doing that, everyone is doing that. You got an AGCT score higher than any general in the goddamned Army—maybe you're a genius, Carlson —but you ain't ever going to be a commissioned officer because you did everything too young. You enlisted too young, got married too young, divorced too young. Shit,

Carlson, what kind of genius is paying child support when they are sixteen?"

"I know," Carlson agreed. "I come from the kind of people who do everything too young."

"Right! And your psychological profile—Christ, it looks like a cartographer's elevation of the Alps." He traced twin peaks in the air with his right hand as high as he could reach sitting down. "In the areas of sensitivity you go higher than any WAAC and in the area of action you'd out-speak Patton." He thought a moment, rubbing his considerable belly against the bar reflectively. "I knew Patton. If they were doing psychological profiles when he was your age, I'd bet a year's pay and allowances his would look like yours. But it's a new Army, son, and even though you got it made now, you ain't got a good future in it. It'll break your fucking heart. I like you. That's why I'm telling you this."

Carlson knew. He had to reach a decision soon. He was twenty-three years old, and though by military measure he had it made, he had to think about his future.

He liked the Army, goddammit. That was the problem. Korea had been a rude, ugly, disappointingly stupid experience, the only war he had ever been in, but he had spent the last nine years of his life in the military, with only a year out of it to get into trouble, and he could honestly tell himself that he had found a home in the Army.

His office was on the choice front side of the headquarters building, on the second floor, overlooking the flagpole and the sunset gun. The lawn was covered with a neat coating of snow, the only area still white around headquarters. All asphalt surfaces had been carefully cleaned and shone wetly in the cold winter sun.

He liked the neatly kept lawn in front of headquarters, the floor of his office waxed nightly, gleaming now in neat swirls of an electric buffer. The large post flag wafted lazily on the morning's slight breeze. A training company with rifles at port arms double-timed down the street smartly toward some training class, the field first sergeant counting out the accelerated cadence loud enough to be heard by every man in the four platoons. Good-looking company, Carlson noted. Then: Hell, that's Charley, his old company! They were still looking sharp. Sergeant Olson had them coming along. Keeping up the tradition of excellence Carlson had established. Looking good, Carlson thought, and watched until his old unit had double-timed around the corner, the guidon bearers out at the intersection as roadblocks. Charley Company never stopped for vehicles and double-timed every mothering step it took in eight weeks.

The training company had been his first assignment after being shipped to the United States from Korea and returned to duty after eighteen weeks in Letterman Hospital at the Presidio where he'd had a beautiful view of San Francisco Bay and the Golden Gate Bridge.

Carlson took over the company knowing that the first eight weeks of a soldier's training were the most important in his military life and accordingly set a pace more along the lines of the Marine Corps or Paratroopers than Army regulations required. Chaplains came to transmit the complaints of some of his men, angry letters were sent to congressmen and to the inspector general, service club hostesses telephoned his commanding officer to complain that Carlson's men could not, in violation of their rights, come to the service club, as men of other training units were able to do.

Other first sergeants threatened to whip Carlson's ass if he ever let one of his companies come over into their company area on graduation night after Charley Company had again won the best training company streamer for its guidon. On those nights, Charley Company Fiftieth was generally hell-bent on turning less proficient companies out of their bunks, usually destroying governmental property when the fight ensued. Charges were sometimes filed. After Carlson's last and most successful training company had turned Baker Company out in a hailstorm in its underwear, including cadre and its first sergeant—a big, black, fifteen-year man who subsequently did whip Carlson's ass—Carlson was given a very casual little court-martial, fined ten dollars, and restricted to the post during duty hours for one week—no lunches in town with the girls from the dental clinics that week—and the proceedings would be on his record. But he had turned out seven consecutive best training companies, sent more men to NCO, and officers training schools than any other first sergeant, confident that the men he sent would be good leaders and more importantly might survive war and contribute to the survival of others. The top of the staff of the company guidon looked as if it was a roost for a congregation of long-tailed roosters, the many-colored streamers all but hiding the company pennant.

Yet it was not for streamers that he trained his companies so hard. When a man was assigned to "C. Co." some wag reading the orders in Receiving Company always concluded by saying, "You better give your hearts to God, meatheads, because your miserable asses definitely belong to Charley Company. You better go take a nice walk right now because you ain't going to walk again nowhere for eight motherfuckin' weeks."

He trained the men so hard because every first sergeant received monthly follow-up reports on how men he had trained were doing in the Army, and from the first cycle, Carlson's men had fewer casualties, fewer serious incidents, fewer crack-ups, more promotions and positive citations than men trained in any other company on the post. And more of them stayed alive. In combat, Carlson knew, you stayed alive by being able to fight well.

It was success with his training companies that had gotten Carlson selected to be the first enlisted adviser on the general's staff—an idea that came down from the Pentagon with the nebulous goal of making the Army more democratic, or something. It was never precisely clear to anyone what his advice was supposed to achieve.

Carlson had no one to whom he had to report or account to for anything, other than the general. He also soon discovered he actually had very little to do. His assignment, office, function, were just Army eyewash. His job was a good idea no one except himself intended to take seriously.

At first, he had gotten a jeep and driver from the motor pool every morning and dropped in on training companies, classes, maintenance facilities, mess halls—he was everywhere, unannounced, taking few notes at the time, counting on his good memory to write up his reports for the general. The top two drawers of his file cabinet were full of neat reports and suggestions he had sent on to the general, all duly processed, properly stamped, endorsed, always replied to, often with a complimentary note of acknowledgment executed for the general by one of his office staff. There was now a letter of commendation in Carlson's 201 personnel file for his work.

But only three of his suggestions of any substance had been implemented on the post. The last to be cut as an order was the first suggestion he had filed, and then only after a trainee demounting the bayonet from his rifle had run the blade up through his chin into his brain. Carlson had always made his trainees remove bayonets from their rifles by sticking them into the ground before trying to free them—the catch often opened up and then the blade came off as a surprise. It was not an elegant military movement, two hundred soldiers sticking their bayonets into the ground, then bending down to work the catches; small pebbles in the earth sometimes scratched the dull finish of the new, short, more efficiently daggerlike blades, but there was no way anyone was going to stab himself. Officers did not like to see two hundred bayonets with rifles on them stuck into the ground and two hundred soldiers' asses stuck up in the air. There was no way to execute the maneuver by the numbers.

There had been a dozen accidents involving men removing bayonets from their rifles since Carlson had filed his first report as the general's enlisted adviser, and it took the death of an eager little black enlistee—not a draftee—out of Georgia, no older than eighteen, before Carlson's observation was made a training order.

Carlson and the general had seen the kid in the emergency room of the post hospital, already dead, the eight-inch blade of the bayonet in his head to the hilt, the handle beneath his chin like Pharaoh's beard, an everlasting look of surprise frozen on his otherwise unseeing, dark round eyes. The general had asked a surgeon present, "You aren't going to bury him with that thing in him like that, are you?" He was assured the bayonet would be removed, which seemed to give the general ease. In his car on the way back to headquarters he offered Carlson an expensive cigar in an aluminum tube and remembered that Carlson had sent him something about the dangers in the way trainees handled their bayonets. Carlson repeated his suggestion in a sentence. The general nodded. "I guess it doesn't matter that it is unmilitary and looks like shit until they are more familiar with their equipment. I'll have an order cut immediately." He was good as his word and the cigar was an Upmann's.

Carlson still wrote out his reports, but by January, 1954, he was spending most of his time reading during what should have been duty hours. The post librarian said he might well read every book in the place if he continued to have such a wonderful job. He had read so much he had grown bored with reading and had begun to try to write—a story about Korea. It was awful. He knew at least enough about writing to know the story was dreadful, and that if he intended to write well he would have to have some better instruction in the discipline than he could get from a book.

The idea of trying to write a story was part of the decision he knew he must make. It fit in with an idea he had to attend helicopter pilots' school. Carlson wanted options.

He had talked about his notion of being a correspondent with a post librarian, an older woman with twenty years in Special Services, and who now was jeopardizing her retirement pension by being in love with a hillbilly corporal young enough to be her son. She had been encouraging, pointing out that the state university, only ninety miles away, had one of the most renowned schools of journalism in the country.

It was true Carlson had only a formal eighth-grade civilian education. But from the first, when he was still a private, the Army had sent him to all manner of schools.

His high AGCT scores assured his commanding officers that he would do well and his graduation would look good on their unit records. He had been to four different leadership schools, all sorts of advanced combat training courses. He had completed correspondence courses from the Army general school for officers up through the rank of captain while he was still a corporal, been tested and awarded equivalency certificates for both a high school diploma and a year of college. He had even successfully completed an extension course in political science offered by the University of Maryland at Heidelberg University in Germany.

How many schools had he gone through since he was a private? Seven—nine? Plus a stint on the boxing team in Germany to have time to work on U.S. Armed Forces Institute correspondence courses in algebra, German, and mechanical drawing. The German was the only course he had not completed with a good passing grade. Something else he could not learn from a book, he'd decided. He had gotten knocked out in the EUCOM semifinals by a novice middleweight from Puerto Rico with an ability to hook with either hand and a pound of scar tissue above his eyes in lieu of eyebrows. Carlson came to after that one with a broken nose, his throat tasting of puke, honestly wondering if USAFI certificates for algebra and mechanical drawing—he had already given up on the German—were worth that much. Otherwise, he was in the best physical condition he had ever been.

By the time his nose had healed he was on orders to be returned temporarily to the United States to participate in one of the first classes of forty officers and noncoms chosen for special combat training. The idea behind the course was that Regular Army men of various ranks would be put through this exotic and demanding training toward making them perfect all-round soldiers. They would go back to their parent units, upgrading those units' effectiveness, and would also form a nucleus of highly trained men who could be called upon individually or collectively for special and dangerous missions requiring a high degree of skill, judgment, discipline, leadership, self-motivation, and techniques for survival. Possibly, they would also be used to operate alone in enemy-held territory in case of renewed hostilities.

Only one man, a young lieutenant, failed to complete the training, dying of heat exhaustion during the third week. All rank was held in abeyance during this period. The man snoring in the bunk next to Carlson's was the ranking officer in the course, a paratrooper major from Brooklyn with the best-conditioned little 135-pound body since an Italian chiseled David out of a rock.

The day they all ran fifteen miles, the major was the man in front of Carlson. They ran in shorts, T-shirts, paratrooper boots, and fatigue caps. On the boxing team Carlson had run seven miles every morning and three every afternoon wearing boots and a sweat suit, his head wrapped in towel; he also worked out and sparred every afternoon. Yet there were times during those fifteen miles when he was running against the pain in his mind and body. So when he saw the barracks ahead at the end of the fifteen he rejoiced. He knew everyone running with him felt the same way. Then the paratrooper physical training instructor who had run with them said, just as they drew abreast of the barracks, expecting to hear the command to halt, *"Okay! We do fifteen more!"* and ran them right on past the barracks, back onto the road.

Carlson soon grew to hate the tidy major's goddamned back—he knew every mark and blemish on his neck, how his hair grew—he hated his mechanical, never-faltering little striding legs like a fucking soccer player's; his arm action made Carlson want to kill the man. His hatred focused on the major, not on the paratrooper physical training instructor or the system that had led to their being run right past the barracks. He wished the little major with the hairy soccer player's body and dark circumcised dick would fall down dead—knowing he could not even have stopped to rest under the guise of helping the man.

Then, somewhere in the last five miles or so of the second fifteen, he felt a rush of love for the major, for all the men running together, that surpassed anything he had ever in his life felt so clearly for another human being. It had nothing to do with sex, blood, or anything he had known in the realm of spiritual brotherhood. He saw the major's little racehorse back and shoulders and legs pumping methodically, his olive drab shorts and undershirt dark with his sweat, and Carlson knew that neither of them was going to stop if they ran forever, that they and all those there would run themselves to death before they would stop unless they were stopped. It did not matter that to run yourself to death would be stupid, that there had been a time back during the second fifteen he had thought seriously that all of them had been chosen by the Army as some kind of defectives who were being used in an experiment to see how much of such training it would take to kill them. No one had made much over the young lieutenant's death. If that was what the Army was up to, then he would run right to the end, extend their study beyond any estimate of human endurance. Happy. That was it. He was happy and as determined as he had ever been. There was an old masturbatory joke when he was a boy in which the punch line ran: "Don't care if I do die, do die, do die." It sang in his brain.

The barracks again came in sight. He heard himself croak aloud, *"Count cadence count!"* Everyone, the majority of men outranking himself and nearly half of them officers, found voice to crack out the cadence with each step twice. He saw the instructor look at him as if he was crazy. There was even a glint of fear in the man's eyes. Then someone else shouted, *"Count cadence count!"* They did it again. Again. They came up the street counting out the cadence at the top of their abused lungs like a bunch of recruits. Carlson's lungs felt on fire. His lungs had felt on fire for miles. It was insane, but it was beautiful.

When they were halted and dismissed they began to laugh and fall on each other, hugging whoever was nearest, laughing, gasping for air; some collapsed on the ground but most did not. Their eyes were washed with tears and running with the stinging sweat from their brows. Everyone's face seemed drawn almost to the bone with pain. Yet they also tried to laugh. Carlson grabbed the major, hugging him; the major grabbed Carlson and they held each other up. They smelled as if every stinking thing in their bodies had been brought to the surface. Carlson felt absolutely clean, in mind and body. Everything he looked at appeared to have an aura so bright he had to keep moving his eyes, as one does when looking near the heart of the sun. He shouted right in the major's face, "Rosen, you're fucking beautiful!" The major shouted back, "So are you, Carlson!"

They received no special insignia or badge for their completion of the course. But in their personnel files there would be a signal that they were a special soldier in the Army's combat repertoire.

In time Carlson knew he would be promoted to the rank of warrant officer with the rights and privileges of a commissioned officer. But he could not as a warrant officer ever be considered a gentleman or hold a combat field command. He could not in a million years become a general or even a colonel. He could only become a chief warrant officer with major's pay.

By going through helicopter pilots' school—helicopters had been seen in Korea to be the cavalry of the future—he could graduate as a warrant officer and could expect promotion to chief warrant within three years. Major's pay at the age of twenty-six or twenty-seven was not bad. He could retire in twenty-one years with three-quarters pay and still only be forty-four, or retire in eleven years at thirty-four with half-pay.

He looked at the stack of books from the library on his desk. There were Kafka, Shaw, Joyce, Steinbeck, Fletcher Pratt's *A Short History of the American Civil War*, and a Britisher's well-written account of the contest in North Africa during World War II between Rommel and O'Connor, in which they fought each other back and forth with equal genius, more often using the captured supplies and equipment of the other than those initially charged to them, so that an uninformed observer would have been hard put to figure out which side represented the Axis powers and which the Allied. Latter-day consensus held that the best two modern field commanders were Rommel and Patton, but Carlson thought just as good a case could be made for O'Connor, and that only his subsequent capture by the enemy in a later campaign and Montgomery's ridiculously puffed publicity in Africa had left O'Connor's achievements sadly overlooked and unhonored.

Carlson cared about the men who fought wars, particularly that one man in seventeen in a modern army who actually did find himself in a position to have to consider the possibility of facing a real enemy who might kill him.

He liked very little of what had been written about Korea. The press almost always had it wrong. Like that nonsense about the Turkish brigade wiping out a North Korean division with naked bayonets. Oh, those fierce Turks! Oh, they were fierce enough, especially when their mobile military whorehouses were far behind their positions. Going through a village they had occupied for a while was not a pretty thing to see. A reading of T. E. Lawrence on such matters still applied in Korea. They had never wiped out a North Korean division with bare steel, not that they might not or would not, given the opportunity, but they never had such a chance in Korea. It was a United Nations division of South Koreans which the Turks went after with their bayonets when the Chinese came down during MacArthur's great Thanksgiving offensive.

The great battle occurred on the day Carlson's division lost eight miles; the poor South Koreans, who had taken the brunt of the Chinese counterattack, were pushed back onto the Turks' bayonets, as the Turks were coming up to the fight from where they had been held in reserve. The Turks thought the South Koreans were North Koreans or just did not give a damn. Yet some people still wrote about the Turks' old-fashioned victory. There were hardly enough First Republic of Korea troops left after that one to muster, what with the Chinese in front and on their sides, and the Turks busy at their behinds with bayonets.

That was the trouble with Korea, it was hardly ever

the way you read about it in the newspapers or heard about it over the radio. General MacArthur only spoke to God and to General Almond, and if his decisions were the product of those discussions, none of the three knew a tenth as much about the kind of war they were trying to fight as did General Smith of the U.S. Marines. Smith commanded the only American units in Korea, which always came out intact as units, bringing their wounded with them, fighting every step of the way.

Carlson thought he would like to write about such things, as he knew and observed and try to get them down straighter than others had gotten them down.

Yet Carlson loved the Army, although he cared for it like the writer Nelson Algren wrote about caring for a city like Chicago: it was like loving a woman with a broken nose. "There are many lovelier lovelies, but never a lovely so real." Carlson had known few lovelies that were any other kind.

Three

AT 1000 HOURS he took his medical forms from his desk, put on his cap, squared it over his eyes, and headed for Dental Clinic No. 1 to complete his medical exam with an up-to-date dental survey to forward with his application for helicopter pilots' school.

Captain Heco would do the survey, Marge, the dentist's assistant, told Carlson. He had gone out with Marge several times. He always thought of her as Marge No. 1, for there was another Marge he used to see who worked at Dental Clinic No. 2.

"Sergeant Cat," Marge No. 1 said, "I've missed you. It's been a while."

He studied her. If she weren't a hillbilly from Missouri, she might have been a movie star. She had won the post Jane Russell Look-Alike Contest. Curiously, Marge from Dental Clinic No. 2 had taken second place. When he had met both Marges he thought they were sisters. Many people assumed they were. They were both brunettes and wore their hair in similar Jane Russell look-alike styles. Marge No. 2 was considerably larger, almost five nine. She could never have children, information which she always passed on in an intimate moment in such a dolefully remorseful way it made her general passivity boring. She never had orgasms, she claimed, nor cared much about doing so. She was what Carlson would call "affectionate." Marge No. 1 was "passionate." She was as direct about her enjoyment of sex as she was about everything else. "Sometimes I wish I had another hole somewhere that ain't been used yet," she told him once. She had been married very young and had a little boy who lived with her parents on their hard-scrabble farm.

"Sergeant Cat, I like it all," she would say, stretching herself like a cat. "All the way, any old way, all the time."

"You're the only man in a long while who understands me and don't put me down," she had told him early on, after they had made it together an amazing seventh time one night. "I can raise a cock given up for dead and I can sing like some bird. I coulda been a good singer like Pretty Kitty Wells if I'd had coachin' and practice. You sure got small hands for a man, you know that? I wonder . . ." And he had been able to get his entire hand inside her, make a fist as she began to move on it, feel the dense, naturally dark hair of her cunt tickle his wrist. Her vagina could hold a man's cock as if it had gums.

"How about tomorrow night?" he asked.

Marge smiled, reaching out to run her fingertips lightly over his lips. "You're too pretty to be a first sergeant and too good to be an officer," she told him. "Why don't you let me adopt you and you can just lay around the house and read and watch TV and wait for me?"

"Now *that* is what I would call having it made." He grinned.

They went in to see the dentist.

Captain Heco was the dentist Marge most often assisted. He was finishing up his military service requirement after graduating from dental school and he did not like the Army. He was from California where his parents had been interned during the Second World War because they were Japanese. Captain Heco had been in Korea. He had been the dentist who put Carlson's front teeth back in with a strong, civilian-style, real-gold bridge. They had snapped off inside his gas mask while he was leading one of his former training companies in a tear-gas assault on a village called Dodge City, which had been built on the post for the purpose of demonstrating techniques of house-to-house and street fighting.

Carlson had met Marge No. 1 when he was in Captain

Heco's chair. She had happily joined in their conspiracy to replace his white metal military bridge with one of gold that would have cost Carlson four hundred dollars in civilian life. The captain used porcelain teeth, too, rather than plastic. He had giggled happily over being able to do good work and screw the Army while he was at it. "Now you have as good a bridge as anyone," the captain said, admiring his work. And that night Carlson had gone out with Marge.

"I won fifty bucks playing golf with the general," Captain Heco cheerfully announced when Carlson was in his chair.

"That must be why he wants to send the clubs he had back to Special Services and get another set," Carlson said.

"I could make a living playing golf with that sausage." Captain Heco grinned.

"Not for long. You'd find yourself on orders for Alaska."

"Yeah," the captain agreed sadly. "You can never have it made in this Army too long. I want Marge to give you a little device so you can insert dental floss under your bridge. Otherwise, Sergeant, you're in good shape. Are you really going to re-up and go to that chopper school?"

"I don't know." He had started to say "sir" but remembered Captain Heco did not like being called "sir." "I'm still trying to make up my mind. Maybe I'll go back to school."

"Well, whatever you do, be sure to floss regularly. Your early dental care was so bad you are going to have to take care of your teeth and gums or you are going to have trouble."

He thanked the captain and they shook hands.

So he and Marge No. 1 spent Friday and Saturday night running up and down old Highway 66, hitting the roadhouses, strip joints, and steak joints, dancing, laughing, loose and loud, and then every night between her sheets, Marge's brown-nippled tits flying around every which way as she ran through an exhausting repertoire of positions, sometimes impossible and hilarious improvisations, both of them coming loudly and obscenely, happily, her big-lipped dark cunt dripping on the sheets, the bed looking afterward as if there had been a fight in it.

"What you oughta goddamned do . . ." Marge No. 1 stopped beating up the pillows and turned to put her arms around him, pressing tightly against him, motoring her pelvis gently but provocatively as she always did. "What you oughta do, soldier, is re-up, go to that whirlybird school, and marry me."

Such a possibility had never crossed Carlson's mind. He was surprised she could think of such a thing. "I thought you liked big cocks," was all he could think to say.

"I like big cocks," she admitted. "I like cock, period. But I like the person they're hung on more than their size, or it's just cock and I ain't never marryin' a cock. I like you, Carlson. Maybe I love you. Feels like. You always treat me real nice, like a lady, whether we go out or stay in. You always talk to me like I had good sense. And I *do!* Only nobody hardly ever notices it except you and Captain Heco." She nibbled Carlson's face. "And I'll tell you something that might surprise you, whether you believe it or not. I wouldn't fuck around on you if I was anywhere I could get to you when I wanted you, even if it took me a week. And if I couldn't get you in a week— hell!—ten days . . . *two* weeks . . . maybe a month—and I did jump on someone, it wouldn't be because I liked the guy more'n you, it would only be 'cause I felt congested and needed to get my rocks off. It would be purely therapeutic."

He held her close, smiled, gently joggled the ass that took first place in the Jane Russell Look-Alike Contest and said, falling into her way of speaking: "I sure do love the way you are."

She kissed him. "And you really like me too. I know," she said.

"I really do," he said. "I really like you, Marge. You're just *fine!*"

She tried to snuggle closer, though they were about as

27

close as they could get. "That's because I'm honest," she decided. "I'm always honest. You're not the prettiest man or the best lay I ever had, but there ain't been no one man I ever thought I could live with 'cept you. Oh, my house wouldn't be all spic and span and little flounces. And I probably can't cook a lot of fancy dishes. But, shit, you grew up pretty strong and smart on the kind of cookin' I can do. And you just look me in the eye and tell me true if any women satisfies you all around like I do."

He had to admit it was true, the warmth coming up from his testicles—or he should say testicle, for his left one had been damaged in Korea, and though it had swollen up large as a grapefruit at the time, it was now about the size of a first-class grape and probably no longer functional. The warmth flooded his heart, rose to his brain, which always felt washed with cool Ozark piny-woods air when he and Marge spent time together; she was the only woman he had ever known with whom he felt entirely free to be himself.

He knew that in civilian clothes he looked like a midwestern university student, and that his boyish face did not jibe with his first sergeant's zebra stripes. Naked, his tattoos made some women wary. He wished his tattoos were not there. He had only been fourteen when he had them put on his arms. But when he spoke to a plastic surgeon about having them removed, he discovered that they would have to be exchanged with patches of skin from other parts of his body that would not show in swimming trunks. And he had decided that he would rather have them symmetrically on his arms than stitched willy-nilly on his ass.

There were also all those scars and skin grafts on his right leg, the myriad little scars on his body and hands, the bridge of his nose, the right side of his jaw. And there was his little left testicle, which always required an explanation in an intimate situation. There were too many things in his life that required an explanation in an intimate situation.

"You're beautiful, but you sure are beat-up for a kid," is how Marge often put it.

She would listen with interest when he told her about a book he had read, some complicated notion or bit of philosophy he was trying to get a handle on, yet excited with him about everything that excited him, but always with a down-to-earth practicality that culminated in her saying or doing something that made him know that what was going on at the moment was perfectly fine and satisfying enough for anyone, certainly herself. She often said, "I could just die happy right now." And she would hold his little testicle in her mouth as if it would melt, and make his cock big again with her never fumbling, never fluttering, always skillful hands.

"I never had big ideas," she said. "I never wanted a whole lot. I have always been able to work to get myself what I need, my own place, car, nice clothes. I don't need nobody to take care of me. But hell, Sergeant Cat, livin' is a lot more than me, me, me. And I like you better than any man I've ever known including my old daddy."

Carlson asked her if he reminded her of her father.

"Shit no! He was just all teeth, legs, Lincoln-lookin' dark hair, liquor, and balls. He really did look like Honest Abe at the table by the light of a kerosene lamp. He was old when I was born. About forty. Used up like men around here get if liquor don't get them first. He had another family over in the next holler. Sometimes there would be a dozen brothers and half-kin around the place. Nearly everyone else was some kind of cousin. Hell, the first six boys ever fucked with me was some kind of brother. But Daddy was always nice to me even if I was just a snotty-nosed bucktoothed girl. If I hadn't become a dental technician I wouldn't a been in no Jane Russell Look-Alike Contest."

Carlson told her that explained it. "You screw like a bucktoothed woman. My stepdad always swore that they were the best. It was about the only thing he ever told me that worked out to be true."

She laughed. "I never heard that one before. Anyway, it's my mother you put me in mind of. She was a genius too. She read books all the time, made up lists and made the old man bring books from the library in town or catch the bookmobile, and made him buy us a whole set of encyclopedias from a travelin' salesman when he wasn't sure he was goin' to have seed money for the next plantin'. He told me once that she was the best danged woman in bed or on her own two feet he'd ever known. She was bucktoothed too," she said and laughed. "And so was you when you were a kid, you said, before you got your teeth broken. Man, our kids could probably eat a roasting ear through a chickenwire fence if we had any," she projected happily. "Sometimes, with you, I feel like I'd like to make a kid on purpose. That would feel so nice. . . .

"Anyway, honey, you think about it, what I just said about what you oughta do. You don't know it, but you need a woman like me. I'd never fuck you up or fuck you over or ever make you feel less a man than you are. I'd be with you more'n any woman when you wanted someone to be with and I'd leave you alone when you wanted to be alone in a way so you wouldn't ever feel lonely or uncared for."

He kissed her as tenderly and deeply as he had ever kissed anyone. "You're a good woman, Marge. The best." He felt as if he might cry.

"I'll call you tomorrow," he promised.

So, that Monday he took the forms for application to helicopter school from his desk drawer, interleafed them with the proper number of carbons, and rolled them into his typewriter.

He had typed in his name, rank, and serial number when the telephone rang. His telephone did not often ring. It was Captain Easter, the general's aide-de-camp. He informed Carlson that a congressional member of the Armed Forces Committee was making a surprise visit to the post and would be attending a meeting of the general's staff at 1400 hours and that Carlson would attend the meeting in Class A uniform, tie not scarf, lowcuts rather than boots. Carlson signified he understood and the captain hung up. At noon he went to his quarters on the post to change uniforms.

He had a beer for lunch standing at the bar in the club next to where the sergeant major sat over a steak sandwich. Carlson would not sit down now until he attended the meeting. The sergeant major had also changed his uniform, but since he would only be greeting the congressman as he came through headquarters, he was not careful about the crease in his trousers and consequently sat. He would sit in any case, Carlson knew.

"That's all you're having for lunch?" the sergeant major asked.

"Yeah," Carlson told him. "I fill my stomach before I go in there and I'll start to dope off and yawn or something." He took a plastic pharmacy vial from his pocket, shook a couple of tiny triangular dexedrine tablets into the cup of his left hand, popped them into his mouth, and washed them down with a sip of 3.2 beer.

"Those things are cunts," said the sergeant major. "They'll wreck your heart even if the Army don't break it. How long have you been eating those things? Since Korea?"

"Since the first week."

"How many?"

"Four, sometimes five. Some days only a couple. I've done as many as twelve a couple of hairy times and eight a few more times than I've done twelve."

"Jesus Christ, kid, if you don't knock that off right now, when you're my age, your heart's going to be the size of a baseball and run like an outboard motor."

"I know," Carlson said.

"You know. But you don't know shit! For a fuckin' genius, Carlson, sometimes you disappoint me greatly."

"I know I do, Sergeant Major. If it's any consolation to you, you are at the head of a pretty important line of folks I respect. I disappoint me too. I've decided to put in for helicopter school."

"Well, if you keep popping them things I ain't goin' to ride with you unless I'm being shot at, and even then I'm not goin' to feel good about it."

Carlson finished his beer and clapped the older man fondly on the back. "Keep alert, Sergeant Major," he said.

"Fuck you, Carlson," the other grumbled, bending close over his steak, so he could see to cut it without putting on his glasses.

Everyone was in the staff meeting room when the general arrived with the congressman, trailed by the general's aide. The general and the congressman were laughing together, each about halfway down a couple of the general's good cigars. They'd obviously had more than a glass of 3.2 beer and a couple of dexies for lunch. Carlson clearly heard the congressman ask the general, "What do you get, General, when you cross a nigger with a Jew?" just before the general's aide called, Attention!" and everyone, although already at attention, tried to become even more so. The general told everyone, "At ease, men. Let's all take seats. This is just an informal meeting."

It had been arranged that Carlson, as the only non-commissioned officer present, would sit at the foot of the conference table directly facing the general. A place was made beside the general for the congressman. Everyone stood behind their chairs waiting for the general to be seated. His aide hovered rigidly one pace to the general's left rear, resplendent in a tailored uniform with the bright gold rope of his office looped over his left shoulder. They all waited until the general asked the congressman, "What do you get?"

"Oh, a janitor who owns his own building," the man replied. The two men laughed.

The general introduced the congressman to his staff and his staff to the congressman.

Then they all sat down.

Before each chair was a shiny red folder stamped in gold with an army insignia surrounded by the crests of all the divisions of which it was comprised. Inside the folder was a detailed formal statement of the Army's mission and a breakdown of how that mission was being accomplished by the individual units. It was a serious-looking folder, heavily documented with statistics, lists of accomplishments from A to Z, like a corporation's annual report, and was primarily, Carlson knew, eyewash.

Carlson studied the man for whom they had all been assembled. He was a medium-sized, florid-faced man with a soft Southern voice, who combed his hair up from the left side and plastered it over the top of his head to hide an almost bald pate. He wore an iridescent pigeon-shit colored silk suit he'd probably had made in Hong Kong in twenty-four hours and expensive two-tone brown and white shoes. His peacock silk tie was tacked to his white shirt with a diamond pin.

The general leaned back in his swivel chair, sucked on his cigar, then said in a cloud of good blue smoke: "The congressman wants to keep this meeting completely informal, so we'll just shoot the breeze together. He has had a fast tour of the post and seen what we are up to here and I'm sure he has some questions he would like to ask based on what he has seen. They're all yours, Congressman."

The man chuckled and cleared his throat. "Well, thank you, General. Gentlemen, I am very pleased to be here today . . ." He smiled, then stared at the table for a long couple of moments as if struggling to think of something further to say. He giggled, stopped himself, cleared his throat again, looked embarrassed. Everyone at the table stared at the speaker with an absolutely unstirring official neutrality that could not in the least be encouraging. When the man spoke again, his voice had gone up a step or two in register. "I haven't prepared a speech. As a new man in the House and on the committee, I don't get too many opportunities to make speeches anyway . . ." He waited for a laugh and got only the merest smile from the men at the table.

". . . it is a puzzle to me," the congressman was saying, "after seeing the level of training and dedication at this camp, how some of our boys failed in Korea to stand up and fight as we have come to expect American boys to do.

33

I know it bothers me and it bothers a lot of good ordinary Americans, men who fought bravely in the last war and mothers who lost sons in that war and in Korea. I guess we are looking for answers to that and assurances that such a thing will never happen again. Maybe some of you gentlemen can enlighten me on that."

There was an unstirring moment of absolute silence. When no one volunteered to enlighten the congressman, the general rocked forward and said: "Well, we all have our theories based on command observations, but maybe we ought to hear from someone who saw it from the other end of the tube. Sergeant, would you please tell us why we did not do as well in Korea as we certainly should have?" It was not a question, however informal the atmosphere was supposed to be; it was a direct order as far as Carlson was concerned.

"Yes, sir!" He was on his feet before he knew it. Tall as a tree, he felt, about twelve feet above the spit-polished toes of his Class A shoes, mentally speeding back to the Scottish Brigade and the lament they played on the night his unit spent holding open the end of the murderous cut below Kunu-ri for three thousand of the seven thousand men who had gone into it that morning to straggle out on foot, past every vehicle in the division which lay wrecked, abandoned, destroyed, and often still burning on the frozen road.

At first he heard himself speaking more than he was aware of actually doing.

"I don't think there was anything intrinsically wrong with the individual soldier in Korea or with the leadership on the ground where the war was fought, though we have, with the help of the press, about convinced ourselves that we no longer have the moral and spiritual fiber of the past. I think that is a lot of bullshit, sir. We got our butts kicked initially by the North Koreans because we were fed piecemeal into the battle, many of us being rushed in from Japan and Germany where we had been occupation troops, more poorly equipped than the North Koreans, far below them in real combat training, and simply because no one had given any of us a sensible explanation

34

about why we were there or what we were expected to accomplish."

"Sergeant," the congressman cut in jovially, "I didn't think a good soldier *had* to have an explanation why he had to do anything, sensible or otherwise."

"Yes, sir!" Carlson was definite. "A *good* soldier *has* to know. A soldier should know what the hell he is doing and why. Sending him someplace like Korea, telling him he is a defender when in fact he must act as an aggressor, will make him very confused. He is not going to trust you. And eventually you are going to make him crazy if you don't get him killed first."

"I am not sure you and I attended the same war, Sergeant," the congressman said. The men at the table laughed lightly.

He could see in the general's face, and in the faces of the men around him, that he had gone too far. But he could not stop himself now that the floodgates had opened up. All the ideas he had stored up on the battlefields of Korea, all the thoughts he had chewed over during the months he'd spent reading on the general's time, came pouring forth.

He talked about General MacArthur's utter lack of understanding of the enemy; about the generally poor training given to the American soldiery; about the lies handed out as Gospel truth; about the foolhardiness of trying to bomb an enemy into submission when it was fighting from a superior moral position that would not be quenched even by atomic weaponry.

"Essentially it boils down to a tenet of Mao Tse-tung," he said. "An honorable victory cannot come from a war fought for dishonorable purposes or by dishonorable means. It has always been the key to his success, our propaganda to the contrary. He also said you have to be ever on guard when fighting a dishonorable enemy against adopting his methods to defeat him lest you become like him. Better to lose than to become like him. We were the dishonorable enemy in Korea. I am sure we did not feel we were. I'm sure even MacArthur did not feel we were. Our President and our allies did not feel we were. But we were. And we were whipped when and where it counted by an army that was equipped for fighting a war thirty years ago—compared to ourselves."

An hour later, still shaking, he was in his office, ripping the application for helicopter pilots' school from his typewriter and dropping it in the wastebasket. He picked up the telephone and dialed the sergeant major's number downstairs. When the older man answered, Carlson asked, "What's the number of the new regulation covering early discharge to attend college? Can you send me a copy? And have Fruchtman run over to personnel and bring me back the necessary forms. Yeah. Thanks."

He then had the operator call the admissions officer at the university renowned for its school of journalism, ninety miles away. The woman he talked to said she would send him application forms for enrollment immediately.

Then he sat down and began to write his report, as the general had ordered when Carlson finally stopped talking. The general wanted everything on record. Carlson wrote it first in longhand, edited it, made several changes, then began to type it up in triplicate.

He worked until nearly ten before he had the report the way he wanted it. There was certainly going to be no one trying to persuade him to reenlist after the general read the report. He had just put in proper subject-to form the essentials of what he had said at the staff meeting.

He put on his cap, squared it automatically over his eyes, hand-carried his report down the hall and dropped it in the general's urgent-in basket.

If you are going to blow a career, blow the bastard, he told himself. But he was not happy. The thing was, goddammit, he loved the Army.

He spent his remaining months in virtual isolation, seeing only Marge No. 1.

Four

Bob Pasetta was seated at the editor's desk in the student newspaper office when Carlson came in with his column for the week and a political cartoon. The column was about Johnny Ace, who had just shot himself prior to going on stage to sing, and about a new female singer who called herself Jaye P. Morgan. The political cartoon lampooned the student government association as a small-time Tammany Hall run out of the Journalism School.

The student newspaper had been taken over by Bob Pasetta right after Christmas, 1954, during Carlson's second term at the university. He and Carlson had rebuilt it as an alternative, irreverent voice on campus. It was an immediate success, even though the Board of Publications withdrew its subsidy after they read the first two editions. The students loved the paper and bought out every edition. The J-School daily tried to ignore the weekly's existence, but after having been scooped on three big local stories, including a suicide in the freshmen women's dorm, it had grudgingly accepted that the maverick paper was indeed alive and trying to practice a sort of journalism that was fast dying everywhere.

Bob put his feet up on his desk, talking on the telephone and reading Carlson's column at the same time. Carlson, meanwhile, stared at the backside of a young woman named Sally Frederickson, with whom he attended a psychology class. He had made a move toward her when she first came into the office looking for an extracurricular activity. They had gone with others for beer at the Shack. He had asked her if she was a virgin. She had said she was and wondered if that was going to stand in the way of their getting to know one another better. Carlson had told her he really liked the shape of her head and her unblinking directness, but that he did not want to take the responsibility for removing her virginity. Subsequently she began dating a promising freshman halfback named Bo Parker. Carlson asked her periodically if she were still a virgin. It became a joke between them. They got along famously, even though she was only seventeen to his twenty-four.

She cranked the mimeograph, smiling at him. He did not like to watch her work. She did not have a talent for things mechanical, but he knew she was not dumb. There was a smudge on her face, and her red hair was coming down from where it had been piled on her head and tucked under a comb. He smiled at her.

"This is nice about Johnny Ace," Bob Pasetta said when he hung up the phone. "The comparison with Elvis and wondering about how it would have been if Johnny Ace had been white and Elvis black is good. But who the hell is Jaye P. Morgan?"

"Beautiful lady! Juicy! You haven't heard her. Easy-riding voice. I thought she was a spade when I first heard her. There's an intelligence and no bullshit behind her voice. A beautiful and real lady."

"So you say here. But that name. That's not serious. Sounds like a stripper."

"She could do that if she wanted. Lady could do anything. Good lady. Some have it and some don't. Johnny Ace did. Jaye P. does. Elvis doesn't. He's just foolin'. Not really."

"Okay. Come on. Let's go over and see what Henry Wallace has to say for himself."

"I don't want to go over and listen to him cop a plea."

"Come on. Some of the S.G.A. crowd and the Young Republicans are planning on shouting him down, I hear."

"I don't care about Henry Wallace, Bob. I would rather stay here and watch Sally mimeo."

The girl looked up and smiled.

"Come on, anyway," Bob insisted. "I may need you for protection."

"Okay," Carlson said.

"I just want the finks to see us there."

Carlson was wearing chinos and an old Army field jacket. Bob had on an old raincoat that was his trademark. He was about a foot taller than Carlson, and looked a little like an Italian "Mr. Hulot."

Henry Wallace was speaking outside. It was a day in March, 1955. He had gotten a pretty good turnout, maybe three hundred people. He had only spoken for about ten minutes when the eggs and produce began to fly. Young men had stationed themselves in the audience strategically, loaded with stuff to throw. It had been planned. It was about as spontaneous as an assassination. There was one young man up in a tree like a sniper. If he'd had a rifle, the speaker would have been dead. Wallace had been invited to speak, to come explain himself. Carlson was shocked when the stuff began to fly from the audience. He asked Bob:

"What the hell kind of threat is Henry Wallace, for chrissake?!"

"Look, Cat. There is Ron Connelly. Right in there with a load of eggs. We should have a camera here!"

"I see a couple of people taking pictures. We can get copies."

"But, damn, I would like to have a picture of Ronnie. That little bastard."

"Look at his face. Oh, he's a killer!"

Connelly was the president-elect of S.G.A. and number one fink on the Board of Student Conduct. A born brown-noser; the number one turd. Another person whom Carlson often asked if *he* were still a virgin. A living pimple who could take shorthand but who would never get shut of an idea if he lived forever.

Anyone with an iota of perception saw that Wallace was never truly more than a centimeter to the left of Harry S Truman, nor enough different from President Eisenhower's own muddled views to call for serious debate. Henry was a sincere professional do-gooder at the end of his rope, seeking now only to be accepted as a decent human being and forgiven his miscalculation in flirting for a time with the American Communist Party when he was running as a third-party candidate for president—though he had never accepted that party's official support and finally rejected the notion entirely.

Pretty girls cradling books like infants against their breasts scurried past with young men in chinos and Thread-n-Needle Street brogues, and hardly gave the scene a second glance. Probably not more than half of the young people on campus could have told you who exactly Henry Wallace was or used to be.

"He's some kind of Communist," an Aggie in cowboy hat and boots explained to his girlfriend, whose all-American butt sprung from her tight tube skirt above the uniform wool sweat socks and dirty saddle shoes.

Not half of those there would know that for all his ill-fitting suit, curled collar wings, and indifferent tie beneath the Iowa farmer's face, Wallace came from a distinguished, moneyed family. His family, after his grandfather had made the fortune, had devoted a lot of time to public service. Henry had come to politics out of the fundamental Christian necessity of putting his money and life where his mouth was. It was simply and utterly the elementary school epitome of what good Americans should do.

After casting his virgin vote for Eisenhower, Carlson felt he had personally been bilked, though he was also certain that Ike by his own rights was as honest and true as Stevenson. Ike, in the long run, was as misguided by his corporate cronies as was Wallace by his Communist supporters, both groups ruthlessly exploiting and corrupting well-meaning men. And if Adlai could not keep the hoods out of the Illinois statehouse, how the hell could he keep them out of the White House? Carlson vowed he would never again squander what ought to be a logical decision between clear and intelligent alternatives on such cheese choices.

An egg splattered on the speaker's platform. Another exploded squarely on the front of the rostrum. The future bombardiers and artillerymen were finding their range.

Wallace faltered in his speech as the stuff whizzed past his head. He tried not to duck. The sponsors on the platform with him were ducking, except for one stalwart young woman built like an upright piano who stood her ground stolidly, even as an egg splattered on her formidable sweatered chest. A young man caught a cabbage in his hands and stared at it as if it were someone's head. He was scared. Wallace lifted his arm to deflect the trajectory of a tomato and it exploded and ran down his arm. Sadness warred with anger on his reddened farmer's features. The garbage continued to arc up out of the crowd. Some of the eggs were obviously ripe. The formidable young woman on the platform covered her mouth and nose with a handkerchief.

Then an egg was lofted which struck Wallace high on the forehead. The putrid yolk and albumen ran over his heavy brows into his eyes. He never looked more like an aging Skeezix than at that moment. He staggered. A low moan rose from the audience. Was actually hitting the man with a rotten egg going too far? It was such a mild, mild day. Bees buzzed aimlessly among the crowd. Suddenly it seemed as if the crowd felt ashamed. Few laughed. There was genuine anger on Wallace's face. Carlson saw it and liked it. For a second it seemed Wallace was casting about for something to throw back or was going down in that crowd to clean someone's clock for them. Then the sadness set in again. The lumpy girl and the evangelic-looking young man leaped to give Wallace support and tried to shield him with their bodies. The young woman caught an egg on the widest part of her beam, which brought a roar of laughter from the crowd.

Where the hell were the school officials, the campus police?

Ron Connelly's face looked pale and grim as an assassin's. Hell, *he* wasn't having any fun, Carlson realized. That little fucker was *serious!* This was not some university prank. The young man's face was set in such a mask of unthinking hatred that Carlson was honestly shocked and frightened. Men's faces in war when their targets could shoot back rarely looked so mean.

What had Wallace been saying when the egg hit his country face?

Something about God. Henry Agard Wallace—a real believer. A Christian. There had been his granddaddy who had made a fortune out in Iowa. Uncle Harry Wallace, who, under Harding, had helped expose the Tea Pot Dome scandal. As early as 1946 Henry A. was arguing that history showed that nations armed to the teeth in peacetime ultimately made war on someone. Henry had asked some valid questions, however half-baked. But who wasn't half-baked in 1946?

Poor fucker, Carlson thought. He would have to write something about all this for his column. Too mean for a cartoon. No humor in it on either side. No wit. No perspective. All just too mean.

Carlson suddenly really wanted to clean Ron Connelly's clock. *Better citizens than that asshole will ever be are killed accidentally*, he thought. He wondered if he could use *that* for a lead to his column. No. Something about Wallace's fumbling for a lost line to God. That would be his lead. It all seemed so out of place on a college campus on such a mild, mild day.

He had expected more of the university than it had so far delivered. He had come there humble, thrilled to have been accepted as a student. Laid against his life before, it seemed so improbable that he could ever be there except perhaps as a laborer. But getting a higher education, beyond learning the rudiments of some boring trade or pursuing equally limiting scholarship, had turned out to be another kind of guerrilla warfare.

Fuck it, he thought, turning away as the crowd was breaking up, even as campus police moved tardily to restore order.

On the fringe of the crowd as they walked back toward the office stood Sally Frederickson.

"What happened, Cat?" she asked.

"Stupidity. Makes me truly wonder if I had been Chinese, coming from so far back as I do, I might not have been relatively better off today. What the hell kind of threat is Henry Wallace to anybody, for chrissake?"

"I don't know," Sally confessed. "But I'm not a virgin anymore. I wanted to tell you this morning in Psych, but you cut class again."

He looked at the young woman.

"Will you buy me a beer?" she asked.

"Yes, I would like to buy a bunch of beer, get away from here somewhere."

"Do you like Henry Wallace or something?"

"He is not a man I greatly admire. But I don't like to see shit like that done to anyone."

"What if he was Hitler?" she posed.

"Well, he isn't Hitler. If he was, those punks would probably have let him speak."

She took his arm and they cut behind the hall where the student newspaper had its office to the parking lot where he had left his car.

Five

THEY STOPPED FOR a six-pack of beer, parked along Spring Creek, a dry gulch except for a trickle at the bottom of it, and made love twice next to a log on the ground among the fallen leaves, once standing against a tree when the sky darkened and it began to rain, and once more in the car after a laughing dash through a downpour, when her red hair was wet and stringy and her face altogether beautiful.

The first time they made love she had her initial orgasm. Reason fled; blinded by his careless blood and their passion, Carlson came with her, in her, and did not care.

He did not care.

They did not discuss the possibility that she would become pregnant.

They had made love again. She did not come.

Standing against the tree with the rain running down their faces she had come for the second time in her life. Stark naked, in the car, the windows steamed by the warm humidity of their lovemaking, they came together, their mouths and tongues slipping each other generous, heartfelt communion.

So tender. So passionate. So happy. So satisfying.

In one of those rare occasions in which everything worked and felt so fine it was as if the experience made the world new, redefined everything both of them thought they knew, and finally proved the validity of knowledge, the creative impulse, the basis for criticism.

"Do the scholars know it all begins with a beautiful fuck?" Carlson asked.

"Oh, it does, doesn't it?!" Sally replied. "Oh, Cat. Oh, baby. I *love* you."

"I love you too," he vowed.

Only then did he regret that he had not had the courage to assume the responsibility of being the first to make love to her.

"Thank you, Bo Parker," he said, watching her pale blue eyes.

"I won't see him anymore," she said.

"Why?"

"What do you mean, 'why'?"

"He's a nice guy, isn't he? You like him?"

"Sure . . ."

"So, why not see him? Best freshman halfback they have had here in ten years. All those social functions you have to attend."

"You *want* me to see him?"

"Jealousy just is not in it for some reason," he said, as much for his own information as not. "Don't misunderstand. It isn't that I don't care for you. Never felt better or more content. You know?"

She was waiting.

"I don't know," he said, "I'm just not jealous of Bo . . . or anyone you would really enjoy seeing. I *want* you to do what you want to do. I trust you to consider my feelings as best you can in whatever you do, I guess. Maybe that is what I learned from Marge No. 1. Maybe that was what she was trying to tell me."

"Who's that?" the girl asked carefully.

"Someone I saw a lot of during the last few months I was in the Army. Good, brilliant hillbilly lady. You would have liked her and she you."

Sally did not seem all that confident about Carlson's contention.

"I am jealous of every girl you have known," she confessed.

"You aren't."

"I am too!"

"That's silly. What do they have to do with you and me? I love you now. I really like you a lot. I desire you, obviously—"

"Or any other girl with a pussy? Admit it, you were primarily just horny. I mean if you had run into any of the other girls you are screwing they would be here with you now, not me."

The accuracy of her judgment upset him, threw him off a bit from the more romantic vision on which he was working.

"Yes. You're right," he agreed. "But that is only an isolated fact. I *was* horny. But it *is* you I came here with. It *is* you I made love to—with—and whom I love now in a way that makes love all new."

She pouted a moment. "I know all about you. I've been sort of poking around."

"You have?" Carlson was flattered.

"Sure. I almost always get what I want."

"I didn't know that." He was even more flattered.

"I'm more than a pretty face, you know."

"Oh, I knew *that*. Who told you you're so pretty?"

"You did when you were humping the hell out of me."

"Oh."

"You know, for the first time in my life I'm really happy. At least in my life as a young woman. I was happy before as a girl sometimes, but today it's as if all the anxieties and worries and bullshit are dispelled. Isn't that wonderful?!"

He drove her home in warm contentment. She kissed his mouth, said "Goodnight," and was out of the car, leaving Carlson smiling in front of the freshman women's dorm. He saw a reflection in the side glass of the car and was startled by how young he looked, like a picture of himself when he was a boy.

Sal-ly. He spread her name gently over his mind. I don't even like redheads, he reminded himself. They have less attractive pubic hair than brunettes. She was of such a fairness she could never tan easily. She was healthy, though small and delicate, a white lady person, not at all his ideal. But he loved her. She pleased and satisfied him. She felt as lovely to his flesh and soul as anyone had ever felt. His ideal was now merely like something he had read about, or perhaps dreamt, while Sally was indisputably, beautifully real.

After that day they were able to tell each other absolutely everything about themselves. For the first time in his life Carlson was able to speak with someone about an incestuous experience he'd had with his mother. He no longer had to make up respectable histories for his ancestors. It was a wonderful relief.

In turn, she explained she had almost had an incestuous relationship with her father. On her sixteenth birthday, he took her to New York as a present. Her mother and younger brother had stayed home.

In New York, her father had taken her to a nightclub and had got her rather drunk, while talking incessantly about how grown-up she was. He had bought her a very grown-up dress for the trip. He kept putting his hand up her dress under the table during dinner and fondling her thighs. She said she had been shocked but wasn't sure what to do, or how to get him to stop.

At first she thought he was just joking. Then he began to talk about What if we were to make love? and laughed too loudly at what he assured her was a joke. But he also told her he and her mother had never gotten along well sexually. Sally said she felt sorry for him and almost decided to let him be the first to have her, only stopping when he put his tongue in her mouth and his fingers touched her beneath her panties. She felt as if she would vomit. She said she had begun to cry and had run out of the place. He followed, apologizing, swearing he had acted so stupidly only because he'd had too much to drink. But Sally knew he had thought about it and had planned the trip so he could screw her.

"It was incredible. After it happened I was able to see how he had been thinking about trying something like that for so long . . . That's what hurt the most, I guess. There was nothing spontaneous about it. It was calculated, a scheme. It was dishonest, evil. It was everything he and men like him do. Goddamn them! Fucking bunch of calculating manipulators. So many men are like that. It's so sick. I feel sorry for him and Mother. But somehow I feel they deserve one another. I love them, but like you, I know I'm mainly alone. We are very different in many, many things, but we meet as equals. I really feel good about that. Every time I see you, every time we talk, every time we make love, I feel stronger and more on my own than before."

Carlson had once mentioned that he had read that Marilyn Monroe removed all the little hairs from her arms and legs to feel perfectly smooth. He wondered aloud what that would feel like. And Sally scandalized the freshman woman's dorm by using a depilatory cream to remove every hair she could reach save her pubes and the hair on her head.

"Everyone said I was crazy," she told him. "They said they wouldn't do something like that for any goddamned man. Am I crazy?" she asked.

"Very. But *smooth!* Very smooth," Carlson assured her.

"Yeah. And wicked?"

"Wicked *and* smooth."

Six

CARLSON HAD COME to the great state university with the same excited innocence that had led him to enlist in the military. His belief that the university actually meant all it said about its dedication to knowledge and learning in its brochures lasted about two months; only long enough for him to learn that the study of journalism had less to do with getting at the roots of things and writing as well and honestly as he was able than it had to do with being a member of the community on a par with a member of one of the local service clubs. Essentially newspapering seemed to be striving to be acceptable to the Junior Chamber of Commerce. That was understandable. Carlson could see that if a newspaper was not acceptable to such groups there would be no advertising money and therefore no newspaper.

So he switched to the study of English, with a writing major, and ran directly into the most tedious game on earth: scholarship in the humanities. English professors snuffled and burbled over aspects of lesser Romantic poets, or the lesser works of major Romantic poets, until Carlson wanted to give them a clonk with *The Illustrated Complete Works of Wordsworth*. (If any poet can live *too* long, Wordsworth came close to exceeding decent limits, if Carlson were asked.)

Burns was Carlson's poet. He wrote a hell of a paper on Burns. The professor, who physically resembled an illustration of Uriah Heep, thought he had discovered a disciple. He was an effeminate gurgler who, during a lecture, could go off on a tangent that would carry over until two subsequent noons. But if you wanted to know *anything* at all about *any* Romantic poet, the lesser the better, he was your man. And he thought he had found in Carlson the genius every professor thinks he or she needs to tear himself or herself away from scholarship long enough to teach a class. Carlson's paper was the best thing on Burns the professor had *ever read anywhere!* He had underlined his comments, then elaborated at length on the back of half of his paper, decorating the margin of the title page with enough A+'s to make Carlson think of a military cemetery on Flag Day.

Afterward, however, it was all downhill. On the first 200-point quiz, he got a tidy 33. The professor insisted he must have been sick—something! He explained he could not read a poem in the way he must to remember what he asked out of context on his quiz, and that his score was a fair representation of his knowledge of the material if that was the way knowledge was going to be measured in the class. He insisted that no one could have written the paper he had on Burns and make such a test score unless something was seriously bothering him. When he made another 33 on the next 200-point quiz, the professor began to wonder if Carlson hadn't cribbed the paper on Burns from someone else. He insisted such was not the case. He accepted that, but was at odds to understand why he could do so well on the one hand and so poorly on the other. Carlson lamely offered that 33 was a mystical number and perhaps, back to back on his quizzes, they might be a sign given to warn him to assign more essay work. He was not convinced, and the paper on Burns and a less good one on Coleridge were all that kept him from failing the course.

Trying to find out what he wanted to know, developing the skills to express the things he thought he saw, the things that puzzled and intrigued him, became for Carlson a new kind of guerrilla warfare. It was as if he had to mine knowledge out of the university against its incorporated will in such a manner that he always felt criminal. And what he learned was hardly ever an answer to a question on anyone's quiz.

In his sophomore year, Carlson was explaining his

quandary to the tiny old poet of the West over breakfast in a mediocre café across from the venerable hall of arts and science.

The old poet was born John G. Neihardt near Sharpsburg, Illinois, on January 8, 1881, third child of Nicolas Nathan and Alice Culler Neihardt. When he was five his father abandoned the family, and John and his mother went to live with his pioneer grandparents in a sod house on the upper Solomon River in Kansas.

Carlson's grandparents had also once lived in a sod house on a homestead on the prairie near Rocky Ford, Kansas, where Carlson's mother was born in 1909. Carlson's father had been killed in an automobile accident when he was two, and he had been more brought up by his grandparents than by his mother.

Though there was a half a century difference in their ages they had met like two new boys in school, trading histories and tales, recalling prairie light and shadow, conjuring up the memories of arrowheads both had prized from the same loam far from the view or call of their houses, among shades of unspoken braves. They shared then a kinship of full-time access to the wisdom of their grandfathers and grandmothers and the effect of a land as broadly sown with spirit stuff as it was with grass and wheat.

John Neihardt was married to a tall, beautiful woman named Mona Martinsen, a sculptress and former student of Rodin, who had been moved to write a letter to the prairie poet after she had first read his work. Both mystics, they were able to conduct a full courtship entirely by mail. They were married in 1908. Their children were named Enid, Sigrud, Hilda, and Alice.

"We exchanged photographs, you understand, before we decided we might get married," the old man explained when he told the story. "But we should have known that was not necessary."

He recalled that in Omaha, the first time they had met in person, Mona stepped down to the station platform where her intended, who was no bigger than a twelve-year-old boy, waited in his best suit, bearing a promised rose so that she would recognize him. She was carrying a volume of his verse so that he would not fail to recognize her. Only he waited for the train that day. Only she stepped down to the platform. They broke into laughter that continued yet.

Now the old man was official poet laureate of the State of Nebraska. A bronze bust of him, executed by his wife, had been placed in the rotunda of the capitol. The bust was some piece of work. You could clearly see the influence of Rodin in it. It was *good*. A bit of the old man's spirit and a lot of Mona Martinsen's love had been poured into it.

"I'd like to talk to you about that story you gave me to read," Neihardt said when Carlson came to his home.

"Yes, sir?"

"It doesn't quite work as a short story, does it?"

"No. It really wasn't a short story. Just writing about some people and a time."

"You know what I think you have there, don't you?"

Carlson waited to see what he would say.

"I think you have the bones of a cracking good novel." He smiled. "That old man and his wife are two of the finest characters I have come across in a long time. And my God, how you write about them! It is really amazing that one so young has such a feel and understanding for those old ones. They must be based on people quite close to you."

"On my grandfather and grandmother on my mother's side."

"They are simply first-rate. Their lives are so harsh, yet you capture all the spunkiness, great spirit, and good humor that keeps them going. You are going to write it, surely?"

"Someday."

"Don't wait too long. I would like to still be around to read it."

Carlson grinned. "I'm not sure you would want to read

52

it if I am ever able to write it the way I think it ought to be written."

The old poet did not understand.

"What I mean," Carlson explained, "is that if I get it down the way I think it should be, I'm not sure it will even be published."

"Oh, don't worry about that. The old man is beautifully profane, especially in contrast to that good woman, but publishers are very liberal about things nowadays. You shouldn't worry about that."

"No. I mean there are other things. I really don't worry about it. I just try to write the stuff the way I think it should be, and I will keep on doing it like that, even if it is never published. I would like to make my living writing, but I am going to live and write anyway. I can always make a living at something. I don't look at my stories as a trade."

"Of course!" the old man cheered. "Of course! You are an artist! You are a writer! Don't feel so guilty about trying to write well. We have all felt that way sometime. You keep going and it will work out. Let's get out of here. Let me show you my horses."

They went out and walked to the stables where the little old man introduced Carlson to each of his horses, describing the various character traits of each animal, explaining that this one was beautiful but stupid and that one intelligent but shy, and so forth. The horses seemed to recognize the old man and like him as much as a horse —not one of the greatly intelligent beasts—can.

"My grandfather always told me that a mule was much smarter than a horse," Carlson said. "He raised mules once. The only time I have seen him cry was when I was a little boy and we took all his mules to the horse and mule auction and saw them sold off when the old man lost his farm and business. He said that a mule will never eat himself sick the way a horse will, never saw his foot off in a barbed-wire fence, nor work harder than it ought. He always said that horses reminded him of damned Irishmen and mules reminded him of black people. The old man was Scottish but always said if he had any other choice he would be black. He always said he figured he was some kind of nigger anyway. Maybe I picked it up from him, and from living a long time in an alley where everyone else was black, but I feel that way too."

The old poet led Carlson to a place behind the house where they sat on large, comfortable chairs. "Tell me more about yourself," he asked.

Carlson explained that his mother had been a part-time prostitute and ever under the influence of his stepfather, a drunk and convicted habitual petty criminal. He told how he had run away from them at fourteen and, with the connivance of his grandmother, managed to enlist in the Navy, spend a year in China and the Pacific right after the Second World War, then after a year or so as a civilian, enlisted in the Army at seventeen to be able to provide for a young wife and a child he could not support with any grace during a time when men with far greater skills and experience were out of work.

"The girl had gotten pregnant and, of course, in our set we either married the girl or ran off and joined the Navy. I had already run off and joined the Navy. And I loved her. So I married her. But it was crazy. It could not last. I'll never forget the eyes of her people when they looked at me. It felt like I couldn't sit down peacefully among them, that I ought to be working at something all the time as penance. So I chose the Army because they promised to send me to Europe."

Carlson also explained that he had never been able to see himself, like nearly all the men of his family except his grandfather, accepting that he must be tied to some machine, manual labor, or trade all his life. "Anything seemed more appealing to me than that. I guess I was just never like most of the kids my age. Anyway, the girl later married someone else who could provide for her and the boy, and he subsequently adopted the child. I understand he is a fine lad. My grandmother keeps me informed. Hell, it was best under the circumstances. I seemed a long way from ever amounting to anything . . . I'm not sure I am so much closer now. But I am the first of my clan to ever be admitted to a university, or even finish high school.

"My trouble is, I'm a romantic," Carlson decided. "Before Korea, the military seemed rather Kiplingesque to me. It offered an escape from everything I knew at home —failures at school and jobs, hopeless love affairs and marriages, marriages in which young women in love grew as worn and tired and unhappy as their own mothers. Sailoring and soldiering were easy by comparison. There was better food than most of us had at home, plenty of good clothes, good shoes and boots, a place to sleep, a chance to succeed at something if you cared. It was my home for almost nine years. I could have learned a trade, but I chose to remain in combat field units. And I still say it beats punching holes in sheetmetal all your life."

Neihardt listened in silence, then offered Carlson a cigarette. As with the Indians, smoking together had large, portentous meaning for the old man. They smoked quietly as the light began to go very quickly, sitting comfortably in the late afternoon until Mrs. Neihardt called them in to supper.

Seven

MEN, CARLSON THOUGHT, generally aged better than women. Women seemed more likely to be eaten by internal bitterness that had cruel pincers. Old men either became sort of lost old boys, failed shadows of youthful promise, or they clung to their rage against others and institutions and so, like Carlson's granddad, went gradually toward death with something of self intact, a touch of humor to make it all bearable, something like wisdom in their eyes. There were women like that, too, Carlson was sure. But when the humor and wisdom were not there, women somehow seemed more lost than men.

Yet there were about twice as many men in the state mental hospital where he worked as there were women. Maybe it was because men had to take responsibility for themselves, as well as for women, children, *and* the community, whereas women remained primarily chattels of men, as demeaning as that was, and therefore did not have to "get it up and get it on" daily, as men were absolutely required to do.

The woman he now saw on the bench on the hospital lawn was a frightened old bird flapping futilely in the neglected cage of memories her mind could no longer knit. Flesh-colored cotton stockings were rolled down around her cadaverous ankles above incongruous blue and white sneakers that wrung from Carlson a desire to try to comfort her, dispel her fear.

Carlson suddenly thought: *She could be my grandmother if my grandmother had let go one last notch of trying.* Once she had been a girl, perhaps pretty, as improbable as that now seemed. He remembered when he had found an old photograph of his grandmother and had asked her embarrassingly who the beautiful girl was. "Why that's *me,* when I was nineteen, just before I married your grandfather," she had exclaimed. "I wasn't always old, you know!" She had been an exceedingly beautiful woman. She could have been the artist Gibson's famous model. By the time she was forty no remnant of that early beauty was left in her face or body. That was a terrifying wonder for Carlson then. Now it was a persistent sadness and regret. His grandfather, an equally handsome man, had aged more gracefully.

Patients strolled aimlessly on the hospital grounds, sat on the state's invariably green benches, squatted and lolled on the grass. They were alone or arranged in child-like groups or huddled silently together, everyone looking off into a personal void. They were all committed to the red brick wall which faced the town and to the wire fences out back. Only occasionally did one wander away and have to be found and returned. Those on the lawn were not considered dangerous. All of them had been put away by someone. All were seemingly ignorant of any rational vanity in their timeless institutional haircuts; the men in shapeless biballs and work shirts, the women lumpy and lost in loose housedresses and aprons. Most were old. Many of the older ones wore the perpetually stunned look of having had their personal devils exorcised by electro-shock, trepanning, prefrontal lobotomies, water treatments, all instruments of a psychomedical exorcism that still awaited the final verdict on their effectiveness.

Carlson worked on CCA, the receiving, violent men's ward, five nights a week, from four P.M. to midnight, to supplement his GI educational benefits. There were women's wings too, run by female attendants, big beefy mamas who rarely had to call for the help of male attendants. The first floor of the building was given over to doctors' and administrative offices, various therapy departments, and a visitors' area.

The building was new, with reinforced glass windows

which cranked open in increments too small for a person to slip through. The building and windows were calculated to give an effect of greater freedom; no iron bars. But no one inside was fooled. The effect was merely eyewash, balm for the consciences of the good citizens on the outside.

On his way upstairs, Carlson said hello to some of the kid patients from CCB, a transitory ward from which patients either went home or were transferred to one of the back wards forever. The kids were emptying the Coke machine in the first-floor hallway. Their leader, by force of his personality, intelligence, and ability to con paint off the walls, was a twelve-year-old killer named Jimmy Sullivan who had stabbed his thirteen-year-old cousin to death with a Boy Scout knife. He had been seeing a psychiatrist at least once a week for over a year and had yet to confess his true reason for killing the girl.

On his own floor, Carlson turned the key, opened the door, and stepped out, pushing the door carefully against heavy resistance at the bottom of it.

The weight turned out to be the crouched gargoyle form of Mr. Collins, who leeringly offered Carlson something vile and viscous he had hawked up, ejaculated, or found, cradled preciously in the nest of a filthy handkerchief. He giggled and leered a come-on of such innocent evil or utterly corrupt innocence every human value was under question.

Mr. Collins had not learned word one. Twisted from birth as badly as the hunchback of Notre Dame, as ugly, he went crablike around the ward in his bagging biballs, scurrying furtively along the walls like a wild animal, trying to keep himself in spare shadows, manic with some curious devilish amusement, or whimpering with fear of things real and imagined.

Carlson tried to imagine what it would be like to be Mr. Collins, to see the world through his eyes, just for a while.

The other patients hated having Mr. Collins on their ward. It was an affront to even their estimates of themselves. The morale on the ward was definitely lower when Mr. Collins was brought over from the old wards.

For the alkies on the ward Mr. Collins was too much like something sprung from their delirium tremens, which they did not care to confront again drunk or sober. For the diagnosed paranoid-schizophrenics—the general catch-all diagnosis for most of the hospital's population—Mr. Collins was a confirmation of their most despairing views of everything.

For all of the joking about Mr. Collins, his existence on this earth was an insult to anyone's theory of creation, a virtual proof of an evil netherworld, confirmation of Satan.

A circus would not have had Mr. Collins. He was often kept in wrist restraints snapped to a leather belt that buckled in the back, to prevent him from publicly masturbating, an urge that always seemed but a tick away. His poor genitals were tattered, perpetually inflamed, worn raw.

"There's livin' proof of what can happen to you if you lope your mule too much," a young alcoholic on very good behavior came up and grinned at Carlson. He was pushing a broom in the hall. He was working his ass off on the ward to make points with the attendants and staff so he might get released. He was almost annoyingly cheerful and uncomplaining. His problem was he was afraid at age thirty he was no longer any good for his pretty little country wife. His problems, of course, were deeper than that, but that is how *he* explained it to the doctor, and how it was written up on his records:

Paranoid-schizophrenic, with suicidal and homicidal tendencies. Low-normal intelligence. Stock clerk in a warehouse. High school education. Married at nineteen. Wife works as waitress part-time. Two children, six and nine, both female. Has been a heavy drinker since age seventeen. Was impotent for last nine months before being committed. Wife has told everyone of their troubles, he says. Her family and parents particularly are "always at him" about it. Wife thinks it must be because of some-

59

thing venereal or that he is "turning queer or something." She says her family always told her "he wasn't ever man enough for her." Patient says wife's family has a reputation in county as lusty, violent people for several generations. He has always been treated as something less than themselves since he married their youngest female relative.

Carlson spent some time almost every night after the patients were in bed recording their medication, making shift reports in all their charts, and so was able to study the histories of all the patients.

Mr. Collins masturbated as simply as a chimp. But a chimp did not get beaten by a zoo keeper for it. Mr. Collins was beaten regularly.

Carlson was sure Mr. Collins' masturbation was an effort at communication, a kind of sharing of the most pleasurable thing he had ever discovered, an effort to join the human race, however misguided. One had only to look closely at the expression on a chimp's face when he was jerking off in a cage before an embarrassed crowd of human onlookers to see a glimmer that the chimp knows at least dimly what he is doing.

Mr. Collins never learned.

Yet, like a chimp, Mr. Collins had to be dressed every day. The task always fell to some luckless cooperative patient, like Ralph, who was pushing the broom, hoping to get out, hoping he was going to be good for his wife again.

Breughel the Elder would have been fascinated by Mr. Collins. He was an imp.

He had no known first name. Rumor had it he was the offspring of a rich family who had made payment for his care in their will and had died. His records did not show where he came from, or his parentage. He was about ten when he was committed. He was now about fifty. No one ever came to visit Mr. Collins. There was another gnarled, stunted little vegetable about forty-seven years old, no larger than a three-year-old child, in a crib on the critical ward who could have been Mr. Collins' kid brother. He had been there since he was a baby. He was known only as Tommy. Carlson tried to think what had been going on forty or fifty years ago that might have fostered such genetic malfunction, and wondered if there could be shown a pattern worldwide. Or maybe the monsters were the product of local pig barons with strange diseases and appetites, or the offspring of women who had mated with beasts or the devil, as many of the older attendants actually believed.

Mr. Collins was back on CCA for shock treatments. The shock did seem to make him keep his hands off himself for a while, quiet him down. His records showed he'd had two hundred shock treatments. But he still had not learned word one. It seemed cruel to shock the shit out of something with little more brain than a monkey. Mr. Collins remembered the room where he got the treatments and did not willingly go in there.

And he saw things when he was not quiet. Again like a chimp, he would become chatteringly agitated at some imagined something he would see on the floor, wall, ceiling, your person, around an inanimate object, and pester everyone about it until he was forced away into a locked room or someone whipped him.

Once Carlson drew a picture of a clawed and winged dragon for Mr. Collins which so satisfied some vision that the little monster began jumping up and down and jabbering until froth flew from his lips and ran down his retarded chin. He had snatched away the drawing and went scampering about the ward as if he were afraid it would be confiscated, which, of course, led directly to the picture's confiscation by the other attendants, who were angry then at Carlson for having "set off" Mr. Collins.

The regular attendants were dedicated to the idea that the ward should be kept as quiet and as clean as if there were no patients on it. For the kind of money the hospital paid, it could only attract men who had failed at everything else or were working there as a second job or, like Carlson and some friends, supplemented their funds while attending the university. Many of the attendants who lived on the grounds were little more than high-level patients themselves. A lot were alcoholics of the milder variety. Many were virtually illiterate. Nearly all were scared.

In spite of the other attendants' disapproval, Carlson continued to show Mr. Collins drawings and photographs, though no more winged and clawed dragons. He showed him pictures of people, objects from ordinary life. Mr. Collins had only the dimmest knowledge of the world beyond the hospital. Curiously, Mr. Collins, unlike the other patients on the ward, save the most disturbed, was not much interested in watching television. In showing him the pictures in magazines, Carlson discovered that Mr. Collins was not greatly interested in mere objects from life outside the hospital. The latest 1955-model Buick left him cold. What he could look at for the longest time, often complaining when the page was turned too quickly, were pictures of women and children and small animals. Photos of dogs and cats especially seemed to connect or excite some area in his brain and he would point at them with his finger and chatter unintelligibly, his eyes almost gentle in a way, the sounds coming from him almost happy. Pictures of men Mr. Collins could live without. He'd seen enough men in real life. Too many of them hurt him. But a picture of President Eisenhower stopped him for a few confused moments. Carlson decided Mr. Collins had confused the President with the Gerber baby, of whom he was inordinately fond.

Perhaps because Carlson took time to show Mr. Collins the pictures, tried to talk to him, and had never hurt him, the monster now awaited each evening at the elevator for Carlson's arrival. How in his ignorance of time he was able to determine when it was time for his shift change was a puzzle, but Carlson had noted it on Mr. Collins' chart as a very hopeful sign which therapists should try to follow up.

No therapist had yet responded.

The other attendants began calling Mr. Collins "Carlson's boyfriend" and continued to query Carlson about his interest in the little monster.

"That sonofabitch ain't never goin' to be nothin' but a kind of jackoff monkey," they would swear. "Why you waste your time? Somebody shoulda put that damn thing to sleep years ago. Just eats up the taxpayers' money to keep a damn useless thing like that alive."

No one liked Mr. Collins. Carlson did not *like* Mr. Collins. But then he did not like his teacher of "Criticism" either. But both creatures fascinated him. Mr. Collins for all his ugliness was more harmless than not. The teacher of "Criticism" could be a dangerous bitch.

By early evening most of the patients were in the sitting room watching the children's television shows. It did not matter what was on the tube, kiddie show, world news, movies, the expressions of the men watching rarely changed, except for those truly very childlike souls who could honestly become entranced by a Popeye cartoon or a wrestling match; they would writhe and rise up out of their chairs empathetically, comment aloud and shout warnings to their heroes. Otherwise it was not certain the others were actually watching. Often it was as if the machine was merely a way of filtering out meandering thoughts, reflecting a diffused illusion of being *in* the real world without having to truly *deal* with it.

The box was just something to sit in front of; both the images seen and one's thoughts softened, diffused, interwoven with an illusion of reality. Then, Carlson realized that it was in the way they watched TV that the mentally disturbed most resembled everyone else watching TV, including the way Carlson himself watched it most of the time. Some men exercised surprisingly good taste when faced with some patently banal crap on the tube; they would drift off to sit in the dining room and smoke or even stare out of a chink in an open window. When the men began doing that they were ready either to get off the ward in a few days or about to have another "blowup." Carlson began making notes on the records regarding a patient's reaction while watching television.

Mr. Babcock, a foxy little man whose primary expression was one of a person about to explode from a stuffing of secrets, was down on his hands and knees sighting a line between the TV and a tiny spired construction he had fashioned from the tinfoil from a cigarette pack. The alignment obviously was critical. Mr. Babcock flattened his cheek against the floor, his skinny buttocks stuck high up in the air. The linoleum had been buffed with a floor waxer and the afternoon light glanced off the wavelike rows of polished wax. Mr. Babcock moved his little machine infinitesimally to the right and rocked back on his heels.

"What do you have there, Mr. Babcock?" Carlson asked.

Mr. Babcock cocked up his aging, unfinished face and winked, put his right index finger in the air and looked infuriatingly smug.

"What's this, Mr. Babcock?" Carlson tapped the man's finger lightly.

But Mr. Babcock was too full of wisdom and secrets to ever have time to explain a thing. At best he would reply in cryptic biblical quotations. Most of the time Mr. Babcock walked around with his right hand higher than his head, his index finger pointing straight up like an antenna. Carlson wondered what he *was* pointing at. But Mr. Babcock had the whole thing figured out. He was the happiest man Carlson had ever seen. Everything was a joke with Mr. Babcock.

"Wish you would let the rest of us in on it," Carlson told the kneeling man.

Ralph swished his push broom up alongside Carlson and observed confidentially, one sane man to another, "I wouldn't of believed this before I got in here. Now there ain't a whole lot I won't believe."

"Me neither," Carlson admitted. "How's it going?"

"Oh, just fine!" Ralph did so want to be believed "well." "It must be goin' to be a full moon tonight. Everybody's been real nervous today. Mr. Morton blacked Mr. Martin's eye 'cause he refused to eat again at the table with Mr. Collins. It does make you feel pretty bad to be put at the table with Mr. Collins. Like eatin' next to a fifty-year-old baby who needs a shave and keeps wantin' to show you his dick."

It was true. Mr. Collins hadn't a clue about spoons, which the men were given to feed themselves with—no forks or knives. Mr. Collins ate with his fingers, played obscenely with his food, missed his mouth as often as he found it, dribbled, spilled, and made disgusting sounds. Whoever on the ward had the regular attendants down on him ended up at the table with Mr. Collins as punishment.

"How are you feeling?" Carlson asked.

"Just fine! I just can't wait to get outta here. My wife talked to the doctor the other day and he said it wouldn't be long now. I've decided to take an electronics course from that ICC correspondence school. Maybe I can learn a real good trade and she can quit work and maybe we can move somewhere else."

"That's good," Carlson said.

"Oh, we got a new patient," Ralph added, as if he were one of the staff. "Attempted suicide. Professor over there at the university. Maybe you know him."

"Okay."

The C-building night nurse, Mrs. Staples, was in the ward chatting and chuckling with Ken and Frankie, the two regular attendants. Frankie had a shy but definite crush on Mrs. Staples, although he was only about half her size, weight, and horsepower. The third townie attendant on the ward was Carl. He was a large, slow-spoken but not dim man, who had once been a patient at the hospital, having sustained some deep personal defeat regarding the breakup of his marriage, about which he was more guarded than any patient. If the three weren't alcoholics, they were serious drinkers of the pint-a-day variety.

Ken was about thirty, a muscular, taciturn man, and the most eager to punch a patient or choke one down. He lived in a small house near the hospital with the wife he had quit high school to marry when she became pregnant.

"If one of these fuckin' nuts ever broke out of here and went and raped my wife, I would kill the sonofabitch with my bare hands. I'd make soup of that sonofabitch!" Ken often vowed.

Mrs. Staples was a large woman, rather pretty in a

coarse, broad way, who carried herself as if she were all precious liquid inside. She had a way of extending her pinkie while drinking a cup of coffee that made Carlson want to tear her skintight uniform right down the front and affect her somehow. (He could not be sure exactly what he would want to do to her.) She was a practical rather than registered nurse, and had more grating little affectations than a pink bedroom in some homemaker's journal. She would go about five nine and weighed at least 160 pounds. For all that, she wore cheap, clattering costume jewelry on duty and high-heeled white pumps rather than regular nurse's oxfords. She did have good legs and big, not unattractive, high hips. Her uniforms were invariably so tight all the buttons were under strain. Her thighs were larger than Frankie was around the waist. He simply went drippy when she was on the ward. But she preferred to play up to Ken, always putting a hand on his naked biceps when giving the evening's instructions. Though Carl was senior man on the ward, it was Ken to whom she addressed her advice and wishes.

Her knowledge of the mentally disturbed, medicine, psychiatry, and life in general was extremely superficial. The key thing was that everyone be in as good humor as herself. So whatever instructions she stroked into Ken's biceps were simply eyewash and could easily be ignored. She would have as little as possible to do with the attendants from the university. They were temporary and dangerous to the normal operation of the hospital. Everyone who worked there permanently was afraid the students would make waves, cause trouble, change whatever it was that the regulars called home. Mrs. Staples, Frankie, and Carl all had staff quarters on the grounds. On the grounds, Mrs. Staples was a queen.

Carlson did not like her but he was as fascinated by her as he was by Mr. Collins. They somehow seemed different ends of the same twisted stick.

He wondered what effect her perfume had on the men on the ward. To get a whiff of her was to think of some good big whore.

"Mr. Collins and Mr. Martin are scheduled for shock

in the morning, so no supper for them tonight, extra sedation at bedtime," Mrs. Staples said pleasantly. "And Ralph Buss will be moving down to CCB after breakfast tomorrow. One of you can tell him tonight."

They all nodded.

All she had said had been written out and posted in clear view not one foot from her small primped head.

"Keep the new patient, Mr. Marshall, in bed until the doctor can see him tomorrow. He can get up to go to the bathroom if one of you goes with him. He is very suicidal."

"Yes, ma'am," they mumbled.

Instructions over, she jangled her bracelets and made leaving noises. No nurse was on the ward at night. She tapped out onto the ward, smiling left and right at the listless men in the rockers, including in her largesse the manic who looked like Rudolf Hess and was now trying to climb a doorjamb, his eyes truly wild and frightening if you did not know him, and even then somewhat frightening. He did not smile back, but tried all the harder to climb the doorjamb.

Stepping around Mr. Babcock, who was still busy as a bee at his tinfoil construction on the floor, she chirped: "My goodness, Mr. Babcock! You shouldn't play on the floor like that!"

"I'll get him up, ma'am," Frankie offered. Mr. Babcock was about the only patient, except for Mr. Collins, whom Frankie felt courageous enough to physically move. Whenever there was trouble, Frankie was always providently at the other end of the ward, or doing something far enough away to not become involved. "You get up off there and sit in a chair like a decent man!" Frankie ordered and hauled the tiny man up and sat him in a rocker. When Mr. Babcock protested that he was doing the work of the Lord and that He would smite Frankie, there was a moment of fundamental fear and confusion in Frankie's terrierlike face. Frankie came from people who believed in proving their faith by handling poisonous snakes. He did not want to challenge any man's Christian faith. "Well, you just act right!" he warned Mr. Babcock. When he looked to see what Mrs. Staples thought of what he had done, she was next to Mr. Collins, who was holding out his handkerchief toward her.

Mr. Collins was offering her the load of whatever he had in that filthy nest. When Mr. Collins caught her eye, Mrs. Staples turned to smile at him, but then caught her breath and made a disgusted sound.

"Ken!" she bellowed.

Frankie ran right up. "What can I do?! What's goin' on here? You darn idiot, you stop that right now!"

Mr. Collins had dug out his abused little dong with his other hand and was vigorously yanking it at Mrs. Staples, a look on his face of sheer primal delight.

Men in adjacent rockers watched and grinned.

Ken, Carlson, and Carl bolted from the ward office. Ken grabbed a handful of leather restraints from the hook beside the ward office door.

Ken lashed the poor monster's hands, shoulders, and head with the leather straps and cuffs until he had forced him to stop what he was doing. He curled in his chair with his hands and arms over his head like an ape. His feet were drawn up into the chair seat. He was crying.

Mrs. Staples said kindly, "Put him in a locked room."

"Good damn thing he's getting shock treatment tomorrow morning," Carl drawled.

"They oughta just cut that damn thing off him," was Ken's opinion.

"I just don't see why the state has to keep something like that alive," Frankie said. "Ought to put him to sleep."

Because, Carlson thought, if it did, how long would it be before people like you or me were put to sleep for some reason?

"The ways of the Lord are mysterious and not for us to question," Mr. Babcock upped to inform them.

"You get away or we'll put you in a locked room too!" Carl warned the little man.

"Put him at Mr. Collins' table tomorrow," Ken said.

"Mr. Collins won't be at table for a few days," Carlson reminded them.

It was always a day or two after a man had shock

before he was ready to rejoin the others in the routine of the ward.

In the dining room two young women from the university were entertaining patients. They were pretty enough young women in sweaters and skirts, penny loafers and athletic socks. One was putting records back in the case that traveled with the portable record player she had brought up from the recreational therapy office. The other girl was finishing a checkers game with Fats Carlstrom. Various young men and women came over from the university as part of required field trips in psychology courses they were taking.

Fats was a farmer who weighed 350 pounds. He was in and out of the hospital about once a year. If the hog market went to hell he was sure to be coming in soon afterward in the custody of at least six deputy sheriffs. No two or three men could move Fats. When the price of hogs went down, Fats would drink for a month or two and go crazy. Crazy, he could wreck a six-room house with his bare hands, raze the thing. He was famous for knocking out a mule with a single punch. When the six deputies and four attendants got Fats into a locked room, he would try to put the bed through the little window in the door unless someone hit him with an entire hypodermic of sodium amytal. And when Fats got crazy, he liked to take off all his clothes, and no number of deputies, attendants, or loved ones could get him to put them back on until he wanted to.

Once he had calmed down, decided to get dressed, he was docile as an elephant. But like an elephant, everyone gave Fats plenty of room. If he ever took it in mind to squash a man against a wall, that man was going to be squashed. In the best of times, Fats, fully aware of his bulk and power, managed to acquire for himself exceptional personal privacy and independence even in a nut hatch. Not many nuts were nutty enough to bother Fats. Simpleminded, ever frightened attendants like Frankie obsequiously solicited his approval. If, after being let out of a locked room onto the ward, he might test the limits by deciding to sit up watching TV stark naked until the thing went off, he sat, while all the other patients were tucked in bed, and no nonsense about what was fair for one was fair for all. The attendants would simply leave Fats alone. When he was ready he would wander back to bed without so much as a "good night" for the attendants.

"Think I gotcha, honey," Fats told the slender young woman sitting opposite him at the table.

"Again!" she squeaked archly. "You're just too good for me."

"Honey, at checkers you ain't no good at all," Fats informed her honestly.

"I used to beat my brother all the time," she protested.

"Um."

"I did!"

"I don't doubt you, honey."

Fats took a tin of Copenhagen snuff from his biball pocket and with a practiced, slow finger dipped out a goodly load and tucked and smoothed it under his lower lip.

"You put that stuff in your *mouth?!*" the young woman squealed in amazement.

"Where'd you have me put it, up my ass?" Fats growled reasonably.

"Well . . ." the young woman stammered. "*I* didn't know. I've never seen anyone do that before. What is that stuff?"

"Snuff. You want a pinch?" He extended the tin to her.

"Uh . . . okay." She felt obligated to taste it.

She placed a tiny pinch in her mouth and made a terrible face.

"Water!" she called. "Oh, it's *awful!*"

She tried to brush the stuff out of her mouth, finally bending over and actually wiping her tongue on her wool skirt.

Fats laughed and laughed and told others who came to see what was going on what had happened.

"That stuff is *awful!*" she complained.

"Now you learned somethin'," Fats congratulated her.

Carlson escorted the young women to the elevator. Two

earnest young women dipping into a world they thought was exceptional, thinking they more represented the world's standard.

"How did you do?" the one that played the records asked the one who had sampled the snuff.

"I don't know. I kind of got the feeling they really resented us or something."

"Me too!"

"Don't feel bad," Carlson advised them. "Loonies are just like anyone else only more so."

"What?" the first young woman snapped. They both seemed amazed that Carlson could speak. Certainly an attendant was not conversant with things psychological.

"They are just men," he said. "They have to resent being treated and talked to as if they are stupid children. The average intelligence of these men works out to be in the high normal range."

"We were just trying to be supportive," the girl said. "And it wasn't easy being half scared all the time." She was a natural blonde, average in every direction, pleasant, with touches of hillbilly ancestry in her face and voice she would no longer recognize nor value.

"I know."

"Are you ever scared?"

"All the time."

"Really?"

"Really," Carlson insisted.

"You go to the university," the girl realized. "I've seen you. You edit the campus humor magazine and write that column in the student newspaper. Why are you working here?"

"I need the money. And when the patients are in bed I can get in some studying. It's interesting."

"Why haven't you ever had a girl from the psych department for your magazine's girl of the month?" the other girl asked; she was large-breasted and very pretty, and she was swelling her possible qualifications at him. "You almost always have someone from a sorority or one of the residence halls. Why don't you have someone who is truly independent?"

"Sure. Stop by the magazine office and we can set up a photo session with one of our photographers. Might be rather provocative if you keep those big black-rimmed glasses on."

"Oh! I didn't mean *me!*" She blushed.

"Why not?" the other insisted. "She's got a sensational figure," she told Carlson. "Really great!"

"Oh, I couldn't . . ." the other said.

"Sure," Carlson said. "Stop by the office. Assert your independence."

"Well . . . maybe."

The young women had become giggly. Carlson held the elevator door for them.

"She'll do it," the blonde assured Carlson.

Eight

MR. MARTIN WANTED Ken to turn off the TV.

"You sit down and shut up or you're going to get your other eye blacked," was Ken's advice.

"They sent out waves that control your mind," Mr. Martin argued. "They watch you!"

"The TV?" Ken grinned.

"The FBI," Mr. Martin explained, exasperated at the other man's ignorance. "They got the TV wired up. They control it all."

Ralph looked up from his copy of *Mechanics Illustrated* and cracked, "Yesterday he said it was the Communists."

"It *is* the Communists, you dumb, ignorant sonofabitch!" Mr. Martin shouted precisely, spraying a bit of spittle in Ralph's direction. "That's what I'm trying to tell you! The FBI's got it rigged to look for Communist acts, only what the FBI's doin' *is* Communist! Don't you darn fools see *that?!* It's the same thing!" His voice had become angrily hysterical, but was yet pleading in utter frustration for understanding.

"The FBI is Communist? Shit, you are fucked up, mister," another patient said.

"Oh, you dumb ignorant bastards! You'll just sit there and let them *do* it to you. Anything they want to do, you'll let them! They control it all already! It's all over, you stupid bastards! It's worse than Hitler. Worse than anything. Worse than the devil! They watch everything. They send out *waves* and read them comin' back. Little bitty itchy waves. I can *feel* them. They're watching all the time. They're makin' us crazy so as to take over everything!" His voice had risen to a hollow scream, cracking with frustration and rage, a middle-aged manic-depressive-paranoid-schizophrenic beset with homicidal furies. He stalked the ward constantly like a caged animal. His grinding fury even under medication this side of a coma was so total and so near the surface everyone was wary of Mr. Martin. He might lash out hysterically and homicidally at anyone anytime. It seemed Thorazine could not really touch what was troubling Mr. Martin. They had him down for electroshock the next morning. The shock would blast him out for a couple of days, leave him subdued and cringing for some time afterward, but it was no cure, and he would soon be his old manic, raging self.

Moreover, Mr. Martin had real trouble going to the toilet because the FBI had something in the bowl to keep an eye on him even there.

"They *ought* to watch you!" was Ken's opinion. "Now you sit the hell down in a chair and shut up and let these other men watch TV or I'm going to kick your ass and put you in a locked room. *You* probably are some kind of damn Communist." He meant it as a joke and took Mr. Martin's upper arm in a tight grip to help him into a chair.

"*Don't call me no Communist!*" Mr. Martin screamed. "*Take your hands off me!*" And he took a wild swing at Ken. As Mr. Martin swung, Ken jiggled him sharply to throw him off balance so the blow just grazed Ken's cheek.

"Now you crazy sonofabitch!" Ken hissed. He hauled the taller bony man around and busted him in the face with a big knobby country fist.

The sound of a man getting hit in the face is always slightly liquid, sickeningly dental, the sound of a butcher chopping bony scrap meat. Carlson winced.

Mr. Martin's face spurted blood. He was surely going to have two black eyes. Ken spun the man around as he tried to fight back. For all his rage and diagnosed homicidal tendencies, Mr. Martin was no fighter. Ken got his right forearm across the man's windpipe and squeezed until Mr. Martin's face turned purple, the manic veins in his forehead swelling like night crawlers. A long plume of breath feathered from his swollen, slack lips, and Ken lowered him to the floor. It was called "choking down."

"Help me get him into a room," Ken said over his shoulder to Carlson.

They dragged the long, limp form of Mr. Martin along the floor, Carlson hauling his feet, Ken supporting the man's head, sliding him along on his ass. Carlson unlocked the door to a quiet room—a padded cell. They dragged Mr. Martin inside and left him, went out, locked the door. Through the tiny observation window Carlson could see the blood from Mr. Martin's nose stain the often-stained padded floor.

"Going to be a wild fuckin' night." Ken grinned, studying a small break in the skin over a knuckle. "Startin' so early on the full moon."

Carlson did not think Ken was calculatedly sadistic. He was like some cops, some killer-soldiers. "If a man wasn't nuts what was he doin' in a nut hatch?" was the extent of Ken's philosophy regarding his work. It was just a job. "They have to be taught a lesson," was his guideline. The lesson Ken himself had learned early was that the world is a tough place where everyone has to look out for himself. You do not give others a lot of shit without risking a busted eye or beak. Standards could be bent a bit here and there, but finally standards had to be maintained. And everyone who deviated had to take his punishment.

The other three regular attendants decided the men were much too disturbed to risk taking them out of doors that day. Carlson had been looking forward to a bit of spirited softball. So had some of the less disturbed patients. Even the very disturbed men liked to watch. CCA usually played the young men from CCB. The men grumbled a bit when they learned they would not be going outside. It was a nice day.

At 7:00 P.M. Carl snapped off the TV set. The men, engrossed in a Popeye cartoon, protested.

"Medicine," Carl announced.

Frankie went around the ward calling, "Medication!"

The men left their chairs and shuffled in from the far reaches of the ward, already drugged to their eyebrows, to form a line along the corridor in front of the locked rooms that led back to the dormitory sleeping quarters.

In the medicine room, Carlson put specified pills for each patient into small paper cups. Frankie stood at the door as each man presented himself and handed the man his cup, watching closely as the man emptied the pills into his palm or mouth and extended the cup for water with which to wash them down. The men then stood like children with their mouths open for Frankie to see that they had taken their medicine. Carlson hated looking into the men's mouths, so Frankie most often worked the door. It was one of the unpleasant things he willingly did to make it up to the others for his scarce ability to read and write. Ken and Carl monitored the line outside.

"Hold it!" Ken commanded.

Ralph had palmed his pills and had only aped swallowing them. He had fooled Frankie. Ken grabbed Ralph's wrist and shook the orange pills out onto the floor.

Carlson felt sick for Ralph. What a stupid trick to try when he was scheduled to go down to CCB the next morning.

"I don't need them things no more," Ralph protested pleadingly. "They just make me dopey. I know I'm going home soon. All these pills'll just make me no good for my wife. Please . . ."

"Shit," Ken said. "It ain't the pills that's your problem there." They all had access to Ralph's records. That he was sexually unsatisfying for his wife was well known. Ralph had a very pretty, fecund-looking wife. "Anytime she needs a little something extra . . ." Ken grinned. "You pick up them pills and eat them."

Ralph bent and retrieved his medication from the floor. "I know I don't need them no more. I'm well . . . or almost." He popped the pills into his mouth and swallowed them dry. Frankie gave him a paper cup of water. "Listen, Mr. Smead," Ralph pleaded with Ken, "I'd appreciate it if you don't put anything about this on my report. I'll tell the doctor about it myself. He *said* he didn't think I needed so much medication no more. I know I don't need them. I feel good without them. Please, huh?"

"Go on. Move on," Ken said coldly. "You think you

got special privileges around here. You ain't home yet, boy. Not by a damn sight."

Ralph moved on. He was scared that the incident might delay his progress out of the hospital. He visibly slumped as he went back toward the day room.

The next man made an elaborate show of taking his pills for Ken's benefit, showing the world his wide-open trap, turning it from side to side like a spotlight. A man old enough to be his father, Carlson felt embarrassed for him—forced to act like a child.

Mr. Babcock came radiantly along, his left hand higher than his ear, forefinger pointing rigidly aloft. He seemed either charged with some kind of current, or, alternately, was folded into a corner like something that had been discarded.

Carlson smiled and tapped the little man on the tip of his upraised finger. "Mr. Babcock, what the hell *is* this?"

"Ask the Lord. For the Lord saw, and in His eyes it was an evil thing. There was no justice under the sun," Mr. Babcock testified in a strong monotone. "He saw there was no man to help and was outraged that no one lent a hand. Amen." His smile widened but his eyes burned as if he had delivered a holy writ.

When the line had ended, Frankie asked Carlson, "You want to take the new man his medicine? You know, him being a professor from the university an' all? The rest of us will take care of the men in the other locked rooms."

"Sure. Okay," Carlson said.

The man's name was Dr. Paul Marshall. An attempted suicide, he was not considered especially dangerous to others. He was only restrained to keep him from hurting himself. Black curly hair frizzed above a weary countenance that was collapsed hopelessly and turned toward the wall. The man was sedated but not sleeping. Large brown eyes rolled warily toward Carlson as he gently touched the man's shoulder.

"Dr. Marshall?" He shook the man a bit. "Time to take your medicine."

"No, thank you," he replied.

"Well, it isn't an option, sir. You have to take the medicine that has been prescribed for you."

"Who are you?"

"My name is Carlson. I'm here to help you if I can."

"What makes you think you can help me?" the older man sneered arrogantly.

"I don't know if I can or not. That is what I am here for. I will do what I can. It kind of boils down to the question of whether or not you want to get well and are willing to try and help yourself. Then, maybe I can help."

"You oversimplify, young man. You really haven't any idea of what you are talking about."

"On the other hand, here I am in this white suit about to give you your medicine and there you are in restraints, strapped to a bed about to take it. Think about that," Carlson suggested.

The professor was dressed in rumpled striped blue cotton pajamas over jockey shorts, which is what he had been wearing when he had been admitted.

A man who wore both his shorts and pajamas to bed, Carlson thought sympathetically.

A man who was soaked with sweat. He smelled acrid and medicinal. Men often sweated a lot when first admitted. The medicine gave them a new odor. But there was something about being "mentally ill" that affected the glands and made new patients or highly disturbed patients smell uniquely bad. They had a kind of death smell upon them. Something was dying in there, Carlson felt certain.

Spontaneously, Carlson unbuckled the man's right wrist from the bed frame. The skin was worn and broken where he had struggled against the restraint.

"I'll put something on your wrist to make it feel better after you take your medicine," Carlson promised.

Dr. Marshall did not seem to be feeling much physical pain. He stared at the worn place on his wrist objectively.

Carlson placed the pills in the man's hand. "What's this?" Marshall asked, dropping the medication.

"Just medicine," Carlson explained, putting the pills

back in his palm. "Some Thorazine and Seconal to help you rest." He guided the man's hand to his lips, which were rimmed with gray scum, saw him place the pills into his mouth, and held the cup of water for him to drink.

"Get them down?" Carlson asked.

The man nodded.

"If you would like to go to the bathroom or anything, I'll take you," Carlson offered.

"Do you know me?" the tall, professorial man inquired.

"Yes, sir. I had your Introductory Psychology class."

"I don't seem to place you."

"Well, I was not often there, sir. I had a lot of cuts in that class."

"How did you do?"

"B-plus."

"Really?"

"Yes, sir."

"Why are you keeping me tied up like this?!" Dr. Marshall suddenly demanded, trying to unstrap his left wrist.

"It is the doctor's orders, sir," Carlson explained. "They want to be sure to keep you down for a while. They will take them off soon. It is more or less routine on a new patient. They want you to rest. They know you are very tired. But why don't you get up and let me take you into the bathroom? You can have a good wash, cool off, stretch your legs a bit."

"You aren't afraid I'll do something crazy?" the man asked sarcastically.

Carlson smiled. "No, sir."

"I might, if I get the chance," he warned.

"Then I guess I just better leave you here as you are."

"Wait. I would like to wash."

"That's what I thought."

Carlson reached over and unbuckled the man's other wrist from the rail and helped him sit up. He was a heavy man, stronger than he looked. Carlson bent and slipped the worn Romeo slippers he found beneath the bed onto the man's feet. He put his arm around him and helped him to his feet where he needed support for a time. He was over six feet tall but a solid 190 beneath a layer of cold porklike fat.

"Hey, Frankie, get me a towel and washcloth for Dr. Marshall, will you?"

"He ain't supposed to be up," Frankie squealed.

"It's okay, Frankie. I'm with him."

"Nurse isn't going to like you gettin' patients up like you do."

"It's okay. I'll take the responsibility. A towel, washcloth, and some soap."

Dr. Marshall had a hard time relieving himself at a urinal. He cupped his hand backward, defensively, around his penis as if he were afraid someone would see it. From the glimpse Carlson got, Dr. Marshall had nothing in that area to be ashamed of. Carlson stood across the room and affected a casual stance of indifference until the professor was able to piss.

At the washbasin, Carlson helped the man take off his soggy pajama jacket and stood by as he methodically began to soap a washcloth and scrub his face and torso. He even washed his hair with the soap, an act that struck Carlson as the most reasonable thing he had yet seen the man do.

When the professor had finished with his front, Carlson offered to wash his back. Dr. Marshall leaned on the washbasin with both hands as Carlson vigorously scrubbed his back until the soft skin was pink.

There was a definite reddened ring around the man's neck from trying to hang himself with a bath towel in his bathroom after having a quarrel with his wife. He needed a shave. His hands were a bookman's, and consequently somewhat obscene. It was something Carlson felt he saw in many scholars—perhaps from a lifetime of probing the vitals of subjects in ways of perverse intimacy under the guise of doing unique work. Or perhaps it was simply that hands that had never known rough labor, even as a hobby, always seemed somewhat obscene to him.

Carlson helped Dr. Marshall with his jacket.

"Feel better?"

"Yes . . . Thank you . . . Uh, look, I don't want to stay here any more!" he blurted, seeming about to cry.

"I'm sorry, sir. There's nothing I can do about your staying or not. I can only try to make you more comfortable while you are here. You will have a chance to speak to one of the doctors Monday morning. There's really nothing you can do until then but try to rest, make the best of your situation."

He reached out and took Dr. Marshall's wrist firmly. The doctor let himself be led a couple of steps, then jerked away strongly, but in the movement of a man not accustomed to violent action. He backed a bit toward the urinals, the fat on his body shaking. Mr. Babcock had come in and was addressing one of the urinals, one hand yet raised higher than his dome as if he were "trucking." He settled down to watch the fun.

"Get your ass out of here, Mr. Babcock!" Carlson ordered. Mr. Babcock scooted.

"Come on now, sir, you have to go back to your room," Carlson said firmly. "I'm sorry. I have been as good to you as I can be now. But you do have to return to your room."

"If I could just make a phone call . . ." he pleaded.

"You can't. A phone call won't clear up your problem. It is going to take more than that. It is going to take time. You had better get it straightened out that you are going to have to spend some time here. Come on, now, let's go."

"I don't *want* to!" The man actually stamped his slippered foot.

Carlson had to smile. It was weird seeing a full professor about sixty years old acting like a spoiled little brat.

"You can only lose in that, sir. Come on. We are going back now." Carlson put out his hand.

The professor took a wild, feminine swing, which Carlson caught in mid-air, carried on to throw the man off balance, then stepped back through, wrenching the man's arm up in a helf-nelson behind his back.

Carlson let him go slowly, then, seeing no further resistance, put his arm around the professor and led him back to his room.

"It's going to be okay," Carlson said as he strapped the man's wrists back to the bed frame. "It seems all bad now, but it will get better. It almost always does. You think about that."

"I wish you didn't have to strap down my hands," the man sobbed.

"I wish I didn't either. I'll leave a note that I think they should take you out of these tomorrow."

Carlson realized the power he had, which the professor now reluctantly accepted. Hell, he might do anything at all to this miserable human being. That possibility was very saddening to Carlson. How could anyone want such power? If orders came down that night from the government that because of some national emergency all patients in mental hospitals were to be liquidated as humanely as possible, say by injecting phenol directly into their hearts as the Germans did at Auschwitz, what would he do?

He wouldn't do it. He was certain. Ken would. Carl and Frankie would. *Are you so sure about yourself?* he asked. *I think so. I hope so.* But he guessed he really didn't know one hundred percent for sure. It seemed very important that one knew for certain what he would do in such circumstances.

He looked at the helpless man in the bed, who was now crying himself to sleep as the Seconal began to take hold, and saw in his mind's eye all the patients in the hospital, all the hospitals everywhere. *I would sure as hell try not to do it. No. I would not do it. Better to be a victim.* Then the alter ego replied: *Better watch it, Sarge, you're really asking for it. Dummy up.*

Nine

THE FOOD CAME up on a rubber-tired cart pushed by a long-term idiot named Earl. He had been pushing that cart every day for years. He had just enough lights to push that cart where it was supposed to go. He rapped at the lookout door of the service elevator, which opened into the kitchen. Frankie opened the doors and passed a well-worn greeting with Earl. The food was in large stainless-steel pans. The attendants unloaded the pans and placed them on the vast kitchen counters for serving. Loaves of bread were taken from the cart and laid on another counter for slicing. The doors from the kitchen to the hallway and the dining room were locked. The faces of patients appeared from time to time in the small windows to see what they were having for dinner. When Earl had gone back down with his cart and the elevator again locked, Carlson unlocked the strongbox which contained the sharp knives and the silverware. Carl carefully counted out the necessary eating tools while Carlson sliced the large loaves of bread that were baked on the grounds. It was pretty good bread, better than you could buy in a store.

"Oh, it's sowbelly and collard greens two times a week," Frankie sang as he loaded the patients' trays.

Carlson finished slicing the bread and put the sharp knife back in the safe. Then the door into the dining room could be unlocked, helpful patients like Ralph could begin taking the food to the tables in the dining room, distributing the spoons and dull case knives with which the men ate.

Carlson took a piece of bread, went over to where Frankie was filling the trays, put a piece of crisp fat meat in the bread and folded it into a sandwich. The staff was forbidden to eat the patients' food. However they often set aside a piece of cake when it was on the menu to have with their coffee when the patients were in bed.

"You eat their food you're goin' to ruin your lovelife," Frankie warned seriously. "That stuff's full of softpeter."

"Saltpeter," Carlson corrected.

"Well, whatever you *call* it, I wouldn't touch a taste of that stuff if I was a young fella your age."

"Doesn't seem to have had any adverse effect so far," Carlson said.

"It will. And if the supervisor catches you, they'll fire you. They don't mind a piece of cake or slice of bread or two, but they catch you eatin' the patients' chow and they'll fire you."

None of the men down for electroshock the next morning were at dinner. They had to be cleaned out so they would not shit on the table when they were hit with the juice.

After the meal, Ralph and his crew cleared the tables, divided up with two men at the sink in the kitchen to wash the trays and cups, while two others swept and mopped the dining room. Then the kitchen was swept and mopped. All eating utensils were counted twice, the patients chased out of the kitchen, the doors locked, the cutlery box opened and the silverware put away, the box locked; then the kitchen was secured.

In the sitting room the men settled again before the television to watch until bedtime. None of the patients from the ward would be going down to the dance.

The dance began at eight o'clock. It might run as late as eleven.

Around ten, Ken returned from the dance. Frankie asked Carlson, "Why don't you go down for an hour? Do you good."

"Okay."

* * *

84

The women sat on folding chairs along one wall of the building's auditorium-gym. The men sat facing them across the hall along the other wall. There was no rule that men and women could not cross the dance floor to sit together, but with only a couple of exceptions they chose to sit apart.

Only about one fourth of those who attended the dance actually danced. The women were more eager to dance than were the men. Many women danced together, either for want of a male partner or out of genuine preference. No man danced with another man. The female attendants would never dance with a male patient but might dance with one of their female patients, and they would dance with the male attendants. Male attendants danced with female patients. The young men from CCB ward danced enthusiastically with all comers—young and old women alike. Jimmy Sullivan, who had murdered his cousin a year ago, was a very mature little dancer, whirling a woman old enough to be his grandmother around with remarkable elegance and style. But the old woman's eyes, like the eyes of most of the patients, were seeing far, far away, or barely seeing at all. So many moved as if stunned, drugged, it was eerie, a scene out of an Edvard Munch painting, the harsh shadows from the overhead gym lights chasing the dancers around the floor.

There were cookies and lemonade on a card table near where the record player was set up on another card table.

Dance in an Asylum.

Carlson leaned in the doorway as he watched. Three lone women dancers glided by—two fluidly, though they were old women, one spastically. A tall angular, emaciated girl with wild black hair cascading over her shoulders and face danced as if killing insects beneath her stomping feet. The attendants kept an eye on her. She danced with her palms flat on her thighs, rubbing her thighs sensuously as she moved. At the end of the room she yanked her shapeless dress over her head, exposing her naked body completely, hiding her head in her dress. Attendants rushed toward her. Patients stopped to laugh and observe. Other patients ignored the entire situation and continued to dance or stare fixedly at something else, or nothing. The girl's hip bones stuck out on either side of her concave belly like those of one nearly starved. Her entire skeleton was visible beneath her pale skin. Her breasts were small and neglected, her bush a wild, sooty triangle across the base of her belly. The whole apparition was mounted on long, birdlike legs, yet she was beautiful, perhaps more so for the pale, fragile vulnerability of her standing at the end of the hall swaying to the music, her dress over her head.

The attendants got her dress down and held her tight, scolded her, then talked to her to get her calmed down. They sat her on a folding chair across the hall. She became dull and disinterested, sitting with her face turned down, staring at the palms of her hands turned up in her lap. Her toes were turned in. She did not move.

Now Jimmy Sullivan was dancing with Doreen, a pretty young patient who worked in one of the offices as part of her therapy. She had gained weight in the hospital and her skirt and sweater were now at least one size too small for her. Jimmy held her at a practiced, respectable distance, making conversation as formally as a regular little gentleman. Only a year earlier he had stabbed his cousin to death with a Boy Scout hunting knife. He had stabbed her repeatedly. When Doreen saw Carlson, she left the boy to come over. She held out her arms. She fit herself closely to him and they moved out onto the floor. She made a good dancer of him. She looked very pretty, having spent time to make up her eyes so they seemed to sparkle out of dark lashes nearly an inch long. The lashes were false, he realized. She had put on stockings, high-heeled black pumps, pulled her thick, dark blond hair back, tied it with a black ribbon, leaving curling tendrils on either side of her face. In the deep vee of the blouse, nestling in the perfumed cleavage of her big breasts, was a tiny gold heart, open, revealing two miniature photos. When she realized what Carlson was looking at, she said:

"Oh, my locket must have come open. Those are my boys. Want to see?" She held up the locket. He took it and looked at the photos of two very dissimilar young boys.

She laughed. "They are Cain and Abel. They have different fathers. My mother takes care of them for me."

One was dark, one fair.

The tiny chain was cutting into the soft flesh of her neck. Carlson returned the locket to the place it had rested, the back of his fingers brushing the tops of her breasts. She made an almost imperceptible sound of "Oh!" and softly shot her pelvis forward against him, touching him, again almost imperceptibly, a couple of times. The sound and the movement were so slight he was not sure if it wasn't his imagination. But he looked into her eyes and knew what he had felt had been real.

"I dream about you," she whispered, barely moving her lips, dancing properly the length of the hall. "In my dreams we do everything. You know how long it has been since I made love with someone?"

"No."

"Three months."

She had been in the hospital for over a year. So, obviously she had been having sex with someone on the grounds.

"How long have you been here?" He smiled.

She did not flinch from the insinuation. "I used to do it with an attendant on CCB. We got caught and he got fired. But I've quit doing it with just anyone. I got to care about a person before I'll do it now. There's nothing wrong with doing it if you really care about someone. I've learned that. Used to be, sometimes I'd do it with some ole boy I didn't even like! Can you imagine that? Anyway, I figured it out and three months is the longest I ever went without doing it since I was twelve. I want you."

"How did you and the guy who got fired manage to get together?" Carlson asked, his face starting to burn.

"Did you hear what I said? I want you. Now."

"I heard. But how?"

"There are places. I had a key to the doctors' offices where I work for a long time. That's where we got caught. But I know a place where we could go right now and not get caught."

87

"Where?"

"The service elevator in this building. No one uses it at this hour. It's open downstairs. There isn't no lock on it except at the floor where there's patients."

Carlson realized she was right.

"It's hotter than shit in it, but you want to try it?" she asked.

"When?"

"Now, honey! What do you think I'm talkin'?"

"Now?"

"Now. You could just leave the dance and go there and wait for me. I could say in a little, 'I'm not feelin' so good' and go back to the ward. Ward's open. No one bothers me no more. Want to?"

"You're sure?" he asked, his voice gone a bit hollow.

"Honey, I'm so wet it's runnin' down my legs. I've been crawlin' the walls for a month. Old lady five fingers don't get it no more. There's no one waitin' for me outside I want more'n you."

When they were turned so there was no one behind them, she kissed his neck beneath his left ear and said, "I love you."

It was very crazy. Carlson realized how crazy it was as he slipped along the first-floor hallway toward the entry to the service elevator in the fire escape stairwell. They had all *talked* about fucking Doreen. Ken claimed he knew someone at the hospital who had and knew several boys on the outside who had before she was committed. They had all speculated on how she would be, vowing what they would do if they ever got the chance. Why was he always the one to do what others talked about doing? It's crazy, he was sure.

Maybe he would just see if she met him there. They didn't actually have to do anything.

Hell, Ken had said she had fucked three of the doctors, even old Dr. Small, who was scared to death of crazies.

He went into the stairwell through a steel fire door, lit a cigarette, waited. If anyone should come along and open the door he could say he was just taking a smoke. The door to the outside had windows in the upper half of it. Carlson could see the old buildings across the empty grounds. The walks were dappled with pools of light from old-fashioned lamps. A stray dog on the grounds trotted along, then stopped suddenly as if listening, looking up at the full moon which was now over the critical wing of the new hospital administration building. Carlson thought of the young man in there who had cut off his penis because it always kept screwing him up, "getting in his way."

He had finished the cigarette and decided she was not coming, when she slipped breathlessly in the door and took his hand.

"I got us a flashlight. It's dark in there," she explained.

Carlson opened the doors to the service elevator. They opened like the steel lips of a mechanical mouth, the upper door rising and the lower going down into the floor. Inside he hauled down on the upper door and the lower one came up too. He pulled down the wooden fencelike safety barrier inside the door but left it partly disengaged so someone could not operate the elevator from outside. Just in case.

Doreen switched on her flashlight, shining it on herself. It was hot as hell in there. They were both already sweating.

"Kiss me," she said.

He kissed her. She kissed as if she would tear out his tongue.

"You kiss good!" she finally exclaimed. "Want me to dance for you?"

"What do you mean?"

"I always wanted to dance naked for someone, for a whole room full of men, feel them all wanting me. It isn't an uncommon feeling. The doctor told me. I don't even have to feel bad about it no more. Lots of women fantasize about doing that. Want me to dance for you?"

"Sure," Carlson agreed huskily.

"You hold the light then." She handed him the flashlight. "I want to make you get hard just watching me dance," she said. "I wish I had some music." She began humming an old roadhouse stripper's tune, "Night Train," as Carlson knelt and played the light over her.

"Do-ta-do-ta-do-ta-do-ta-do-ta—voom-voom," she hummed, peeling off her blouse, lifting her thick hair off her neck with both hands while she ground and bumped her hips toward Carlson.

He played the light over her face and breasts. A roll of pale fat bulged above the tight waistband of her skirt.

She unhooked her black brassiere and shook her big floppy tits free. "Voom-voom . . ."

He played the light on her bare tits as she lifted them as if in an offering, twirling the tips of her forefingers on the large, erect nipples. Then she bent her face and was able to kiss each nipple, actually sucking them.

How about that? Carlson asked himself.

"Do-ta-do-ta-do-ta-do-ta—voom-voom," she hummed and bumped.

He played the light on her middle as she unzipped and skinned out of her tight skirt like a snake shedding skin, then kicking high but not prettily with first one meaty leg then the other in a would-be ballet or modern dance movement. On one level, Carlson suddenly felt very sorry for the poor deluded young woman. On another level he shone the light full on the crotch of her blue nylon panties from which peeked a wealth of dark pubic hair when she kicked so high.

She squatted in front of Carlson with her legs apart, rocking her big ass back and forth, tapping the bulge in her blue panties teasingly with her fingertips, cocking her head quizzically as if to ask if he wanted her to take them off.

"Do-ta-do-ta-do-ta—voom-voom," she sang.

Off came the panties. Then, wearing only her black garter belt, stockings, and shoes, she began dancing furiously, fucking the air wildly toward all four corners of the compass, grabbing the air to her as if pulling imaginary ropes. The cellulite in her ass was dimpled like the distant surface of the moon. Her skin shone with sweat in the dark box in which she performed.

"Do you like me?" she demanded.

"Yes!" he told her.

90

"Tell me."

"I like your big flying butt, your bouncing tits, your big hairy cunt. I like you. I like your legs and your face."

"Do you really want me?" She continued to dance, teasingly closer, then backing off or spinning away.

"Yes."

"Tell me."

"I want you."

"Tell me what you want to do to me."

"Fuck you. I want to fuck you."

"Are you hard?"

"Sorta."

"Show me your cock. Make it hard for me. Do-ta-do-ta-do-ta-do-ta—voom-voom."

He took out his cock, stroking it with his right hand while playing the light over her sweating naked flesh with his left.

"Um, it's pretty!" she observed as he shined the light on himself to show her he was hard.

She danced over and ground her cunt at him a few inches from his cock and said, "Kiss it."

He grasped her ass with both hands, dropping the light, and kissed her big pussy.

She dropped to her knees and propped the light so they could see each other better and popped his cock in her mouth, sucking deeply for a few minutes, then getting astride him and sinking his cock deep into her big wet cunt.

"Fuck the shit out of me, honey!" she cried.

He rolled her over onto the floor and fucked her hard. Her ass pitched like a small boat on a stormy sea.

"Kiss me! Suck my tits! Fuck me! Don't let me scream when I come. I go off like a siren. Put your hand over my mouth when I come. It has been *so long* since I had a good one. *Oh-do-me-good-Daddy!*"

Her cunt was very large. Carlson was puffing, fucking all sides of her and to the depth, the best he was able.

"Honey," she crooned, "you fuck good. If any of my husbands had been like you, I'd be happily married yet.

Um, don't stop! Shove your finger up my ass, will ya? I wish you had three dicks."

"So do I!" Carlson assured her.

"Do you really like me?" she asked.

"I do! I really like how you are," Carlson vowed, fucking her hard again. *Woman could accommodate a battalion of Greek Marines*, he thought. "Can you come?" he wondered.

"I been comin' since you got in me," she insisted. "I come all the time. But I can pop it too. Do me hard and close until I can't hardly move, grind that bone above your dick into me hard and I'll make it with you."

"Hadn't I better pull out?" he asked.

"They tied my tubes first time I was in here," she said. "Oh, that's it! Do it! Oh, yes, do it! honey! Fuck me *hard!* Hard! Tear my ass up! I'm comin'! Come with me!"

They came together. His juice flowed out of her cunt and down the crack of her ass.

"Whoo, baby, you flooded me," she sighed.

They were both sticky with sweat.

"Boy, I needed that," she sighed, sitting up, beginning to get herself together. "If you come see me when I get out of here, we can spend the whole night together, fuck our brains out. Would you like that?"

"Sure," he said, wondering if he would.

"You do really like me? I'm not just another dumb cunt, am I?"

"I like you. You aren't dumb. I liked that a lot, really."

"Am I better than them little college girls over at the university?" she wanted to know.

"You're real good, Doreen. You're great!"

"My pud's not too big and sloppy after having them kids?"

"I like it big and sloppy. I mean you're just fine. Real good, baby."

"I wish we *could* spend the whole night together. I'd just like to do everything with you. After three months once just isn't enough. But I guess it will have to do for now. We'll go out together when I get out, won't we?"

"We will. First thing."

"Promise?"

"Promise."

"Seal it with a big kiss."

He kissed her.

"We better go," he said, checking his watch.

Outside in the stairwell, she said, "I'm glad you respect me and relate to me as a person. That's why I let you."

"Thank you," he said.

"I really love you, James."

"James?"

"Yeah." She laughed. "Didn't I tell you, you remind me of James Dean."

"Oh."

In the hallway the rush of night air was so cool it made him shudder. His whites were rumpled and soiled from his having been on the floor of the elevator. She had wiped back a stray hair from her brow and given him a quick kiss and walked partly away down the hall, her clothes not so neat as before, but otherwise so unchanged he had to recall some detail of what had transpired between them to assure himself that they had fucked at all. He could see her at the far end of the corridor about to go up in the elevator. She blew him a kiss, smiled, and wiggled her fingers at him.

Like Chinese food, he thought; an hour later and you will be hungry again.

Doreen. Christ she had a big cunt.

Crazy! Carlson, you are crazy to be fucking some crazy young woman. *Popular psychology for you and me, baby, he told her in his mind, just isn't for people like us. It is for somebody else. For somebody who somehow gives more of a shit. Good fuck. Dumb show. Yeah, I love you too. What the hell.*

On the way home after midnight, Carlson and the three other college men were all beat. It had been a night of walkers and talkers. Everyone in the car pool except Tom

Allen, who was driving, tried to catch a few winks of sleep as they headed back along the highway. Tom was uncommonly chipper, whistling.

"What the hell's with you?" Wade Gordon wanted to know. "You been into the paraldehyde or something?"

"Damnedest thing happened to me. You won't believe it. If I tell you bastards you gotta promise to never tell anyone else. It could be my ass."

"You saw a ghost!" Wade guessed.

"Better than that. I met Doreen in the hall comin' up from the dance, all hot and bothered, and she took me to the service elevator and I fucked the shit out of her. Man, she's wild! She says she loves my ass. Says if any of her husbands had been like me she'd be married yet."

"She is crazy, you know," Carlson reminded him. He saw that the knees of Tom's whites were stained and his clothes rumpled. "You could really get your ass in trouble screwing a patient. Jesus Christ!"

"But shit-oh-my-dear that girl likes to fuck."

"Maybe she's just lonely," Carlson said.

Ten

CARLSON WAS COMPELLED to tell Sally about the incident with Doreen at the hospital. It puzzled him that he had to tell her about it; that was not at all like him.

"I don't care," she said after several moments of thought. "Yes. I don't care," she affirmed. Yet she did not look happy.

"I'm sorry," Carlson told her.

"Why? Why are you sorry?"

"Because I've hurt you."

"Yeah, you've hurt me. I don't know why. I really don't care . . . intellectually. Emotionally I guess I'm conditioned to be hurt by it. I know you love me. I know that more than anything I've ever known. It's like being rich, I think. It's like money in the bank. I'm not repelled by your confession." She laughed. "It is a confession, isn't it? 'Sally, I screwed someone else when you were home.' That poor girl. Actually, I'm not repelled at all. In fact, I'm rather excited by it—her doing a striptease while you shined a flashlight on her. Want me to do a strip for you?"

"No."

"Why not? I think I could do a great strip."

She skinned out of her light blue sweater, tossing it lightly into the backseat of the car. Off came her clean white bra; flinging it into the backseat, she got up on her knees on the seat and shook her nice, pale, pink-tipped boobs at Carlson.

There were pearls of tears in the corners of her eyes.

"Sally," Carlson pleaded.

"How do you like it so far?" she demanded.

"Come on, Sal."

She unzipped her light blue skirt and rolled and bumped her belly at him as she knelt on the car seat.

It was late afternoon. He had picked her up after her last class. They were parked where they had parked the first time they had made love. It had turned cooler the last couple of days. Leaves were starting to fall. The light in the late afternoon was at the first remarkable slant of autumn.

"Come on, Sally, don't. I'm sorry."

"Don't I excite you?" She peeled her skirt and panties down to her knees, then sat down, took them off, tossed them into the backseat. She braced her shoulders against the back of the front seat to thrust her bare belly wildly up at Carlson, rubbing her hands over her body, over her sex and breasts. She was beautiful, poignant, dearly pathetic, cute even—with scuffed saddle shoes, heavy athletic socks on her feet, otherwise stark naked in the front seat of the car on an autumn afternoon of painter's light, leaves falling so the memory of the smell of burning leaves and football afternoons was like a kind of drunkenness.

"Don't you want to fuck me? How can you resist?" Tears now coursed down her cheeks in two distinct rivulets. "I want you to fuck me! Fuck me like you did her."

"No." He clasped her buttocks in both hands and dropped his face between her white thighs. "I want to make love to you because I love you more than anything or anyone ever. I love you. I want *you!* . . . Because you are very, very dear to me and always will be." He kissed the wrinkly pink lips beneath the golden bush of hair. He found the eternal taste of the sea within her—a taste that tied him to some nonspecific, transcendental reality, a truth beyond his ability to verbalize or explain. Thinking of falling leaves and the first remarkable light of autumn, he was lost in his tender feelings for the young woman.

"Take off all your clothes too," she requested.

It was rather crazy. It was a day when other cars were likely to come and park along the creek road. But Carlson stripped while Sally put first one foot and then the other up on the seat to remove her shoes and socks.

"Everything," she insisted. "I like to feel the hair on your legs with my feet when we do it," she said.

It was sweet. It was love and it was fucking of a very high order. Each touch and movement was electric, effortless, lovely. Every kiss was like falling through space together. It was so sweet it was corny.

"I love you so much," Carlson told her.

"I feel like I'm connected to you," she said. "It's like your cock is part of *me*, and my cunt is part of you. Like our molecules have blended together or something, like one nerve system. I want you to come in me. I want to have your baby."

"That's crazy, darling."

"No, it isn't. Trust me. I want it. *Now!* It doesn't matter if we get married ever. I want to have your baby. Let's come together and you come in me. Promise?"

"Okay."

"Yes. It's okay. Very okay." She snaked her arms around his ears and pulled his face down to kiss him long and lovingly. She caressed the calves of his legs with her bare feet.

They came together, crying out, she screaming, and lay together blinded, throbbing, moving together for the space of an exquisite lifetime—a full lifetime, for it was the kind of coming that puts the slip on time. Almost dying can cause the same effect. People always speak of their entire lifetime passing before their eyes. It was that kind of coming. Carlson had experienced something like it only once before. If he experienced such a thing a couple more times in his lifetime, he thought it would be exceptional. He didn't think most people ever experienced such a feeling.

They lay together, he on top of her, on the car seat and dozed for a little while. It was only when they awakened that his flaccid penis was finally squeezed from her. Even then she sought to cradle it in the lips of her vagina.

"I hope I have your baby," she said. "I hope it's a boy."

"If you do have one, a girl would be all right," he replied.

"I want a little boy like you were."

"I was a strange little boy. What the hell would you do with it?" he wanted to know.

"Take him into the bathtub with me and wash his tummy."

"Take me into the bathtub with you and let me wash your tummy," he suggested.

"Can we? Really?! Can we go away together sometime soon? It wouldn't have to be expensive. Just drive down to Lake of the Ozarks and get a cabin on the lake or something. Sleep together every night all night, for several nights. Oh, I'd love that!"

"So would I. Sure we can. You just figure out when you can get away and I'll take a long weekend."

"But maybe you will hate me." She became concerned.

"Now why the hell would I hate you?"

"I can't cook. I couldn't make you breakfast. Oh, I guess I can scramble an egg and make bacon, but I don't do it well. I mean my eggs never come out nice and fluffy and the bacon is always half done at the ends and burnt in the middle. I'm hopeless. I can't cook and I can't sew. You *will* hate me."

"No I won't. I can cook *and* sew."

"Can you really?"

"Sure."

"I *do* love you. You've got tattoos, and you can cook, and sew, and make love to me so beautifully. Let's go soon. I love you so much I ache. I love you more than I do me. I truly do. I always heard or read about that, but I never felt it until now."

"I love you more than I love myself too," he said.

"You ever feel like that before?" she asked.

"Once." He would not lie to her.

"The girl you knew in the Army?"

"Yes."

"I don't want to think about that. I don't want to talk about other women. This time was just perfect. Hold me tight. Kiss me. Love me."

But the perfect moment had passed and they would never know it together again.

Eleven

THE MEETING OF the Bard's Lair was held that night in the home of the chairman of the English department. It was a club of writers and poets who met to read their work, drink a lot, and discuss literature. There were only male club members, most of them faculty. Carlson had been the first undergraduate elected president of the club.

He was arguing with an English professor, a published writer and poet named Levy, about Mrs. Browning's work. They had both had a few drinks.

"I say she doesn't know shit about love, the countryside, or much of anything else!" Carlson contended. "Hers is a purely sentimental view. Nothing she writes about falls close enough to the heart of the matter."

Levy was also a Milton scholar, another subject they might argue violently about.

"In all of critical history no one has made the absurd, uninformed, callow claim you have just made!" Levy was certain.

"Then they sure as hell should have! Take that poem about the milkmaid and the farm boy. It is pure bucolic nonsense. A dizzy upper middle-class woman's view of what goes on down on the farm. Shit! There's no regard in her sentimentality for the fact that the kids' diets were lousy, that they might well have had cowpox—certainly angry red bumps on their asses—and that their matings when they took place were more than likely a furtive jumping on one another in the back of a barn. Man, have you ever *been* on a near-feudal farm?"

"Have *you?*"

"Yes. We were on maneuvers one spring outside of

Rosenheim, Germany. Pulled our tanks off into the woods on some high ground overlooking a hop field and a traditional farm. We watched the girls working in the hop field through our binoculars and waved at them. Good, big strapping *frauleins* with sunburnt arms, rosy cheeks, asses like Percherons. We figured we could slip down there after dark and trade some C-rations and cigarettes for whatever they had. And we did.

"We arrived when the family was sitting down to supper. Fourteen people eating on a big scrubbed wooden kitchen table—no dishes. Just eating off the table. Three generations there. Big bottles of beer. They made their own beer and dark bread. We traded for the beer and bread and some lean Nazi ham. Great fucking ham. Then I went outside with one of the girls we had waved at. She was a niece of the owner. She and the others slept in the barn. All the men in the place had a right to the girls— the uncles, the owner, the cousins.

"She was a healthy, ignorant sort. Hoisting her skirts was of no great moment for her. Nor was taking it up the butt. All in a day's work, as it were. The situation worked. The beer was excellent. So was the bread. The ham was great. The fucking had no more meaning than anything else. Maybe it shouldn't. But the point is, Mrs. Browning does not know shit about country love among the peasantry."

"You do grow tiresome, Carlson. You really do. I think we should put it to a vote, you're growing tiresome." Levy was drunk enough to throw an almost full can of Budweiser at Carlson's head, which Carlson ducked and saw tumble past to smack the chairman of the English department's favorite Picasso print.

Carlson laughed. Education was a joke. Yet it *was* an education. It just dawned on him. He felt he was almost one of the gentlemen. A major insight, he supposed. Then he wondered if he might cry. He never felt more alone or less happy in his life.

His faculty advisor and a member of the club called out to inform Carlson that he was wanted on the telephone.

It was his roommate, Jeff Steele.

"Tom broke a mirror in the men's crapper beneath the library," he reported. "You better get over here. We took pictures with a brownie camera. There was a little old campus cop behind the hole. He was scared shitless. Had a gun and everything, but he got up and ran. Get over here, Cat."

Carlson went back into the living room, half laughing, half crying.

"Gentlemen, I must go. It seems there is—or was—a see-through mirror installed in the men's toilet at the library. It has been broken."

"My God!" someone said. "Whatever for?"

"I don't believe it. Is it some prank?"

"A what?" the chairman of the English department kept asking as Carlson left.

"Absurd!" someone insisted.

They were in the toilet in the tunnel which passed through the lower level of the library between the main campus and the new campus. There were Jeff Steele, Tom Allen, and Wade Gordon.

All three worked with Carlson at the state mental hospital; they shared a car pool, driving back and forth together each day, and had become friends.

Wade was in engineering. He was a methodical, soft-spoken young man, forever baiting his best friend, Tom Allen, with whom he'd gone to high school in some small town.

"Look at this, Cat!" Tom showed him the hole in the masonry wall that had been behind one of the mirrors above the sinks in the restroom. Inside the hole was a stool, table, and telephone so a voyeur could sit and observe the toilet through a mirror.

"Why the hell would anyone want to do that?" Carlson wondered, truly. It had been such a lot of trouble to make that hole and spy place, cost a lot, too.

"Who the hell knows?" Tom said. "The fuckin' place is crazy, man."

"It is just crazy."

"What are we going to do?" Steele wondered.

"Do we have photographs?"

"Yeah."

"Okay. Let's go over to our place and call Bob Pasetta and talk about this," Carlson said.

"Man, Cat, you should have seen that old fucker that was in there when we busted that place. I thought he would shit! Went pale as a sheet. He was scared!"

Bob arrived at the converted garage and someone gave him a beer.

"I think we should call *The New York Times*," was Wade's suggestion.

"Maybe," Carlson said. "I think first we should call the dean of men and see what he has to say about this."

"Shit, man, you call that fucker about this and they'll have our butts in jail before morning," was Tom's opinion.

When they voted, Steele and Bob Pasetta voted with Carlson to talk to the dean before calling *The New York Times*.

Carlson made the call. It was then two o'clock in the morning. The dean denied any knowledge of any sort of two-way mirror in any toilet on campus. Carlson would have to speak with the vice-president of the university about this. The dean would telephone the vice-president and get back to Carlson.

Within an hour the dean called to say that Carlson and the others had an appointment with the vice-president of the university at 8 A.M. the next morning and that if they had to miss any classes they would be excused.

"Have you told anyone else about this?" the man inquired.

"We were about to call *The New York Times*, inasmuch as the local newspaper is under the control of the university, but we thought we would give the school a chance to explain first," Carlson said.

"Well, Jarl, I'm glad you are acting responsibly in this thing. I am sure it will be taken into consideration by the vice-president."

"Oh, we *will* call *The New York Times* if we don't get some damned good answers."

"Well, Jarl, I can assure you that I have no knowledge on this matter. I'm as surprised as you are."

They hung up.

"That lousy piece of shit," Carlson told the others. "He's lying like a bastard. And he's scared."

"I still think we ought to call *The Times*, man," Tom Allen said. "You don't know these fuckers. They'll hang your ass in this pigfucking country and look for justification later."

"Well, still the right thing is to confront the vice-president with this and hear what he has to say," Carlson said.

"Cat's right," Bob Pasetta said.

"Okay. Who's going to go in there tomorrow?"

"I think you and Bob and one of us who was in the crapper should go," Jeff Steele suggested.

Bob Pasetta did not seem eager.

"What's the matter?" Carlson asked him.

He was embarrassed. He was going to refuse, Carlson could see it. He loved his friend and was pained for him.

"What is it, Bob?"

"If you guys want me to go, I will," he said wearily. "But I'll tell you the truth, I would rather not. I'm ready to graduate with honors. There's a scholarship for graduate study. I'll do it if you want me to, but I would honestly rather not. I hope you understand. I know I'm copping out . . ."

"Forget it," Carlson told him and went over and put his arm around him, but he knew as he did it that they would never really be close friends again.

"I'm in enough trouble already," Wade said. "I mean the engineering department is super damned conservative. They would be upset as hell if I get my ass into some crazy shit like this. I'd like to skip it."

"Okay. Tom? Jeff?" Carlson said.

"I'll go with you," Jeff Steele said.

"Better count me out," Tom said. "What we should have done was call *The Times*."

Jeff Steele had an idea. "I'll call Bill Campbell. He'd like to hear about this."

Campbell was an opposition campus politician and law student. It might be good to have Campbell along.

Carlson called Sally to tell her what happened but the girl on the phone at her dorm would not call anyone to the telephone at that hour unless it was a family emergency. Nor could he convince her it was a family emergency.

Promptly at eight o'clock the next morning Carlson, Jeff Steele, and Campbell presented themselves to the secretary in Vice-President Green's office. They had taken the time on the way to notice that police barricades now closed off the men's toilet in the tunnel between campuses under the library.

This is how the world ends, Carlson thought absurdly as they went into the vice-president's office.

He was a shirtsleeve kind of administrator. A hard-working, no-nonsense kind of character. Mr. Green was the unsung man who actually ran the university. The president lived up in the big house, had published a couple of fairly well-received books, and was a glad-hand-out in all directions. He did not actually know anything about how the university was operated. He was a front for men like Joe Green.

"Come in. Come in. Sit down." He waved brusquely at the chairs before his desk in the small office. "Now, what is this all about?"

Seated behind his desk with a pad open on the pull-out extension of the desk was the chief of campus police, Gene Wright. Carlson knew about Wright from Dr. Turner, his professor of philosophy. After class one day, Carlson asked about the long jagged scar on the doctor's forehead. He always made a point of talking to Turner, savoring the intellectual stimulation of their conversations. Turner was a friend of John Neihardt, another bond between himself and Carlson. The portly, good-natured professor would speak to the younger man as an equal, talking often of his years in China, of warlords, trains and towns under attack, the occupation by the Japanese, internment in a concentration camp. When he spoke of torture and hunger one day, Carlson had asked if the scar dated back to his time in the Japanese camp.

The doctor fingered the place. "No. That happened right here. Oh, about five or six years back there was a famous criminal case in town. A babysitter for a family over in the best part of town"—he said a well-known local family name—"was raped and killed. Everyone knew that the somewhat demented son of that family had done the job on her. But that family was so powerful the police went out and collected a black man, a town drunk who slept every Saturday night on the courthouse lawn, beat him with nightsticks until he confessed.

"Now he was an illiterate. And when his first and then his second confession did not hold up in court, they kept going back to him and beating him until they got one that would hold up. We all knew the man was being framed. The whole town knew. Dr. Neihardt and some others from the university went to the police station to protest. I was elected spokesman. The police chief was a local fascist named Eugene Wright. He is now the head of our campus police. Wonderful character. He would not let us present our protest or answer the list of questions we had drawn up. Instead he had a deputy, a big sucker who was supposed to be able to knock down a mule, come and disperse us. He had on a pair of those yellow leather workgloves. He hit me in the forehead and split it open. There was also a slight fracture. Huge man. The chief got scared after that and fired him. He went back to his farm. But I hear now he has been having some problems and is in the state hospital."

Carlson had wondered if the man could have been the patient they called Fats.

Now he tried to concentrate on what the vice-president of the university was saying.

"I understand you boys are in a little trouble." Green would begin on a tack like that.

"No, sir. We are here just to find out why there is a two-way spy mirror in the men's john under the library," Carlson said.

"Well, it isn't there now, is it?" Green said sarcastically.

"No, sir."

"Did you boys break that mirror?" Wright asked.

"That is immaterial to why we are here," Carlson said. "We want to know why it was there."

"There has been a problem with homosexuals on campus," Green said wearily.

"*That* much of a problem?" Campbell asked. His voice was exaggeratedly southern, stentorian; you could hear echoes of Pitchfork Ben Tillman in it. "Goodness, I wasn't aware that we were so overrun with queers around here. I do wonder, though, what the daddies of some of them good old Aggie boys are goin' to say when they go home and tell them: 'Pa, you know what we've got up there at the great state U? We got a peeper in the poop-house!' "

Carlson and Steele could not help but grin. Campbell leaned back in his chair and actually put his feet against the front of the vice-president's desk. Carlson thought *that* was going a bit far, but he did admire the man's audacity.

"Well, I'm sure *if* you fellas aren't a bit that way yourselves, you will understand and want to help us," Wright suggested.

"Well, we aren't a bit that way ourselves, and you damned well know it," Steele let him know. "You're trying to play some interrogation game you learned at the FBI Academy, first threaten and then befriend. Hell, we've all studied the same manual in the military on the interrogation of prisoners. Now, we did not come here as some wetass-behind-the-ears punks."

"We'd just like to know if the governor of the state is aware of that damned thing in the crapper," Campbell said.

"And philosophically," Carlson added, "we would like to know—since that thing was designed to catch queers— on which side of the dirty glass do you think the greater perversion is possibly committed?"

"Well, the governor does not have to be bothered with crap like this," Green replied. "I run this school, and the board of trustees have given me the responsibility for the protection of students at this school."

"The board of trustees are aware that a two-way mirror was put in the toilet and that you have a man behind it all the time the library is open?"

"It is not important if they know exactly about such measures or not," Green snapped. "I don't have to answer to you people!"

"Yes, you do," Carlson insisted. "We are not only here as students. I am here as a representative of two campus publications. Campbell represents the law school journal, and Steele is on the student council."

"You are here because you have damaged university property," Wright countered.

"In a pig's ass we are. We called you, not the other way around. One, you would have to prove that we were the individuals who actually broke the thing and you would have to produce your witnesses. Have you a witness? I understand that there was a campus cop in back of the mirror. Do you want to call him in and see if he can identify us?"

"You . . . think you're pretty smart, don't you, boy?" Wright snarled at Campbell.

"I think you people are shaking in your shit. I think the last thing you want is for this to hit the newspapers," Campbell said.

"Have you spoken to any of the news media?" Green humbled himself to ask.

"No," Carlson said. "We agreed to wait until we had talked to you and gotten your best explanation for what has been going on. Do you also have such mirrors in the women's toilets on campus?"

Green looked quickly at Wright and then said, "*No!* Of course we don't!"

"I don't see why," Carlson argued. "I know of at least three lesbians on the faculty here. In fact, I know more lesbians on campus than I know homosexual men."

"Give me their names and we'll have them out of here in a day," Wright promised.

"No. That's nuts! They don't bother anyone."

"Well, we just want to rid the campus of this blight," Green said. "We had a scandal here back in forty-eight, lost an assistant dean and uncovered a card file of homosexuals that went down to the School of Mines in the southern part of the state."

"We know about that, but it just seems to us that if we have a problem of such magnitude that it warrants a device like that mirror, we have a problem that should be brought out in the open and discussed by the student body generally."

"We are running a university here," Green said toughly. "Not a hospital or a debating society."

"Oh. I see what is desired is that we should shut up, keep our hands down, and show up and make passing grades even if we have to cheat a bit or use a paper that has been in fraternity or sorority files for six years—all those good healthy American ways of getting by—and don't ask any real questions at all, right?" Carlson said heatedly.

"This *isn't* a democracy. I have to run this school. You haven't any idea what goes on on this campus. Suicides, girls getting pregnant, faculty members—dammit, do you know just last week, right in that tunnel down there, some damned queer caught a little eight-year-old girl coming home from school and jacked off on her shoulder? She had to run all the way home with that stuff on her sweater. If we don't catch that bastard before that little girl's father does, we are going to have a killing. Can you imagine the trauma that little girl will suffer all her life because some goddamned animal did that to her?"

"Yes," Carlson admitted. "Again, if there is a problem, wouldn't all of us being aware that some geek or queer is going to jump out of the bushes any minute be useful in stopping the problem?"

"We don't see any reason to rile up the community when we can take care of such things ourselves."

"By putting a two-way mirror in the donnikers?" Campbell said.

"Only the one!" Wright insisted. "And now you've ruined that," he added with genuine sorrow.

"What do you do with the men you catch in there?" Carlson asked.

"Well, I can promise you they don't stay around here very long!" Wright said and grinned grimly.

"In other words, you kick the shit out of them and run them out of town," Carlson said.

"I'm only saying they don't stay around here after we have caught them," Wright replied.

"Jesus Christ!" Campbell cried. "Do Missouri and Iowa and Ohio State and Michigan and all those other great state universities know you are sendin' this army of beat-up queers their way?"

"What you men must understand," Green almost pleaded, "is that we have many minors here. If a young woman is raped or molested on campus and we haven't taken every precaution against such a thing, her parents are going to want to know the reason why. Or a young man less secure than yourselves. We could even be sued. We believe we know what we have to do to maintain order here and create the proper climate for this university to function."

"We do appreciate the special problems of running this place, I am sure," Carlson said. "But we also don't think your methods, as exemplified by that damned mirror, are an answer. It begs the question whether the ends justify the means."

"Our consciences are perfectly clear on that score. You can be sure of that."

"I am only sure that your primary response is to sweep the whole thing under the carpet so it's important that news of this situation gets to more objective newspapers than the school-controlled daily and the school-controlled radio and television station," Carlson said.

"If this thing goes any further than right here and now," Green said coldly, "I promise you, Carlson, you will never graduate from this institution."

"That has long since ceased to be my fondest desire," he replied, just as coldly.

"All right. You all get back to your classes. You will be hearing from me about this. And what I said to Carlson goes for all of you."

"You really are an asshole, aren't you, Mr. Green," Campbell drawled.

Green stood in his shirtsleeves, both fists on his desk, supporting his weight on rigid arms, and said nothing.

They went over to the Student Union together and took a booth where they could talk.

"What are you going to do?" Jeff Steele asked.

"Call the *St. Louis Post Dispatch* and the *Democrat* and *The New York Times*, tell the whole story," Carlson said.

Campbell scratched his head beneath his railroader's cap. "Well, Cat, that was fun. But I ain't goin' no further with this. I live in student housing with my wife and kid and dog. I don't think this is issue enough to sacrifice my law career for. I plan on being in the state government in a few years, a judge one day. We made our point. They aren't going to put that thing back in there . . . until we've gone, anyway."

Steele said, "I'm with you, Cat, whatever you think we should do. My old man will kill me, but . . ."

"Forget it, Jeff. I'll do this. I think we should make the situation public. I'll write a note to Green, taking responsibility for all further action."

"You always did want to play Mark Antony or Coriolanus," Campbell accused Carlson.

"Maybe. But I'm going to do this. I think it is a serious thing. I don't give a damn about graduating from this school."

"You think other schools are better?" Campbell asked.

"Probably not. I don't care."

"Well, okay. It's all yours now, then."

They got up and went off to their classes.

Carlson went to the magazine office. He wrote out a

statement for the vice-president and put it into the intra-university mail. Then he telephoned the *St. Louis Post Dispatch* and gave them the story. Within an hour the television stations in St. Louis were calling him.

Sally came into the office in the middle of the afternoon. She looked flushed. She threw herself in his arms and kissed him.

"You heard," he said.

"Heard?! My darling, I have been over at the god-damned Student Health Service all morning answering questions of that asshole. He's just a fink! He had a tape recorder going in his damned desk the whole time I was there. They called me out of my first class. He asked me all sorts of things about you. He tried to scare me by saying that he knew we were sleeping together and that I was still under eighteen, all sorts of shit like that."

"What did you do?"

She laughed.

"I played dumb, let the crud look at my knees, stuck out my tits, blushed, and swore on a stock of Bibles that we are just good friends. I said you are the nicest person I know. I confused him, by God! It is degrading how dumb such people think you are."

"I know, baby. I know. I love you."

"I know they are going to tell my parents something. I just know it. My dad will go through the roof."

"Let's get out of here, okay? For a while. I have to go to work tonight."

"Okay, baby. I love you. I did good for you today."

"I'm sure you did. I'm very proud of you."

Before they could get out of the door, however, they were confronted by the big girl who had shared the podium with Henry Wallace back when he had tried to speak at the university. She was trailed by three other spotty young people, one of whom had a beard and wore sandals.

"Cat, we are a delegation of the Young Socialists on campus and we would like to talk to you for a minute," she said. "We know what has happened and we think this is a prime opportunity to break the back of the fascist administration on this campus once and for all. We want you to know that we are all behind you and that you can count on us to serve you in this battle any way we can. We stand ready to follow you. If you can come tonight and tell us what we should do, we will do it. We also have some ideas you might like to hear."

He looked at Sally. He knew he looked so sad, so appalled, for her face was a mirror of his own.

"I'm not leading any goddamned socialist revolution on this campus or anywhere. You people did not break the mirror. Nor would you have if you had known it was there. I can only take responsibility for my own actions and responses and try to protect those around me who might also get hurt by association. I don't expect to be entirely successful, but it's all I really believe in doing now. In fact, I don't trust you people. You don't operate out of passion, or even reason unless reason happens to fall conveniently within your dogmas. What rights do you think homosexuals should have? What rights do you think heterosexuals should have? Should anyone fuck without approval of some damned authority?"

"We just thought you could use our support," the heavy young woman said.

"I'm sorry," Carlson said. "I really would not know what to do with it."

He and Sally went out and turned away up the hallway.

"*Nihilist!*" the kid with the beard and sandals spat after him.

He looked at Sally and felt married to her. Was that what true marriage was? That feeling that another being was a physical part of yourself, and you a part of her? Her flesh, warmth, breath, and earthly reality had never seemed more real, more beautiful, more desirably abundant.

They raced out along the gravel road to where they usually parked. Carlson saw a new blue Ford coupe in his rearview mirror with two men in the front seat.

"We're being followed," he told Sally. "I can't believe this! How can they be so dumb!"

"Maybe they want to be seen," she suggested.

"Yeah." He sped up until the gravel was flying back at the other car about half a mile behind, then he threw the Ford into a bootlegger's turn, skidding around on the two lanes of gravel and, gearing down, headed back the other way toward the car that had been following them.

"Bastards!" he called as they passed and gave the stoic-faced men the finger.

They went to a drive-in restaurant on the main highway and ordered hamburgers, french fries, milkshakes.

"I want you so bad," Sally said.

"I want you too."

"I'll sneak out of my dorm tonight and meet you after you get off work," she suggested.

"That's crazy, Sal. You have to be very careful now. Obviously we are going to be watched."

"I don't care. I'll do it. I want to be with you. My dad is sure to come and take me away, unless you take me away first."

"He would have us arrested," Carlson explained. "You are only seventeen."

"I don't care. I love you. Will you meet me when you get off work? My roommate can cover for me. I promise. Please."

"Okay."

She got up on her knees to kiss him on the lips.

"I'll meet you at your place when you get home."

"Here. I'll give you the key," he told her.

"Don't worry, darling, it's better to be daring on the side of what you want than it is to be too careful for security," she said.

"How do you know that?" he wondered.

"Oh, I'm getting a pretty good education here lately."

"I love you a lot," he told her.

Twelve

THAT AFTERNOON, Jeff Steele was waiting for Carlson in
their converted garage.

"I've been talking to Campbell, Cat, and I think I am
going to move in over at his place until I can find another
place to live."

"Okay."

"I don't want you to think I'm copping out on you
exactly, but that is kind of what I am doin'. I don't want
to get kicked out of school, man. There was a ticket on
my car this afternoon because the parking sticker was a
couple of inches off the prescribed place for it to be. I
swear. And Campbell received a notice that all his grades
were suspended until he returned some overdue library
books. I just think I better move out."

"I said it was okay," Carlson said.

"You think I'm an asshole, don't you?"

"No. I honestly don't. I think you are doing what you
need to do. I am doing what I need to do. Tom and Wade
are doing what they need to do. Bob Pasetta is doing what
he needs to do. Green and Wright are going to do what
they need to do."

"And you aren't pissed off?"

"No. I'm not even exactly pissed off at Green and
Wright."

"Bullshit!" Jeff Steele said. "You just want to seem cool
as hell. You know, we're a little pissed off at *you*, when
you come down to it. We resent your making a big deal
out of this. It was our thing."

114

"You called me," Carlson reminded him.

"Yeah. But we don't see it as a congressional issue. We sure as hell don't want to get our butts burned for some damned principle. It isn't fun now," Jeff Steele said.

"You won't get anything burned. You will all put your diplomas up on your walls and live happily ever after."

"What's wrong with that?" he wanted to know.

"Nothing. I just can't do it that way."

"That's why we're pissed off at you. Even Bob Pasetta resents you now. What you're doing isn't right."

"Why not?" Carlson said. "To you it is a prank. I actually *do* want the people in authority to comment on which side of that mirror they think the greater perversion is being committed."

"Yeah, and that's why we're pissed off at you. You make us feel *we* should be demanding the answer too. The fucking world is the way it is and we have to get along in it. They aren't going to let you stay here. I don't give a shit what you do now. Man, the story was on this afternoon's news. And it will be on again tonight."

In fact, there was a television camera crew waiting at the hospital, wanting to interview Carlson before he went on the ward.

"Did you in fact break this two-way mirror in the men's restroom yourself?" the interviewer asked.

"That is not important. What is important is that the thing was there and had been there for quite some time."

"What did the vice-president of the school tell you its purpose was?"

"To catch homosexuals, after which they would be shaken up enough to frighten them out of town forever. The chief of campus police explained that their pictures would be put on file and sent to every law enforcement office and school in the state."

"Are you a homosexual yourself?"

"No. Are you?"

"That is all. Thank you. This is Quentin Quisenberry outside the State Hospital, speaking to Jarl Cat Carlson,

115

the student at the university who reported that someone
had broken a two-way mirror in a men's restroom on
campus, allegedly installed there to catch homosexuals."

Sally was waiting for Carlson when he got home from
the hospital. Jeff Steele was there long enough to finish
packing and putting his things in the car.

"Take 'er easy, Cat," Steele said.

"Always try, man."

That was their good-bye.

"He's moving out," Carlson explained to Sally.

"Oh."

When they made love later, Carlson could not get a
full erection. He could fuck and come, but he never got
as hard as he usually did.

"What's wrong, sweetheart?" Sally asked.

"I don't know. Maybe I'm tired, or too tense about
things. I don't know. That was awful. I'm sorry."

"It's all right, baby." She stroked his brow. "Go to
sleep. You will wake up and we can make love like
always."

But when he awoke the next morning and did enter
her cunt, his erection began to fail until it was as it had
been the night before.

"This happened once before," he explained. "When I
was in the Army and got turned down for Officer's Candidate School. I'm sorry."

"*I'm* sorry. I feel bad for you."

"Don't feel bad for me," he said. "I love you."

"I love you too." She was crying softly. "I feel like
it's my fault. We could always do that, no matter what."

"Now we can't, it seems."

"I feel something is wrong with me now."

"Don't be silly. It's me. Let it go!"

"Okay. Okay. I'm sorry. But I feel so rotten."

"Me too," he said. "We better shower so you can get
to your first class."

"Screw my classes. Just hold me and make me feel
better. Touch me. Make me come."

He made love to her with his hand and his mouth until she had an orgasm. But that did not make her feel better for long. She was truly worried. Always before, they had been able to make love really well.

"What do you think is the matter, Cat?" she asked when they were in the shower together.

"I'm becoming middle class," he joked.

"What does *that* mean?"

"We never *do* anything actually. Remember, I said this to you before. We just talk about things. Talk about things all the time, offer opinions, answers, when in fact we are the most powerless people anywhere. More powerless for the illusion of having power, for believing we are able to make meaningful decisions, affect the outcome of history. It's a joke. A cruel joke. An illusion. Maybe I just realized how impotent we really are."

"You aren't impotent. You *do* something. You have stood up to these bastards here."

"It is meaningless, baby, and it won't change anything. Tom and Wade and Campbell and Steele are right, you know. Get the fucking degree and get out and get on with your life. Taking a stand is bullshit. Maybe, in truth, I am just looking for the publicity of the thing. I don't know. I know that what I have done and seem determined to do is stupid, yet I *have* to do it, have to see it through, whatever the goddamned cost."

"I think you're wonderful."

They kissed in the shower, the water running off their heads into their mouths.

"I'll see you after class today. We can go somewhere then. It'll be okay. I know it will," she said.

By her last class that day, Sally's father had come to take her out of school. Only by throwing a screaming tantrum had she been able to get his permission to see Carlson to say good-bye.

He was in the magazine office. Her father waited in the car outside, which was loaded with all her things.

"I'll stay with you if you want me to," she sobbed.

"They can't pull me away from you. I'll tell them I'm pregnant."

"Are you?" he asked.

"No," she said. "I love you and we'll stay in touch and when this shit is over, we'll see each other. Oh, Cat, I love you so. And I'm so angry and scared. I'm being treated like a child."

"I know. What did your father say?"

"The sonofabitch said the director of the Student Health Service called him and said I was not doing well in my classes, which is true, and that I was associating with a group on campus he was sure the good doctor would not approve of, and suggested he come down and talk. The dean of women told him what happened with you, and said it might be better if I dropped out for a semester. So that's what was decided."

"I'll see you again, Sally. I love you. I will always love you. It has all been good. No jealousy. No pain. I can't say that about anything else in my life, about anyone. It has all been just good, Sally."

They heard the horn honk insistently outside. They kissed. He patted her on the butt and promised to write to her regularly.

Carlson walked Sally down the hall, down the stairs, and told her good-bye at the front door.

He watched her get into the Chrysler driven by the small man who was her father. She sat staring straight ahead as they drove off. Then the window on her side slid down and Carlson saw her arm come out. She waved her hand.

That afternoon he was called by the head of the Board of Publications and told he was to stop the press run on that month's magazine.

"What the hell for?" he wanted to know.

"We have learned that you are running some material that was not submitted for approval."

"You're crazy. We are running nothing you haven't seen. We never have."

"I have been told you are, and I want the publication stopped and the offending material taken out," the man insisted.

Carlson had told everyone that they would not run anything on the mirror business until a later issue.

"I want to know what you are referring to," Carlson demanded.

"There are two center-spreads, cartoon material, that I have not seen."

"That is bullshit, sir! We are running a retrospective of center-spreads this month since we are a bit short on copy. We are running two center-spreads that were published in the magazine years ago and were done by two now very famous cartoonists. You have seen them and okayed them. We saw no reason to resubmit them to you. They are reprints of already approved material."

"The rules are that I must see and approve of *every* bit of material that is published *each* month. You did not fulfill your responsibility."

"Look, you and I both know this is just bullshit, just some kind of harassment. I'm not about to stop publication in the middle of the press run for some shit like this. And you tell Dr. Green and the assholes that have put you up to this cheap shit that if they want the center-spreads taken out, they can go stop the press run and take them out."

"You're fired, Cat. I am relieving you of your editorship right now," the man said.

"Oh, stick it up your ugly ass!" Carlson slammed down the phone.

It was all set up. A young no-talent hanger-on at the magazine named Gil Parker had already been approached and was waiting to come claim the editorship, remove the supposedly offensive material, and generally kill one of the best humor magazines that had ever sprung up on a college campus.

A little later *The New York Times* telephoned.

The next day Carlson received in writing a summons to appear before the Board of Student Conduct to explain his irresponsible actions while editor of the humor magazine, and his rude and insulting behavior to the faculty advisor and head of the Board of Publications.

"Gotcha!" Carlson said aloud after reading the letter.

All grades and class privileges will be suspended until disposition of this matter has been made by the Board of Student Conduct.

He had to smile. The ruse was so transparent. But it would work. He couldn't afford a lawyer.

"Fuck it," he decided.

The dean of men sat at the head of the long oval table. In the middle was Ron Connelly, the student representative on the board. There was a classics professor Carlson knew vaguely. The rest of the board, including two women faculty members, were from departments in the university outside arts and science. Carlson did not know them.

The dean smiled and introduced the man to his left as president of the board. A man from engineering, it seemed.

"What kind of grades do you make, son?" the president of the board asked as Carlson took his place at the foot of the table.

"A's and D's mainly, with the odd B and C."

"How do you explain the seemingly wide disparity in your grades?" the president asked him.

The woman directly to Carlson's left, a mousy-colored woman with a pink sweater thrown over her shoulders, was staring very intently at him as he spoke. He felt like some sort of specimen under glass. He thought suddenly of how he had felt when he was called to speak before the officers and the congressman before he left the Army.

I keep doing the same gaddamned things, he realized.

"Well, if a subject is interesting to me, I make an A. If it is boring to me, I make a D. If it is boring but also a snap, I will usually make a B. If it is just difficult without being overly interesting, or is not well taught, I will make a C."

"What are your best subjects?" someone else asked.

"Creative writing, religions, literature, art, psychology, but that last is because it is mainly a snap."

"You think psychology is a snap?" the woman next to him asked archly. And he knew what *her* field was.

"Yes, ma'am."

"Have you ever considered seeking psychological help yourself, Mr. Carlson?" she asked.

"No."

"Would you avail yourself of it if you were offered the chance, let's say by the Student Health Service?"

"I will go to a shrink if you will," he said. "But not to the Student Health Service. The former director of it resigned because of the crap that is being done over there. It is nothing but a recording studio for the offices of the deans. It is just as insidious as the spy mirror we had here in the library john."

"We are not here, young man, to discuss the deplorable incident you got yourself involved in recently," the president said. "We are here to ascertain if you should remain in this university after committing a direct violation of our regulations concerning publications on campus, and insulting your immediate faculty superior in the process. We understand you swore at him. Used profane language."

They voted to close the hearing, and the president informed Carlson that he would be notified of the board's findings.

Later that afternoon he was informed that the board had voted unanimously to suspend him from the university for one year. At the end of the year he could reappear before the board and request reinstatement on a probationary basis.

That was it. He would lose his GI educational allowance. It was all over. He might as well have been kicked out irrevocably. Motherfuckers always got to cover their asses and make themselves feel like they are being fair.

It had begun to rain that afternoon; now it was pouring. He ran to his car, getting soaked before he was able to pile into it and close the door.

He had no desire to tell anyone good-bye. Not even

121

John Neihardt. He would write him a letter later. Now, all he wanted to do was get the hell out of there—go, go.

Where would he go?

Probably Chicago? Why not? Try to get a job on a newspaper or on *Playboy* magazine. It was starting to be quite big, *Playboy*. It was just a glorified college humor magazine. They had even reprinted one of his cartoons in a survey they did of college humor.

He was halfway home when he realized that the car radio was playing Fats Domino's "Ain't That a Shame." He sang along with Fats.

Fucking Chicago. Pig-sticker for the world. City of big shoulders and all of that.

"She-caw-go," he said aloud.

Thirteen

HE HADN'T FOUND a job. It seemed there was something on called a "recession." No one at the university had mentioned it. Oh, he had heard and read about it, but the students weren't actually touched significantly by it, the professors and lecturers were still able to debate the merits of the new Plymouths, Chevys, and Fords they were buying, their talk about real estate and insurance. But in Chicago, that December, 1955, it was cold as a well-digger's ass in the Klondike, and well-diggers and ex-students were all out of work, it seemed, willing to take any sort of job.

Carlson got three days' work loading out quarters of beef at a packing plant where union dock workers were on strike. Then one morning the early arrivers got the shit beaten out of them by the strikers and Carlson turned around, took the El back to Hyde Park, and did not go back.

Campbell's brother had an ex-girl friend who let him sleep on her couch in a one-room kitchenette flat with a bath, about four blocks from Chicago U. It had been arranged from the university, with Campbell calling her on the telephone, promising it would only be a temporary arrangement.

Carlson had first tried to find a job at *Playboy* magazine. He wore his suit and had shined his brown cowboy boots. He had worn his tie. He had carried a portfolio of his cartoons.

No one at Playboy actually looked at his work.

A handsome, brassy woman with a cultivated accent explained to Carlson that he was not the Playboy type of employee. This, from merely reading his application, look-ing at his suit and footgear. His tie hadn't been a lot of help either.

"We wish to create a certain image, a particular, identi-fiable, and desirable image in our magazine," she ex-plained, as if the effort was giving her a great pain in her left tit. At any rate, she cuddled it in her right hand as if, had Carlson been a bit more the Playboy type, she would wrench the massive thing out of its jacket and give it to him to bite.

He replied humbly: "I didn't suppose I had to actually hang beside my work in the magazine. I mean, I'll show you mine if Hugh Hefner will show you his. But then maybe he already has . . ."

She quit playing with her breast and excused herself, letting him know once more he was definitely not the type they were looking for.

"I guess what surprised me most," he explained to Margaret Archer, the lanky young woman who let him share her apartment, "was how fucking serious everyone was. God! No one was having any fun. All very posh, pre-tentious, we-are-going-to-kick-the-stuffing-out-of-*Esquire* attitude. Why the hell can't anyone have some success and have some fun at it?"

She didn't know.

"Why can't a good feeling, an intelligent feeling, a sense of good fun prevail in a goddamned company?" he asked her.

She hadn't a clue. She poured him a drink to make him feel better, nodding gravely and with sympathy as he spoke.

In desperation one afternoon he applied for work as an attendant at Lucy Raines Allen Memorial Hospital.

"Why do you want to work here?" the pleasant young interviewer asked.

"I need the job. I worked on the receiving ward of a state hospital for a year and thought maybe you could use me here."

"But you aren't looking for a long-term job with us, are you?"

"No, ma'am. I hope to get a job on a magazine or newspaper, something in art or writing. But I need a job. I'm almost broke. I'm living on the couch of a friend of a friend.

She smiled. "We don't like to go to the trouble of training someone and having them leave soon after. If we hire you, you have to go through the nurse's aide training program, which takes two weeks, including your physical and administrative processing."

"I understand." He was ready to leave.

"The job only pays forty-seven fifty a week after deductions." She smiled. "Do you still want it?"

"Yes. I mean, yes!"

She laughed. "Okay. You come here at eight A.M. Monday, and I will start your processing."

"Thank you," he said sincerely and shook her hand.

With twelve bucks left, his total worth except for his car, which had sat parked at the curb for more than two weeks because he didn't want to buy gasoline, and his portable typewriter, he felt surprisingly rich.

He was in the bathtub when Margaret came home from her job. She saw the small bouquet of flowers he had put in a water tumbler on the table in the apartment's single large room.

The hot water was wonderful.

"Who brought the flowers?" she called out to him. "It is snowing again, goddammit!"

"I got a job. Not much of a job, but something," he said.

"Great! I was beginning to worry." She came and opened the door.

"Hi." He grinned.

"Hi." She spoke from the doorway, not quite facing him, her eyes focused on a distant corner of the living room. Carlson continued to grin, splashing water on his chest while reaching for the soap.

Theirs had been a surprisingly unsexual relationship, especially considering the small, cramped living space they shared. Margaret was modest in the extreme, he thought, as he contemplated her tall frame. She was extra careful in the mornings and at night, doing her best to appear fully clothed before him, dressing and undressing soundlessly in the bathroom, scurrying past him in a long navy blue wool bathrobe she had tied meticulously around her lean body.

This was the first time since he had come to live with her that she had allowed physical intimacy between them. Yet he liked her. He responded to her warm interest in him, to her sympathetic reaction to his problems, to her quick intelligence. Looking back on his life, he decided he had never had a female friend before. He had been close to many women, but the closeness was always tied to sex. It was not so with Margaret. He liked being with her without thinking of fucking her. She made him feel comfortable.

"Want to go out to eat tonight?" he said. "We'll celebrate—my treat."

"You better save your money. Anyway, I've been invited to go over to these people's place at Chicago U for dinner. Come with me. They are very intellectual types, the guy is studying philosophy at the school."

"Okay," he decided. "You're right about the money." Then, "I'm getting out of the tub now," he warned. She walked quickly into the other room, closing the door behind her.

He dried himself before the little electric heater she used to heat the otherwise freezing bathroom. There was ice along the sills of the windows in her apartment. Ice on the inside of the glass.

Not the faintest glimmer of sunshine had touched Chicago since he had arrived. Gray day deepened into dark frozen night. The wind off the lake could frostbite your naked ears during a four-block walk. The snow was swarthy with soot and slag. At least one wino a night froze to death in a Hyde Park alley where they made tiny Hoovervilles out of cartons and crates, or in some doorway, curled rigidly in the corner like the stiff dead cats of everyone's memory.

This city makes us objects, Carlson thought, as he put on his clothes. *As soon as we are dead it becomes apparent that we are, indeed, objects. Only upright, babbling, consuming, seeking, working, hustling are we able to pass as something more than objects.*

Dostoevski would have been at home in Chicago that winter of 1955. He would be at home in Chicago winter and summer, but *that* winter was a natural for him if he could keep his feet on the glazed sidewalks in the gusts of wind that would sweep a dumpy bundle of a woman half a block in a precarious, heart-stopping ice dance before she could catch a pole or piece of fence to save herself from a certain broken hip.

Carlson steadied the tall girl by an elbow as they crossed the street and turned up an alley about a block from the campus.

They went down into the cellar of an old building, wending their way along a narrow, dimly lit corridor through which snaked the pipes and vents of the building, a maze of rusting, flaking, disorganized piping, ductwork, fuzzy with lint and dust. The place was dank yet pleasantly warm, warmer than Margaret's apartment. Behind the huge furnace there was a plywood wall with a brightly painted green door rigged in the middle of it. Margaret knocked at the door.

It was opened by a small, long-haired girl in a wrinkled wool skirt and stained gray sweater. She had a pretty young face and long straight dark blond hair. She wore ankle-high rubber boots that had a rim of white salt stain around the soles, as did every pedestrian's shoes. Her stockings were patterned and had several snags in them.

The room was dimly lit by a blue light bulb which turned the dim lumps of furniture crowded in the small space into sickly shapes while managing to bleed away all sense of warmth from being adjacent to the furnace. Carlson was led by Margaret, and their hostess, Madeline, to be introduced to Jack. Jack looked like an emaciated Rasputin. His fingers were long and either dirty or ink-stained. Great rashers of notepaper covered with minute handwriting littered the floor all about him. He extended his hand and Carlson took it when they were introduced.

"Margaret tells me you are a writer?" he said, inhaling his cigarette.

"I write," Carlson replied.

"You read this?" the young man wondered, showing Carlson the back of an edition of Jack Kerouac's novel, *On the Road*. "They say he wrote it all on one long sheet of paper, on a paper roll."

"That's one way to do it," Carlson could see. "I read it."

"What did you think of it?"

"Well, at first I was very excited about it. I mean, it was about a lot of things I and some of my friends could genuinely relate to. Then I discovered that Kerouac was damned near thirty before he took step one on the road. We were twelve, thirteen, fourteen, fifteen, when we were doing much the same thing. I no longer respected his trip. It began to seem like prolonged adolescence to me. Just another middle-class kid playing with himself, amazed at his audacity. Do you know what I mean?"

Jack nodded sagely, then proceeded to tell Carlson what *he* thought about Kerouac's novel. How the book definitely heralded a new reality, an end to all old realities, and how it was like Dostoevski's work.

He was still holding forth when Madeline announced supper. Jack produced a half-gallon of California mountain red wine to go with the Spanish rice his wife had made, and they had good crusty Russian bread from a nearby Jewish bakery.

Bohemians.

During supper Jack explained that they had had to get married. "Our parents would never allow us to just live together." They were living on what each set of parents contributed regularly to their upkeep. "My mother would die if she could see this place," Jack said, and giggled.

"Especially considering what she sends us each month." Madeline giggled with him.

They talked more books until about midnight when a sleepy Margaret and a tired Carlson went home.

They trudged back to Margaret's apartment in silence. Margaret's quietness came only from fatigue. Carlson's was generated by a mixture of tiredness, despair, and hate.

Goddamned little fuckers, he raged, *living in that artificial, artsy-craftsy poverty while I'm breaking my ass for a lousy forty-seven dollars and fifty cents a week.* He felt hopeless. Life was closing in on him, he was sliding back to the poverty and unskilled labor he had known as a child and had sworn to escape.

Next day, still in a sullen mood, he rented a room at the Hyde Park YMCA and moved his stuff into it. Margaret had not wanted him to go.

"You're not in my way here," she said. "I like having someone around when I come home. Besides, I'm not charging you rent and you could use the extra money."

"You're sweet," Carlson said, caressing her cheek. "I have to go. I don't feel right staying with you, especially for free. Please understand. We'll see each other. I'll call."

In all the weeks he had lived with her, they had not fucked once. Looking at the plain, earnest-faced girl before him, he thought again of how odd that was. True, his mind had been on Sally. But it was also true that for him sex and Margaret did not seem to mix.

The room at the Y was a cell with a single window overlooking an air shaft. The wall above his narrow bed was cracked in dozens of places. He would count the cracks sideways first, then up and down, trying to fall asleep. It always took a very long time.

Why do all Y's come with an old, hollow-voiced eunuch-like deskman and gym equipment man? he wondered. Invariably they made you feel criminal or diseased.

He bought a large bottle of white shoe polish and spent much of the weekend turning a pair of chukka boots into the white footwear he was required to wear on his new job at the hospital. He sat at the small desk in the room and wrote a letter to Sally. It was the first time since arriving in Chicago that he felt secure enough to take the time from hunting for a job, or thinking about getting a job, to write to her. It seemed years had passed since they had last touched, or looked into each other's face. Years. He looked at his reflection in the grimy glass of his window, saw he looked no older, that in fact he looked astonishingly young and well. Could he really be twenty-six years old?

It was hard to write about his feelings. They seemed to have become numb, drastically changed.

> I love you but I feel deadened. It is cold and very grim here. Snow is the color of asphalt. People are the color of asphalt, right out of Nelson Algren. It is worlds away from the time we shared. I think of you back in your bed, in your home where it is tidy, proper and warm, and I feel like a character in a book by Algren or Dostoevski. I love you, but it has a strange distant allure like the tropics when I am trying to stretch my last nine bucks.

He told her about his new job then and became more hopeful. He told her about going to Playboy and described the interview. He said he wanted to telephone her when he got his first pay, and asked if it would be all right to do so.

He went down to the lobby to read a newspaper. He had neglected to keep up with what was going on in the world while he had been unemployed. There were always newspapers in the lobby. He found a deep chair in the corner and that day's *Daily News.* He had tried all the papers for a job. Most of the reporters came from other papers with considerable experience or came out of the city news bureau.

He had also put in an application for work at the local employment agency, his first choices being writing or anything in commercial art for which he might be qualified.

City of Big Shoulders, my ass. City of pipe-sucking squares who taught seminars at this or that college when they weren't writing self-righteous columns. Even the black newspapers were striving for a country-club air. Photos of pretty black young women in formal gowns and young men in tuxedos attending "fêtes" and "soirees." Shit! No wonder Richard Wright left the joint for Paris and never came back.

"Call *this* the good life!" some creep said, and killed two little sisters in the park on Christmas Eve. And the cops reacted to public outrage, like cops anywhere, and found a suspect within less than a fortnight, an illiterate working in a Salvation Army warehouse. They arrested him on suspicion and hung his dumb ass over a door in a station house, throbbed his testicles with a nightstick until he signed a confession.

"*Kick him again, he ain't got a dime,*" was an old Chicago saying, Nelson Algren had written.

Carlson thought most men could incorporate that into their family crest.

Fourteen

THERE WERE FOURTEEN women in the class with Carlson at the hospital. Most of the women were young, poor, lacking a high school diploma, foreign-born, or black. Carlson became a passing source of pride for the young women. They were proud that *their* man was smart, that he could make a perfect hospital bed faster than any of them. As he was the only male in the class, the young women shared his company, physical strength, and friendship, rather than one or two of them vying for his attention, as might have been the case had there been another male present. Among his classmates, his sex became entirely secondary to his mind, ability, and greater physical strength. He wondered and worried about the situation, feeling both freed and threatened by the young women's attitude toward him.

At times he felt as if he were a kind of mascot of the class. Then he decided that mascots do not lead normal, happy, or satisfying individualistic lives. To be a pet was a limited pleasure and ultimately debilitating spiritually.

It was obvious to him that long-standing fears of being less masculine than he thought he ought to be had begun to haunt him somewhat. He did not fear that he was a homosexual. He had no desire to have sex with another man. But he wondered if his body was beginning to fail to produce "enough" of the male hormone. A fear of possibly being sexually "inferior" to other men cast a shadow across his thoughts. He was honest enough to look back to see that he had always had that fear to some degree, from the time he was a toddler. Without word one, he had been afraid that he was "not like" the big grown-up men around him. And though he grew up admiring those men, after puberty he did not truly aspire to be like them. He had himself rated for larger, more important, interesting things. Perhaps he felt guilty about *that*.

Then, there were all the years he had spent in the military.

The military reduced life to an insane rote that was complicated without being really complex; a kind of obsessive drill that often turned an otherwise average brain into the mind of a duck.

Then, he argued, here *I* am, critical and bitter, living in a goddamn YMCA that smells like a bus station urinal, beating my meat, wondering if my cock is shrinking, if I am masculine enough, if I'm nuts, working for about forty-five lousy bucks a week, and feeling guilty as shit because even now I insist I am somehow rated for better things than my peers, my antecedents, the asshole jacking off in the next crummy room.

Sally had not answered his first letter, nor his second or third. Suspecting her mail was being censored, he called her at home and spoke with a soft-voiced woman who said Sally was not there but she would tell her Carlson called and give her Carlson's telephone number in Chicago. The woman hung up before he could ask who she was, and the next time he called her voice had grown much less soft.

Sally was not home, the woman had no idea why Carlson had not heard from her. He should not call again. If Sally wanted to speak to him, she would telephone. The receiver banged in his ear.

Oh, Sally, he thought, *I'm never going to see you again.* A part of his youth seemed to have gotten lost along with her.

He had not called Margaret all this time. In late January, she called him, inviting him to dinner at her apartment. Out of loneliness he went. He liked this intelligent young woman, but he could no more think of loving her— or even fucking her—that he could think of it with an elderly maiden aunt.

He began to develop a yearning lust for an attractive,

well-built blond pediatrician, whom he met after being assigned to the children's orthopedic ward. (The rationale for his assignment was that he was strong and would be a boon in handling patients in heavy casts.) He knew the doctor to whom he was attracted was also rather drawn to him, though she was puzzled by being attracted to an orderly; like nurses' aides, orderlies were nearly nonpersons in the hierarchy of the hospital, where the lowest of doctors was more powerful than both church and state.

Back in the classroom, while learning to give mouth-to-mouth resuscitation, using the intriguing life-size female mannikin they all called "Annie"—anatomically correct as to lungs, oral, vaginal and anal cavities, breasts, and extremities, even blessed with a nice head of human hair—Carlson began to become aroused.

He fantasized about balling as many of his classmates as he could, showing no favoritism. All for one and one for all! The fat, the ugly, the terminally acned, the stupid, along with the pretty—the Puerto Rican wife with a luminous beauty and the big, swinging, high-assed West Indian black with thighs like twin bundles of snakes. But all he actually did was blow into Annie's mouth hole and make her chest rise and fall with his breath.

In the snack bar he usually sat alone, stealing glances at Dr. Caroline Palmer, the children's doctor, as she sat more often than not with a Jewish doctor who had enormous pale hands covered with black hair. The surgeon's nails were perfectly manicured. He clearly lusted after Dr. Palmer quite as strongly as Carlson. Did she date the doctor? She seemed reticent with him, wary. Once she caught Carlson staring at her and their eyes met for a very long time as the pale surgeon continued talking urgently. He finally noticed he had lost her attention and turned his head to glance toward where she was looking, saw Carlson, turned back and said something to Dr. Palmer that caused her to look back at the large doctor and reply to whatever he said with a shrug, and not look Carlson's way again.

Dr. Palmer was always pleasant in her dealings with

others on the staff, wonderful with her young patients. She smiled a lot. She seemed very self-contained, aware of the space she occupied, and she commanded that space with a gentle insistence. She had a definite reserve, the pleasantness that made everyone want to help her, and also the power to keep the rest of the world from running over her. She always wore very pretty, very expensive, very high-heeled shoes, which made her good, solid legs and bottom as beautiful in their resultant deformity as was fashionably possible.

Going down in the elevator on his lunch break a few days later, Carlson found himself alone with Dr. Palmer. She smiled and said, "Hello."

"Hello," he said.

"Busy morning," she observed.

"Yes," he agreed.

There had been a bus accident the night before.

"Are you married, Doctor?" he asked.

She looked at him for a few seconds as if deciding whether she was going to reveal such intimate information or not. She finally said: "No. I'm divorced."

"Oh. Children?"

Again she seemed annoyed at his questioning her so intimately.

"No. No, I don't."

He almost said, "I'm sorry," but realized that was always a stupid response to such a revelation. He felt stupid, awkward in any case. He should not have intruded upon her with such questions. The only thing to do, he decided, was to be as honest and direct as possible.

"You didn't want kids," he said, more a statement than a question.

"Well, really! No. We didn't. We were very young. I was still in school. No, I didn't want children. Not now. Someday perhaps. Maybe I just feel I *should* have children because I am able, which seems a lousy reason really. Is there anything else you would care to know about me?" But she partially smiled.

"Virtually everything," he replied.

That turned her head. She looked at him quizzically. "You are presumptuous, aren't you?"

"Entirely. Incorrigible, too. I have report cards from kindergarten through sixth grade to prove that."

"Really? What are you doing working here . . ."

"As an orderly? I'm a noted brain surgeon in disguise. I'm really the heir to a great fortune, hiding out from my disgusting family and the responsibility of riches." Then he said, "Is your friend joining you for lunch?"

"Impertinent as hell, too, aren't you?" But again she was smiling. "Yes. Would you care to join us?" she asked.

"Never. Are you in love?"

"*What!* . . . What a remarkable thought!" She was walking away, shaking her pretty head. Carlson trailed along.

"Well, he's in love with you."

"So are his wife and two kids."

"Whatever. *He* is."

"Maybe I'll tell him you said so," she shot over her shoulder.

During lunch she pointedly avoided looking at Carlson though he had placed himself in the lunchroom so he could see her. She seemed utterly engrossed in conversation with the large surgeon.

I wouldn't want those big, damned hands prowling around inside me, Carlson decided. Not if my life depended on it. He could not believe that any surgeon with manicured and laquered nails could be worth a damn.

He could imagine Dr. Palmer's thighs in good hosiery beneath her wool skirt, how her panties, plump with her sex, were a tight skin between her closely pressed hot flesh. She also had large breasts. Her hands were small but beautifully kept, extremely competent.

Shit, he told himself and left the lunchroom.

Yet, at approximately three-thirty that afternoon he asked Dr. Palmer to have dinner with him.

He had been called to move a youngster in a full body cast from the room where casts were being applied to a bed on the children's ward. Dr. Palmer came along to supervise the bed placement of the little boy. When the job was done and the child reported he was comfortable, Dr. Palmer and Carlson walked from the ward together.

As she was talking about the case, he blurted: "Have dinner with me . . . please."

She glanced sharply at him, replying automatically: "I can't."

"Why not?" he demanded.

"Why . . . I just can't. I never thought of it. I . . . Well, goodness . . ." She laughed. "I'm sorry I just never thought about . . . I'm older than you."

"Not by much. What's two or three years or four, or whatever? Look!" He stopped her by taking her arm and turning her as they passed a glass wall behind which there was a curtain drawn, so their reflections were mirrored in the glass. "You don't *look* any older than me. In fact, we are sort of pretty together." He cocked his head one way as she cocked hers the other.

"You're right," she agreed. "But, really, I can't," she said.

"Okay." He gloomily accepted her judgment.

Then, at five minutes to five, Dr. Palmer passed Carlson in the corridor, went several steps past after nodding, half-smiling, then turned and said:

"Hey! Listen, why don't you let me make you dinner Friday night."

He wasn't sure he had heard her right. She was almost laughing at the stunned look on his face as he gathered his wits.

"Yes!" he blurted. He walked back toward her. She was smiling. He was smiling. "I was thinking after I asked you to dinner," he said, "that I probably can't *afford* to feed you as you are accustomed or as I would like."

"I realized what a sacrifice it would be for you to take me out to a restaurant on your salary," she replied softly. "I was really touched."

"No pity?"

"No! You are very sweet. Besides, I haven't cooked a

meal for anyone in ages. I really want to do it. Is seven all right?"

"Perfect."

He wet the bristles of his hairbrush in the small basin in his room and brushed his blue wool blazer. The gray flannel slacks he'd had cleaned were now about two inches too big around the waist, he was surprised to see. A white shirt, reverse rep tie, and freshly shined brown cowboy boots completed his ensemble for dinner with Dr. Palmer. He carried his old trench coat over his shoulder and went down to see if his car would start. He had not started up the car in two weeks. It sat on a dim side of the street, covered with city grime, looking like a huge lump of pigeon poop. It sat low on the back springs because of all the books and things he still had in the trunk and, covered by an army blanket, on the backseat.

The car started immediately. He felt lifted, gratified.

Vroom-vroom-vroom, he goosed the engine to full-throated life. Whatever God *is*, he is a V-8 at heart, he thought. The windshield was layered with city grime. Carlson worked the wipers furiously until they succeeded in scraping a couple of wedges down the underlying glass, out of which he could see.

Dr. Palmer lived out on the Near North Side in a nice apartment building within walking distance of the lake, next to a small neighborhood park behind a wrought-iron fence.

The lower lobby was guarded by an elderly man in a worn monogrammed blue jacket with gold lapels, sporting a blue and gold military style cap. The lighting in the lobby picked up the gold paint on the decor's trim and the soft glow of the marble or fake marble floor between paths of carpet.

"Dr. Palmer, please?" Carlson told the doorman.

"Dr. Caroline Palmer, is she expecting you?"

"Yes."

"That's the fourth floor."

"Thank you."

The apartment door was at the far corner of the floor from the elevator. Above the bell was a brass plate: *Caroline M. Palmer, M.D.* The nameplate made Carlson smile.

Dr. Palmer answered the door wearing a lovely, floor-length Chinese brocade dress that was slit to above the knee. She was smiling. Her makeup was much heavier than she wore during the day at the hospital, her eyelids darkened sexily, her eyelashes seemingly twice as long as they had been a few hours before. Her lipstick was thick, deep red and very liquid-looking. She had pulled some of her hair up on the sides to accent the Oriental look, gathered it in a bouquet of curls, and decorated it with some small bell-like white flowers that hung from a delicate miniature branch.

"Hello, please come in," she said, her voice softer and lower than it was professionally, almost a hesitant, shy little-girl voice. He blinked a couple of times, thrusting the suddenly very ordinary half dozen long-stemmed roses at her.

"Oh! They are beautiful!" she exclaimed. "I love long-stem roses. Where did you get them this time of year? They must have cost a fortune. I must put them in water right away."

The roses had cost a dollar and a quarter each at the florist in the lobby of the Parker House on Michigan Avenue. He had stopped there after getting off work to buy them and had carried them home on the El, which had not done them much good.

She actually rushed them to the kitchen, which was at the other end of the apartment. He thought how wonderful she looked, hurrying away bearing his flowers in both hands before her. He felt almost faint at how beautiful she was.

"Well!" Dr. Palmer said, moving to his side, having taken care of his flowers.

"This is nice. It feels good to be in your place," he said. "Real good."

"I'm so glad you like it. Would you like a drink?"

"Yes, thanks."

"What would you like?"

"Oh . . . How about a Scotch and soda?"

"That's easy. I was afraid you were going to ask me for something exotic or Texan or something. Light or heavy on the soda?" she asked.

"About half and half."

"Good. I think I'll have the same thing," she decided.

He felt at home, yet far from anything he had ever called home.

"Aren't those kind of boots difficult to walk in?" she asked, sitting beside him on the couch after placing their drinks on the low glass-topped coffee table before them. She crossed her legs, and the slit in her red silk brocade Chinese dress slid up to reveal a peek of the lower band of her stockings.

"No. I've always worn them. I was a boy sailor and I even wore black cowboy boots with my uniform on liberty."

"I was a boy sailor," she repeated his words. "You have said things like that before to me. It is a remarkable arrangement of words. 'I was a boy sailor.' Maybe the reason I wanted to invite you here tonight is because things like that have haunted me. Who *are* you? Where do you come from? Why are you working as an orderly in a hospital when you obviously could do something else? What do you *mean* you were a boy sailor?"

He laughed. "It might take a whole night to tell you about my life."

She reached over and squeezed his hand tightly. "That's all right. We can talk for hours during dinner." She patted his hand briskly. "I hope you like stuffed baked lake trout."

The table was set with a yellow cloth and napkins, which looked nice against Dr. Palmer's dress. She had placed one of the long-stemmed roses in a tall slender vase in the center of the table, having removed something she'd had there when Carlson came in. He was pleased by her thoughtfulness.

The food was beautiful. The fish was served with broccoli under a cheese sauce. She produced a bottle of champagne, which she said someone had given her for Christmas, and which she had saved for a special occasion.

They ate and exchanged stories of their lives, eager, intimate trading of details that revealed similar ideas and emotional responses. It is a great game, such conversation, Carlson thought. Intimate conversation when you are falling in love is the most erotic exposing of self there is, he was sure.

The dessert was a fruit compote sprinkled with shredded coconut, which she called Ambrosia.

Then they went back into the living room and drank brandy from tiny crude crystal glasses from Mexico that had bubbles caught in the glass and did not sit perfectly on the table. He reached across, took her drink from her hand, and told her he had wanted to kiss her for so long it was a kind of pain.

"No . . ." she protested automatically, but not irrevocably, for she let him draw her closer, and when he placed the fingers of his right hand beneath her chin there was no physical resistance. When their lips met, their eyes still open and searching each other's, her mouth became soft, giving, opened to receive his kiss. His tongue found hers as if there had never been any question about anything.

"I have wanted to do that for so long," he breathed when they finally let the kiss go. Her hands held him as tightly as he held her. Both of them were breathing hard and feeling dizzy.

"I know," she said. "I know. When I would be near you at the hospital, I could feel the heat coming off you. I swear I could. I thought about you a lot, though I didn't want to. I'll explain that. Don't worry." She touched his lips with her fingers. "I wanted you to. I just didn't understand it."

"And now you do?"

"No."

"But can we make love?" he asked.

"Yes."

They kissed again. It was not as electric as the first kiss, nor would it ever be, but it was a remarkable, swimming, deep, eternal kiss. Carlson's leg was wet where the head of his penis lay against it.

"It's funny," she said. "I have slept with a couple of men since I was divorced from my husband, but you are the first man I've wanted like this. Do you understand?"

"I think so."

"I hope so. The others were just something I had to do . . . almost like an experiment. I hadn't had any sexual experience to speak of before I was married. I wondered. I was curious. The first guy I couldn't speak to afterward or even stand! It was terrible. Poor guy. He really liked me. The second I went through in my bitch stage, you know? I mean I became a raving bitch in heat for about three weeks. I couldn't get enough and the guy was very thrilled and very flattered, and then one day I had to tell him that I liked him a lot, but that there had to be more to a relationship than just sex, and that was really all it was between us, it felt like to me. We never really saw each other except professionally afterward."

"And the doctor?"

"He's a good surgeon, a friend. He wants to sleep with me, but I don't want it."

They kissed again.

"Will you take me to bed now?" she said.

"Yes," he replied. "Thank you."

She undressed in the walk-through dressing area between the bedroom and the bath. He waited in his shorts for her to come out. She emerged wearing a bias-cut gown of ivory satin, which gathered her large breasts into a draped bodice that offered them like gifts nested in satin. They kissed and got into the bed.

They began to make love. She tugged to get his shorts off. He helped her and tossed them out of the bed. He helped her shed the gown and threw off the covers in the warm room to look at her beautiful body. He kissed her mouth, breasts, belly, went down on her, parting her wet bush with his fingers, parting her inflamed lovely vaginal lips with his tongue, finding her little clitoris.

"No one has ever done that," she said. "Oh, it feels wonderful! My God!"

He went down on her until she wrapped her legs around him, crying out repeatedly, arching her back and fucking his face until she came. She screamed. Then screamed again.

She was still shaking as if having a little fit when he slid up beside her to see her face in the tousled blond hair, the little branch of bell-like flowers now broken in the tangle. Her face was sweaty and beautiful, her lipstick long since kissed off her lips and distributed as a blush to her cheeks, breasts.

"Oh!" she cried when he entered her. "No one ever did that to me before," she said again.

"Did you like it?"

"Oh, yes! Oh, yes, my darling!" She searched for his mouth with her own, her tongue a sweet reward as she tasted herself from his lips.

They fucked long and lovingly, telling each other how good it felt. Just before he was about to come he realized. "Do you have a diaphragm in?"

"Do it!" she demanded. "Please do it!"

He came in her. He did not think that she came again.

"It's all right," she assured him when they lay side by side afterward in each other's arms, aware of their smells beneath the overriding musky scent of her perfume. "I'm pretty regular on the rhythm method. I have a diaphragm, of course; I just didn't want to spoil tonight with it. I knew it was okay. Do you think I am a calculating bitch?"

"Hopefully," he replied.

They laughed. Then she made love to him, getting on top of him and riding his cock to two orgasms before he got really excited and came with her the third time.

"I can only come when I'm on top, or in a position where you can touch my clitoris while we make love," she explained. "But I have never come like I did when you were—what do you call it—going down on me?"

"Yes."

"Can I go down on you?"

"I think it's sleeping."

"I don't care. I want to put you in my mouth too."

Her technique was basic, but inspired and very sweet. She sucked him a long time, until he pulled her face back up and kissed her.

143

"Okay?" she asked.

"Entirely," he told her.

They slept in each other's arms for a couple of hours. She woke up with a start and he caught her and held her and asked: "Have a bad dream?"

"I don't know," she said sleepily.

He cuddled her, kissed her, touched her. Their fluids had made the hair between her legs feel matted and stiff.

"I think I'd like to take a shower," she said.

That sounded like a good idea, he agreed.

"Do you know it is four in the morning?" She giggled as they prepared to shower together, she tucking her hair beneath a large bath towel. "It's absolutely sinful," she whispered..

"The doorman will wonder what's going on up here, Doctor."

"He doesn't know diddly," she replied, using a phrase she had picked up from him already. "Or even half of it," she added, kissing him happily.

"I love you, Doctor!" he exclaimed. "Really nice ass, you know?"

"*Great* ass! Great tits too," she replied proudly.

"And great in bed," he added.

"Am I?" she asked, pressing herself tight against him. "Yes."

"No bull? Really good?"

"*Really* good."

"That's nice. I always thought I was pretty hot stuff myself. No one ever had complaints. Sometimes they would go out of their heads. But I was never sure until now. I'm good, and you're wonderful, Jarl Catlin Carlson. I feel wonderful, and—yes, I do love you. To hell with it. *I-love-you!*" She had raised her voice in the shower to a moderate yell.

He kissed her mouth as the shower nearly drowned them both.

The dried each other happily, with care.

"Let's put on warm clothes and go out for a walk."

"You are a romantic, aren't you, Doctor?"

"Terribly tonight. Or this morning. Please, let's go see what is out there at five A.M."

"Out there? My dear, out there are cats . . . and cat burglars going home to sleep, cops sneaking a sleep in a car on a corner, strays of all kinds, the lost and drunken, milkmen. And paperboys, if they still throw the morning papers, making up their routes. Exhausted rapists and murderers returning from their night's work. Salesmen rolling into town to be that early bird that catches the worm, looking for a quick pick-me-up, a bath, a shave, a splash of bay rum on the jowls, then look out Chicago!"

"Let's go out for a walk anyway," she insisted. "I want us to always do crazy things. Loving, romantic things."

"Okay. You are absolutely right. The rapists and murderers are probably too tired to worry about anyway."

So they were. There were the cats, the milkmen, and cops cooping in a police car at the corner of the little park. The air was cold, yet Carlson felt perhaps there was a southerly whiff of spring in that morning's air.

The doorman stirred himself and smiled at them wearily when they returned, as he had when they went out. "Good morning again, Henry," Dr. Palmer said cheerfully, her voice like a little girl's.

"I don't want you to live at the Y," she told Carlson bossily later when they ate breakfast, so late she called it brunch. Neither had to go to the hospital that day. "I would like you to move in here."

"You want me to live with you?" Carlson replied.

"Yes. No. I want us to live together. Scandalous, huh? My parents would never understand. My ex-husband would shit, as you say, but . . ."

"Are you sure?" he wanted to know.

"Yes. I'm sure," she said.

"Okay," he agreed.

"Good. That's settled. Now give me a kiss. You have jam on your mouth," she said.

Later, he asked: "Can I have a brass plate beneath the bell too?"

"What? Uh . . . Sure, I guess so. Why not?"

She had been so shaky on that he had to smile. "Never mind. I was just teasing. That would not be smart in any direction, pretty lady. I'm sorry."

"I don't mind. I can understand why you would ask that. Listen, darling, there is a saying in Mexico, '*Mi casa es su casa*.' I mean that."

"I know the saying. I lived down there, remember, before I was a boy sailor."

"Hey boy sailor, will you do something for me even with the jam on your lips?"

"Anything."

She whispered in his ear: "Please go down on me again. No one ever did that. Just watching you talk makes me hot. Please."

"Of course. With pleasure. Any time."

"Promise?"

"Promise."

Right there on the floor, beside the breakfast table, with strawberry jam on his lips, he went down on her until she came big, then kissed her while his mouth was still smeary with her juices and fucked her hard as they protested their love for one another.

Sunday, they slept late, had another brunch. That afternoon he moved his things into her apartment, storing some of them downstairs in the locked cage that was hers in the cellar. She wore jeans and a big sweater and windbreaker to help him move.

They made love and watched the Chicago Bears and New York Giants play a football game that was like trench warfare. Then they dressed warmly in jackets, caps, and gloves to go out and walk over to the lake, strolling along it in love, seeing the cityscape and the gray lake where slabs of ice were stacked up on top of each other higher than their heads. Carlson no longer felt like one of the subterraneans, no longer one with the stray cats and derelicts.

As if reading his thoughts, she said: "Things are going to be different for you now. I really believe it. You'll see."

"I think so too," he said. "Thank you."

"For nothing! Thank *you!*"

Their kiss was cold. Their breaths smelled like the indoors in the cold. So they turned without discussing it and walked arm in arm back to the apartment.

Fifteen

"LET THERE BE no misunderstanding, when all this is settled the Princess will be mine, quoth the Black Pirate," Carlson told Dr. Caroline Palmer fiercely.

"What?"

"Saw that on TV last night. That's what it is all about, isn't it?"

"I'm not sure what you mean."

"Well, you know."

"Happy?" she wondered, snuggling on the couch with him.

"Sure. You?"

"Oh very! Very!" she vowed. "But you seem troubled, more manic than happy. Is something wrong?"

"Maybe I am incapable of sustained happiness," he said. "Maybe a few days at a time is my limit."

"Oh, I hope not. I have been happy these last two weeks."

"Me too! I love you. I love it here with you. I feel rich. I don't even feel too guilty about your significantly greater contribution to our livelihood. But, you know, one nice thing about poverty is that it is a damn good excuse for not being able to solve all your problems. With the essentials taken care of, more than enough to live on, you have to face the possibility that you are going to fail badly all on your own."

"Do you worry about failure so much?" she asked.

"Constantly."

"My God, darling, please don't worry. You are intelligent and talented, a beautiful, wonderful lover, funny and wise and sweet and gentle and strong, passionate about the things that count, honest, I think, in a sense that is more important than always just telling the truth. You have integrity without being some kind of fanatic. My God! You are just about the most perfect man I know. Before I knew you, my father held that honor. I just now realized that you've replaced him in that. I love you very much."

"But, looking at it from a different point of view—let's say, from the point of view of your own colleagues—I am a rather countrified hospital orderly who earns forty-seven dollars and fifty cents a week. Or, why do you think we are so careful toward each other now at the hospital?"

She thought a while. "You're right. We will have to do something about that."

"Don't make any gestures on ridiculous principle. You could lose your job, then where would we be?" He grinned.

She looked shocked.

"Poor people learn to think like that," he explained.

"Listen, let's go out and do something tonight," she suggested. "Let's go out!"

"I am very broke, you know," he said.

"You! *We* aren't broke. Let's go out. What would you really like to do?"

"Hear some real blues," he said. "I miss it. Love it. Best thing when you feel like this. Delta blues. River blues. Kansas City blues. St. Louis blues. Chicago blues. Blues anyway." He sang: "My woman left me, an' she didn't say a mumblin' word . . . yeh."

"We can go to the Jazz Limited or the Eleven-Eleven Club," she suggested excitedly.

"And go bummin' North Clark and South State? See the strippers?"

"Yes!" I've never been in those kinds of places. I've never seen a stripper."

"You're joking?"

"No, I'm not."

"Okay," he said. "I've never gone bummin' with a nice girl before."

"What shall I wear?" she wondered.

He laughed.

It wasn't all that much fun to go bummin' with a nice girl, he discovered.

Bummin' categorically is an illicit pleasure. It is blowing a week's pay when someone is looking to repossess your car or coming for the rent. And you are away from all that. You are where the strippers' naked thighs are the gates to long-held fantasies; where the beers all taste like golden nectar from the land of sky-blue waters; where the drummers lay down a beat that lies just next to your heart and the sound of a cornet can honestly elevate your soul, while in no way altering the certainty of your own morality. But then it is all right. Whatever happens is all right!

The girls up there on the runway and the bartenders and the owners and the street are all after your little hoard of money. It's a straight deal. It's a straighter deal than you can get in any house of finance with the advice of an accountant. It's a straighter deal than you can get when you buy anything else on this earth from a company. It's a better deal than you have ever gotten from any government anywhere, anytime. That's it. The tricks and attempts at larceny are so obvious they foster a kind of sympathy for victim and jack roller alike. A kind of sympathy for all of us who aren't incorporated.

"What do you *see* in all this, darling?" Caroline just wanted him to tell her.

Carlson tried to describe the feeling of anonymity among like souls, blowing money you couldn't really afford to lose.

"Have you ever slept with one of those girls?" she wondered, meaning the strippers who doubled as bar girls and sat with the customers when they were not dancing.

He explained that the girls could be felt-up and they

often told great gossipy stories about your favorite athletes or local politicians. A surprising number admitted to a year or two of college. More were hillbillies out of Kentucky. Chicago seemed cluttered with hillbillies out of Kentucky that season; hillbillies and Hungarian "freedom fighters" who had never *seen* a Russian tank. A girl Carlson had met a long time ago, a statuesque beauty named Jacqueline, had a master's degree in anthropology from Purdue, a dime-a-day little drug habit, and would give you a half-and-half in her dressing room for fifty dollars. She would ask for a hundred. But offer her fifty and she would lead you back. If she was hungrier, she might take twenty-five for the same service, Carlson was sure, but she would not put a penny's worth of her heart in it for twenty-five, he also knew.

"But they all look so tired and tawdry, even the young ones," Caroline argued. "I can't imagine you ever going with one of them."

"I didn't all that often," he explained. "I have rarely been able to afford those kind of ladies."

"It's just so sordid. Even this whiskey sour is lousy."

"It is supposed to be. I see what you mean, though. I really do. I mean here with you now, it is pretty mean and unromantic—"

"*Unromantic?!*"

"Well, yeah. That's the word. What else? But, look, with you they don't even see me—us. We aren't bummin', see? We are voyeurs. It's spoiled."

They went to the Eleven-Eleven Club, near Jazz Limited, where George Brunnis still played some trombone and laved his ulcer with vodka and milk, a mixed drink. There they ran into a couple who were Caroline's friends, Milt and Myra Abrams. They joined them at their table.

Between sets, the clarinetist, a humorously dour young man in thick glasses, a neighbor of Milt and Myra, came over and sat with them. He did not drink. He taught music a few days a week at the University of Illinois in Chicago. He and Milt were funny together.

Carlson liked Milt and Myra immediately. Milt was a slight, very good-looking professional artist—with a fine technique, it turned out—who had a show in one of the best galleries in Chicago at the moment. Myra was a sexy, very pretty, juicy mother of two, with great legs, large tits, and a way of dancing close that was inspiring; she was a natural, instinctive flirt who never did anything to put her husband down or make him disloyal, and who also had the ability to generate the trust and friendship of women.

Caroline had lived near them when she first came to Chicago. The couple's two children called her "Aunt Caroline."

Milt and Myra also accepted Carlson immediately. It was as if Caroline's love and desire for him were the most perfect credentials he could possess.

"Where have you two been?" Myra wondered, eyeing Carlson openly.

"We went bumming," Caroline reported.

"Bummin'," Carlson corrected. "It was a mistake," he explained, catching a knowing and surprised look from Milt, who smiled.

"Whose idea was that?" Milt asked.

"It was mutual," Caroline said.

"Milt would never take me bummin' with him," Myra accused her spouse.

"He's a wiser man than me," Carlson said.

"I hated it!" Caroline said. "I don't see what men see in that sort of thing. It's a total gyp. The drinks are ghastly . . ."

"Next time call me," Milt told Carlson.

"Promise." Carlson reached across and he and Milt shook hands.

"Where did you get him?" Myra asked Caroline while looking at Carlson. "He's a hunk."

"At the hospital. We live together."

"No kidding?! Well! Milt, they are *living* together," she said. "Has our little Caroline hit the jackpot, darling?"

"I heard. I see. So, when do they get married like decent people?" he joked.

"You have to understand," Myra explained, reaching

across the table to lay a warm squeeze on Carlson's sleeve, "we sort of adopted Caroline. We feel like her parents."

"We haven't discussed it," Carlson explained. "We've only lived together a couple of weeks."

"A couple of *weeks,* Myra!" Milt cried, "Do you hear this! I don't listen! A *couple* of weeks! I should have lived to hear from her own mouth these words!"

"Come with me," Myra ordered Caroline. "I need to powder my nose and I want to speak to you privately." Caroline got up dutifully to follow Myra. Myra turned back and touched Carlson, who was standing. "Actually, I want to ask her how good you are in bed. I love *all* the intimate details!"

"What do you do at the hospital?" Milt asked. "You a doctor?"

Carlson laughed. "No. No doctor. An orderly." He quickly explained about getting kicked out of school, about being a soldier for so long before that, about being a writer and an artist-cartoonist, and not being able to find a job in Chicago, about going around to all the papers.

"I know where there's a job on a paper near here. Would you mind working in the suburbs?" Milt asked.

"I don't know. Where?"

"I just heard about this today. My neighbor—works for the *News-Leader* in Waukegan. They've just gone through a big strike and hassle with the union. They lost some reporters and are looking for a couple of guys. You should look into it right away."

"I will. Thanks!"

Christ, he felt good. He really liked Milt and Myra. He wanted to see Milt's paintings. He remembered there was a painting of the bridge over the Chicago River on Michigan in Caroline's apartment which he admired; it had been signed "Abrams." Good name. Good painting. Milt was one of those destined for success. He also had great taste in clothes, Carlson observed. Up-to-the-minute in style.

When Myra and Caroline returned, Myra teased Carlson: "Milt, you would not believe what this innocent little doctor told me. We could take lessons."

"So, how do you like my best friends?" Caroline inquired happily. "Cat thought all my friends were some kind of squares," she told Milt and Myra.

"I love them," he said.

"So do I!" She laughed.

"I just realized who Milt reminds me of," Carlson said. "Lenny Bruce."

"Oh, my God!" Myra shrieked. "Now you've done it. He thinks he *is* Lenny Bruce. Now that's what he will do all night, his Lenny Bruce routine."

"I don't know why you say that, you dumb broad. You just come in to see the show or are you working the room?"

"Don't ever do this again," she asked Carlson. "Can I see your tattoos? Anything?"

"What?"

"Oh, listen, in the john Caroline told me *all* about you!"

She laughed.

"Tattoos?" Milt said. "*Mein Gott!* Jews can't get into heaven with a tattoo. Did you know that?"

"No," Carlson confessed.

"Listen," Milt said suddenly, "what are you two doing after here?"

They looked at each other.

"Home," Caroline said. "Why?"

"Why don't you come home with us and use our guest bedroom and we'll get some stuff and cook it tomorrow and not shave and watch television or something. We haven't seen you in months. Since it got so cold. The kids would love to see you."

Caroline looked at Carlson.

"Sure." He grinned.

"Wonderful!" Myra cried and clapped her hands.

Caroline snuggled up to Carlson as he drove the Ford toward Waukegan. The car was cold. It took a while for the heater to warm the automobile. He followed the lights of Milt's Ford station wagon. When you have kids, you buy a station wagon.

"I really like them," he told Caroline.

"I'm so glad. I knew you would. They're my best friends on earth. They like you too. I can't believe the things Myra asked me in the ladies room."

"Like what?"

"If you were as good in bed as you looked. And if you made me happy. And some other things when I told her there has never been anyone for me like you."

A wave of tenderness washed over Carlson that dipped into his deepest places. He pulled her closer to him and put his hand between her coat and skirt along her warm thigh. He could feel her stocking top beneath the material of her dress.

"No one has ever said something like that to me," he told her. "It makes me feel as if I might cry."

"Don't cry. It's true. I love you, mister."

"I love you, Doctor."

He drove silently for a while, then he told her about the possibility of a job that Sam had mentioned.

"Oh, that's wonderful! I knew you would get a break soon. I just knew it! And it was by meeting Milt and Myra. I feel very good about this. Don't you?"

"Grandma always told me never to count my chickens before they et cetera."

"You're right. But I still feel very hopeful."

The Abrams' house was in a suburban development of many winding roads with names like Hawthorne Circle. The structures were so alike you had to remember numbers and street names or you would never find your way home. The landscaping had not yet become lawns and where there was no snow the yards were frozen tufts of brown grass. The shrubs were hardly as high as an elephant's eye. Most of the trees were propped up by supporting sticks.

But the houses were well designed, clean, bright, and livable in a modern style.

Carlson observed, "It feels like we are married, doesn't it?" when they made love in the guest room that night.

"It always feels so good," she replied.

Then they heard Milt and Myra making love in the next room and realized they had been heard also. They giggled together beneath the covers.

It was a lovely day. They did nothing. They read the Sunday papers sprawling around the living room, Myra using the small of Carlson's back for a pillow as if they had known each other forever. She flirted all day, often laying her big soft breasts on Carlson somewhere, giving him a spontaneous hug. They grilled hamburgers outside on charcoal though it was so cold Myra wore mittens and boots, a fur coat and stocking cap. It was Milt's idea to cook out.

"Really fuck up the neighbors, man. They'll think it's springtime."

Their kids thought it was nuts.

It was just right.

They dashed inside with their hamburgers and ate them by the fireplace.

Later, in the laziest part of the afternoon, Milt and Carlson watched a football game between the Redskins and Bears. Myra and Caroline went into the kitchen to drink coffee and talk.

Before they left, Milt showed Carlson some of his work. The stuff he was working on at the moment was at his studio, but everything he showed was good.

"When you two get married, I'll give you one," he said when Caroline and Myra came into the room.

Monday morning Carlson called and got an appointment that afternoon to see the city editor of the paper in Waukegan. He left work early, changing into slacks, shirt, tie, and sports jacket, and drove to Waukegan.

The editor looked at the samples of his work, chuckled over stuff in the humor magazine Carlson had edited, liked the makeup of the student paper Carlson had redesigned, and asked when he could start work. Carlson told him he could start the next morning.

"The job pays a hundred and ten a week, to start," the editor said.

Carlson hadn't even thought to ask.

He was a newspaper reporter.

On the way home he bought a bottle of ten-dollar French champagne and six roses for Caroline. It was only the second time he had bought her flowers.

Sixteen

"THERE ARE THE upstate thieves and there are the down-state thieves," the managing editor explained Illinois politics to Carlson. "That's all you need to remember. Forget Democrats and Republicans. You can't understand anything that way."

Carlson *had* been puzzled when both the Democratic and the Republican candidate for mayor had offered him a fifty-dollar bill to ensure each got as much ink in the paper as the other, should Carlson ever be doing a story on them. All reporters, he discovered, were similarly offered money for space in the newspaper. The two top reporters were given a hundred dollars each. It was not a bribe. Neither candidate sought to influence the reporter's personal choice. They just wanted to be sure that they got about as much ink as the other. Pro or con really did not matter. Carlson did not accept the fifty from either candidate and was now worried that he would be considered naively idealistic, bordering on stupid, by managing and city editors, copy desk editors, reporters, and probably the owner of the paper. He would have to be watched.

He told Caroline about it that night, pulling her close, turning her to face him in bed.

She put her head on his shoulder. "Why do you let everything bother you?" she said. "Learn to accept what is and live with it."

"I can't," he said. "I try, but things stay with me. My whole life comes back to taunt me when something goes wrong."

He had told Caroline everything about himself, even

what troubled him the most: the loss of his son and the loss of his college education. Both seemed to represent terrible negative steps he could never erase.

She kissed him now, softly at first, then more hungrily. He hauled up her nightgown beneath the covers, tugging it over her head so her warm body pressed against his own. Her flesh was so soft and smooth. Her pubic delta was a lovely dense contrast. He entered her waiting wet cunt.

After they made love she idly traced the hairs down the middle of his belly with her fingertips and told him: "If your feelings about yourself bother you so much, why don't you see a shrink? I could arrange it, if you like."

"What do I need a shrink for if I have you?" he countered. "And I'm afraid I would either con the shrink and just be wasting his and my time, or he will discover that I *am* a hopelessly immoral, unregenerate bastard, and *then* where would I be?"

"Oh, Jarl. I never saw anyone who could make the simplest decisions of life so overwhelming. Why suffer?"

"Maybe I need to suffer. I mean it. Maybe I *need* to examine everything by running it through the house of mirrors that is me. Man, *I* don't know! I just always have. Maybe it is Swedish. I mean, I can recognize how I'm happy as a lark on the one hand, that here I' am in a lovely spot, clean fragrant sheets, soft pillows, a woman I'd rather love than any I have ever known, whose pussy feels and tastes so *good* to me—a fulfillment all around, beyond any I can verbalize, a satisfying experience outside of language, beyond morality, sans hope *or* depression, past or future, something more immediately good than breakfast food in a box. I'm happy, Caroline. I have moved from a place of genuine fear and loathing to a place of happiness in one lovely jump. But what you must realize is: I will always be troubled by something a lot of the time, however happy I may be."

"Okay. I just hate to see you in pain," she said, and snuggled closer to his naked body.

* * *

Carlson had been with the paper for almost six months, rising from rewrite man and taker of obituaries to a general assignments reporter. He also had become the paper's military editor, though such an office did not actually exist. His beat covered Fort Sheridan, the Great Lakes Naval Training Center, the Greater Chicago Civil Defense District, and everything else pertaining to the military.

When there was an ugly murder on the naval base, Carlson was able, through acquaintances he had developed there, to find out who the parties were and where they lived, and was able to get the story, even though all information to the news media was immediately blocked by the FBI.

A pretty young woman who worked for her uncle, a civilian orthodontist on the base, was shot to death in his offices, apparently by him. The man then killed himself by putting the barrel of a .38 caliber pistol in his mouth and pulling the trigger, after putting the "closed" sign on the office door and locking it.

Obviously, uncle and niece were emotionally involved beyond their interest in corrective dentistry.

The girl's husband drove a mail truck. To avoid the Chicago reporters the young man was whisked by the FBI to stay with his parents in the country.

But Carlson tracked the young man down, parlaying a few scraps of information and a lot of bluff to discover from the man's landlady that he often visited his parents in a small town about forty miles from the base. The name of the family was not all that common. With the possibilities narrowed down to three, Carlson set out in the heavy fog.

It was nearly midnight when he arrived at the small frame house. In the yard was a Pontiac sedan about three years old and a shiny midnight-blue '48 Mercury club coupe with spotless whitewall tires. The young husband's landlady had told Carlson the boy drove an old coupe, which he always kept shining like new. Carlson knew he was where he wanted to be.

He parked along the street rather than pull in behind

the two cars in the driveway, then got out and went up to the door. He felt like a bastard, yet excited at the prospect of scooping the Chicago papers in such a juicy murder case. He knocked on the door.

A woman wearing an apron over her dress opened the door and said: "Yes?"

"I would like to talk with Andy, Mrs. Wotjas. I am Jarl Carlson of the Waukegan *News-Leader*. I know the FBI has told you not to talk to reporters, but I found out about the situation, and though I do understand and sympathize with all of you in this terrible time, I think you should talk to me about it and get as accurate and true a picture in the papers as possible before the Chicago reporters get hold of this and blow it up into something awful." He appealed to their country pride with the specter of filthy big city reporters.

"Well, I just don't know, Mr. Uh . . ."

"Carlson, ma'am."

"Mr. Carlson. Will you just wait a minute?"

"Sure."

She left the door slightly ajar. Presently she returned and reluctantly let him inside the small living room. There was a slight, balding older man in a red cardigan and flannel shirt standing beside a distraught young man, short, with a stocky, muscular build and a shock of thick, unruly red hair. He could have been one of Carlson's cousins. He had a sprinkling of freckles on his nose. A kind of all-American midwestern youth who surely worked as diligently for the post office as he did keeping his car impeccable. Carlson was willing to bet that the car ran like a watch and had been hotted-up knowledgeably. He liked the young man immediately. What he was about to do was cruel, but probably less cruel than everything that would come later and linger even after his wife was buried.

They sat down. The woman offered Carlson coffee, for which he was grateful.

"There are questions I have to ask you," Carlson explained. "I hope they are not too painful for you to try and answer. I am really sorry this has happened."

"Me, too," the young man managed.

"Do you have any idea why this could have happened?"

"No, sir. I don't," he said sincerely.

It crossed Carlson's mind that the young man honestly had not considered that his wife and his uncle were having an affair.

"There was never anything your wife said to indicate there was any kind of problem between her and her uncle?"

"No, sir. They were always laughing and joking together when they were around each other. Everyone liked him. And everyone liked Linda."

Linda Wotjas.

The young man really could not understand it. Was he so simple? Until a few hours ago that young man thought the world was his, with a lot of hard work and dedication. He was *too* good a boy, Carlson thought. Too good. Too innocent. Old happy uncle peering into people's eyes, thinking what kind of thoughts? Uncle was married and had two children. Looking at the dentist's picture that the woman brought from another part of the house and the picture of his wife and kids, Carlson instinctively felt the uncle had just eased the young woman into whatever it was that happened. He looked like a cross between Joe McCarthy and Vice-President Nixon. Yeah, hit her with the gas, get her panties off, then convince her it is love or some damn thing.

"May I borrow these photographs?" Carlson asked. "I will return them to you tomorrow. I will give you a receipt for them, to guarantee their safe handling and prompt return. It will just save us bothering you any further and maybe getting not so flattering photos."

"Well, I guess it's all right. What do you think, Daddy?" the woman asked the man in the sweater on the couch.

"What does it matter now?" he wondered.

Carlson asked Andy about his schooling, how he and Linda had met, courted, got married. The young man seemed to like to talk about his life with the girl.

He hauled out his wallet and dug out several photographs of a very pretty young woman with a new hairdo at her high school graduation, and one photo showing her in a revealing tight bikini taken on a summer day beside the lake. A very pretty, voluptuous girl, pursued by men all her life. Yet there was an innocence in her expression in both pictures; like her husband, she seemed unbelievably ignorant of what was going on. How could she not, for example, know that her yellow bathing suit when wet, as it was in this picture, did not reflect quite enough light? There was a distinct slight shadow of her not unremarkable pudenda clearly visible. She did not look as if she really knew. But she would have had to, wouldn't she?

Uncle looked as devious as the tunnels of a pocket gopher.

"Just take a sniff of this, Linda. It's really better than beer or anything, honey. Of course it won't hurt you. Doesn't hurt our patients, does it? Just try it."

Gobbling that sweet young pussy. Getting the old joint out and all *day* to get it up and get it into the darling tight hole. And no responsibility at all! Hump, hump, hump, her lifeless bare knees reacting only to his considerable weight, kissing her lifeless lips, mauling her nice little titties—do anything to her—huff-huff-huff. In the office, the door locked, the venetian blinds closed. Oh, rapturous joy!

Then she woke up too soon. And it was *all* over.

Maybe it all began innocently with his doing some free dental work on her teeth. Her husband said she had always been afraid of going to the dentist before she went to work for her uncle. He had been surprised when she took the job.

"More coffee, Mr. Carlson?" Mrs. Wotjas asked.

"No thank you, ma'am. I think I have bothered you folks long enough." He folded the unobtrusive squares of paper he had been taking notes on in his own kind of shorthand. The 8½ by 11-inch sheets of newsprint folded in half each way formed a nonthreatening pad for notes when interviewing. It was just a bit of casual paper he pulled from his pocket. Yet he could get a considerable story on a segment of paper one fourth the size of the sheet.

He told the family good-bye, shaking hands with each

solemnly. They all smiled, as if he were taking their pictures.

It was funny, he thought, *poor people, Midwesterners and Southerners particularly, always smiled when they had their pictures taken, except at the scenes of accidents and funerals. Give them some time to pull themselves together, break out the camera, and eight times out of ten they will smile, however inappropriately.*

He went back to the paper where the city editor sat like a great toad-shaped thunderstorm in the slot of the city desk. Everyone else had gone. Carlson showed him the pictures and sat down to write the story for the morning edition.

The city editor waited to read it. He read it, marked it up, put a head on it, and sent it down to the composing room. It would run on the front page with the pictures enlarged and prominent, with Carlson's by-line.

"Good job, Carlson," the city editor said in the dry, begrudging way he had of offering anyone praise.

It was better than a show of enthusiasm. It pleased Carlson enormously.

"Good night," Carlson said.

They would not actually walk down the stairs together. Carlson waited to watch the older man wrap his portly form in a heavy overcoat, turn a wool scarf around his throat, and place a brown homburg squarely on his silver hair.

"Good night, son," the man said and went down the stairs.

Carlson had a press pass for one night at the 1956 National Democratic Convention being held in Chicago's Cow Palace. He was told to go and write "color."

So he interviewed the hookers polling delegates in the outer lobby, the hallways, and along upstairs ramps. Some had even gained badges to get onto the convention floor.

It was the conviction of the whores, many of whom

had worked both the Democratic and Republican conventions, that the Democrats were "better sports."

He interviewed delegates so drunk they were not certain what town they were in. But most could remember for whom they were supposed to cast their votes. He found a delegate passed out in the outer lobby against a post in a monkey suit hiked up on his pale fat legs, and learned later that the man was discovered to be dead of a heart attack when the hall was being swept out the next morning.

The most stirring moment of the convention came when the name of a young senator from Massachusetts, John Fitzgerald Kennedy, was put in nomination for the office of Vice-President of the United States. Carlson had never heard of the man. But when his name was put in nomination a searchlight in the darkened auditorium scanned the floor trying to find him and discovered him in the balcony. He stood with his beautiful young wife beside him, laughing and waving to the crowd. That he was up on the balcony like a regular person pleased Carlson and everyone there. That he was young, slim, and handsome was an exciting thing too. Too many politicians were gray old men with bellies and trouble with their bowels or prostates, no matter how leathery tan their hides had been.

When Carlson got back to his newspaper, even the garrulous city editor was impressed with young Kennedy and offered the pontifical observation that he would be the first Catholic President of the United States.

Carlson had gotten on the floor and was behind the two-story podium where Adlai Stevenson waited for the precise psychological moment to ascend to the rostrum and lead the Democrats back to the White House. Carlson would not forget the look in the man's eyes. It was not greed or fear, but something akin to both, something unique to the politician, perhaps the same thing that led Carlson himself to despair of being worthy of association with his fellow men. But then there was the confidence too, which caused the candidate to mount the steps to his greater destiny, to answer the call of the people.

"Stevenson is no Lincoln," Carlson scrawled on a fold of paper in his palm.

Since Stevenson had lost in 1952 to General Eisenhower, the Saturday morning quarterbacks had decided his manner and speeches were too intellectual and witty for general consumption in America. This time they hired various speechwriters to help him tone down his addresses to better reach the grassroots voter. There was John Steinbeck sitting out at Northwestern adding ideas and words on Stevenson's behalf. Carlson had tried to interview Steinbeck about his contribution, but Steinbeck would not talk to him.

Carlson felt that beneath the brave display and surface fire, Stevenson knew he had even less of a chance against the General this time around.

Carlson went back and wrote a story that began with the hookers and ended with the hookers, with an emotional peak around the nomination for Vice-President, dwelling on John Kennedy and leaving Stevenson of little more importance than the dead delegate in the outer lobby in his rucked-up suit. It was a good story. He described the moments waiting beside the man, saw into his pores, and concluded publicly: "Stevenson is no Lincoln." It was the kind of story that broke a lot of journalistic rules, one that the city editor huffed and puffed over as he read it, then threw a headline on it and sent it down the tube to be set in type, with Carlson's by-line above it.

He was amazed to discover how happy he was. After work, he would hang out at the Burgundy Room in Waukegan with the other reporters. At night, he entertained Caroline with great intellectual arguments, sitting at the small table in the kitchen, watching her cook dinner.

"Go to night court or a police station some night," he was saying, "any night. Well, you have seen an emergency room at a city hospital. The same thing. See that and the problems in *Marjorie Morningstar* and *The Man in the Gray Flannel Suit* will appear as remote to most of these people as the backside of the moon. Why the hell is such shit so popular? Or as Nelson Algren put it in an interview recently: 'If *The Man in the Gray Flannel Suit* was marrying *Marjorie Morningstar* on my front porch tomorrow morning, I wouldn't go to the wedding.' "

Caroline did not see the humor in that or find its meaning as essential as Carlson did. She did not like Algren's work. She knew he wrote beautifully but did not think most people wanted to read about the kind of things he wrote about.

"Just because things are popular doesn't mean something's wrong with them," she insisted, waving a spatula at him.

Oh, no, wrong, wrong! Carlson was off again, with examples from Mark Twain, quotes from *Moby Dick,* references to Pieter Breughel.

He was still at it while they finished the stuffed pork chops in Italian sauce, one of his favorites. Dinner over, Caroline kissed the top of his head. "Let's go to bed. All this talk makes me horny."

When they were undressed, she asked softly, shyly: "Please eat me."

She came, thrusting her cunt against his mouth as he churned her vagina with two fingers. He turned her over and entered her from behind, then before he came, he stopped, lubricated her asshole and his cock with K.Y. jelly from the tube in the drawer of the nightstand, and slowly entered her rectum. It had been another thing she had never done before. But she had been very willing to try it. Now it was an occasional passionate addition to their lovemaking.

The way she offered her asshole to him was a unique and touching experience that created a desire to be tender and caring toward her, and he was always careful to enter her slowly, letting her dilate to receive him: when his cock was in the tight anal passage, he could feel her playing with herself so that she would come again with him. She had developed an amazing ability to turn her head around enough to be kissed on the lips.

But this time he stopped and had her turn over so he could face her, kiss her, and tell her he loved her when he came in her. He had never been in her bottom before face to face. It was good.

They showered together afterward and returned to bed. They lay in each other's arms and told each other they were happy, content.

"But next time we do that," he suggested, "would you be on top and just let me lie still a bit? I would like to feel what that was like."

She thought a second to see if she could picture what he was talking about. "You mean fuck me in the ass, only like we do sometimes when I'm on top and you hardly move until the end?"

"Yeah."

"Okay."

"I love you!"

"You know I'll try anything with you . . . once."

"That's why I love you. I saw that written on a wall in a latrine at the hospital."

"You did not!"

"I really do like fucking you, you know?"

"I *do* know. I like that you do. I like fucking you too."

She would never be comfortable using the word "fuck"; there was a resistance to it deeply ingrained in her.

"I love you, Dr. Caroline Palmer," he said. He fell asleep with his bare bottom against hers and his feet up against her calves.

Seventeen

A NIKE ANTI-AIRCRAFT missile escaped during a routine drill from one of the many missile sites around Chicago, and fell into Lake Michigan.

"Was it armed?" was Carlson's first question to the commander of the missile site.

"No, sir," the bespectacled young captain replied. "There was no danger in that missile at all. Unless, of course, it happened to fall on someone." He smiled confidently.

"None?" Carlson persisted.

"No, sir! There is absolutely no possibility of it exploding, or any nuclear reaction occurring, or any kind of pollution from the missile in its present configuration. A key has to be turned by missile site commander to arm the missiles. He lives with that key around his neck."

"You said, 'No nuclear reaction or pollution'?" Carlson repeated.

The captain paled. He looked as if he wished *he* was at the bottom of the lake, then became very flushed of face.

Carlson had a nationwide scoop.

CHICAGO MISSILES HAVE ATOMIC WARHEADS!
NO DANGER, GENERAL DECLARES

Until that morning no one had known that the many sites ringing and within Chicago had missiles with atomic warheads on them. No matter what assurances various generals and functionaries declared on the side of public safety, people in "Chicagoland," as one of the big city papers often liked to put it, did not feel safe.

"It's just another damned example of the government doing what it darn well pleases and telling us nothing, and only 'fessing-up after they been caught at it," a woman with blue hair declared at a checkout line at a local supermarket. "I'm just fed up with this sort of thing. Who knows what else the damned government is doing to us and not telling us—*with our money too!*" That was the crowning indignity.

Even less upset individuals, willing to accept that the atomic warheads might be necessary militarily to protect the nation from enemy bombers, wished that the government had been able to be more honest with them.

"You say they got them things on top of buildings right downtown?" A local fireman was incredulous. "Man, has anyone thought what would happen if there was another Chicago fire?"

"They say an atomic warhead in that case is safer than a conventional one, unless it is armed," Carlson said.

"Who says? How do they know? They ever tested those things in a fire as hot as a city block can get if it takes off?"

A farmer from out in Lake County called the paper to report that there was one of those missile sites on some land he had sold to the government and he had cows grazing near it. Would the atomic missiles do anything bad to his cows or their milk? He wanted someone to tell him.

An organization called Friends of the Lake tried to file an injunction against the government to get all missiles removed from places where firing them or other accidents might let them fall into the lake.

Students at Chicago U., where work on the first atomic bombs was done, filed a protest with the city and the federal government. Then students at Northwestern put together a big papier-mâché cartoon of the whole thing and got their picture in the paper.

"I don't care about it!" a recently immigrated Hungarian freedom fighter declared in North Chicago. "I love this country. They let me come here to live. I got a good job. My family is pretty happy. My boy, he is running around with a bad crowd I don't like, but this is a good country. I love Uncle Sam. You can put it in the newspaper. If Uncle Sam wants to put atomic bombs on my roof, it's okay with me. You can put it in the paper I said so, just so he keeps the Communists and niggers away from me, I don't care."

Carlson put it in the paper.

Finally it was decided that the mayors from all the outlying suburbs and towns where the main number of missile sites were located should be junketed at government expense down to Fort Bliss at El Paso to visit the NIKE missilemen in training and see a demonstration of the missile in action. Carlson was the only reporter invited.

He crept into the apartment, rather drunk. He crawled into bed beside Caroline.

"Why are you so late?" she asked sleepily.

"I got to drinking with some of the boys."

"I called the Burgundy Room, you weren't there."

"We were there early. We went out and got some pizza at a place and bummed a bit. I'm sorry."

"I wanted us to have a night together before your big trip. This will be the first time we have been apart."

"I know. I'm sorry. I was just sort of keyed-up about everything, I guess. Wanted to drink with the guys."

He kissed her. It was just a peck, but she opened her mouth and drew him insistently into a deep, passionate kiss.

"You aren't seeing someone else, are you?" she asked.

"No. Why do you ask that?"

"I just wondered, that's all. I mean, we aren't married, are we?"

"No. But I'm not seeing anyone else. Are you?"

"Don't be silly," she said as she pressed closer and opened her mouth in another wet, long kiss.

He was going to have to make love to her.

He thought to go down on her, but when he started toward the other end of the bed, she stopped him and said, "No. Be in me. I want to feel you in me."

171

And tired as he was, he loved her and was able to be in her.

God, she was so much better, so much more open and loving than anyone he had ever known. She was particularly passionate that night. She and Myra had been talking or she had been reading something, he guessed. He was pleased, delighted, felt very tender and loving to the beautiful treasure of a woman beneath him, fucking him like a snake, digging it. Then he realized she was going to come. It started like a small earthquake rumbling deep in her throat and built to a crescendo that broke into a shrill scream at its height. It was the first time she had come while they fucked in the missionary position without either him or her touching her clitoris.

"Oh, baby, I love you so!" he cried, coming in her. It felt as if the lower half of his spine had melted and been ejaculated out of his cock. It was wonderful but rather painful. They lay exhausted together, he between her legs, their arms wrapped around each other, kissing each other blindly while trying to breathe. The covers were off the bed.

When they could straighten up the bed and prepare to sleep, they were happy. They looked at each other with renewed wonder.

"We really did it, didn't we?" she asked.

"We really did," he assured her.

"You know I didn't have any diaphragm in, don't you?"

"I didn't think you did. I'm sorry. I just didn't care."

"You didn't?! Oh, I'm so glad! Neither did I! Oh, Jarl, I love you so much. That was so good, wasn't it?"

"Just perfect."

"Just perfect," she repeated.

He was up at four-thirty the next morning, tired, slightly hung over. Caroline had providently packed his bag the night before. She was a marvelous packer of bags. He showered and shaved as quickly as possible. But he realized Caroline had gotten up when he heard her in the kitchen.

"You should eat something," she said, setting a plate of bacon and scrambled eggs and a stack of toast at his place at the small breakfast table in the kitchen.

"You should have stayed in bed," he scolded her.

"I want to do this," she said.

He put his arms around her, slipped his hands beneath her robe.

"You feel good to me, Doctor."

"Um." She let him kiss her.

"Um, *good* coffee!" he exclaimed. Usually her coffee tasted like hospital coffee.

"It's new. French market blend with chicory. It *is* good, isn't it? I'm always looking out for you."

"That's true, love," he agreed.

She sat on his lap when he had finished gulping down his eggs, had eaten all but one strip of bacon and still held a wedge of toast and strawberry jam.

"I would like to get married, I think," she said, putting her arms over his shoulders, locking them beyond his neck, leaning back to look into his eyes as she spoke.

"Oh?" was all he could think to say. Then he grinned. "You've been asked?"

"Not yet. But I have been thinking about it and I think a certain fella I've been seeing ought to make an honest woman of me. I mean, I'm not complaining. We are very good as we are. And Milt and Myra understand. But we can't have people from the hospital in for a party or even a dinner for fear they will find out we are living together and damage my reputation." She became direct. "Really, darling, you are doing well now. It isn't a matter of money or ego anymore. It doesn't matter if someone from the hospital recognized you as the former sexy orderly on orthopedics. I want everyone to see how much in love we are, how happy, how well you and I have done. Do you see? I love you. I'm proud of you, of us—I am proud of *us!* I want to have people in, let them see us. The women will be envious. You'll like that. I promise. Anyway, please think about it. Will you?"

"Of course," he said. "I will. I do. I really would like to be married to you," he explained. "Really! It is like a perfect dream come true to think about it. I mean we *are* together." He put his hand under her robe and touched her bare thighs, her soft pouting belly, played with the fringe of long silky public hair that was a blonde puff in her lap. "To be able to do this with you the rest of my life . . ."

"But?" she asked.

"No buts," he insisted. "I *want* to. If I can, I will. But it is an enormous responsibility. I mean, I don't ever want to hurt you. Your future means more to me than my own in a way. But you know I don't accept the world on the same terms as most people. I am never entirely satisfied with being comfortable and happy and in love."

"Listen, you lunkhead, knowing you has made me a better, more patient human being. Do you know that? I love you and I would like to be married to you."

"I would like to be married to you, too," he vowed.

The downstairs buzzer sounded. She got up and spoke into the intercom. "He'll be right down."

"When would you want to do this?" he asked.

"Oh, there's no rush. I don't know. What about June? My folks would probably want to come down. I don't think dads are supposed to pay for a girl's second marriage. Sorry about that." She shrugged.

"I would want Milt to be my best man," he said.

"Oh, he would love it!" she exclaimed. "I would ask Myra to be my matron of honor."

"Can they do it? You know?"

"Oh sure! I think so. I'll speak to them. They aren't orthodox."

"We could convert, of course," he said. "Naturally, I don't want the operation."

"Don't be silly! Anyway, you never needed to be circumcised. Maybe you could fake it."

"Like to fake it right here and now."

"Go to Texas, you crazy person."

"Give me a kiss first."

"There!"

He put his hand under her robe and slapped her bare bottom a couple of times.

"Sadistic bastard. I love you." She kissed him again,

better than the last time. "Hurry home, darling. Write well. Have a nice time," she called from the door as he got into the elevator.

An Army sergeant got out of the shiny olive-drab sedan, saluted, and opened the back door for Carlson as he approached.

"Sergeant Heller, sir. May I take your bag?"

Carlson let him take his bag and stow it in the trunk of the car. He felt funny sitting in the backseat like an officer, being chauffeured so formally. He wished he had insisted on sitting in the front.

"Lots of fog this morning," he observed.

"Yes, sir. It's supposed to burn off though."

"That's good."

Carlson lit a cigarette and then offered one to the driver.

"No, thanks, sir," he said, without taking his eyes off the road. "It's against regulations while we are driving."

"Oh. Things have tightened up a lot since I was in the Army."

"Yes, sir."

This was definitely a VIP trip. Sergeants usually drove field-grade officers. The sergeant sat at attention, like a Park Avenue chauffeur.

Very well, Carlson decided. He sat back and relaxed and thought of Caroline as he idly stared out through the fog at the ghostly houses sitting on the narrow yards so close together he could imagine coursing the entire block via adjacent bathroom windows. He saw himself scrambling through the startled lives of the inhabitants, now mostly middle-aged people, the husbands breakfasting in undershirt and trousers perhaps, the women in housecoats and curlers, all the children grown, gone away. The people who owned these houses were where they would be until they died. That was it, their greatest economic achievement beyond staying alive—those narrow little houses of no more than five rooms and a bath, a nickel's worth of yard in front and a one-car garage out back with access off the alley. This was it.

Yet, it was an amazing achievement, for the houses were the products of years of working for someone else, saving, doing without, and not getting really sick or injured for at least twenty years. The lives of the people who lived in those houses fell within the universal parameters of living for working people anywhere in the western world. There was a sadness to it. It was like a wash of gray and faded work clothes hung on a backyard line, of a size and bent that tells you the body that wears them is getting old and heavy and less agile than when dreams were new and the houses smelled of new boards and fresh paint. Now the entire neighborhood was forever permeated with the scent of corned beef and cabbage.

Suddenly, he loved America, loved Chicago, loved those people in hard-earned homes. He loved them and shared their despair. That so many were unaware of the terrain of their own despair, sitting there being conned by ownership of the Ford and the big TV was the sad thing, the possibly hopeless thing.

It was ridiculous for him to be sitting on the backseat of the staff car, being chauffeured to a story.

Eighteen

BY THE TIME they got to O'Hare the fog had lifted. The sun was bright, the sky blue. Jet aircraft regularly were launched like bolts into a sky that was dotted with fluffy white clouds. Though his breath was still visible in the air, Carlson felt winter was finally over.

The driver went to the military end of the airport, pulling up in front of the Military Air Transport Service waiting room—a small one-story frame building like any orderly room or supply room structure on any fort or base in the world. Familiarity with the place made Carlson feel at home. There were no mysteries in the physical process if such a building was the staging point for the coming journey. Sitting in sight some yards away was a silver MATS DC 3, around which a ground and flight crew were making last-minute checks.

By 7:30 A.M. the forty passengers had been assembled with their single pieces of baggage to be handled and their smaller hand-carried kits. They were greeted by a public relations major, a captain, and an Army chaplain who would be accompanying them on the trip. Everyone was shaking hands and introducing themselves, checking in. The baggage was stowed on the plane, the pilot and flight crew went aboard.

Passengers were boarded, once again their names were checked off against a master list by the sergeant at the door of the plane. Jokes were made about the relative beauty of the sergeant-stewardess.

The plane was cold from having sat in a cold hangar all night, but it was beginning to warm up from being in the sun.

"There will be some heat soon," the major promised. "When we get going, it'll warm up. We'll have donuts and coffee once we are in the air. We'll be flying from here over Kansas City, Wichita, Oklahoma City, and will land to refuel at Amarillo, then on to El Paso."

Carlson had a seat by himself and watched the takeoff from the window, feeling good about the trip, curious as to what his reaction would ultimately be. That was the great anticipatory aspect of being a reporter. Without that first wonder he would not have liked the job. Already he was describing the other passengers in his mind. There was General Clark, retired Army, now an advisor for Chicago's Civil Defense program. A portly man in a good tweed sports jacket, with a light blue sweater under it, gray gabardine slacks, brown suede shoes. Across the aisle was the scientist, a doctor of physics from the university, working on nuclear fusion, who had recently returned from Russia where he had seen some of the work they were doing in the field. Carlson would want to talk to him later.

The patchwork of the land below was always amazing to see. So fertile a land. So much of it yet uninhabited. Only one tenth of the land of China was arable. It looked as if nearly ninety percent of the U.S. was capable of supporting some kind of crop. We are a very rich country. *We don't even understand our riches*, Carlson thought.

They passed over Wichita. The airport Carlson's grandfather had scraped out of the prairie with teams of mules was now headquarters of a SAC bomber command. The new airport was on the other side of the city, big, sprawling, modern. He was sure people no longer packed a picnic to go out and watch the airplanes take off and land as they had when he was a boy, when Walter Beech was still his own test pilot.

When they got out of the plane at Amarillo during the stop for refueling, the sudden heat outside was a shock to bones still attuned to a Chicago winter. Inside the small airport the men stood around looking slightly stunned, displaced, objects of minor interest to local citizens and airport idlers. The airport reminded Carlson of Wichita's airport before it became the headquarters of the bomber command. He had not seen the new Wichita airport on the west side of town. The old one had been on the east. Nothing made quite as much difference in Wichita when he was a boy as whether you lived on the east (most desirable) or west side of town.

Towns can be funny. In the early days, it had been the west side of town that had grown up, been the boom side, the site of great homes of the rail, cattle, and wheat magnates. The city park was over there. Then came the oil, gas, and aircraft magnates, and they chose to live on the east side; the west became neglected. Now, with the airport and new developments starting up on the west side, it could swing back to become the dominant side again. Some of that he thought standing in the Amarillo airport. More of it while taking a leak in the men's room, on the wall of which, above the urinal to which he addressed his need, was written:

Please don't throw toothpicks in the toilets. Amarillo crabs can pole-vault.

Beneath that was written:

Aggies—please do not eat the yellow snow in the urinals.

Lo, the poor Aggies everywhere.

Carlson was glad he had his all-purpose Swedish khaki twill suit with him. It was not any cooler actually than the other suit he owned, but it so stood up in heat, cold, abuse, and natural disasters that it had to be considered a mistake by the company that imported the miracle. It was a handsome product, exceedingly well made, sold at a fair price. Carlson knew it had been an error by the American importing company when he tried to purchase a second one in a different color. "Sorry, that particular item is no longer being carried—*care-eed*," a clerk sung at him. Why wasn't so great a suit being care-eeed? He wrote a piece about that for his paper. There was considerable controversy when the piece was printed because

Sweden was also an important advertising account. The head of advertising was furious. He still glared at Carlson whenever they passed in the offices. Perhaps, Carlson just realized, *that* was the beginning of his being accused both jocularly and seriously of being some kind of Communist.

The accusations were part of the national climate in 1957. Only the week before, he had covered a story about a divorced Catholic music teacher who shot the hell out of her house and yard and terrified her neighbors with a 12-gauge shotgun because her ex-husband, who was twisted in her memory into being a Communist, was coming back to both spy on her and try to get in bed with her and their two daughters. The neighbors had called the police. Her apartment was heaped with literature about the Communist menace in America. Photos of the Pope, Joe McCarthy, and J. Edgar Hoover were framed atop the bureau in her bedroom. Man! Looking at the poor madwoman, who could hardly ever have been the object of any man's natural lust, as she shook with near convulsive rage, her domain shattered now by the pellets of five shotgun loads, Carlson wanted to grab her, hug her tight, and tell her that it was all right, that she was safe. Man. Her daughters were there, no beauties either, each had legs like members of a field hockey team. Poor fuckless girls. Poor woman. Man! Sleeping in the same fuckless room with pictures of the Pope, Joe McCarthy, and J. Edgar Hoover. No wonder the lady was beginning to look like Hoover herself. And nuttier than a Peanut Plank.

Carlson stopped at the newsstand in the Amarillo airport where General Clark was purchasing a package of Tums for his tummy and bought himself a Peanut Plank candy bar.

"I should never eat donuts," the general complained. "Always gives me heartburn. I never learn."

"Did you know the missiles were mounted with atomic warheads, General?" Carlson asked him. It seemed as good a place to ask as any.

"No. Well, no, I didn't actually know they were armed with such warheads. It doesn't really seem an important consideration, though. If the damned things weren't for our greater good, you don't think we would have them there, do you?"

"That's what I'm trying to figure out," Carlson said, breaking off a chunk of Peanut Plank between his teeth. The teeth were the good ones the Army dentist had taken upon himself to make for him.

"Well, you can rest assured that the Army is doing its very best to protect you and yours, night and day. In war there are certain risks we have to take, naturally. Certain calculated risks for the greater good. War is not a thing we can always stop and have a debate about and vote on."

"I was not aware, sir, that we were in a war."

"Oh yes! Oh yes. That is how the Russians trick you. We are in a war all right. An undeclared war. But those are the worst kind, don't you know?"

"My thinking is that as long as the bombs and shells are not falling on you and you are not killing or being killed, you are still ahead of the game."

"That's exactly it! That's why we have missiles around Chicago and our cities, our early warning system. We have to be ready and the enemy has to know we are ready, so we can buy time and perhaps achieve a chance to make a real peace."

"Yes, sir," Carlson said.

The general clapped Carlson on the shoulder. "Good boy."

It's all quite mad, isn't it? Carlson asked himself and got back on the airplane.

Below, Apaches raced over the lion-colored desert in dusty pickup trucks toward the Chiricahua Mountains. Grandsons of some of the fiercest warriors ever, kicking up rooster trails of dust behind their Chevys, Fords, and Dodges. Amazing landscape! Beautiful. The air so clear.

In the time when Carlson's own grandfather had been a man not much younger than Carlson, the Apaches and the United States were in a real undeclared war in which people killed people. He was astonished to discover he was thinking about events which happened only about eighty years ago.

The plane landed in El Paso. There was an air-conditioned Army bus waiting to take them to the fort. They were taken to the officers mess where they were greeted by the commander of the fort, Major General Stone. He wore Army dress blues with a starched white shirt. He shook every man's hand and read their name tags. He apologized that the bar was not open during duty hours but invited them nevertheless to have lunch with the other officers of the post. The men took trays and passed through a cafeteria-style lunch line, choosing anything they wished, and joined officers sitting at four-man tables.

Carlson sat with a young first lieutenant and a captain. Both were missilemen. They seemed so young to Carlson. He realized that for the first time he was on an Army post and he was older than most of the ordinary soldiers and about the same age as most successful captains.

But it was a new Army. There was a junior executive air among such officers.

The men at the table with Carlson were married. They were automatic patriots, being patriots in the way they were Christians. They were from the southern states, as were most of the white soldiers. They were not West Pointers. The captain was Virginia Military Academy and the first lieutenant was Auburn ROTC. They each had served a tour of duty in Korea after the truce. They were not interested in what happened in Korea before they arrived. It was as if all that had gone before them had no bearing on what existed or now might logically occur in the future.

They were not aware of the moves that led immediately to the North Koreans invading the South. They did not know that President Syngman Rhee had lost the election just preceding the invasion but refused to leave office, and with American support remained as President. They did not know and did not care.

Carlson couldn't wait for lunch to be over.

After they ate, the visitors were taken to field-grade officers' cottages on the post that had two rooms and a bath and a small front yard, with patio, all of it taken care of by a Filipino houseboy in a white mess coat, who stood at attention with his broom and dust pan at his side like weapons.

There was also a small kitchen and wet bar in the cottage. Most of the men were assigned a cottage with one or two roommates. Carlson had a cottage by himself.

He told the houseboy he would unpack for himself and take a rest.

The chaplain stopped by as Carlson was putting his things away to see if he was pleased with his accommodations.

"We thought that as you would want to be writing, you should have privacy, so we did not put someone in with you."

"That was very thoughtful. Thanks. The place is just fine."

"Anything at all you need or want, just let me know. It has been arranged that you can use the post telephone-telegraph circuits to send your dispatches back to your paper if you like."

"That's good. Thanks."

When the chaplain had gone, Carlson unlimbered his typewriter and banged out a lead piece about the trip down with the group and their arrival at the fort. When he was finished, he had about half an hour to lie down and rest before they were to assemble again with General Clark for cocktails and induction into the Loyal Order of the Oozelfinch, a mythical Texas bird that flew backward to keep the sand out of his eyes.

The Rotary Club right down to the snappy brass buttons on your diapers. Carlson smiled.

Each inductee was presented with an elaborate parchment scroll by the general. Champagne was poured and the men toasted each other.

But something was wrong. Something was not quite working for Carlson.

The group was photographed by Army photographers for posterity.

The general told stories of the early development of the U.S. missile program.

"After the war we brought all the German rocket experts we captured over there and they thought they were going to be killed. Really! They were scared! Werner von Braun, the whole lot. We had them here under house arrest, as it were, while they worked on our rockets. When they had the first birds ready to fly, we brought down a lot of congressmen and government people to witness the first firing of the Redstone rocket. We built a big set of bleachers from which the men could observe the firing.

"Von Braun and his boys were very nervous. Time for launch came. The rocket went up about thirty feet above the ground, laid over on its side, and went screaming down range to blow up. A disaster!" The general was laughing. "You should have seen the faces of the Germans. They were absolutely certain we were going to kill them. It took considerable assurance to convince them that we were not going to. There were many disappointments in our program in those early days," the general concluded, almost wistfully.

The phone rang early the next morning. It was the P.R. major reminding everyone cheerily that it was time to "rise and shine" and assemble at officers' mess at 0800 to proceed to the airstrip to take light planes out to Red Canyon Range Camp and White Sands near Alamogordo, New Mexico.

"It's going to be hot later in the day, so dress accordingly," the major warned.

Carlson got dressed, walked over to the officers' mess. He had bacon, scrambled eggs, and gratefully mixed some of the medicinal brandy one of the mayors brought along into his orange juice.

Nineteen

THEY WERE DRIVEN out to a fort airstrip where six high-winged monoplanes with large engines stood ready to jump them out to Red Canyon Range Camp in the desert. The planes were of Canadian manufacture and called for recognition purposes Beavers. Humpty, rather old-fashioned planes of the kind that can carry six or eight passengers and their gear into outbacks anywhere on earth. Strong planes with short takeoff and landing requirements.

They dropped out of the sky onto the desert, disgorged the passengers, and leaped off again back to Fort Bliss. *The men who flew those planes had a good job in the Army*, Carlson thought. Most of them were warrant officers rather than commissioned officers. If Carlson had stayed in the Army, he might have been operating in a similar capacity, or flying helicopters. There was a moment of envy. Then he thought of the bully-boy, junior executive, defensive kind of attitude he had picked up on in the mess and weighed his life against that and was glad to be out of it. He allowed himself a moment of feeling rich and almost important. It was because of his work that all the mayors and others were down there at government expense.

In a big shed the group was taken around the assembly area for the NIKE-Titan rockets and shown on a cut-away full-size model how the missile worked. The public relations officers were constantly monitoring the group, reminding them which areas and materials were restricted and where they might use their many cameras. The working of the atomic warhead on the missiles was explained.

And they were told of an even superior anti-aircraft rocket soon to be installed called the NIKE-Zeus.

Indoctrination and a visit to a working missile control site down in a deep, bombproof, reinforced concrete bunker where the men were ready to run an actual intercept mission took the remainder of the morning. All the various fail-safe devices were explained in detail. They saw the tracking radar lock onto a target as the crew ran a dry mission. Had it been an actual mission, TWA would have been missing its midday coast-to-coast.

Outside again, where the day was heating up rapidly, mirages were visible across the sands. As Carlson watched, with the scientist at his elbow, a dust devil danced across the desert first this way, then that. The wind, when it reached them, lifted the scientist's thin, combed-down straight hair. They smiled at each other as the devil disintegrated. A faint bit of grit pelted them momentarily.

"It is eerie to find all this secret military boogity-joogity out here in the desert. Wonder what the Indians think about it?" Carlson asked.

The scientist shook his head to indicate that he hadn't a notion of which he could speak regarding Indians, but he patted Carlson on the shoulder to let him know he considered the question worthy of thought.

Carlson walked over to the public relations major. "That radar atop the missile control bunker seems different from any radar I have ever seen." He pointed to a large, curved, platter-shaped framework moving slowly up and down while rotating on an axis. In its center was a busier, smaller framework and dish sweeping rapidly side to side and up and down. Wheels within wheels, as it were. At least those were the first words upon seeing it that jumped to Carlson's mind.

"That is the key to our intercept capacity," the major said proudly.

The scientist was already reaching for his camera.

"Sorry," the major restrained him. "That is *definitely* top secret. The Ruskies would give a lot for a photo of that thing. You bet! That is the highest-developed operational radar in the world. Ten years ahead of anybody." There was pride that would not be misplaced in a new father or at least ownership in the invention.

The radar worked away there, with nearly imperceptible variations, like a living thing. It worked around-the-clock. Indefatigable, ominous, amoral, the robot eye of a system that could reach out and destroy any known aircraft on earth, miles from the target.

It was hot now. Some men took off their jackets and carried them over their arms. It was still windy. Men who had worn neckties stood with the ends whipping wildly around their necks. The grit came in gusts that made sense of the mythical Oozelfinch's ability to fly backward in the desert wind.

"The mission will be piped through the loudspeakers here so you can hear the missile site commander issue his orders for the intercept and destruction of the intruder," the general said over a bullhorn. He then handed the instrument to the P.R. major.

"Gentlemen, you are privileged to be the first non-governmental civilians to observe the intercept and destruction of an intruding aircraft by the NIKE-Titan missile. Now I want to emphasize that this missile crew does not presently know when or where the aircraft will come from or at what altitude and speed it will be flying. Because you are here, of course, they know they will be running a mission sometime this afternoon; otherwise it is just as it would be if they were on station around Chicago. When they pick up the aircraft I will tell you, and you can follow the mission on loudspeakers. I will try to interpret what is going on for you. Naturally, we will be using conventional warheads, not nuclear. It should not be long now."

Some men nervously lit up cigarettes. The scientist stood with his hands folded behind his buttocks gazing calmly about the skies. The sun glinted off his half-rim glasses.

"I should have brought a cap," he said.

Carlson felt excited. It was like the kickoff of a championship game. He felt as he had before his first parachute jump, his first ride in an airplane, ride on a train—an almost sexual excitement that was not sexual at all. But he felt close to all those on the hilltop, those he liked and respected and those he did not care for at all, one with the soldiers and their general, half-a-one with the general's aide-de-camp. It was just hard for him to feel any positive human thing for an aide-de-camp.

We are like boys, Carlson thought. All of us. Even the scientist. All possibilities are held suspended, all imagination suspended for the event, the act, this thing we are here to do and see according to our respective stations.

"We have a contact!" the P.R. major exclaimed.

Over the loudspeakers poured a quantity of commands in a jargon Carlson could not quickly decipher.

The secret radar had swung and locked on something coming in from their right as they stood facing south. The P.R. major told them to all watch the southwestern sky.

Then there it was.

An old World War II B-17 came lumbering into view like a bird from another era. Carlson wondered if it had a pinup picture of some leggy lady painted on its nose and bombs for missions flown and German or Jap flags for fighter planes shot down painted on her fuselage. There was no question that she was a sitting duck against such sophisticated weaponry as the missile represented. Hell, a good anti-aircraft gunner could take that bomber out of the sky from where they stood. Carlson felt sorry for the old plane.

But that was not the point.

The plane was being flown purposely low so they could see the intercept.

When the plane was clearly in view, the command "Fire!" was heard. But the missile was already on its way.

A collective sound of awe rose from the throats of the men on the hillside as the rocket sped away as fast as the tongue of a frog snatching a fly out of the air. Then there was a silent burst of flame in the sky and everyone loosed a cheer as if the home team had just scored on a long pass play. Someone was waving his jacket. Someone had thrown his hat in the air. Then they heard the distant explosion. The sky was already clearing, a bit of debris from the intercept fell into the ground haze.

My God! Carlson thought.

"There is another bandit!" the P.R. major screamed. "We have a contact. It is coming very fast. Look to the southwest!" They all turned to look and something very small and very fast was streaking along at a much higher altitude, high enough to leave a contrail.

The earth below them shook again with the nearby rocket's launching blast, and again there was the direct reaching out from where they were to the target in a matter of two or three seconds, it seemed, then the intercept, the distant silent burst in the high sky, the bit of debris trickling down. The men were cheering madly, like boys, many of them now waving their jackets. Carlson had gotten himself next to General Clark to see if he could pick up a quote. The general seemed stunned. Then, very soberly, he pronounced: "The day of the cannon is over, gentlemen." That was all he said. He went further into retirement, not unhappily.

In the newspaper that night on the financial page was this headline:

GRIM VIEW OF FUTURE
WORLD POVERTY

The World Bank, soberly assessing the problems of ameliorating the lot of the have-not countries, predicts that although some gains have been made in reducing poverty, there will still be at least 600 million "absolute poor" by the end of the century.

All that money spent on weaponry, Carlson thought, to annihilate each other when no one wants to die.

He wanted very much to talk to Caroline. He called her through the post switchboard and reversed the charges. He heard her sleepy voice answer and tell the operator that, yes, she would accept the charges.

"What's wrong?" she demanded. "Are you all right?"

"Yes. I love you."

"That is what you are calling me about in the middle of the night?"

"Yes. I love you. And I feel lonely."

"And you are a little drunk, aren't you?"

"A little."

"Are you behaving yourself?" she asked with a tone of concern in her voice that touched him across the sleeping miles.

"Yes." He told her about the missiles.

"I've been having bad dreams while you've been gone. This is the first time we haven't slept together in a long time," she said.

"I know."

"I masturbated tonight before I got to sleep thinking about you," she said.

"You *did?!*" He was pleased, amused, touched by her confession. "I will jerk off and think of you before I go to sleep then," he vowed.

"I wish you were here so I could do it for you," she said.

"I'll be home tomorrow night," he told her.

"Then why not wait and we can make love all week-end?" she suggested.

"Okay. I love you."

"Love you." She made the sound of a kiss in the phone before they hung up.

He thought of Caroline in bed back in Chicago. *I'm no good for you, darling,* he told her as he stroked his cock in the dark in the officer's cottage in Texas. *I love you more than anything,* he told her. *I miss you and want you. I would rather be able to be the husband you deserve than anything on this earth. But I'm no kind of good husband. That makes me sad. I love you but, God, I don't want to hurt you, and I will. I will . . .*

Twenty

THE STORIES ON the missiles were well received. Several papers across the nation picked them up and ran them. Carlson was already getting mail locally and some phone calls. About one letter or call out of ten was from a nut who was sure Carlson was some kind of Communist or pinko or traitor to the United States.

Two months after he filed the last story in the series, he handed in his resignation from the paper.

The managing editor was shocked.

"What the hell is this?" he demanded.

"I want to quit," Carlson explained.

"Quit?! Jesus Christ, son, what the hell is wrong? You having woman trouble or something?"

"No. Hell, no. Look, I know it sounds crazy, but—"

"Crazy is right! Hell, boy, the publisher wants you to have lunch with him tomorrow. Maybe you don't realize how well you've done."

"I realize, I think. See, sir, my thinking is this: I can work here for the rest of my life and never have a story like the missiles thing again. I could hang on and wait until a spot opens on a Chicago paper, cover the police beat there. And so on. But I want to write about things like the missiles *most* of the time. I want to write about what interests me. Writing about the school board, clubs, local politics is not how I want to make my living all my life."

"Yeah." He looked disgusted, as if Carlson had failed him personally. "Well, I'll tell the publisher you've given your notice."

"The notice is pretty flexible. I'll be glad to stay until you get someone else," Carlson offered.

"No problem. I've got a drawer full of applications from hot-rocks out of journalism schools looking for a job."

"I know."

"Well, you did good work. It doesn't matter what else I think," the older man said.

"Thanks," Carlson replied.

They shook hands.

The managing editor never looked directly at him again as long as he was there.

The other reporters, upon learning of Carlson's resignation, began treating him the way members of a football team treat an injured player—ignoring his existence as much as possible while mumbling things like: "How's it goin', Cat?" when they had to pass by. Only the young reporter covering city hall, Mary Devlin, was understanding and personally appreciative of what Carlson had done.

"You're right. You can write. Move on. Shit, give it a try," she said, after inviting Carlson for an after-work drink.

Carlson did not have to explain a thing to Mary.

But how to tell Caroline?

Carlson had had several drinks by the time he parked his car a couple of blocks from the apartment and walked home in the gloaming of the streetlights' first glow.

Caroline never asked him where he had been when he came home a couple of hours late. If he was going to be really late, he would have called, or if they'd had plans for the evening, he would have called also.

Seeing her coming into the living room in her Chinese housecoat as he entered the apartment made the knowledge of the crazy thing he had done seem enormous in the face of her vulnerability. She came toward him pinning her hair up over one ear, and lifted her luscious lips to be kissed.

I wish I could die, he thought. *What the fuck am I doing? What is wrong with me?*

Her arms slithered around his neck. Her lips opened slowly and sexily over his.

Caroline had obviously been aroused before he arrived home. Her perfume had been liberally applied and the drugging scent of it rose in virtual fumes from her warm, naked body beneath the long red silk brocade coat.

"I love you," she breathed against his mouth. "I want you."

"I want you too," he told her.

"Right," she said, playing all around his lips and teeth and mouth with her tongue.

"Regular little slut this evening, aren't you?" he teased.

"Very. It must be a virus or something. I have wanted you ever since coffee break this morning. I couldn't wait for you to get home. And you're late. I almost had given up and started without you."

"You are a beautiful woman, Caroline."

She had also put on her big-time eyelashes and some kind of gloss to make her lips look perpetually wet. He commented on her mouth.

"All the better to eat you with, my dear," she purred.

He unfastened the knotted buttons and loops on the shoulder of her dress, found the little ties along the side under the arm, and opened her gown. Beneath she wore black stockings and a lace garter belt which framed her perfumed bush.

Carlson kissed his way down her belly, feeling her rotate her pelvis forward to offer him her cunt to kiss. He was not really turned on, but pulled her down on the floor to eat her with all the love and inspiration he had ever known. She became very loud, heaving herself around in the cradle of his arms, fucking his face, coming wildly up off the floor, screaming, coming, laughing, and doing it all over again. He did not know how many times she'd had an orgasm, nor did she.

He only stopped when she weakly implored: "Please, darling, no more."

They lay in the dark on the floor in each other's arms. She kissed his face, which was slick with the fluids from her body and smelled of her sex.

193

"You taste good!" he told her. "I could do that with you forever."

"Um! You'll get me excited again, talking like that."

He started to make love to her once more.

"No. I'm wonderful," she told him. "Just hold me until we get too cold, then we can go to bed. Are you hungry?" she asked, suddenly concerned.

He laughed.

"Don't say it," she said in an embarrassed small voice.

"Okay," he agreed.

They lay there on the floor. The fluids on his face felt as if they had dried into a thin powdery mask. He liked the smell and taste of her on his face.

It was not the time to tell her he had given his notice at the newspaper.

Once under the warm covers, Carlson could not sleep. He made love to Caroline again, lying virtually at a right angle to her body within her widespread legs to drive his cock as deeply into her as he could. Now and then he hurt her a little. When he came, he felt as if he had ejaculated the end of his spine which had turned liquid.

When they awakened at six-thirty, they made love again in the missionary position and she did not come, but asked him to let her get on top of him to ride his dying erection to her own climax.

They hardly spoke to one another as they rushed to get ready for work.

It was not until the evening after he came home late from work again that he was able to tell Caroline that he had quit his job.

He was late because he had gone with skinny little Mary Devlin to have a drink.

Caroline was in bed when he got home. There was a tuna casserole, and the heating instructions on the kitchen table were signed "Love."

He crawled into bed beside Caroline, trying not to awaken her. She stirred, mumbled something, and turned over to take him in her naked arms to offer him a good-night kiss, all without opening her eyes.

He kissed her.

"Caroline?"

"No," she replied.

"Sorry. I just wanted to tell you something."

"Can't it wait until the morning?"

"Sure."

"Good. Love you. Good night." She turned back over and snuggled her bare bottom into his lap. He put his right hand on her stomach and told her he loved her. They went to sleep.

In his dream he was very afraid, very alone, very crazy and frightened. It was something he had felt before so many times in the past it was a tiresome dream and he awakened without rest, glad to see another day.

"I quit my job at the paper," he told her as they were showering and dressing for work.

"You did what?" she asked rhetorically. "You quit your job? What happened, darling?" The last with true concern, as she stood in her underwear, stockings, garter belt, and shoes. She looked so beautiful to him then.

He could see her jawline was just beginning to go soft, not fat, just soft. She was a full-grown woman who made him feel that morning that he was just a boy as they stood there. She often made him feel like that. Before it was always exciting, kind of illicit.

He explained to her how he knew if he worked there another fifteen years he would never have a story like the one on the missiles.

"I don't want to be a copy editor or city editor someday. I don't want to be the managing editor. I know now if I owned a paper, I could not run it the way I would want to run a paper. It would go broke in a short time. You can only try to slip a little truth in the so-called impartial facts. The advertising is everything and that depends on the favor and interests of the advertisers, which ultimately means you cannot alienate the business community, the church community, the leaders of the town. It's a defeating proposition all the way."

"But what are you going to do?" she agonized for him.

"I don't know," he confessed.

She was trying to get her half-slip and skirt on, then her blouse.

"I just don't understand," she insisted. "We have been so *happy*. God, I have been happy. You were happy. Why didn't we discuss this?"

"I don't know. I guess I didn't know I was going to do it until I did it. I'm sorry. I just didn't think."

"That is a problem! Too damned often when I should be involved in a decision about something, you just don't think. Well, just what does this mean, 'I quit my job'?" She really wanted to know.

"I'm not sure."

"Wonderful! You will let me know, won't you?" She was dressed. She furiously made up her face.

He put his arms around her from behind.

"I know I love you," he said.

"For God's sake, don't. Not now."

"I'm sorry," he said. "I hoped you would understand."

"I will certainly try. For my own sake as much as for yours. I'm going to be late. Will you be here this evening at a decent hour for a change?"

"Yes."

"Good. We can talk about this then."

He caught her before she got away and tried to kiss her good-bye. She turned her mouth away, so he caught her soft cheek.

"I know it's crazy, I guess," he said. "But my loving you hasn't been. Not at all."

"I wish I could be so sure," she replied, but relented and gave him a peck on the lips before she left.

Carlson got home early and decided to make dinner for Caroline. He took out a packet of cut-up chicken and began to make chicken cacciatore. He would serve it with boiled noodles and a crisp salad. He worked happily, anticipating her pleasure and forgiveness. But in his anxiety he made mistakes that annoyed him. He cut his finger. He spilled things. Anxiety was taking its toll. He felt tired now and wondered when he would feel rested again. He thought he looked haggard. He still did not know what he was going to do. It was hard to think.

Caroline was only partially pleased by his cooking when she arrived.

"I'll clean up the kitchen," he promised.

"I need a drink," she said.

"Sit down. I'll get you one," he insisted, taking her arm, guiding her to an easy chair, seeing her into it as solicitously as if she were a dear old aunt.

She burst out in a laugh, then she began to cry, throwing her arms around his neck.

"You crazy, aggravating big dope. Oh, Christ, I love you. For better or worse. I don't even know what I got angry about. Why the hell should I get angry? I don't really care what you do for a living. If you want to write or draw and paint, or work on your cartoons, it's really fine with me. If you just want to work on your own stuff, we can easily get by on what I earn. I don't know why I got angry, darling. It was a shock. I guess I resented not being consulted beforehand. I don't really care if you quit. I love you so. Kiss me."

He kissed her.

"Just keep kissing me a lot, darling. Even when I am old and ugly."

"You will never be ugly," he assured her. "Now relax, I'll get you a drink and finish dinner."

"Let me help," she offered.

"Hell no. This is my treat," he said.

"Make the drink a double," she begged.

They got about half drunk before dinner, had a fine time with the food. Afterward he sent her off to take a hot bath while he cleaned up the mess in the kitchen.

She was fluffing up her pubic hair as he had so often seen her do, when he came into the bedroom. Her robe hung from her shoulders. Her head was in a towel.

They made love before she got around to drying her hair.

197

Then, in bed later, she said, "I don't care if you want to work in a gas station the rest of your life. Don't work at all. I love you, I just want us to be together."

He said, "I don't know what the hell I'm going to do. It just seemed necessary to quit when I did. I wish I could just go and live in Mexico like a Mexican and really try to write and paint as best I can."

"Why Mexico?" she wondered.

"It's cheap. If a Mexican family can live all year on two hundred bucks and change, I could last quite a while on a grand, if I had a grand."

"Please don't talk like that, darling. It makes my skin crawl. That's what I'm complaining about. That's what makes me crazy. There is no place for *me* in your thoughts like that. I told you, you don't have to go off to Mexico and live on beans. You can stay here, be comfortable, be loved and cared for by a pretty woman who loves you. What goddamned writer or artist do you know ever had such a great damned offer?"

"None," he agreed. "God, you make me happy. You make me so happy, darling."

"You make me happy, too, most of the time," she confessed.

But his mention of Mexico was more than a notion of beneficial monetary exchange rates. It was something else he could not explain exactly. He would have to think about it. Her loving proximity confused the issue enormously.

It was definitely something else, he reminded himself before he fell asleep that night.

Twenty-One

THERE IS A line in Woody Guthrie's autobiography, *Bound for Glory*, that runs something like: "No matter where I am, I always feel like I ought to be someplace else." That was Carlson's feeling. The why of it was the puzzle. Oh, even *he* could lay out psychological explanations for his feelings. But such explanations proved nothing, psychology would not catch it. Woody would understand, Carlson felt.

"I got to go," he told Caroline that night and began to cry. "I don't understand it, I just do," he said.

"Why?" she wanted to know.

"No *reason*. I *want* to stay. I love you. I want to go on with you forever. I *want* to marry you and have the kind of life you want and deserve. I really do. I honestly do. I *do*! But I can't. I can't be what I would have to be to have it, to do right by you. Don't you see?"

"No. Frankly, I don't see at all." She too had begun to weep. "Is there someone else?"

"Christ no! I love you. No one has meant to me the things you have meant, made me think, feel, to really want to be like everyone else, straight and sincere . . . even in the hypocrisy of it . . ."

"*Fuck that!*" she shouted and slapped his face hard. "I'm tired of that crap. I'm tired of hearing about it! You and me! That's what this is about! *You* and *me*."

"But we don't live in a vacuum," he pleaded. "It never is just you and me."

Christ, he thought, *we even sound like a soap opera.*

"So," she said, "what are you going to do, go back and live with the poor? I don't think you could do that. That would be no more honest than your 'passing' as a member of the middle class, as you have so often put it. You *aren't* lower class anymore. You don't have to live like that. I'd think you're trying to would be an affront, an insult to them."

"I've thought about that. I could not go as something I was not. But I would have to work for my bread. I'd have to take ordinary jobs. When I leave here, I'm right back to where I was before I met you. Don't you know that? You are what has made the difference in my life. I could still be in that hospital making forty-seven-fifty, or whatever it was every week, instead of sleeping here soft, you making love to me, getting a little fat, spending days unable to write enough about anything to make it live longer than a few editions."

"I told you, you could just stay here and write the great American novel or whatever. You don't have to do *anything*. Marry me, and we will live happily ever after, don't you see that, you goddamned hillbilly?" She wiped away his tears. He wiped away hers. Her mascara had run.

They kissed. Her lips were swollen and wet with her tears and sweet saliva.

"I know that," he told her. "I *do* know that. That is why I feel so crazy. I know if I go, I will not be happy again for a long, long time, maybe not ever again. Certainly never like this. I know that, Caroline."

"Then stay. Be my love. I want no other. Stay. Make love to me. Okay?"

They began there with their clothes on and made love all the way through the house, ending up in the dark, naked in the bed, making love by the light of a large fragrant candle.

Even as he was in her, so happy he could not conceive of any higher happiness, he knew he *had* to leave her, that he had to go.

Such happiness and beauty are not for me, he thought cornily. But why? Am I destined to only know it, experience it, and never stay with it? Is there some design to my own madness that makes better sense?

"I don't know," he said aloud, coming in her, with her

as she cried out in the candlelight. *I don't know!* he cried out in his mind. *I don't know. I've got to see. See what? Whatever. Keep going!*

But afterward, much later, lying entwined in the bed, in the dark, he told her again he thought he had to leave.

"Where would you go?" she asked wearily.

"I don't know. Mexico, San Francisco, maybe. I don't know. Just go."

"Well, maybe you just need to get something out of your system," she said resignedly. "Maybe you just need to go away for a while by yourself and think about things, 'see,' as you say."

"Yeah!" He leaped at the easy explanation like a drowning man for a rope. "Maybe I just need to drive the highways for a while. I love you and I want you. I just want to feel as good about myself as I feel about you. There is nothing about you that I do not adore. You know that, don't you?"

"Well, if you don't feel that way, you put on a terrific act, darling. Yes, I do know you love me. That's why this is so hard to understand. But I will try if you don't stay too long. When do you want to leave?"

Faced suddenly with the certainty of it, he was no longer so sure he *had* to go. He looked at her. She was actually saying he could go, that she loved him and that he could come back if he did not stay away too long. God, he loved her.

"Well, my two weeks' notice is up at the end of next week. We could go off for the weekend together and I could leave Monday morning, I guess."

"Okay. But let's not go away anywhere," she said. "Let's stay right here and not see anyone and do like we did the first weekend we spent together. Go for a crazy early walk."

"Anything. This time I will bring the champagne," he said.

"That's a deal."

They slept peacefully in each other's arms.

Things did not have to be so goddamned painful, he

thought, *if there was love and understanding. God, life could be great,* couldn't it? He felt good to finally be so corny and easy in his mind.

Their weekend was quiet, easy, intimate. They made love often, passionately, tenderly, desperately. The only rough moments came when Myra telephoned and Caroline tried to explain what Carlson was doing. She finally gave up, telling Myra she would call Monday.

Sunday night they dressed for dinner in the apartment. Caroline made herself especially beautiful for him. He put on slacks, a clean shirt, his blazer. She had the whole apartment cast in a pink, flattering glow with candles in glass windshields. But he did not comment except to tell her repeatedly how very beautiful she was that evening, and how very much he loved her. They did not speak of future plans, possibilities, trips to take, things to do together. Carlson was aware of how deeply the lack of such talk cut into the volume of their conversation. It was quiet for long periods of time. They each consciously tried to make the other feel as good as possible. The next-to-last time they made love, each was so intent on the other's satisfaction that neither was really satisfied. The last time they made love, Monday morning, was tearful, anxious, frantic, and both strived excruciatingly to come together. Finally they did. Then, it was a race for Caroline to get dressed, out of the apartment and to the hospital.

"Should I give you this?" he asked, holding out the key to her apartment.

"I don't know," she said, not knowing whether to take it or not.

"You better," he said.

"Yes. I guess so. You might lose it. I guess you know my number."

They embraced again, kissed, vowed again their love for one another.

"I'm going to be late again," she sniffed, flicking tears from her eyes as she hurried to get out of the apartment. "Please don't be here when I come back to surprise me," she asked. "If you change your mind, darling, please call me and tell me. I couldn't stand it otherwise."

"I promise. I'm sorry," he said.

"Well, so am I. But you have to do what you think you must do, I guess. Take care, my love."

"You, too," he said.

Then she was gone. The apartment was silent. He felt utterly abandoned, as sad as he had ever been. It was completely crazy, his going away. But so was staying.

He had not packed when she was there. He did not plan to take more than one big B-4 bag, a box of books, his typewriter, and some drawing materials. He packed and carried the stuff downstairs past the curious doorman and loaded it in his car.

"You takin' another trip, Mr. Carlson?" the man asked.

"That's right."

"Well, you have a good trip, hear?"

"Thanks."

"Yes, sir."

It was cloudy and had begun to rain when he got over to U.S. 30 and turned west out of Chicago. He drove all day, crossed Iowa with its curbed highways like streets, stopping only for gasoline. He was somewhere along the Platte River in Nebraska when he stopped at a roadside diner.

The hamburger was good and greasy. He washed it down with cold milk and had cherry pie and coffee for dessert. Realizing that Caroline would be home at that hour, eating alone, getting ready for bed alone, caused him to panic, want to turn around and drive directly back to her. It was the hardest thing he had ever done not to do just that. Instead, he sat in the car, took out a pad and pencil and wrote her a long letter, told her all the truths of his life he had rarely told any other person. He had not told anyone else all of it, not his fears, self-doubts, shameful experiences. He wanted her to know *everything* about him. He told her of lies he had created and let her believe about him. He had to express his terrible feeling of lack of self-worth in light of his love and respect for her. He concluded: "I guess I feel like this in general in relation to all good people like you. But in relation to you it seems painfully critical. I want to get over this feeling if I can. I love you and want to be with you and be happy and confident that I will not hurt you the rest of our lives . . ."

He finished the letter, put it in an envelope, put a stamp on it. In the middle of some sleepy little podunk place he stopped to put the letter in a mailbox. It had rained off and on along his route, sometimes hard so his windshield wipers could hardly sweep it away. Often it was just good hard midwestern rain with drops like little bomb bursts on the road and in the gutters, ditches, rainsoaked fields.

Finally, after fighting sleep for twenty miles that seemed like a thousand, he pulled off along the road under a big grandfatherly tree older than the state itself, old and full of Plains Indian spirit stuff. He felt safe there even in the rag-top car, with great bolts of lightning ripping the pitch-black rumbling sky overhead. His troubled dreams drifted to visions of Caroline.

He started up and drove off after about an hour, again heading west. Once more he stopped at a place where he could get out and look back and see the whole panorama of the great old tree, the Platte twinkling beneath the cottonwoods with alders along its bank, the sky streaked with gold, orange, blue, and black.

Then he drove on.

Book II

Twenty–Two

FOR A HUNDRED miles he had been teased by the billboards advertising something called Little America until it began looming in his mind as an oasis of multiple delights and refreshment against the relentlessly boring miles. It seemed a place of historical importance, an outpost in the desolate West, an amusement park, purveyor of delicious foods and cold drinks.

Carlson's disappointment when he saw the place was infuriating. His desire to kill, lay waste to the fraudulent place in the face of the billboards' extravagant promise, had to be weighed against his need for food and a cold drink of water, to wash his face. Set in the middle of nowhere at all, it was just a sprawling red brick building of faintly colonial scantlings housing a very ordinary and predictable truckstop café, dispenser of overpriced, bland, portion-controlled processed food and all the usual roadside slop. It was an exclusive disappointment, calculatedly venal for lack of an alternative for miles. The gasoline prices were the highest Carlson had seen in the United States.

"Everything has to be trucked in," the waitress, who had to field his complaint, explained. It was a question she had obviously answered often when travelers complained of the prices.

Carlson mailed Caroline a silly postcard from the place.

Driving away, he decided that overstatement of products and services should be a punishable offense, and anyone found guilty of fraudulent overstatement regarding goods and services should be required to spend thirty days to life at Little America. That would stop it, he was certain.

In the mountains, as he reached the summit of the highway, before the drop down into Cheyenne, it began to snow. A late spring snow. He pulled into a café to have breakfast. Silver-dollar-size pancakes, link sausage, and coffee cost three dollars—another outpost with a virtual monopoly.

"We have to have everything trucked out to us," the waitress explained wearily.

The cashier took his ten-dollar bill, returning him seven silver dollars, which were heavy as hell in his pocket. Yet he could not bring himself to ask to have them exchanged for paper currency. There was just something seemingly more valuable about hard money.

What had begun as a little fine spit of snow had quickly grown into a storm of wet cotton-batting wads by the time he started down the winding mountain grade.

Forget the brakes! he cautioned himself, getting the car into second gear, steering very gently, gently, easing the clutch in, slipping into low very carefully when he thought he was carrying too much speed coming up on a curve. The decision had to be made long before he reached the curve. On the off side of the highway the drop went down a long, long way. It was interesting and challenging driving. It made him feel good to be able to concentrate on it and do it well. The heavy wet snow packed up under his windshield wipers. There were no car tracks in the snow ahead, no way to see the edge of the roadway. He had to interpolate from the position of the signs alongside the highway and try to see the change in depth of snow between the roadway and the shoulder.

At the foot of the mountain on the runout toward Cheyenne, cars were stopped behind two highway patrol cruisers for over a mile. Obviously the road had been closed until the arrival of a snowplow. People in the cars and the troopers looked at him as he eased the Ford down the line, shifting up into high now that he could again see the roadway.

The sun was out in the valley. The snow on his car began to melt and slide off the hood and windshield in large wet chunks, exploding on the highway in the slipstream of the car.

He stopped for the night in a frontier-type hotel in a town that boasted that Mark Twain had spent the night there. Carlson might, indeed, have had the very bed in which Mark had slept. The bed had age enough and the horsehair-stuffed mattress was ancient. The wallpaper was a venerable pattern, in keeping with the narrowness of the accommodations. Forty-watt unfrosted bulbs burned in the converted gaslight wall sconces. The floors creaked. A copy of the *Territorial Enterprise*, published that very week, was available in the lobby. Twain had once worked for the paper.

Something about the place made him want Caroline, then want any woman, to couple with female flesh and juice, to come in a squirming female body. He went downstairs, bought a Coke, and made an inquiry of the night clerk behind the desk, who disclaimed any real knowledge of the availability of women thereabouts.

In half an hour an entirely ordinary woman of about forty was knocking discreetly, yet with some urgency, at his door. She clutched a kimono around her plump body, glancing up and down the hall furtively.

She asked: "You wanted to talk to me?"

"Yes," Carlson admitted.

"Then let me in," she demanded anxiously, again glancing up and down the dim, narrow hallway, pushing her way inside. She closed the door behind her.

Once inside, it seemed poor taste to Carlson to refuse to go to bed with her on the grounds she was not entirely what he had expected and was perhaps a bit older than he thought a prostitute ought to be.

She wasn't so bad, Carlson decided, handing over the ten bucks she requested before she made another move.

She doffed her kimono and started to haul her slip up over her thighs.

"Did you lock the door?" she asked as if she had never

met such a dumb sonofabitch in her whorish life. If a man did not know how to conduct himself in the presence of a decent desert whore, just what the hell did he know?

She lay on the bed, skidded her slip over her belly and butt, and waited for him to get as naked as he was going to get to collect her service.

Her hands were rough and red, her face careworn and devoid of makeup. She looked like the mother of so many of his chums when he was a boy. *He* probably had an aunt who looked just like this woman. She probably worked in the kitchen of the hotel, a nearby restaurant, some ordinary line of work, taking care of guests like himself to earn a little something extra. That too was an old western tradition. It did not have the same kind of negative connotation working in an outright whorehouse would have. She was a sturdily broad beamed woman, with good muscle tone, very pale skin, dark auburn hair, a dusting of freckles, a vaguely Irish face, large, soft breasts.

She let Carlson tug her slip up over her head, scolding him for "mussing" her hair. Her belly was round, soft, pale as the full moon, curiously unmarked by childbirth. Her rather unattractively clabbered-looking fat ass was offset by a truly lush, wide bush across her lap that was touched with reddish glints in it like flame.

She did her job thoroughly if not particularly excitingly or inspiringly. A good straight fucking woman who had always accepted her responsibilities and did the best she could. No frills. But no cheating either. She genuinely grunted when he was whipping it to her, while she strongly ground her body up beneath him. When he came, she quickened her movements to run out his pleasure to the end.

When he told her: "Thank you, that felt good," she replied: "That's what it was supposed to do."

And she was gone.

She could have been there in that hotel back in Mark Twain's time. She would have been no different. The thought made Carlson feel a curious kinship with Twain.

He slept beautifully beneath heavy covers when the heat went off in the place late at night.

He awakened thinking for sure that he could smell the ozone from the snow up in the mountains. Outside birds were singing.

Breakfast was dark, dry country ham, pancakes, ice-cold milk, good strong coffee, and there was nothing "portion-controlled" about it beyond the cook's best judgment of what was fair for the money.

Out West the various American air forces seemed to practice furiously every sparkling clear day. High above, silently, two high-flying airliners or strategic bombers left vaporous contrails across the firmament, while lower a flight of swift jet-fighters flew a seemingly mock intercept. Beyond the sound of the fighters' jet motors it sounded as if they were ripping a canvas as broad as the sky. The sound reverberating in the ground shook the car in which Carlson was traveling, vibrated his very bones, and left him a bit breathless in their audio wake.

It snowed again in the Sierra, touching the branches of the giant redwoods with painterly touches of white, releasing an exhilarating level of ozone in the crisp, clear air, sponsoring a rush of love in the breast so expansive it was a burden to have to contain it.

"Joy!" Carlson cried aloud to the ancient trees that bordered a tumbling crystal stream. He pulled the car over to stop, and got out.

The automobile creaked and bubbled momentarily and then sat silently. All the sounds of the forest began to come to his ears above the violent tumbling of the stream. Looking down he saw two trout wriggling past in the clear water. He wished to drink the water. He racked his brain to figure out how to do it. He walked a short distance from the car along the bank, hoping to find a discarded soft-drink bottle, some kind of container. Then he remembered there was an old funnel in the trunk of his car in case he had to pour in emergency gasoline. He got it out and found a length of twine back there. He plugged the spout of the funnel with a rag and a short stick, fashioning a bail to the funnel with the twine. Then he was able to go out to the edge of the stream, stand on a rock to lower the funnel into the torrent. He carefully hauled up a cup of cold, fresh mountain stream water. He repeated the process until he felt full and cold inside from drinking water.

He thought of perhaps one day living in such a place, away from everything, with Caroline, wearing jeans and boots, flannel shirts, making love among the old big trees and animals of the forest, having children, seeing them grow up in such a place, with their home-haircuts and knowledge of the great woods. He had seen a bear and a coyote and several deer and raccoon along the road as he was driving.

He sat on a stump to smoke a cigarette. It tasted both good and filthy in that environment. He put it out, griding it to nothing beneath his heel in the soft, moist earth.

The forest was not paradise. It required large skills to survive in the woods, to eat, protect oneself from the elements and other animals looking to dine.

Well, it was beautiful there anyway. But now he grew cold. The sun had been blocked by one of the great trees. It was cold up there, out of the light of the sun.

He slung his funnel-cup into the backseat of the car, started up, and drove on toward San Francisco. Memory of the taste of the water would last forever, reigning as a measure of all other water everywhere.

The top of the convertible had become stretched by the wind when he had driven fast across long open stretches of highway. Now it sagged down and lifted, snapping loudly on its supporting bows. He turned on the radio. He could pick up a station only faintly crackling some distance away. He turned it off. Imagine a place where your radio did not work! He was thrilled by that, as much as he would have liked to have heard another human voice.

It was very dark in the woods when he stopped at a log-cabin café for his main meal that day. The people were friendly. Sitting at the counter, he had grilled fresh trout, boiled new potatoes, green beans, a dish of homemade coleslaw, and a wedge of great homemade apple pie topped with a chunk of Cheddar cheese, and coffee. The people were like foreigners. They had never lived any-place else. Oh, the husband had gone to war, been in Africa, Sicily, and Italy before coming back to the woods to marry the woman who did the cooking here. Their two gangling boys came in to take their supper at the counter too, playing some songs on the jukebox with slugs they took from the cash register.

Carlson asked about land thereabouts for sale.

"Oh, there's plenty of land if you got the price," the husband allowed. "You can get a right nice little place overlooking the lake for five–ten thousand. Time to buy, if you got the money. This place will be built up like hell pretty soon. There's nothin' we can do to stop it. Developers are already comin' around sniffin' things out. I wouldn't want to live anywhere else. But how it was when I was a boy and how it is for my boys ain't never going to be so again in a few years. You can just smell it in the air."

The air simply smelled good to Carlson.

He told them he was driving to San Francisco.

"You won't make it tonight. I sure wouldn't sleep in that rag-top car out along the road," the man said. "Bears are awake and out and around. Saw one just the other day."

"They'll open up a regular sedan, even if it's locked, if they think there's something to eat inside," one of the man's sons explained.

"Go through that rag-top in one swipe," the other insisted.

Carlson wound up spending five dollars for a bed in one of the ice-cold cabins beside the place. There was a little iron stove in there, plenty of wood and kindling. He got a fire going and stoked the stove for the night. The sheets were like ice when he crawled between them, but he was asleep before he got them warm. He woke up once and saw the fire in the little isinglass window of the heater; the light it cast on the wall of the cabin was pleasant. He heard rustling outside around the cabin and got up to look out the window. There was a family of raccoons trying to get into the café's garbage cans. The lids seemed chained down. He went back to his bed and slept soundly until bright daylight.

"Well, it's a beautiful day for traveling," the wife said cheerfully as he had bacon and eggs for breakfast.

Running down into San Francisco from the mountains he crossed valleys of grapevines owned by wine companies, acres of all kinds of lush produce, irrigated by elaborate systems, kept from frost by huge smudge pots and enormous propellers on towers. There is a sense of Kansas and the Lower Rio Grande Valley of Texas in the agricultural towns that dot the bottomland and delta of the Sacramento River Valley. Carlson recaptured the feeling of his relatives back in Kansas that California *was* the promised land.

He thought of an uncle of his who had tried four times to move to California. Four times he packed up a trailer with his belongings, sold what would not fit in the trailer, said good-bye to friends and relatives, and drove off to live forever in California. He never lasted out there longer than three months. Once, the last time he tried to move to California, he sold his house, everything, and counting on the money as a stake to buy a similar place out West, took his family and the family dog. He was back inside of three months, a look of wondering defeat in his eyes, as if he just could not understand why he could not catch on in California. He bought back his house, having to borrow money to do it, and had remained there ever since, though every now and then he would start talking about the farms and opportunities in those lush, irrigated California valleys. His wife would just look at him, put her arms around him, and then he would stop talking.

The people in the fields and the little towns, the pickup trucks angled into the curb before "Good Eats" cafés, the hot, wide streets, old bank buildings and mortuaries all looked like Kansas and Texas. The people who had built those towns and lived in them often had roots going back along the Okies' track to Kansas, Oklahoma, and Texas, to dusty blown-out places. The kids on the streets could have been found in Newton, El Dorado, Guthrie, Tulsa, Wichita Falls, Panhandle.

Outside one of the towns Carlson saw a young man in a military uniform hitchhiking and stopped to give him a lift. The young man had reminded him of himself.

The uniform was a police trainee's clothes.

"I wouldn't be hitching," the young man explained earnestly, "but my danged ole car broke down and I got to get back into the city. I just came home for the weekend, but my danged ole car wouldn't start this morning. You goin' to San Francisco?" he asked.

Carlson said he was.

"That's just fine," the young man said, sitting back, taking out a pack of cigarettes and shaking out one to offer Carlson.

"Thanks." Carlson took the cigarette and lit it with the car's lighter.

"Yes, sir, my life sure has been different since I found the Lord." The young man smiled at Carlson.

"Oh?" Carlson said warily. The last thing he wanted was to be trapped in a car with an evangelistic cop.

"Sure has!" the young man said cheerfully. "Before, I wasn't nothing. Couldn't *keep* a job. Couldn't keep a girl friend. No friends. I was a poor wretched soul. Then the good Lord came into my life and everything's been changed. Like when I went in to take the civil service tests to be a highway patrolman, I flat dang failed the shit out of them. But the testing officer suggested I might go someplace else to look for a job in police work. And I saw this advertisement for policemen up in Novato, you know, and I drove all the way there wondering what the dickens the good Lord had in mind for me now. But I was accepted there and am in training now. My whole life's changed, praise God. How about you—you a Christian man?"

"Oh, sure, nominally," Carlson said.

"What does that mean, nominally?" the young man asked suspiciously.

"It means if I was going to go take a civil service examination I would put 'Christian' in the slot where they want a religious preference. Just to forestall debate," he added.

"Um . . . well, I can't say I know what the devil you are talkin' about. I never knowed a nominal Christian before. That some kind of Lutheran or something?"

"Something like that," Carlson told him.

He seemed satisfied.

The young man also told him how to get to the address in Stockton where Margaret Archer had an apartment. She was working for the *San Francisco Chronicle* now, had been for months. She had dropped him a postcard with her new address when she moved. He had telephoned her before he left Chicago to say he was probably going to be in San Francisco. She had told him to be certain to call her as soon as he got into town.

Maybe he would go to the *Chronicle* and see about a job in San Francisco for a while. He had always liked the city. He had left for the Pacific and China from San Francisco when he was just a boy, when he could not imagine that anything that floated could be as large as the ship he had left upon.

Even the smell of the place at night when he pulled into town and wandered around Chinatown looking for Margaret's address was familiar to him, ever embedded in his senses. He was not happy, but part of him, a frightened part to be sure, a wondering, wandering part, felt suddenly at home.

The apartment house was on a steep street next to a small alley. It was painted gray and had bay windows out over the street from the second floor upward. He found a place to park not too far away and walked back. He rang the bell beneath the tiny placard upon which was scrawled: *M. Archer*. The wall spoke to him, a tinny version of Margaret's voice. He identified himself.

"Cat. Just a moment. I'll buzz the door."

Presently, when the door buzzed, he pushed it open and went inside. The hallway smelled of cooking odors, certainly some kind of cabbage, or a near relative to cabbage. Maybe a cooking smell he had whiffed in China. Margaret's apartment was on the second floor.

It was just one sitting room with a Murphy bed in the wall, a kitchenette and bath. But it was on the corner, with one of those bay windows over the street.

Margaret looked thinner. There seemed to be dark circles under her eyes. She wore a brown skirt and sweater he thought he remembered from Chicago.

She smoothed down her hair with that characteristic gesture he had seen her use before. She wore no makeup, as usual, and her dark brown hair was twisted into a bun at the nape of her neck. In Chicago, she had worn her hair loose sometimes and it had softened her long pale face. He'd wondered from time to time why she didn't take more trouble with her looks; she could have been an attractive woman if she tried. Some lipstick wouldn't hurt, he decided. She could resemble Sophia Loren, if she wanted to.

But she seemed determined to hang on to her plainness, to hide behind it. She wore such nondescript clothes, and he had never seen jewelry on her.

He wanted to hug her, to tell her it was okay. *He* was so damned glad to see her, plain dress and all. In her presence, he could feel the tensions of the past weeks recede. Even Caroline's memory stung a little less.

Except for Campbell's brother, a man Margaret had always dismissed in conversations, Carlson could never recall her being involved with a man. Thinking of Caroline, remembering the warmth of her body, aching for it, Carlson was struck anew by Margaret's lack of sexuality.

What the hell was it? He liked her, damn it, so why did he never feel desire for her? Maybe it was her lack of femininity. She seemed to deny her womanliness. She never flirted, never said or did anything that called attention to her sex. He wanted to tell her that men would find her attractive if only . . . If only what? If only she took better care of the way she looked and acted? How the hell could you say that?

He took her hands in his. "I'm so damned glad to see you," he said.

She smiled, leaving her hands in his for a few moments.

"So what have you been up to?" he asked.

She was working in the classified department of the paper, she explained.

"I also write the column that tells what's going on around the Bay," she said. "It's a sop to advertisers. Sometimes I do a feature on somebody or some store or something if it can be made interesting as a straight feature story. But I don't make much money.

"My dad died. I just got back from the funeral. I may go back home and help Mom. She kind of needs me."

"I'm sorry. I didn't know."

"Heart attack. Went out fishing and ate a bag of donuts, got gas, and had a heart attack. My brother came into their cabin and found him dead."

"That's too bad. My grandfather always said donuts will kill you. Anyway, he was fishing. You told me he liked that." He wanted to look on the bright side.

Margaret had told him her father was an alcoholic who had once had a masterpiece of delirium tremens on an airliner which resulted in the plane having to land especially to put him off.

"He hadn't taken a drink in almost two years either," she added, as if she had been reading Carlson's thoughts.

He felt suddenly as if he were trembling uncontollably, realizing finally the whole room and everything in it was trembling.

"Oh, we're having an earthquake," she explained. "It began yesterday. Really shook bad a couple of times. Broke windows all over town. Brought down some cornices. Shook some people out of their beds."

It was more like an enormous subway train rumbling than any actual sound. Carlson was not afraid. He was curious. It was an experience.

There had never been anything like a romance between them. They had never kissed more passionately than would a brother and sister at a family reunion. That time in Chicago Carlson had gone from Sally to Caroline. But suddenly he was very aware of Margaret's large soft breasts pressing against him, jiggling gently in the tremors that shook them and the city. He felt the wide bones of her hips and was aware of her solid athletic haunches. Her lips were soft, however prim.

They held each other until the tremors stopped.

"Welcome to San Francisco," she said. "Hungry?"

"Yes. Very."

"Well, I don't have anything much here, I'm sorry. But we can go out and eat."

"Good! I would like that. It seems to have stopped," he said, regarding the earthquake.

"That's the fifth time since it began," she said.

"I kind of like it," he said. "Reminds us of our mortality and the fragility of our most presumptuous enterprises."

She smiled. "I'll bet whatever else you do, one day you'll be a teacher."

She shrugged into the same navy blue coat with fur collar she had worn in Chicago and wound a long black cashmere scarf around her neck so it hung down fore and aft.

They walked down the hill and drifted toward Broadway. She was a plain young woman, a bit horsey, too masculine in stride, voice, and attitude, though the bones and flesh were really good. *Haul all that up in understated but sexy clothes and she could look like Sophia Loren, or at least very good*, he thought.

"How long are you going to stay?" she asked.

"I don't know. Maybe forever. I just don't know. I take it the job situation on the *Chronicle* is not good."

"Terrible! You would hate it anyway, even if you could get a job there, and you can't. No one walks in and gets a job on the *Chron*. It's a Hearst paper, baby. You don't have to pledge allegiance beside your desk in the morning, but goddamned near. Loyalty is everything, generally and specifically. It's sick."

"There aren't any good newspapers any more," he said. "They have lost their voices. The Chicago *Daily News* hires reporters who smoke pipes and calls them 'pundits.' They write about problems that fall near enough the hearts of the readers who have been addled for so long they can't find their asses with a flashlight."

"I guess that is why I am seriously thinking about going back home for a while," she said.

Over soup and sandwiches at the Co-Existence Bagel Shop, he told her why he had quit his job. She seemed to understand. Margaret had always understood, almost by instinct, what drove him. That's why he could tell her anything, be more free with her than anyone, even Caroline.

"You should be able to write what you want, draw and paint what you want," Margaret said now.

"Yeah. I guess I decided it does not matter what I do otherwise, if I can do that. Yet, working on a paper, particularly if I could get on the police beat, gives you access to a lot of life you would not otherwise see. Covering the school board and clubs is a waste of time for someone who wants to write about something that matters."

"The people who turn up in a police station do?" she asked.

"Hell, yes! You know that. Dostoevski, Chekhov, Babel, Victor Hugo, even Hemingway and Faulkner, everyone who has written meaningfully writes about the kind of people who wash up at some night desk or another, who are all victims of some kind, even when they are guilty of a crime," he insisted. "You know that, don't you?"

As they talked, the cups on the table began to jiggle. Carlson's cappuccino sloshed into the saucer. The whole room was trembling. Faint dust was visibly shaken from the building's ceiling and walls. The lighting fixtures could be seen to shiver. All talk in the place ceased for the length of the tremor, everyone froze in his place. It almost seemed as if the entire city held its collective breath.

Then it stopped. Soon there were the sounds of the sirens on firetrucks and police cars racing to where someone was hurt or damage done.

"If this is like the great earthquake of oh-six," Margaret wondered, "would you want to be here? We could leave in your car."

"Yes," he said. "Even then, I want to be here. I'm not ready to leave. I guess if I knew for certain that I would be killed if I stayed, I would leave right now. But I don't want to be anywhere else just because we are having earthquakes. Do you want to leave? If you want to, I'll take you."

She didn't have a car.

"No. I just wondered."

They walked back toward her room in the fog. The fog had come in thick. Fog horns on the bay moaned like lonely bull sea lions. Shadowy ships with lights like halos above their decks moved cautiously on the water.

They walked up to an overpass near her place and stood in the fog to look out over that part of the city. It was cold and they put their arms around each other.

They strolled arm in arm back to her place. He hadn't even thought of where he would stay that night. He had just assumed she would have a couch or something for him to sleep on.

She did have a couch, but it was small and very lumpy-looking.

"We can sleep together," she said. "I trust you."

She got ready for bed. Slept in blue pajamas. Carlson slept in his shorts and a T-shirt.

There was another brotherly-sisterly kiss and then it was "good night."

She liked for him to snuggle up to her back and put his arm around her, but removed his hand from where the blade of it rested under the weight of her breasts, patting it like a pup after placing it on a very neutral site between her lower ribs and her flat stomach.

"Be good." She chuckled awkwardly.

Jesus Christ, he thought. *Be good.*

But he slept deeply, in a jumble of dreams, visions, fears. He dreamed of Caroline and she seemed in some kind of trouble.

The process of a full bladder and whatever he was subsequently dreaming caused him to have an erection.

Barely aware of where he was or with whom, he gently hunched the sleeping mound of warm flesh nearest to the tip of his engorged member—

And was awakened by a singular burst of energy and profanity that lifted Margaret directly from a curling prone position in the bed to an enraged young woman in rumpled blue man-tailored P.J.'s standing beside the bed.

He had but touched her ass with his cock, each entity being encased in sturdy cotton broadcloth and knit.

"I told you to be good, goddammit!" she said indignantly.

"Oh, fuck you!" he snapped in return.

"You would like to!" she challenged as if it were a criminal accusation.

"Look, come to bed. I'll never touch you again. I just have to piss."

He got up and went to the toilet.

"I don't like to be goosed," she said when he came back. She was as far over on one side of the bed as she could be. He got in on the other, patted her shoulder, and said he was sorry, then turned away, careful not to touch her in any way.

Again he dreamed that Caroline was in trouble. Partially awakening in the first light he decided he would telephone her that day.

When Margaret went off to work, he settled on the lumpy couch and asked the operator to ring Caroline at her office and tell him the charges when he had finished talking. Someone else answered and said Dr. Palmer was not in. Nor did she expect her in the rest of the day. He became frightened because of the dreams and telephoned her at home. There was no answer. Finally, he called Milt and Myra's number. Myra answered. She sounded very cold to him, very distant.

"My, where's Caroline?" he asked.

There was silence for a long time. "I don't think I should tell you," she said.

"What the hell is it, My? What happened?"

"I promised if you called not to tell you."

"Tell me, My! Jesus Christ. Listen, I'm starting back right now anyway. Something's happened."

"Caroline is in the hospital . . . Nothing happened. I mean there wasn't any accident or anything. She's all right. Just weak and needs to rest."

"What happened?"

"She was pregnant, you know. No, she said you didn't know. She had an abortion. A friend of hers did it. Right after you left. She hemorrhaged and had to go into the hospital for a scrape. She's okay now. She will be home in a few days. You're a real bastard, you know that?" she said.

"I *didn't* know. Christ! I love her, My. Please tell her I am coming right back. I'll drive night and day. I'll be there, in a couple of days."

"I'll tell her I talked to you," My promised. "I'll tell her what you said. But, I don't know, mister, if I was her I would tell you to go take a flying fuck. There are certain responsibilities in a relationship with someone you care about that you don't seem to know anything about."

"I know, My. I'm sorry. Man, I hurt like hell for her."

"Sure, like people hurt for the Jews during Hitler."

"No, My, dammit! *No!* I love her. I would die for her, don't you know that? I would!"

"But you can't live for her like you should, can you? I'll tell her you called. She may forgive you, but I don't think I ever will."

"My, I'm sorry."

"Grow up!" she advised. " 'Sorry' don't get shit here." She hung up.

He had to get started immediately. The operator called him back and told him what the charges were. He called Margaret and told her he had to leave immediately for Chicago and that he was leaving the money for the long distance call he had made on the table by the telephone.

"Well, keep in touch," she said.

"I will. You too. It was nice to have shared an earthquake or two with you."

"Yeah. Good-bye, Cat."

"Good-bye," he replied.

Twenty–Three

WITHIN AN HOUR he was out of the city, driving as fast as possible back to Chicago. He had decided to take the southern route to avoid being delayed by snow.

He was into the desert by evening, having stopped only for gasoline, eating a candy bar for dinner. He passed huge fenced-off portions of the desert where thousands of warplanes, fighters, and bombers of all denominations were parked as if awaiting crews. Thousands of planes sat there in the dry desert air, the setting sun glinting off their Plexiglas windows, turrets, and canopies. The amount of money the planes represented was incalculable to Carlson. Millions and millions. *What would happen to all those planes?* he wondered.

Along the side of the road past the planes a lone coyote loped, looking hungry. Or Carlson, being hungry, imagined that the coyote looked hungry.

He had only a little money left. Enough to get him to Chicago if he did not spend anything on lodging and very little on food.

When he checked the oil it was black, needed changing, and it was low. He bought a quart of the cheapest oil the station had and three candy bars.

The car was not running as well as it ought. It sounded as if it needed new plugs and points.

He began worrying that the engine would break down. Driving was especially tiring because of the exercise of will he deemed necessary to keep the engine running. When he was dangerously close to falling asleep at the wheel, he would pull over to catch a few winks beside the highway, then plow on and wash his face when he had to stop next for gas. His hands felt permanently bent to the grip of the steering wheel. When he stopped, he still felt as if he were moving. When he slept along the highway, big trucks would blast by and the air they displaced would rock his car.

In a gas station toilet he looked at his face in the mirror. His hair was dirty, matted, tangled when he wet it and combed it. His eyes were bloodshot. His shirt filthy, trousers stained. He looked like a bum. He tried to remember how it had been living in the apartment with Caroline, dressing nicely every day to go to the paper, making love with her, going out with Milt and Myra to dinner and dancing.

Man, what are you doing? he asked his poor relation in the mirror.

I don't know, he confessed. *Going to see Caroline. Got to see Caroline;* he saw his lips actually form the words in the glass.

He had gone to San Francisco and not even seen Jack Kerouac, Ferlinghetti, Gregory Corso, or Allen Ginsberg.

He wanted to smash the image before him with his fist; he drew it up and threatened his image with it. Then, he realized how crazy and ugly he was being, and stopped. He got back into the car and continued doggedly to try and get to Chicago.

Finally he could stand it no longer, felt he was starving, and stopped at a Mexican joint along the highway that had no pretensions. He had two enchiladas, beans, and a bottle of ice-cold beer for seventy-five cents. It was the greatest bargain he could recall finding in his entire life. With a tortilla provided for the purpose, he sopped up the last bit of beans and hot chili gravy and left his plate so clean that the stout little Mexican woman who took it away smiled. "Good beans, *mamacita*," he told her. He felt bad that he dared not leave her a tip. Not even a dime.

As he drove, he tried to recall where every dollar he had spent on the trip had gone. He begrudged so many expenditures that had seemed okay on the way out of Chicago and that now seemed sheer extravagance.

He was afraid the car was not going to make it.

In the panhandle of Texas he ran into a snowstorm that made the one in the mountains seem as nothing in retrospect. Semi-trucks were at odd angles in the ditches. It had snowed all night. A train was stopped in drifts along an adjacent track, the passengers long since taken away. Into the little town he crept between walls of snow higher than the car. Cross streets were approached with great caution and no way to know what was lurking in either crossing direction. He went through the entire town and saw nothing but snow and the odd car or truck at the intersections. Outside of town he stopped to inquire about the road conditions.

"Well," the native drawled, "it's open for now, but I wouldn't be going anywhere."

"I have to. My wife is sick and I got to get home," Carlson said. Caroline *was* a kind of wife, he reasoned in his mind.

"Well, I guess if she was real sick, I'd chance it," the young man beneath a snow-covered cowboy hat said. "It stopped for a while, long enough for the plows to get through, but now it's startin' again."

Carlson gassed up and bounced over the potholes the grader had scraped along the roadside.

It was snowing so hard he could barely see after he had been on the road fifteen minutes. He wondered if he ought to turn back. The snow was driven by the wind out there on the flat and could form drifts burying a car in an hour.

He put on his lights and ahead he saw another car's lights come on in the snow. He slowed to a crawl, as he and the other approached. As if of one mind, they stopped, rolled down their windows, and said almost simultaneously:

"How is it back from where you came?"

"It's bad," the cowboy said. "How's it back your way?"

"Just like this," Carlson told him.

"Well, good luck then," the man said, a rawboned purely Texas face with a cigarette dangling on his tobacco-stained lower lip.

"Good luck to you," Carlson called.

They rolled up their windows and crept slowly away

in opposite directions. For a while he could see the other car's tracks, then he could not see them. He used the telephone poles along one side of the road and the plowed pile of snow along the sides as his guide and kept driving.

He did not know when he crossed the border into Kansas. But then he was in Dodge City and it had stopped snowing and the sun was shining brightly. The air was full of ozone. The town streets were much like those in the little town he had passed before, mostly just walls of snow along which he could slowly creep up to each intersection. At the main intersection there was a policeman directing traffic. People in cars who knew the policeman called out things to him that made them both smile.

The car was running terribly. There was no way it was going to make it to Chicago. He decided to take a slight detour to Wichita, stop at his grandmother's long enough to get the car fixed and see if he could borrow some money from her. Maybe he could even get a plane to Chicago. He drove the next hours in a panic, kept repeating what he had to do and hoped to do over and over in his mind. He kept seeing Caroline in a hospital bed.

His grandmother had moved since he had last visited her and was now living in half of a small duplex owned by a woman she knew from her church. It was on a street named Laurel in a neighborhood where all the streets were named after trees. It was no longer a "good" neighborhood, lying just off the east-west main drag and too near the problems of downtown. But some pretty good old trees still lived on the street and the houses, though small, were fairly well kept and lived in by their owners for the most part.

He parked in front of the house with two front doors and went up and rang the one with the number distinguished by an "A" after it.

There she was, tiny now, with the smiling face, the smile not entirely masking her wariness and suspicion. He embraced her and gave her a peck on her thin, dry lips. She smelled old and sour. She was well into her seventies, he realized. His grandfather had been dead almost four years. The end of another world, a more unequivocal set of values, or whatever it was that gave America great promise. Now the survivors were floundering, up shit creek without a paddle.

For Carlson, his grandmother was irrevocably, inseparably imbued with the memory of her husband. He looked at her again, seeing her standing there in her doorway, no longer part of the large, crazily sane old man. She was smaller than he ever remembered. She cocked her head and said:

"Come in off the porch. The neighbors will see and wonder something, me huggin' a nice-lookin' young man like you." She smiled at him happily.

The living room was narrow, no more than ten feet wide. There was a couch there, an old easy chair with crocheted antimacassars on the back and on each worn arm. There was a small metal-cased television set turned on to some morning soap opera. It seemed strange that his grandmother should have a television.

She switched the set off and apologized weakly:

"It helps keep me company. I got it on sale. I don't watch too much, but maybe more than I should. I just can't read so good as I use to. My eyes aren't so good. I'm gettin' cataracts."

"But you can have them taken off," he said.

"Yes. And I will when they get worse. My insurance will cover most of the expense. Thank God I kept my insurance, no matter how tough things got . . . I sure was surprised to get your telephone call. I thought you were in Chicago, workin' on a newspaper."

"I quit. I wish now I hadn't, but I did. It seemed like a good idea at the time."

"Well, you never were very good about keepin' a job, or stickin' to somethin'." She giggled a little to take some of the sting out of her judgment.

"I guess not. Look, Grandma, I stopped because my car is really in bad shape. And I'm broke as I can be. My— Caroline, the woman I live with, is sick and in the hospital in Chicago, and I just have to get back there. I was wondering——"

She cut him off. "If I could lend you some money?" She

shook her old gray head, smiling wryly to herself. "I shoulda knowed if it was you comin' to see me, it was to try and get some money out of me. You know all the times you just had to 'borrow' some money from me? You never paid back once."

"I know, Grandma," he said contritely. "I'm sorry. I just seem to ship from one damned disaster to the next."

"Just like your mother," she said. "Can't ever keep a good job when you can get one and *never* put anything aside."

"I know. But, can you help me or not?"

"I don't know . . . Maybe. How much? I don't have much. I took out of my savings to help Sam and he ain't paid me back yet. He will. He's always good about that."

The idea of getting enough for a plane ticket was out of the question now. Her implication was plain.

"Well, I need a tune-up and oil change and some gas money to get me to Chicago. I don't know exactly. But probably not more than fifty bucks."

"Well, I guess I could let you have that. But I was hopin' you would be able to stay a little. I haven't seen you since your grandpa died. You don't hardly write."

"I'm sorry, Grandma. I really am. But like I said, I'm kind of always between some crisis or another. It's hard just taking care of myself. The only peace I've known has been the last year with Caroline. She's a doctor. She's shown me there is another kind of life I really don't know much about."

"Then why did you leave it? Let me get you a cold drink. I got iced tea or lemonade."

He chose lemonade and they went into her kitchen where he sat at an oilcloth-covered table. The lemonade had been made with some kind of concentrate and tasted metallic.

"You didn't make this," he said.

"Well, I did. I just don't like to squeeze lemons no more since I fell on the ice and cracked my right wrist. It's just never been much good since they took it out of the cast. Sometimes I can hardly hold an iron."

"You should get a mechanical squeezer," he suggested.

"Yeah. If I was able to get all the things I should get, I'd be sittin' right pretty, don't you know. Maybe you'll get me one for my birthday," she teased. For he hadn't remembered her birthday since he was a little boy.

He tried to answer her question: "I love Caroline more than any woman I have ever known. She is really a great lady, Grandma. But I'm not a great man. Maybe I never will be. At least not by the standards Caroline has grown up in and lives by. I wish I was like her, but I'm not. I'm not really like anyone in that kind of successful, middle-class milieu—"

"Speak English," she warned. "If you want me to make head or tail of what you're talkin' about."

"I'm not like those good people. I'm a kind of perennial bastard. I know it and am trying to make some kind of peace with that. I *want* all the things and maybe the kind of life people like Caroline have. I truly do. But I can't *do* it! Not their way. I try. I can talk to them and love them and not seem all that much different from them. But a lot of the time I am thinking about where I've come from, where I've been, what I've done, and I feel like a white nigger passing in an unknowing society. I mean, these are *good* people by any acceptable measure, but I am really not one of them."

"I just don't know what in the world you are talkin' about," the old woman said. "Ever since you were a little boy, you always acted like you thought you were better than everybody else. You were too good to do what your cousins and others did. I don't know. You are so like your mother was sometimes, I wonder if there is any hope for you."

"I wonder too, Grandma."

"Well, it's never too late for you to come to Christ and let *Him* help you carry your burden."

"Yeah."

"Well, it's true and if you didn't think you knew so much, you'd be able to see it and get the help of the Lord. I was hopin' you'd be able to stay awhile. A lot of people would like to see you. Ain't you even going to see your cousins and your son? Why, Mark was over here just a

230

week or so ago. I see him regular. He's a nice boy. Looks just like his dad. You knew Sharon and he are alone now?"

"No."

"She looks just fine. I like her a lot more now than when you was married to her. She's grown up."

"I'm not surprised. She was only seventeen when she had the baby."

"Well, he's eleven now and he'll be very upset if you don't take the time to see him while you're here."

"Okay. Can I use your phone to call Chicago?"

"Well, I guess. But just talk a minute or two. I can't afford no big telephone bill. I share the line with Mrs. Mathews next door. It's cheaper that way."

"Right," he said.

This time he telephoned the hospital and found Caroline had a phone in her room.

"Hello," she said wearily, cautiously.

"Caroline, I'm sorry. I'm on my way there. My car broke down and I'll get it fixed and be there in a couple of days."

"Why?"

"Because I love you! I want to be with you. I want to marry you."

There was silence on the line for a long time.

Then she said very carefully, but there was a hint of tears in her voice: "I'm not sure I want to marry you."

"Oh, baby, listen. I love you. Why didn't you tell me?"

"I'm angry that Myra told you," she said, her voice sounding genuinely angry for the length of the sentence. "Would you have married me, made an honest woman of me?"

"Yes! I love you."

"That's what I thought. That happened once to you. I didn't want that. I wanted you to decide to marry me because you wanted to marry me."

"I do! I *want* to. I will. Please, Caroline. I go nuts sometimes. I'm sorry. I don't understand it. Maybe I'm really sick in the head. I don't know. I know I love you and I want you and don't ever want to lose you."

"Well, I wish you had realized that before you left. It

seems such a long time ago now. It seems years ago actually, like something that happened in my past."

"Oh, baby, Caroline, listen. Please, I love you. Forgive me. Let me try to be the kind of man you want and need and deserve . . . Caroline?"

"I just don't know. I really don't."

"But how are you?" he said quickly.

"I'm okay. It was nothing that dramatic. I'm weak, but I'll be going home in a couple of days. I'll be fine."

"I just wish I had known."

"No! I am definite about that. I would not have married you if the reason you wanted to was because I was pregnant. I know if I had to decide right now, I wouldn't marry you. I don't want to marry you. Maybe I will again, but I can't tell. I know when you come back—and there's no hurry, I'm okay—we aren't going back to how things were. We aren't going to live together again until *I* know what I want. I know I want a real relationship, a stable relationship, a home and a husband. I don't want what we had. It was wonderful, I guess. It certainly must have seemed so. But now it seems there was a lot of hurt in it, a lot of anxiety and pain, of not knowing where or what the next day would really bring in our relationship."

"Do you love me?" he asked.

"Sure. Sure I love you," she said matter-of-factly, refusing to give in to the sentimental appeal inherent in his voice and question. "I love you. I would like for us to be able to be together forever. But I am not going back to what we had under any conditions. I want you to act like a grown man, the healthy, strong, intelligent man that you are. I'm tired of feeling like a kind of surrogate mother or big sister. I'm tired of having to deal with your emotional binges. I want you, but I want you to take care of me and my needs, work together for a mutually agreed-upon future. I want children and you don't know how this ripped me emotionally. Nothing could have made me happier than to have had a child with you. If we are going to be together again, I have to be confident that I'm going to be taken care of, too. That it will be a real partnership."

"Okay," he said. "I do understand how you feel. I'm

sorry I have just sort of run over you. I guess I just don't know how to live any other way."

"You don't have to rush back. There is nothing you can do now. If we get back together, it is going to be a slow process.

"I've got to hang up now," she said suddenly.

"Okay. I'm sorry. I love you."

Clearly her hurt was the more serious one.

"That was not a very quick phone call," his grandmother scolded him.

"I know."

He was suddenly exhausted. Simply putting one foot in front of another required absolute concentration. He lay down on the couch.

"What's the matter with you?" his grandmother asked.

"I'm tired. I've got to rest. I didn't realize how tired I was."

"You look very pale."

"I'll be all right. I just have to rest."

He more fainted than slept, then came to in a terrible guilt-ridden kind of dreaming in which he sweat and stank and awakened to the sick, acrid smell of himself and thought he was back on the ward at the funny farm. That was where he had smelled that odor, he realized. God! He smelled like a lunatic. And he sank into deep despair, sleeping again, this time dully, curling at the depths of utter despair, his hands plunged prayerfully between his thighs as he had seen the clinically insane do. A part of his frayed mind *knew* what he was doing, yet he was unable to do otherwise. It was like being half dead, or half alive. He just lay there. During the night his grandmother covered him with a sheet.

The next morning, she had to go to her job taking care of an old woman who was a member of her church. She wakened him to tell him she was leaving, that there was stuff for breakfast in the kitchen, and laid some other bed-clothes on the foot of the couch.

"I sure hope you aren't sick," she said.

"I'll be all right," he said.

He put a bottom sheet on the couch, took off his stinking clothes, and lay back down. He lay there all that day, dozing, having nightmares, sweating so profusely it left a salt-rimed yellowing stain on the bottom sheet.

He knew he was nuts. He knew he just had to stay there and work it out or be locked up. That was the single certainty to which he could cling.

I will get all right or I won't, he repeatedly told himself.

At one point he turned on the television set. It was early in the morning. He stared at the banal shows as if they were magic. He masturbated frequently, virtually every hour until he felt he had hurt himself, until his cock was so sore he could barely touch it, yet masturbated one more time, ejaculating nothing. He had masturbated over the women in soap operas, commercials, over the bleached-blond amazon on a children's show who had enormous cantilevered tits. The star of the show was an ex-burlesque comedian and Carlson recognized the roots of much of his humor came from the raunchy *schtick* of those early years. When he could not possibly masturbate again, he slept.

His loneliness was infinite.

For three days he lay on his grandmother's couch, masturbating, sinking lower into the feeling of worthlessness, of being able to do nothing. He was able to get up and wash himself, though he could not manage to take a full bath. His body looked weak, emaciated, and flabby at the same time. He tried to eat once and had to spit the food out. It tasted like garbage. It made him retch. Milk was rotten to drink. He drank water to wash the tastes from his mouth and padded back to flop down on the couch.

On the fourth day he got up at the insistence of his grandmother and put on clothes, yet fell back down after she had stripped the stained sheets from the couch and lay there until noon with one arm over his eyes.

At about two P.M. he told himself: "Well, you can lie here and die or be carted off to a bin, or you can get up and see what the hell you can still do in this fucking world."

He got up. He felt weak. He washed his face for a long

time under the cold water in the kitchen sink, soaked his matted hair, let it run on his neck. Then he dried his face and combed his wet hair with the big blue comb his grandmother, who also washed her face at the sink, used. There was an old watery mirror over the sink. There was a toilet in her room, but the only bathroom in the house was in Mrs. Mathew's side of the duplex. He had been a small child the last time his grandmother had her own bathroom.

But she had a small personal scale in the kitchen because she had to watch her weight. He got on the scale. He had lost almost fifteen pounds since he left Chicago. He felt empty. But he felt lean and tight with himself.

"All you can do, sonofabitch, is try," he told himself. "You ain't dead yet."

New priorities.

He started by making himself a large bologna sandwich on cracked wheat bread, which was the only bread his grandmother would eat, piled thick with lettuce and mayonnaise. He washed it down with a glass of ersatz lemonade.

That afternoon he took tools and removed the carburetor from his car. He sat on the front porch to disassemble the carburetor and clean it.

While he worked, it began to rain. Clouds boiled up out of the east. Leaves of the trees along the street turned bottoms up. He could smell the rain coming. The first large drops stained the sidewalks. Soon it was pouring off the overfilled gutters of the porch roof in sheets. Lightning sizzled through the glower above. Thunder exploded and rumbled off like a furious, grumbling beast.

Carlson continued to work. He enjoyed the smell of the cooling rain. He honestly did not care if a bolt of lightning struck him or not, so he was no longer afraid of it at all. He sighed a lot. It was good to be alive, he knew, but it wasn't all *that* big a deal.

Twenty–Four

LIFE IS OFTEN reduced for most of us to simply putting one foot in front of another and going some place to ask someone for a chance to do what we know we can do. All pretension, elaborate dreams, heartfelt hopes, everything is reduced to just putting one foot in front of another and going some place and asking for that chance. Carlson had been there so many times, from so early on, instinct carried him through the heat to the doorway of Ross Hubbard's Laugh Line. Ross had reprinted many of the cartoons and jokes from the humor magazine Carlson had edited at the university.

Ross was a pleasant man with a thick red beard and a kind of Santa Claus aspect about him and a jolly approach to life. He also happened to be looking for someone to help edit and paste up his *Laugh Line.* Carlson explained he did not want a permanent job but would be glad to help out for a while, until Ross could find someone good to work full-time.

The pay was one hundred dollars a week and Ross also bought a few cartoons from Carlson at twenty-five dollars a shot.

The smell of freshly set type, the fixative with which he spritzed it so it would not smear, the familiar odor of rubber cement all became boosts to Carlson's confidence.

He was good at layout and paste-up, fast. He realized how good he was feeling, in spite of how bad he felt about Caroline and what had happened. Let a person do what he is really able to do well, and he cheers right up, he reasoned as he worked.

The car needed more work than could be done in a few days. The transmission needed rebuilding and new head gaskets needed to be installed; it also had to have new plugs, points, a really thorough tune-up. He was stuck there anyway, so he had gone to work.

Then he had gone to see his son.

The boy was so open and eager and beautiful, just to see his son coming toward him was to be touched ir-revocably by regret for all the years Carlson had not seen him. His mother, even more beautiful than when she was a girl, waited smilingly on their stoop. The boy's hair was combed nicely and he was dressed to go visiting.

Carlson wasn't certain what was appropriate, but then the boy was in his arms and slender child's arms were wrapped fiercely around Carlson's neck. Carlson felt his eyes go misty. He saw Sharon's face. Her smile seemed fixed. Then, he and the boy were standing on the sidewalk hand in hand.

"Would you like to come in for an iced tea?" Sharon asked.

"Uh, no. I think we better move along," Carlson said. "We don't want to be late for the movie."

They went to the Miller Theater on Broadway.

"Did you used to come here when you were a boy?" the child asked.

"Sure. Used to sneak in with my buddy Greg. One of us would buy a ticket and then let the other in through one of the emergency exits. The theater had to have more people in it than it does now, though. The usher would see the door open and come look for you. So we had to hide in the crowd, get down on the floor, sometimes under the seats until the usher gave up trying to find us. But don't you try it," he warned.

"I won't," the boy promised.

Carlson had loaded them up with popcorn and candy bars and Cokes.

After the show, they went and had banana splits at the Candy Kitchen and played the jukebox.

"Did you and Mom used to come here when you were in school?" the boy asked.

"Yes. We used to come here and drive the Greek who owned the place crazy because he didn't want any jitter-bugging in the aisles."

"Did you love Mom then?" he wondered.

"Sure. Let me tell you something about love. I still love your mom. You don't stop loving someone just because you can't live together always. There's no limit on the amount of room in you for loving. You can love more than one person, you know?"

The boy looked puzzled, but interested.

"Don't you and your mom talk about such things?" Carlson wondered.

"Sometimes."

"Well, you love your mom, and all her sisters, and her parents and a lot of other people, don't you?"

"Sure . . ."

"Well, just because you can love one person very much doesn't mean you can't love others, too."

"Why can't you and Mom live together?" he wanted to know.

"I don't like to work in one place forever, you know. I need to be able to go and see things. I'm trying to be able to work for myself, not for someone else. Maybe I will never be able to do it, but that is what I want to do and I will keep trying all my life to do that. When I try to take a job and settle down, it doesn't last. I lose interest in it. I get to feeling rotten and start doing dumb-ass things that upset people I love very much. Do you understand?"

"I guess. Grandma says you're just too lazy to live."

Carlson laughed. "Yow. She always said that. Well, by her way of looking at it, I am. I don't want to work in a factory all my life. I don't want to be a foreman of a department, stamping airplane parts out of aluminum. I want to tell stories that people will pay to read, make pictures that people want to see. I'll do a lot of hard things

238

to let me continue to try to do that. One of the hardest things I've had to do was move on from a place when I really wanted to stay there and get to know someone like you and be a part of a real family."

"I wish you would stay and be a family with us," the boy said, ice cream in the corners of his mouth.

"Well, that would be nice." Carlson watched the boy eat. "But your mom wouldn't think that was such a hot idea, I'd bet."

"Why?"

"Well, I'm just not the kind of fella your mom really wants for a husband."

"She has a picture of you in her bedroom."

"Really?"

"Sure."

"Well, that's probably just so you could know what your real father looked like."

"Will you come to school with me Monday?" the boy asked. "I'd like to show the kids I have a real dad. We're practicing our class play."

"Well, I'll speak with your mom about it, okay?" Carlson said.

"Okay." He seemed happy.

All the years. But what would Carlson have done for the boy had he been there? Nothing worth a damn. It was better that he was in the Army and sending an allotment for help in the boy's care.

He felt he should have stayed away now. He had let his grandmother convince him that he should see the boy. He *wanted* to see the boy, but hard-headed reason told him that if he was not going to stay and be a proper father to him, he should have just gotten in and out of town without seeing him. But then his grandmother would have told everyone he had been there and the boy would have felt terrible because his natural father had not come to see him.

And that too is what country western life is made of. All those flaky grandmothers who just say any damn thing at all with great moral conviction. I mean, they don't lie!

Carlson's uncle had an illegitimate daughter by a woman he had met when he was bootlegging at night out of a house next to the old 400-Club. His grandmother kept in touch with the girl and her mother and never forgot her at Christmas or on her birthday. As far as the old woman was concerned, the girl was just another granddaughter. The woman, fortunately, was married to a very understanding man.

When Carlson delivered the boy back to his home, Sharon invited him in for coffee. Sharon had always been a coffee and cigarette fiend. They sat at the kitchen table and studied each other warily, drank coffee and smoked.

"Will you ask her?" the boy insisted.

"Ask me what?" Sharon looked at Carlson, a frown growing between her eyes, behind her glasses.

"Mark wondered if I could go to the rehearsal of his class play on Monday?" Carlson explained. "I told him he would have to ask you and we would have to think if it was a good idea or not."

"Well, I guess if you really want to go with us . . ." She thought. "He would like to show you to his friends. To prove you exist."

"Then, if you think it is really okay, I will be glad to go."

"Boy!" Mark exclaimed, and gave his mother a big hug.

"Why don't you run outside and play a while and let us talk. Just for a while," his mother said. "Hon?"

"All right," the boy said reluctantly. He went and got the gun and holster Carlson had bought for him and crammed an old battered cowboy hat on his tow head and galloped out the kitchen door.

"I'm sorry," Carlson said. "I told my grandmother I didn't think this was such a hot idea. But she had already set it up."

"What do you think of him?" she asked.

"Beautiful! He is really a good, sweet boy. Almost breaks your heart in a way, you know? Makes me wish a million things that never were and maybe never will be now. You have done a great job."

"Thanks. He *is* good. I like him a lot. I'm glad you and he met, finally. Now at least you are a real person. Some things are just hurtful no matter what you do. We'll survive."

"Sure. Well, it's good to see you. You really look great. You are prettier now than you ever were before."

"You would tell me that in any case. You always flatter women."

"No flattery. You were a beautiful little girl, but you are a better-looking woman."

She had cut her long hair and it curled all over her head, leaving her neck bare. The back of her neck was smooth and vulnerable-looking.

"You seeing somebody now?"

"Um, hm. A nice man. He wants to marry me."

"And you?"

"I'm not sure I want to be married again. We are doing pretty well now. I'm an executive secretary. We have what we need. I just don't know if I want to put another man first in my life, before Mark, you know. And he would like children. I guess I would too. I just don't know. Let's talk about something else."

"Sure."

"What are your plans now?"

"Oh, I've thought of going back to school and getting my degree. But I don't know. A college degree doesn't mean anything to me now; yet if I had one, I might be able to teach. I look at Mark and I want everything everyone else has. I sit in this kitchen with you and I want you and everything that goes with you. I wonder if I could get a job on the local paper. I envy you and everyone who sticks to things, makes it where they are, has a real family, retires to the Ozarks or something. But then when I say it, it scares the hell out of me."

"You're just the same. You haven't changed much. Oh, I don't mean that critically. You are how you are. You have learned a lot, and gotten more relaxed and interesting, but you will never settle down."

"I don't know. I'd like to. I just don't know how to do it. I wish I did."

"Well, you are still too damned good-looking. My sisters and Ma may not like you, but they still say you were the best-looking guy I ever went with."

"How are they?"

"Fine. Jean finally got married. They have a great house with a swimming pool and everything."

She looked at her watch.

"I better go," Carlson said.

"No, that's okay. I just have to think about fixing something for dinner. You want to stay?"

"Uh, sure. Sure! I would love to."

"What shall we have? I can just get to the store . . ."

"Listen. Why don't I go out and buy some barbecued chicken and ribs and bring them back here? And some roasted ears and watermelon, and—"

"This isn't watermelon season." She laughed.

"Well, ice cream then."

"All right. I never refuse a chance *not* to cook."

Sharon had never been what Carlson would have called a good or inspired cook.

"I'm better than I used to be," she vowed, as if reading his thoughts.

"I'm sure. But I'll just take Mark and drive over and get some good pit barbecue. That place still there, Chub's?"

"Still there. Getting fancy though. Looks like a regular restaurant now. But the pit is still out back like always."

"Good. We'll just be a minute."

"Well, if I'm not cooking, we don't have to hurry. Let's have another cigarette and some coffee."

He leaned over to light her cigarette and she grasped his hand with her fingers to guide him and he looked at her eyes and was stirred with desire for her. She knew it. She had a very level, unblinking way of acknowledging such feeling in herself that was more revealing than most women's expression of grand passion.

They smoked around the moment. When he impulsively reached over to squeeze her hand during an animated remembrance, she said quickly, "Don't," and continued the conversation.

It was good being there during dinner and washing up afterward.

They watched TV together in the living room, Carlson and the boy sitting on the couch and Sharon on the floor between them.

Then it was time for the boy to go to bed.

He got into his pajamas and came out with a favorite teddy bear, ready to be tucked in.

He sort of hung around, looking shy.

"I think he would like to kiss you good night," she said.

"I was just hoping he might," Carlson said.

He embraced the boy, who hugged him again around the neck fiercely. They kissed and Carlson told him "good night," giving him a gentle swat on the rear.

"Come tuck me in too," the boy asked.

So Carlson went with the young woman to tuck the boy into his bed in his room.

"Sleep tight," she said before turning out the light.

"I'm sure glad you're here, Pop," the boy said.

"So am I," he replied.

Back in the living room Sharon said, "He's so happy."

"I know. Me too," Carlson admitted. "But—"

She stopped his words with her fingers on his lips.

"Just enjoy what is."

"Okay."

They talked for another hour, then Carlson got up to leave. On his way out they peeked in on the boy. He was sleeping happily.

"Isn't he beautiful?" she asked.

"Very. And so is his mother."

There was a studio portrait of Carlson when he was fifteen on Sharon's dresser. It stopped him by her bedroom door.

"I didn't have it up for a long time, naturally," she explained. "But when my marriage broke up and Mark got older and wanted to know what his real dad looked like, I got it out and put it up."

"Could I have ever looked that pretty?" Carlson wondered. "That's a face bullies would just love to smash."

"You were very pretty until you smiled. You look better with your teeth fixed."

He bent down and kissed her gently on the lips.

"The boy is just great," he said. "You should be proud."

"I am; good night."

"See you Monday," he said.

He got outside and felt like crying. Something was wrong with him. Something was broken deep inside.

He drove home through a light ground fog, his eyes misting over.

He wondered what would happen to them all.

Sunday his grandmother was pleased that he got up as promised to go to church with her. Sunday was going to be her day. He was going to take her out to dinner and a movie that evening.

By the summer of 1957, the church had prospered, as had the city, as had the nation. The church had started in a basement covered with a tarpaper roof. It grew to a full-fledged little stucco tabernacle, then was sold and razed and an apartment house grew in its place. When Carlson was a boy and he and his chums played in the rubble of the church, however delicious, there was a feeling in Carlson's heart that the play was sacrilegious and that he would surely be punished for it.

The present church had been bought from the Presbyterians. It was a small granite fortress along the lines of a Scottish castle. The Presbyterians had had a magnificent pipe organ built above the baptistry, rising behind the minister like the golden horns of God. The Church of Christ tore the pipes out and put in solid brown double-breasted paneling like the deacons' coats, dumping the organ in the cellar until it could be sold. In the Church of Christ you could only get to heaven a cappella. No instrumental music was permitted, not any place. There were no instruments mentioned in the New Testament and therefore there was no instrumental music in the church. Carlson had once tried to point out to his grandmother that there was no mention in the New Testament of the First Federal Savings and Loan Co., Inc., but that half the deacons and elders of the congregation were affiliated with *that* organization.

"Oh, you're just tryin' to start an argument with me," she had complained. "If they aren't good enough men or if the First Federal isn't a decent company, God'll take care of them." She had every confidence.

Actually, Carlson liked going to church. He liked the light that streamed in from the high windows, the smell of polished wood warmed by the sun, the hymnals, the scrubbed congregation. He liked the pretty young girls dressed as for a party, who flirted the least little bit, yet eyed him warily, for they knew he was a prodigal if ever there was one, and dangerous. He liked feeling dangerous in that congregation. It was the perfect place to feel dangerous.

He liked the singing as it swelled and got itself together a cappella after the songleader gave them the pitch with his little pitch pipe. That pitch pipe worried the hell out of Carlson and he used to challenge his grandmother about it. If it wasn't a *musical* instrument, he would *eat* it. And if it was a musical instrument, it was just as sinful as a pipe organ.

Hello, pretty lady, Carlson mentally greeted a former fellow student of a hundred Sunday school classes ago. *God has been kind to you!* And two little children on each side, white gloves clasping white gloves. Her husband was one of the younger deacons.

"Hello, Mrs. Mac," she greeted Carlson's grandmother cheerfully. "It is so good to see you."

"Hello, Nancy. Nice to see you and little Diane and Nina. You remember Jarl, don't you? You used to be in Sunday school together."

"I certainly do." The beauty smiled like an advertisement for orange juice and toothpaste. No one should be *that* healthy.

They had been in love one mad summer when they were six. Nothing had come of it except he had given her his Sunday handkerchief when she had gotten a nosebleed in class. And he had only blown his nose on one corner of it.

245

They shook hands, smiling at one another.

"It is so nice to see you again here," she breathed. "God bless you."

"God bless *you!*" Carlson said. "Pretty girl," he told his grandmother.

She whispered: "They say she and Stanley are having problems. It is too bad because they are two of the young leaders in the congregation."

Carlson clucked sympathetically. Divorce was also a mortal sin in the eyes of the church. You could be forgiven for it, but you would never be truly clean again. And no one wanted their son or daughter to marry a divorced man or woman. People would whisper behind their funeral-parlor fans about so-and-so being divorced in tones you would think were reserved for dope fiends and ex-cons.

And a cappella they all went up to glory; the basses brump-brumping along under all and echoing the tenor's clarion efforts like distant heavy thunder. *Shall we gather at the river? The river? The river? Shall we gather at the river? That glorious rived of blood? Bawluddddddddah . . .*

Then it was time to take communion and pass the plate for collection.

Carlson's grandmother slipped her dollar into the plate, trying to hide its folded denomination with her gloved hand. He noticed that the fingers of both gloves had been mended. The dollar was also old and worn.

Why don't the poor ever get new money? he wondered, flagging his own damned dollar right onto the middle of the plate. The sermon wasn't worth a dollar. He liked a minister who got down and wrestled with sin. This big Texas turkey would not have lasted a single fall with any sort of right devil. The late Reverend Wing, when Carlson was a boy, would throw the good book at the devil, jump on him and stomp him, bite him and put the skunk to rout! You could feel the relief when Satan was driven right out the door. Oh glory, glory, it was too. The only way the new minister would be able to rid them of the devil was to lull the old bastard to sleep. Not worth a dollar.

Then they sang the invitation, but no one went up to

repent and be baptized. Brother Dave was in trouble. You could see the pleading look of desperation in his face. "Please won't someone wend their way to Jesus? Why not now? Why not today? Just put up your hands there, right where you sit, while we pray. Just put up your hands and say in your heart: I'm sorry, Jesus! I'm sorry, Jesus! I've sinned and fallen away. Take me back, Jesus! Forgive me, Jesus! Just raise your hands while we pray."

Carlson cut a glance around the congregation and did not see a hand raised. Up went his own hand.

"I see you, brother!" Brother Dave cried as if he had found the original tablets given to Moses. "I see you! We're praying for you, brother. The Lord hears your prayer. Let's all offer our prayers for the brother who has called out that he is a sinner, fallen from the grace of God, and wants to be forgiven and accepted back into the fold. Amen."

Well, it was little enough to do.

But his grandmother looked definitely suspicious. So he winked at her and smiled. Her lips squeezed together into a thin line and she shook her head.

There was no running out after services. His grandmother wanted him to hang around and shake hands with people. He hung around and smiled and shook hands. A lot of people came up and said, "God bless you," often looking entirely past him for someone else to rush to and bless.

"Let's go," he urged his grandmother.

"Just a minute. You only come to church with me once in a dozen years and you want to run right out and not say hello to anybody."

There was a nice clean, deaconish-looking man before Carlson, offering his hand.

"Jarl, I want you to meet Mr. Withers. This is my grandson."

"I'm pleased to meet you, sir," Carlson said.

"I'm happy to meet you. I've heard a lot about you," the man said.

Carlson did not stop to wonder how. They shook hands and stood awkwardly for a moment before the man excused himself. He wore a good blue suit—one of those iron serge suits that will last a lifetime and form part of a decent inheritance. The man's collars were starched and impeccably ironed. He carried a bag of something in his left hand, like a kid carries a sack of penny candy.

That evening Carlson took his grandmother to dinner at the Hickory Pit, where the waitresses wore old-fashioned long dresses and served all the homemade bread or biscuits you could eat.

Afterward they went to a movie: *The Gunfight at the O.K. Corral*. His grandmother sat patiently through the film; when it was over and they were walking out, Carlson asked her: "Well, Grandma, how did you like it?"

"It was all right, I guess. But that wasn't Dodge City and that gunfight didn't happen like that."

She had been a girl and a young bride in Dodge City; her husband had been a deputy marshal in Dodge at one time.

"The things back then weren't never like they always show in some picture show. There weren't that many bullets in the whole dang state. It's all pretty wrong."

On the way home, his grandmother said: "I'd like to ask you something. I guess you'll think I'm nuts, but I'd like to ask."

"Sure, Grandma, what is it?"

"What would you think if I got married again?"

He smiled, grinned, saw she was serious, and sobered up.

"Well, hell, I don't know. This is kind of sudden, isn't it?" he teased.

"No, it isn't. We have been keepin' company kind of for the last year or better. I met his children, who are all grown and livin' out West. His mother, who is still livin,' approves—I met him when I took care of her winter before last, when she fell and broke some ribs. She's over ninety. He is a little younger than me, but he asked me and I just wonder what you think?"

"That man you had me meet this morning?"

"Yes." She giggled. "Mr. Withers."

"Well, he's a nice-looking clean old man," Carlson said. "Why do you want to do this?" he wondered.

"Well, pshaw, I was married to a good man over fifty years. I just don't like livin' and sleepin' alone."

He thought about that and was touched. He reached over and patted her hands folded quietly in her lap, like a child waiting for his permission.

"How's he fixed?" he asked like a practical parent.

"Well, he's got a nice little house with a garden out back, a nearly new Chevrolet car, he don't have no debts, and he's got his social security and a pension from the company he worked for. He's a heck of a lot better off than your grandfather ever was, I can tell you."

"I think then that if you want to get married again, you ought to do it," Carlson said.

"You don't think I'm just being an old fool?"

"Grandma, the only time you have done anything really foolish is when you've loaned me money," he told her.

She laughed. "That's sure so!"

She sighed. She had been wanting to talk to him about Mr. Withers for days. His own life was always too important. He felt sorry he was so thoughtless and was suddenly very tender toward the tiny woman who could make her underwear or a shirt from a old coat lining, and a good peppery gravy out of thin air and a bit of bacon grease.

He loved the idea that the old girl wasn't done yet. She was going to get married. Who the hell had a grandma almost eighty who was going to marry for the second time?

"We're a wild bunch," he told her and gave her a sharp pinch where she bulged beneath her girdle. She slapped his hand away. "Just stop that!"

On Monday he attended Mark's class play practice with Sharon. They all went to the Burger Shop afterward and had big double-decker hamburgers with everything, thick milkshakes, french fries, and onion rings.

"I'll break out in pimples." Sharon laughed.

"Remember when we used to come here?" Carlson asked. It was always after a drive-in movie during which they had made out like bandits. His fingers would still smell of her body when he stuffed a french fry into his mouth. He could still see how she tilted up a bottle of beer, how the brown top fit against her sexy mouth.

"Never knew a girl who could give me a hard-on just watchin' how she drank from a bottle," he had said then.

But now, such reminiscences were completely out of place. He put them out of his mind and concentrated on the boy. It would be the last time he saw him for a while. He did not know how long. He promised he would write often, knowing he would not.

Later, he helped Sharon tuck the boy in and kissed him good night.

Sharon and he had a cup of coffee and smoked cigarettes in the kitchen. He took her in his arms for the last time and kissed her. She was passive and uncomplaining. He promised again to write and left.

Twenty–Five

IT WAS THE second time he had driven the new Kansas turnpike, a beautiful banked highway without billboards or telephone poles along its length. It was fast. There was no speed limit save the highway patrolman's judgment as to what was safe. There was a minimum speed limit, with slow traffic urged to keep to the right. The rejuvenated Ford clung to the banked curves at seventy-five miles an hour and felt as if it were a great sled.

When the governor had opened the highway a photo went around the country because the governor's party roared right off the end of the marvel into a muddy Oklahoma field where it ended abruptly. Oklahoma had not finished its end of the interstate project. Up to the axles in mud sat the governor's big black Cadillac and the state troopers' motorcycles.

Carlson had the radio tuned to a station that played the top forty tunes in America or in the state, it was never clear exactly where the top forty came from.

Carlson was pleased that Fats Domino's "Blueberry Hill" was still hanging in there.

The drive back to Chicago seemed to go much more quickly than the drive out. Carlson drove all day, his mind a virtual blank, concentrating on the road with the radio blaring in his ear. At night he would fall into heavy, dreamless sleep.

At the outskirts of the city, he could no longer keep his mind off Caroline. He pulled into a small diner, ordered a hamburger and coffee, and sat for a long time hunched over his coffee cup. What would he say to her when he finally saw her again?

Would she really be glad to see him? He had called her before leaving Wichita and she sounded cordial if not exactly full of love. Yes, she was pleased to hear he was coming to Chicago. No, it didn't matter when he showed up; he should just call the hospital or the apartment to let her know he had arrived.

She told him that the employment agency he had registered with when he first came to Chicago had sent a card about a newspaper job. Carlson had called them too from Wichita. Long-distance, he had set up an appointment for the job interview.

He had called Caroline back to tell her about it, to give her concrete proof that he was trying to be a solid citizen. Now he decided to get the interview over with before he saw Caroline. If he got the job, it would be another good mark on his record. He drove to a large motel to celebrate his decision, feeling that a good night's rest in large, clean, thoroughly impersonal surroundings would sufficiently empty his head of worries to make a good impression with his prospective employer. It was worth the extra cost.

You had to pass a used-car lot, two chicken and catfish joints, and companies of various kinds to find the ordinary red-brick office and plant.

This was headquarters for the publishers of an advertisers' chain of weekly throwaway papers across the nation. Some of the papers were actually sold for a nickel or dime in places where there was little or no competition from a good daily or weekly newspaper. But primarily they were not worth any money as to news content and were solely mediums for paid advertising space, sold cheaper than the local papers' rates in the same area.

The chain wanted an editor for a paper it owned in downstate Illinois, Lincoln country.

Carlson pushed in the door to the large outer office where half a dozen women were busy clipping ads from newspapers, answering telephones and taking walk-in advertising from customers at an L-shaped oak desk which divided the room—business on the one side, customers and the curious or merely wandering desperate on the other.

Around the high room, on all the walls, were life-sized portraits of middle-aged men. Completely banked around the upper reaches of the room, nearly all the portraits in gilt frames were rendered with a fixed stare of patriotic fervor in their eyes like the eyes of the angry eagle of *E Pluribus Unum.*

Uncle Sams! The room was ringed with life-size portraits of Uncle Sam! All were painted professionally, in oils.

One of the women noticed Carlson swiveling around gawking at the two dozen or so portraits. None was like the traditional old Uncle Sam of everyone's memory, the canny Yankee trader with the New England Protestant whiskers, in the suit and top hat made from a flag. There were some odd Uncle Sam pictures in a flag suit, but all had shaved and put on weight and grown shorter in stature. Chumps and automobile dealers every one.

"Can I help you?" the woman asked with a note of concern.

Carlson gestured at all the Uncle Sams arrayed above them. He knew there was a desperate look in his eyes.

"Uncle Sams," the woman told him as if she were somehow threatened.

"But why?" he veritably squawked.

"Mr. McGregor ran a contest for a new Uncle Sam," she explained.

"And these were the top entries," he guessed aloud.

"And the winner?" His eyes strayed upward directly above, in the center of the room, facing the street.

"That's it," she said.

Indeed, he thought.

There was the life-size portrait of *the* new Uncle Sam. Incredible. Hilarious. Chilling. Sad. Scary as hell. Uncle Sam had shrunk to about five eight in his Adler Elevator shoes and had obviously overindulged with the country club's prime ribs and twelve-year-old Scotch beyond a point of any decent return. The tubby little bastard was a walking hymn to gout beneath a silver crewcut, with a mean, flabby face and frightened, conniving eyes. The artist had to have been a marvelous visionary, a perfectly subtle critic of existing American society and its corporate leaders. And the chumps on the selection committee and Mr. McGregor had bought it; seen themselves in it; gone for it totally! The artist had to have known.

The New Uncle Sam was leaning formally, but without weight, upon a waist-high Gothic pillar, casually holding an open Bible in his left hand as if teaching a hard lesson to everyone. His right hand was gesturing at his right side —a kind of parody of a famous painting of Thomas Jefferson; wasn't there somewhere the same ridiculous pose by Warren G. Harding in an official painting? The New Uncle Sam could have been teaching an adult Sunday school class at the wealthy First Baptist Church. He wore a single-breasted blue suit, button-down white broadcloth shirt with a narrow red tie. He looked just like Charley Wilson of General Motors, Carlson realized. The very image.

Surely the artist who had won the contest for the New Uncle Sam was somewhere having a beer with his winnings and falling on the floor with laughter at having put over such a thing on the people who had conceived of and sponsored the crazy contest. He could *not* have been serious . . . could he? No, Carlson decided. It was too frightening to contemplate.

The New Uncle Sam.

"Can I *help* you?" The woman really wanted to know.

"Oh, uh, yes, ma'am. I have an appointment to see Mr. McGregor," Carlson replied.

She directed him to the publisher's office, down a corridor along the left wall. The man's name and title were on the door in gilt.

When Carlson was passed on into the inner office by the man's secretary, an aging woman who was armored with spikes of loyalty to her boss that made her seem a human porcupine, he almost broke into laughter. Mr. McGregor *was* the New Uncle Sam. He should have known.

Carlson was dressed in sincere clothes. He had on his gray pinstriped Robert Hall single-breasted suit, shined brown cowboy boots, a blue oxfordcloth shirt and reverse rep-striped tie. He carried two portfolios, one filled with examples of his writing and one filled with examples of his artwork.

The man who was the New Uncle Sam studied the examples of Carlson's work in both portfolios non-committally.

He closed the last portfolio and cleared his throat and looked Carlson right in the eyes with an eaglelike gaze.

"How come you did not graduate?" he asked.

"My GI Bill ran out," Carlson said, shading the truth by leaving out the pertinent reason for his having lost his educational benefits. "My parents are deceased," he explained.

McGregor cleared his throat again. "What are your politics?"

"I voted for Eisenhower," Carlson reported without elaboration. He had voted for Eisenhower the *first* time, and had been so disappointed in how that turned out he was sure he would never vote again until he was offered something other than the traditional cream cheese choices or provided with a space to vote "None of the Above."

"A registered Republican?" the man asked, a decision obviously beginning to form beneath his silver crewcut.

"Yes, sir," Carlson said sincerely.

"When can you start?" McGregor asked.

"Why, right away, sir," Carlton said, with more surprise than he felt. Man, if the Russians were any smarter than chumps like McGregor, they could run such individuals like Pavlov's dog. Problem was, he decided, that the Russians and Mr. McGregor were brothers so alike they might have once been joined at the hip.

McGregor wanted to talk politics. He was explaining how he owned a ranch in Arizona near that of the state Senator, a man named Goldwater who, Mac was betting, would be the eventual President and savior of the United States.

"I'm sorry," Carlson said. "I never heard of him."

"Well, you remember his name. He's going to take this country by the scruff of the neck and give it a good shake

255

that will put everything back into its proper place, restore the Republic."

"Yes, sir," Carlson said.

"Right! Well, you be down in Decatur Monday morning. I'll have my accountant, Mr. Small, meet you there and stay around for a few days until you get things organized. We'll see how you do."

"Yes, sir. Thank you, sir," Carlson said and stood up.

They shook hands. Carlson knew he had a good handshake, strong and dry and calm. It wasn't something he had studied, it was just something that a couple of people had commented on. McGregor looked as if he were the kind of man who judged someone by their handshake; McGregor was easy.

That artist had to have known, Carlson decided as he went back out through the lobby, knowing full well he could never take the job.

He rang the bell at Caroline's apartment that evening bearing a dozen roses in cellophane.

She accepted the roses cautiously, seeming to fear that in accepting them she was making some kind of unwanted commitment. But they were roses and she was gracious, letting him kiss her on the cheek.

"I love you," she explained wearily when he had taken her in his arms inside the doorway and protested his love for her. "I take it you got the job?" she said.

"I have to go down there Monday," he said, avoiding a direct answer.

She could not see how his editing a newspaper in Decatur was going to permit them to work out their problems in Chicago. But there was a continuing recession and jobs were very hard to get outside of the professions and exotic engineering disciplines so she tried to sound pleased that, at least, he was working regularly again.

In time, Carlson hoped to be able to explain to Caroline that he could not possibly work for the New Uncle Sam, not even for her sake. That garbage was no more a newspaper than toilet tissue. Anyway, he would never last on the job. He would not be able to keep a serious face and there was no way he could keep up his conservative good-boy act. But he did not want to mar their first evening with arguments about his inability to settle into gainful employment. He kept silent as she talked herself into being glad about the position in Decatur.

They went out to a nearby place for homemade soup and warm cornbread and sweet butter. The place was run by a strange young woman built along pioneer scantlings, whose two small children played on the floor in the tiny soup and sandwich store. Everyone referred to her as "the hippie." She called the place Earthmother's. She closed early to take the children to wherever she lived and put them to bed. She made good soup. That night Caroline and Carlson had the cream of watercress. It was delicious. The cornbread was good. A nice supper.

Later, they sat on the couch in her apartment.

She let him kiss her, reluctantly letting his tongue into her mouth, finally responding in spite of herself. He placed his hand on her breast. She covered it with her own, mumbled, "Don't," but when he insisted, she relaxed and let him fondle her breast urgently, desperately.

"Please don't," she asked as he reached beneath her skirt and forced his hand between her thighs above the tops of her stockings.

"I want to," he breathed. "I want you."

"I don't want to," she explained, trying to keep his hand away from her sex.

His fingers touched the film of her panties.

"You're wet!" he exclaimed.

"No!" She tossed her head.

He caught her mouth with his lips and kissed her again. His fingers found their way beneath the elastic of her panties and found their way into her hot, wet pie.

"Goddamn you," she hissed, but relaxed and partially opened her thighs. She returned his kiss.

"I don't want to do this," she told him as he got between her legs on the floor beside the couch.

"I'm sorry," he said. "I just want you so. I *need* you."

"Don't you dare come in me," she warned, as his cock

slid up into her familiar cunt. For a few minutes he felt at home, finally able to relax. He felt as if he had not been able to relax since he was last in her.

"Don't you come in me!" she reminded him.

He helped her to move her bottom with his hands.

"Fuck me, Caroline," he begged. "Please fuck me."

She dutifully moved as he wished her to do, began to become aroused herself.

"Boy, you better not come in me. Not a drop, you hear?" she panted.

"I won't. I promise," he said, fucking her hard, driving the air from her as he felt his cock swell to painful proportions inside her.

"Be careful," she breathed. "You're hurting me."

He ceased banging so hard and deeply into her, tried to make the experience last forever. He felt her start to move as she did when she was about to come. He quickened his movements, felt himself start to come, the gathering in his tight testicles, the ejaculate starting up the channel. She was almost there.

"*No!*" she cried out and twisted away from him as he yanked his cock out of her and came all over her pubic hair.

"I didn't come in you!" he exclaimed. "I didn't! I wouldn't. Don't you believe me?"

She waved that it didn't matter and tried to curl up on the floor. She was crying. He forced her to turn over so he could go down on her, hoping to give her pleasure.

"For God's sake, stop it!" she cried out. "Just stop!"

"What is it?" he pleaded, scooting back up to look into her twisted face. Tears were wet and flowing on her face. "Please," he begged. "I'm sorry. I just want to please you."

She shook her head. "You don't know how any more. That was not what I wanted. Don't you understand?"

"No, I don't know, Caroline. I wish I knew. I wish I could do what you need. Tell me. I love you."

"It doesn't matter," she said, sniffing deeply, starting to get control of herself. "I guess I am just being emotional." She patted his face, smiled. "There has been so much hurt, so much disappointment. It did feel good for a little while. I'm sorry. I wish it could be lovely and forever."

He touched her as if to initiate sex again.

She removed his hand gently. "No. Please. Let's don't. I'm okay now. You go downstate and we will stay in touch. Maybe it will work out. I want you to know I want it, too. I am not very hopeful, but I hope it will work out."

"I love you," he said.

She kissed his mouth gently. "Let me up. I want to go wash."

She would not let him stay and shower with her. She went with him to the door, kissed him, and wished him luck in Decatur.

"I love you, Caroline," he said.

"I know." She smiled. "Good night."

The doorman told him good night without bothering to look at him. He was no longer a resident in the building. He wondered if Caroline had other men guests now. He had not asked her. He was sure she did not. Yet it felt over. His hopes and dreams involving her seemed hopeless indeed. He felt that on some level she was at that moment regretting having ever gotten involved with him. That was the hard knowledge. That is what really hurt. He never felt more impotent, alone, outside.

There was nothing to keep him in Chicago. He drove to a small motel outside the city, not having the heart to spend money on another night in luxurious surroundings. The place he had now was clean if fraying at the edges. He slept badly.

The next morning he headed the '50 Ford convertible toward the Rio Grande Valley of Texas where he had come of age following the oilfields with his mother and stepfather. He was going to find any sort of a job to feed himself and concentrate his energies on writing great, exciting stories of shrimp fishermen, roughnecks, retired generals who sold insurance, border jackals, and border hustlers. He wanted to see Mexico again.

On the way south he stopped in Ohio to visit Margaret

Archer, with whom he had maintained a correspondence, even from Wichita. She had returned to her family and was living with her mother now.

Carlson had never been able to write to a girl without somehow getting turned on to her. The act of communication affected him in an oddly sexual way. And Margaret's letters were always so *wishful*. She clearly cared about him, liked him very much. He figured he would stop and say hello while he was in the neighborhood.

Pretty soon a week had passed and Carlson was still there. Margaret had this new little sports car, a beautiful English thing with wire wheels she let him drive as they went visiting all her friends so she could show off Carlson. He was enjoying himself, glad to be out of his old green Ford.

They played a lot of tennis on private courts near a place called Hog Creek. As he batted the ball toward Margaret, Carlson's mind dwelled on her recently widowed mother, a sexy, feminine woman of fifty who wore black beautifully, the net bodice drawing attention to her large breasts. Perhaps Margaret was simply a late bloomer, he thought. How could such a plain young woman have a mother virtually bursting her widow's weeds?

One day, after a game of tennis, chewing on the grasses along Hog Creek, Margaret said, "Take me with you."

"You're out of your mind," he said. "I don't know what I am going to do. I don't have a job. I may end up washing dishes or pumping gas. I'm just going down to Mexico and write until I get it right. Or as right as I can."

"I want to go with you."

"You would hate it."

"I want to go."

He looked at her.

At the university he had been a close friend of the old poet of the West, John Neihardt. In spite of the great disparity of their ages, they talked as brothers for hours at a time. John and his wife were in their late seventies, yet there was a romantic love between them of such power that he could not cross the room nor could she without touching and saying, "Darling." Once John Neihardt had confided, "It took me ten years to learn to love that woman. She would never leave me alone. Had to go everywhere with me. There was a prizefight once. About ten miles away. We did not have a car or horse then. I walked. She walked with me. All the way there and back, with never a complaint."

Carlson put his hand on Margaret's arm. "If it gets too rough, you will have to come back," he said.

He hadn't realized his offer was taken as a proposal of marriage. It was simply not in Margaret's mores to just live with a man. Nor was it in her mother's. That night, Margaret's mother kissed him and called him "son." She said she was sorry they were not having a real wedding but that it was probably all right, what with her husband so recently "gone."

"Whatever makes you happy, dears," she said, smiling bravely.

She handed Carlson a check for a thousand dollars. It seemed like a fortune to him; he had about a hundred and a half in his pocket, and owed two payments on the Ford.

The next night, it was the family—brothers, sister, sister-in-law—everyone chuckling and drinking a great deal. Margaret's older brother said in that half-teasing way they all used with each other, "I don't know: I think he loves her car more than he does her."

Everyone laughed. But it was *close*. He did love that car. He loved everything that was going on there. The car, the house, the close-knit family, the laughter, the teasing, all the *things* they had. And he liked Margaret, dammit, he liked her a lot. He just didn't want to get married and settle into conformity.

Earlier that day they had gone to see the Archers' family doctor, who had given them medical certificates and stopped to confide to Carlson: "She is a *good* girl. Do you understand? A very *good* girl," he emphasized.

Carlson assured the older man he had always considered her so.

Perhaps it was Margaret's very niceness that made it

impossible for him to walk away. Assumptions were being made all around him by these good people and he felt trapped by their kindly suppositions.

Within a day there was a "surprise" engagement party given by Margaret's friends. People she had known since childhood congregated around Carlson, telling him how lucky he was, raising their glasses to drink to their happiness and his good fortune.

He tried to slow things down. "Did you tell your mother I don't know what I'm going to do?" he asked Margaret. "That I don't even have a job lined up?"

She said, "I told her I was going with you. That I loved you and you loved me and you were the man I wanted."

His head filled with John Neihardt and the poet's long romance with his wife—mixed in with visions of Margaret's mother's black net before his eyes—Carlson stayed. In spite of the old Army adage that you never screw your friends, he decided to give Margaret as much time as he was willing to give himself as a writer.

He had never really touched her. Her mother was ever-vigilant inside the house, and outside Margaret would only exchange chaste little kisses, allowing his hand to wander over her breasts but not farther below. She never relaxed her body around him, no matter how often they talked of sex. She told him her older brother had been a virgin when he got married—and he'd spent a couple of years in the Army. She was a *good* girl, exactly as the family's doctor had said.

They were married by the acting mayor of the town, who had never married anyone before. Margaret's mother wept. Her family kissed both of them after the ceremony, and then they all walked to the wedding lunch in the town's most expensive restaurant.

With Margaret's MG roadster hooked onto a tow-bar behind Carlson's old Ford, they headed south via the spine of the Blue Ridge Mountains. They stopped for a dinner of home-cured ham in a hillbilly joint along the way.

Come nightfall, Carlson found a motel in Kentucky

and ran a mile down the road to a liquor store to buy a bottle of champagne while Margaret prepared for bed.

She came from the bathroom after about an hour in a pale blue nightgown. Her mother's Arpège did not have the same effect on her suntanned skin. Her deflowerment was so excruciatingly painful that Carlson performed his duty as quickly as possible, losing full erection during the process, never to regain it again until he hit the *putacasas* of Matamoros, Mexico, just across the bridge from Brownsville, Texas.

He lay in the dark, listening to his wife's sobs subsiding into snores, drinking the tepid champagne from the bottle, wondering, with the worst case of indigestion he had ever known burning his guts: *What the hell have I gotten myself into now?*

It all fell into place. In Chicago, Margaret always wore expensive but dull clothes. Her mother bought her a new wardrobe twice a year. Looking back, he remembered that all of Margaret's clothes were black or gray. Fifteen cashmere sweaters, all the shade of a sparrow. Mama couldn't stand the competition. She had kept Margaret plain, decided at some early age that she *was* plain. While Mama wore the diamonds, the pearls, the lacy net, the silk hosiery, and most expensive underwear, Margaret wore no jewelry and pristine white panties. Her hosiery always bagged at the knees, got twisted, sprouted runners.

Man, man, Carlson told himself in the dark. *What have you gotten yourself into now?*

She had the bones and flesh of Sophia Loren, but she was so damned plain. *Not her fault,* he thought. Not her fault at all. Still, there he was.

When they pulled away from the motel, Margaret was already pregnant. They would not learn this, of course, until some weeks later in Texas when Margaret started throwing up each morning so regularly you could set a clock by it. She thought it was the heat at first and was in her seventh week of pregnancy when the doctor told them the news. Carlson retreated into a depressed silence and made frequent trips to the prostitutes in Mexico. Margaret continued to throw up relentlessly almost to the end of her term.

Carlson had stayed beer-drunk all the way down to Texas, taking the Huey Long Bridge at Baton Rouge in the driving rain at ninety-five miles an hour, with Margaret's MG whipping behind on the tow bar like a tin can, seldom even looking at his wife sitting sullenly against the glass, wrapped in cashmere and unhappiness. Margaret was convinced he hated her, that he was determined to kill them both.

The day he pulled into Brownsville, Texas, he walked into the newspaper office and came out with a job as reporter and assistant Sunday editor at one hundred five dollars for a fifty-two-hour week. The paper was owned by a man who had a chain of what he called "Freedom" newspapers, the title somehow justifying in *his* mind the pay and hours. Yet it was a good job. The editor ran an easy newsroom. Carlson covered the police beat and the courts, and spent as many hours as possible across the river with the girls of Boystown.

He was particularly fond of a *puta* noted for the elaborate makeup and costume she brought to her calling. Her costume, a series of specially made gowns latticed up the sides to display her fine body, and her makeup with wings of black, gold, blue, and sequins around her eyes, her hair bleached out like sisal, were as superbly designed for catching as Yogi Berra's mitt. Yet she was not happy in her work. A city girl, she met disappointment on the border where the American trade looked for whores who reminded them of their secretaries and the daughters of their friends. Carlson loved her, for all her carping about the tastes of his fellows. She had pride in her calling and a triptych mirror above the bed to see how she was doing, along with an air-conditioner in her crib window.

So they did eight months on the border. Margaret suffered terribly from the intense heat that hit one's brain when stepping out of the air-conditioning like a hammer of hell. She grew large with child, worried about the .45 automatic Carlson slept with beside the bed, never understanding that under Texas law there *were* situations under which some sonsofbitches could reasonably be shot, particularly if caught crawling through your window on a moonless night.

Carlson was trying to write. He sent a couple of stories off to a writing workshop at Columbia University, and received in return an offer to enroll on a scholarship. In Margaret's eighth month, they sold the Ford and, averaging four hundred miles a day in her MG, drove to New York. Their son, Luke, was born four weeks after they arrived. Margaret's mother had to pick up the tab, after a scalding attack on Carlson that ended with her asking:

"What would you do if I didn't have the money?"

When he replied, "I'd steal it," she wrote him off forever.

Rationally, he denied to himself the guilt Margaret and her family laid on him, yet it ate at his vitals till he felt like a man who had swallowed a badger.

"Welcome to the middle class," he congratulated himself one morning in the mirror while Margaret was still in the hospital.

And the pattern of their lives was set.

Twenty–Six

IT WAS MARGARET'S decision to move to Brooklyn, to a small, dark, one-bedroom apartment in an old six-story house in Brooklyn Heights. It was all they could afford, she told Carlson. He was too weary to argue.

There was no question of his taking the scholarship at Columbia. He wrote a terse letter declining the offer and went to look for a job to support his wife and child. He found work with surprising ease through an employment agency, in the art department of a large Manhattan department store. He wrote nights, working at the kitchen table, because he had sworn to himself that nothing would make him stop writing and also because the book kept him away from Margaret's sullen, resentful silences.

Six months after Luke was born, Margaret had gotten a part-time job selling printing for a Brooklyn firm. Her family owned a very successful midwestern printing company, and it had been easy for her to make the connection in New York.

Carlson barely tolerated his own job. It was impossible for him to take seriously all the executives, who had started with the company twenty to thirty years before, who still took their suits off the store racks, still were thrilled to receive a solid gold watch after twenty-five years of service, bequeathed with great solemnity by the store president at a companywide dinner.

He had refused, absolutely, to join the store's cherished profit-sharing plan. His argument was: "I know it is a good deal for someone who is going to stay here for twenty years. But if I let you believe that was my ambition, I would be lying. I *need* these few extra dollars at this time in my life. I don't need the couple of hundred in savings they will eventually represent."

But the art department's manager, Captain Oliver, could be caught regularly staring at the stubborn sliver of white at the top of his profit-sharing thermometer with the look of a man silently grinding his teeth. He didn't like that bit of white that kept *his* thermometer from being one hundred percent.

Captain wasn't the man's name. He was in the local Army reserve unit and changed into uniform at the office every Tuesday when his unit drilled. When Carlson first came to work there, Captain noted he had been a platoon sergeant in Korea and tried to interest him in joining the reserves. He spoke of the need for a public relations officer in his unit, seeing no reason Carlson could not be directly commissioned as a first lieutenant. Carlson had thanked him, promising to think about it.

The professionally kind man in the store's personnel department also tried his hand at convincing Carlson of the benefits of profit sharing. "But the way the store's stock is rising, it really is a good deal," he said.

"Yes, it is, if I work for the company for five, ten, twenty years. But for me to let you think that will be the case is ridiculous. I'm leaving long before that."

"I understand and appreciate what you're saying," the man with the masters in psychology told him. If they had been on the same side of the desk, Carlson had the feeling the man would have patted his knee. "We all feel like that. But it is amazing how many of us end up making a career here."

That was true. Carlson had worked in worse places. The level of performance required rarely exceeded the meager salaries paid. Still . . . "Well," he said, "if I *am* still here next year, I promise to participate in profit sharing."

The man had lost the battle but Carlson had lost the war. Behind the man's forced smile, Carlson could see his own days were numbered. That sliver of white on the art department thermometer was intolerable. It was particularly so in view of the fact that the Teamsters Union was outside the doors every day trying to organize the department store workers, most of them clerks who worked for forty-five dollars per week, plus commission on sales. All employees were excused from work to view a company anti-union film that followed a company stockholders' report to all profit-sharers. The meeting only lacked badges and paper hats to make the phony bonhommie totally disgusting. All the little profit-sharers clapped their hands like trained seals thrown a sardine during recitation by the steel-gray men of figures they did not understand by half. Call it anything, it still looked like a kind of slavery to Carlson. None of the stock was negotiable. Employees could only cash it in when they left the company. In the meantime, the Teamsters offered more beer and skittles each week than anyone not on the dais was then getting.

A week later, the art department was excused for an hour to take a psychological test administered by a young woman. Carlson finished his in ten minutes and handed it in, then went to the cafeteria for coffee, feeling the young woman thought he was a showoff. He knew the test would show he had enormous peaks in the areas of physical action and intellectual curiosity. Such peaks, in fact, that he would be labeled a troublemaker. He had taken enough tests to know how he broke on their graphs. It had been the same in the Army when he was up for direct commission to first lieutenant, with top ratings by all his superiors. Approval went all the way through to the Pentagon, where someone with a test-reading overlay found that his peaks went completely off the scale of acceptability. It was going to be the same here.

Three weeks before Christmas he was given notice. The excuse was that the department was no longer functioning economically and the area he was working in was being turned over to a different office. But two men over whom he had seniority were kept on.

He went home and told Margaret he was not going to work for anyone again. He was going to finish the novel he had been pecking at for a year even if they had to go on welfare. She had a better idea. There was an account

268

at the company where she worked that her firm could not continue with, the margin of profit being too low. She could handle this herself and net about three hundred a month. She was sure they could get other accounts as well. He could do the artwork and still write his novel.

So, with three hundred dollars in the bank, they went into business, forming a partnership called Grafiks. When they could not have borrowed a dime anywhere on the rational side of any small loan company, they found the Brooklyn Trust Company ready to make them a small business loan of $2,500 and completely finance a new Ford station wagon they decided they needed to make deliveries. Margaret walked out of the bank with an order for posters and a series of mailing pieces.

Grafiks was an immediate success, mostly due to Margaret's inflexible honesty in business, an anachronism in New York, and perhaps due in part to Carlson's ability to come up repeatedly with ideas that convinced a regiment of *schlock* merchants, drug wholesalers, and non-profit organizations that Grafiks could catch the human eye. After his stint at the department store, he knew how general merchandisers thought. It was never a matter of aesthetics; it was always color, power, and occasionally humor.

Carlson was grateful for Margaret's business acumen, grateful for the freedom she brought into their lives. On their own, they were making more money than they had earned at two jobs. Yet, away from the business, their life was not a success.

She did not like him to touch her, did not want hugs or kisses, could not wait for him to finish fucking on the rare times they had sex. Yet she was a passionate person, a deeply feeling person. A couple of times when she had gotten drunk, her sexual desire had been almost frighteningly powerful. If she cared, she could have been a beautiful, voluptuous woman. It seemed to Carlson that she hated the female inside her, kept her womanliness imprisoned in some corner of herself, despising everything it represented.

He thought that if Margaret would ever let her femaleness come out, she would feel she had lost some uniqueness, some superiority. He couldn't figure it out, so mostly he let it alone.

In 1960, they had another child, a girl named Jean.

Because of the new baby and their newfound affluence, they moved from their cramped one-bedroom Brooklyn Heights apartment to a large, sunny, three-bedroom place in Park Slope, overlooking Prospect Park. Carlson used one of the smaller bedrooms as his study, the room where he wrote.

By then, almost two years after they started Grafiks, the Carlsons were able to hire a full-time maid to take care of the two children while Margaret worked, took a three-week vacation in Scandinavia, bought a new car, went to Manhattan to dinner at least once a month.

It was not enough for Carlson. *It's the damn lethargy that gets you,* he thought, *settling into that complacent middle-class life, surrounded by things!*

It's like goo inside you and all over you. It's a soft, thick heavy gunk that weights you down and oppresses you. And you begin seeing yourself living with it the rest of your life because you know you're going to live, yessir, you know that's the one thing you do. You're going to live, no matter what. Life goes on, like they say, and you ooze through your days. When you begin to feel too uncomfortable, you pull your cap down over your ears, put your hands in your pockets, and walk until the feeling passes, and then you take up again where the ooze left off and pretend like you can make it. You go another week, or month, oozing along like a slug, and then walk again. And again. For maybe forty years—Carlson figured he had maybe forty more lethargic years to get through yet, to live out emptily.

Twenty–Seven

IT WAS A cold morning and bad weather and there was nowhere to go, but Carlson didn't care. He had to get out. The walls had been closing him in for days and his mind had begun to feel stretched to the end of some psychic sort of sanity-saving tether. You could call it restlessness, boredom, a hundred things, and still not put a real name to it because it came packaged within, and around, the general condition of his life. That is, what Carlson felt inside his bones was a deep dissatisfaction with everything, including himself, and it had become a malaise finally more concrete than simple mood.

"I'm going out," he muttered to Margaret as he slung on his mackinaw.

"Have you finished?" She meant with his part of the ad they were working on. He had been in the middle of the layout when the whole thing became a blur in front of his eyes and totally nonsensical.

"No." He was going, pulling his ski cap from his pocket.

"We promised it this afternoon."

"I didn't promise anything." He was going out the door.

"Where are you going?"

He didn't bother to answer and only heard her curse trailing him down the hall. "You sonofabitch."

Outside, he pulled his cap down over his ears and started walking hard with his hands in his coat pockets, looking straight ahead. Snow had fallen most of the night in light flurries and covered the streets with soft whiteness until the traffic had come along to ruin it. It was now a dirty slush on the sidewalks and turning gray on the windowsills of the brownstones. Small flakes were still coming down tentatively but making no impression except as a slight blur in the air before vanishing.

The novel Carlson had written was like the snow too, light and of no consequence. He had burned it to make it vanish, but his failure with it still pulled at him. Margaret had been angry and disappointed with him. You wasted your time like that, she said; how could you? A slap in the face. She meant, of course, how could *she* have wasted her time. And how dare he let her down. She had felt deceived and selfishly concerned about herself, not him. So, okay, fine, but what about him? How the hell did she think he felt?

It was the same old story, two people living together like strangers with an invisible barbed-wire barricade between them, and there was no solace or sympathy, or even a facade of warmth where either could warm their cold backsides. They were left to themselves and the paradoxical rage and lethargy that kind of separateness created.

He had started out as nothing, a dirt-poor kid from nowhere, not knowing a thing, where he was going or who he was, but after half a lifetime he thought he had discovered himself. After all the hits and misses, and God knows he had covered the field, he thought he knew he was, at last—at least—a writer. It had been a sudden, wonderful feeling to finally see himself in a suitable frame, to see his image clearly for the first time. And since he was a writer, it naturally followed he could write. But that first novel he had struggled to finish, hoping to the end, proved he couldn't. His lack of ability was so glaringly obvious it knocked the props out from under him. The mirror image of the writer was shattered. To be sure, he tried to pick up the pieces. He didn't give it up completely all at once, but one of the broken pieces, the one with the spark in the heart, was missing. And the picture wouldn't come together again.

He had burned the manuscript of that first novel, his failure, with a chunk of ice in his bowels, and Margaret's fiery resentment by his side. What he had written was no damned good, and the pain of discovery ate at him.

He had walked several miles, in the park and around Grand Army Plaza, and had crossed from Flatbush Avenue to Sterling Place before he was aware of where he was. The once-quiet and sedate neighborhood was running down but still dotted with churches and funeral parlors, places for the dead and the watchers of the dead. The gutters were brimming with slush, and sleet was coming down out of low gray clouds. A light wind was blowing small snow flurries around the corners of buildings.

Then something caught Carlson's eye, in the upper right corner of sight, coming from the sky. Something totally out of whack and shockingly immense, and it appeared too quickly. The mind wouldn't detail the sight at the time but Carlson would recall it later in slow motion, a huge silver shape that suddenly loomed above the street and seemed to hover for a second at the top edge of a building. But not for a second, or even an instant. It came from the overcast sky too quickly and with too much of a rush to even hover or be held in view distinctly. Only in memory could you see it distinguished for what it was, and perhaps only then because of photographs after the fact and you felt compelled to respond: Yes! That's what it was! That's it!

At the time it was more like a gigantic warning in the air, a presence of threat suddenly calling forth unexpected alarm in the body. It was also instant fear and disbelief, a flat stop of the heart.

Later the newspapers would say it was a DC-8 Jet Mainliner, 150 feet long and 42 feet high with a wingspan of 142 feet, carrying six tons of cargo, seventy-seven passengers, and seven crew members. Each of its four J-75 engines, they would say, delivered a maximum thrust of 15,900 pounds, and the plane itself was probably dropping through the atmosphere at about 765 feet a second. It would speed the length of a football field in the blink of an eye.

Carlson thought the colossal thing was coming down right on him and that it had zeroed in on him like a giant shark with a blunt jaw about to take his head off, and it was crazy because it was something totally out of place and not something that should have been in the streets at all. A monstrous roar came with it, and a satellite to it, a wing, was sailing alongside, easing out from it. It might have been that Carlson saw faces in the zipper row of windows and heads in the cockpit eyes of the beast. He at least *felt* human beings inside some disastrous fate and he knew their minds were stricken and disbelieving, too.

As he went flat to the sidewalk he realized the thing would miss him but he went down anyway as a great ball of fire screamed past his head.

On the sidewalk ahead two men were bending over setting up Christmas trees and didn't know it was coming. A street sweeper shoveling snow barely had time to look up. He might have seen it enough to know it was engulfing him—had engulfed him, in fact, as he looked. He was killed quicker than thought, but his soul might have lingered apart from his already obliterated body long enough to remark. Before these men, though, a parked car was the first to be hit, or caught up. It was swept ahead of the hurtling missile but as far as any eye might see, the men and car were all in one and annihilated together instantaneously. Only a few sprigs of a Christmas tree would be found later under the snow.

The giant plane had already strafed the tops of ten four-story tenement buildings and was plummeting in flames. A tail section sideswiped a delicatessen and a Chinese laundry. The owner of the laundry was ironing a shirt when his store window was shattered and his face was singed in a sudden blow of heat. A man in the delicatessen was biting into a pickle when a sharp piece of debris sliced through his hand leaving two fingers still holding the pickle for a moment before falling away. At the same time in a block of apartments just passed by the plane a little girl was playing on the floor with her doll as the ceiling above her head came crashing down.

Carlson was flattened on the sidewalk but with his eyes open and seeing. Even if the crash happened too fast, in less than a second, the whole scene was still before him and his mind was registering it. He was also lying in a havoc of air because the impending disaster carried with it its own disturbance of wind as if in advance of a cyclone. His face was blasted, but it was a storm that hit and passed very quickly.

The doomed plane had popped startlingly from the overcast sky, streaming flames, and descended furiously. It was already breaking into flying chunks and spraying destruction without warning. Then the great bulk of it seemed to skip, or take a jump in the air. Carlson thought it flapped like a giant bat just before it hit the spire of the Good Shepherd Church and crashed massively into that solid Gothic structure. There was the roar, the sound of impact, the jarring of the collision through the nerve cells in the ground, and then a terrific explosion, a showering of wreckage, and a billowing of flames three stories high.

At that moment ninety-three people were already dead but no one knew it yet. No one had screamed. The rear of the plane's fuselage had plunged into the intersection of Seventh Avenue and Sterling Place and set fire to two blocks of brownstones. Flaming rivulets raced down the slopes of Sterling Place, enveloped parked cars, and, as the fire reached gasoline tanks, set off a chain of popping explosions. People streamed out of their threatened apartments and flooded the streets with panic. Some were in the cold in their pajamas or only in their sweaters. Small children had been carried out barefoot. Cripples were being helped and dragged through the snow. The spraying wreckage had ignited roofs, so the skyline was aglow with yellow flames.

Carlson found himself running to the remains of the church, but the fire was raging there and the heat was too intense, and he had to stand back and watch what was left of the passenger section of the plane burn. There was no sound from that section anyway. Only later sixty-two bodies would be picked from the ashes but too horribly mutilated and burned for identification. Also a ninety-year-old caretaker of the church was supposedly buried in that mess, but no part of him would ever be found and he would be listed simply as missing.

A siren was sounding. A policeman had appeared, obviously shaken, and was frantically calling for emergency help. In fifteen minutes the first firemen would arrive, and then more. The scene would turn into a seven-alarm fire with two hundred and fifty firemen bringing along more than fifty pieces of firefighting equipment and it would be some hours before the flames would be contained.

Some bodies were lying in the street and Carlson helped carry them to a nearby garage and lay them out on the cold cement floor. The people coming out of the burning buildings were running in fear and shock at first and then aimlessly searching for relatives, shivering in the winter air. Some were huddling together for warmth, and Carlson put his mackinaw around an old woman freezing in a thin nightgown. Her lips were blue and she thanked him with her eyes, and it was the last he saw of his coat. An arm sticking up out of a snowbank claimed his attention next and he went to work clawing the snow away from what he presumed to be a buried body, but it turned out to be only an arm severed at the shoulder and the unattached body was nowhere around. He took the arm by itself to the garage morgue. A fingerprint could tell who it was.

"Help me!" someone screamed at him. "Help me! Help me!" A fat woman was pulling at his elbow and Carlson tried to respond. He shook her and tried to calm her, but the woman was in shock and screaming for no reason, it seemed, and he finally had to lead her to someone else and leave her. The funeral parlors were taking people in off the street and giving them a warm place to stay. A little diner was handing out free cups of hot coffee, but now the area was beginning to fill with the curious and the onlookers of tragedy from the nearby neighborhoods. Some were already boldly looting the vacated apartments not yet burning. Traffic was blocked and snarled in the surrounding streets and horns were blaring. The police were coming in fast, though, and working to seal off the streets and keep the crowds back out of the way.

Carlson was pushed back by a policeman. "But I'm trying to help," Carlson said.

"Then stay back," the policeman said, "keep outta the way."

But Carlson couldn't. He ran back into the worst part of the scene and helped carry more bodies into the garage. He was beginning to feel very cold without his coat but he didn't care. This was a human tragedy and he felt compelled to do what he could. He didn't care either that the task first at hand was gruesome. What did that matter now?

The dead were lined in rows and an effort was made to straighten them respectfully, but some had to be laid out as they had been found, in torturous positions. There were no blankets to cover them and wouldn't be for a while yet, so death was displayed in full view. And its perfect stillness in the bodies was quietening. Carlson was touched by the climate of the skin when he carried one. Though certainly not warm, neither was the feel clammy as he might have imagined, but rather human. The limpness of the bodies, however, spoke for their ultimate helplessness. And the expressions on the corpses told something too. Some appeared serene as if peacefully asleep, while some were in various states of distortion, but all were immediately recognizable as thoughtless and totally without spirit. The expressions proclaimed absolutely that there was nothing of any content whatsoever behind them. Even the grinning ones. The joke that might have provoked the grin had not even been a phantom.

Without life a body was simply abstract. And hardly that.

Apparently no one had been trapped inside the burning apartment buildings. At that time of day most people were at work, and the rest were alerted by the explosions and noise. Still, many firemen and a few others risked their lives in the spreading flames and choking smoke to search the buildings and make sure. The looting was quickly stopped. One bleary-eyed junkie struggling down some steps with a TV set was tackled by several outraged women and nearly had his hair pulled out before a policeman could get him away.

The elementary school full of a thousand children two blocks away had been missed completely, but parents ran to the school anyway to make sure and hugged their children with great relief when they found them safe and still the same.

When the police finally contained the crowds behind barriers, several priests were allowed to go through with holy oils. Carlson watched them go from body to body in the garage and felt a letdown. That seemed so beside the point now and too late, Carlson thought, all too late. Then, suddenly, he realized he was cold and tired and his clothes were smeared with blood. His hands were black and numb. Someone handed him a cup of hot coffee and he took it gratefully.

He was leaning against a far wall in the garage when the ambulances arrived and began loading the bodies to take them away. A priest made a point of coming over to him, and asking him in condolence, "Someone close to you, my son?" He assumed Carlson had lost someone in the rows of bodies and was in a state of shock perhaps. He put a kindly hand on Carlson's shoulder.

But Carlson shook his head. "No."

"No?" The priest seemed confused and turned away saying, "God is merciful."

After the bodies were taken away, Carlson was left alone in the garage. The coffee had turned cold in his cup but he still held it. For the first time in his life, it seemed, he was struck with his own mortality as a real part of his body, but it seemed attached inside him very delicately, as if by tiny, fragile strings. His mortality hung inside his chest by a few threads and it wouldn't take anything to break them. He could be bumped slightly, barely jarred, and they would snap just like that. His life would be over, and it wouldn't take anything near like what had just happened with the giant plane. It could be something light and small, like a dart. It wouldn't take anything—

The church was still a raging inferno, and the buildings for blocks were still blazing, the streets cluttered with debris and burned cars, but the firemen were there en masse and working hard, pumping foam as well as water, and they had delineated the area where the fire could be contained. It was all going to be brought under control.

The mayor and several city officials had collected in one spot and were being interviewed by newsmen. Carlson walking by could hear the mayor pointlessly proclaiming a fact, that it was a tragedy, and one of the officials was already bringing to bear his officialdom and demanding a complete investigation into every detail of this whole affair. They would see to it that something like this never happened again, he said. And his face was silhouetted by the fires yet burning behind him.

A reporter stepped from the group and stopped Carlson, who looked like he had been involved somehow. "Hey, you didn't by any chance see it happen, did you?"

Carlson paused. "Yes."

The reporter was insanely excited. An eyewitness was quotable. "You did? What did you see? What did it look like?"

"It looked"—Carlson couldn't say it—"I don't know. It didn't look like anything I'd ever seen before."

"You saw the plane coming down, though?"

"Something like that."

"What did you think?"

"I thought it was coming right at me."

"What did you feel, frightened?"

"Yeah—and alone." Carlson ducked his head then and walked on.

Miraculously, there was one survivor from the plane, an eleven-year-old boy who had been thrown clear of the crash and into a soft snowbank. From his hospital bed he was able to describe the last desperate minute of the flight before the crash, and he was quoted in the newspaper the next day:

"It looked like a picture right out of a fairy tale," he said. "It was a beautiful sight."

Carlson stood at the edge of the crowd watching the firemen battle the roaring flames. Water from their hoses was running in rivers down the streets and people were wading in it ankle-deep. The snow had stopped falling, but it was still winter and very cold.

Nearly a hundred human beings had just been killed instantly and for no reason right in front of him, and he had been left alive. Why? Why spare him, and for what? He wasn't worthy to be selected, singled out, like that. Why for him, and not those others, the continuing gift of precious breath and lively movement?

It was the eternal conundrum.

Then Carlson mused, *probably just so I can torture myself feeling this way.*

He didn't know it, but that passing thought skipping lightly through his brain was actually a slip of humility, and the first step down the right path.

The next step would be to quit taking himself too seriously so much.

Life was too short to waste, to let ooze away from you over, say, forty more lethargic years. There might not be forty.

The startling tragedy in the streets behind him had certainly shown him that. A giant specter of death had loomed from the sky, hovered a moment in his mind, sent a ball of fire screaming past his head, and then shocked his senses like nothing in this world ever had before.

And he was still shaken, but he was on his feet and making his way home. He didn't know how long it would take him to get there. He had gone away farther than he knew, but he was on his way back now and something told him he would make it. All he had to do was forget a lot and try.

When Margaret heard him coming in the door, she had been building up to it, and she started in, "You sonofa-bitch—" But the sight of him stopped her.

He was standing in the doorway as if he had just come through a bombing. His clothes were bloody and black. His eyes were red and wild, and he was holding himself, shivering violently. Without a coat, the cold had penetrated to his bones and lowered his body temperature dangerously. Before leaving the crash scene he had waded in water and been made wet from the spraying mist of the fire hoses.

Margaret was shocked. The plane crash was all over the news, all that had been on for the last three hours, and she immediately connected him with it, knew he had somehow been caught in it.

He half grinned. "About that ad," he said, but no more. His legs were quaking and going out from under him.

"Cat!" She rushed to support him and felt his freezing skin and the shudders racking him.

"That ad," he said again as his eyes rolled back.

Two days later, still in bed, Carlson read through the newspaper accounts of the disaster and looked at the pictures of the wreckage and burning buildings. The cause of the crash had been a midair collision with another passenger jet, and that plane had gone down on Staten Island, killing eighty more people. It was the worst air disaster in history.

But the accounts of it and the pictures couldn't give any meaning to what had happened, not the way Carlson remembered it. You could read the newspapers and glean facts, but you couldn't feel what happened, you would never understand the feelings of anyone involved. There was no real understanding in the journalistic method.

Well, Carlson had been through the journalism thing. Still, an event of such consequence, a matter that concerned the deaths and affected the lives of so many demanded a better telling and a different accounting.

Carlson saw then what writing was about: It was one individual bringing to bear upon life his own views, his own personal feelings and ideas and thoughts, and doing it as honestly as he could. And as intelligently and sensitively as his mind and soul would allow. With luck, you express for others what they think and feel too. But the essential thing is what *you* think and feel.

When Margaret came in to change clothes, he was smiling.

"My," she said, "don't you look pleased. Feeling better?"

"Yes, fine."

As she pulled off her blouse, she turned away, self-conscious of her breasts before his eyes. "Then you'll be all right," she said, "while I go over to Jarvis's. Need an approval on their new brochure copy—okay?"

"Sure. I may get up."

"Don't do too much yet. You're still a little pale."

"I may scribble a little."

"Oh?" She looked at him curiously, then took a change of clothes with her into the bathroom. She had not undressed completely in front of him for many months now, which irked Carlson, and he knew she knew it. It was some kind of new, false modesty with her, as if she were trying to be a proper virgin again, or at least regress into some kind of adolescent sense of decency. Her body wasn't particularly that appealing to Carlson any more, so it didn't really matter, except a naked female body was interesting, even hers, and he would have rather enjoyed looking at it than not.

"Well, if you're going to scribble," she talked through the door, "you might look at that ad again. It's still where you left it, and they're still waiting."

When he didn't answer, she looked out the door. "But you don't feel like it yet, do you?"

"No." Then he figured he might as well get it out and over with right then. Later wouldn't be any better. He hesitated only slightly. "I'm through with ads, Margaret. I'm never going to do another ad again, and I'm not going to finish that one waiting."

She didn't blink, but stared a moment, then pulled her head back behind the door and finished dressing.

She came out, pulling at her stockings. "Would you mind repeating that? I'm not sure I heard you."

"No, I think you heard me. No more idiot fucking ads."

"And what's that supposed to mean?"

"Just what it sounds like. I'm through doing idiot fucking ads, period."

"Then what are you going to work at?" She was trying to contain her growing irritation and sound reasonable.

"Nothing that involves work for somebody else."

"But you're going to do something?"

"Not for somebody else, never again."

Margaret jerked her stocking and caused a run. "Oh, for God's sake, Jarl, make sense and quit sounding like a little boy trying to get his way!"

"I'm through working. Now, can you understand that?"

"All right, but what are you going to do, just lie in bed all the time and play with yourself? Or what?"

"I'm going to write."

"Shit!"

"Ah, ah." Carlson wagged his finger playfully at her. "You said a bad word."

Margaret sagged down in a chair beside the bed and frowned. "You're going to write, and not work, is that what you've decided?"

"Yes."

"And what am I supposed to do?"

"Whatever you want to. You can quit working too."

"And how are we supposed to eat? How do the children get fed, out of garbage cans? Where do we find their clothes, on trees? How the goddamn hell do we pay the goddamn rent?!" Her voice rose with her anger but she remained sitting.

"Don't worry about it."

"Don't worry?!" She stopped to control her voice and started again lower. "To merely ask the obvious questions seems to me only sensible. So let me repeat it sensibly: How are we going to live if neither of us works?"

"We'll manage. It doesn't matter."

"But how?"

"Some things will take care of themselves. The other things we'll take as they come."

"So, just that stupidly simple?"

"Why not? We'll manage and things'll work out."

She crossed her stockinged legs and rocked her foot. "Cat, you're out of your mind. I think something happened to you with that plane crash. Something knocked you in the head, didn't it? Or your mind snapped and you don't know it."

"Well, I think something did happen to me, but I wasn't conked in the head. I've never been more sane, or seen as clearly." He was sitting relaxed back against the headboard.

"You're going to have to explain it to me better than that, because I don't think I understand you now at all. I thought we were on the right track for once. You had gotten rid of some of your romantic notions about pretending to be a writer. You were working steadily. Well, at least working more often than not. We are doing well with the business. Now this!" She hit the arm of her chair and tried to contain her anger. "You can't stand for anything to be normal, can you? If everything's running smoothly, then you've got to throw your weight around and rock the boat. You have to upset everything and especially me. You can't just stand to see me halfway contented, can you? That's it, isn't it?"

Carlson patted the air between them. "Hold it, hold it. You want me to explain, then listen."

She folded her arms defiantly. "All right. I'll listen. Convince me."

"Well, I probably can't convince you, so I'm not going to try. But I'll try to explain, and you don't have to understand if you don't want to. That's up to you. I know what I'm going to do—what I have to do." He paused and, when she continued to hold her tongue, went on. "Now, I'm not purposely trying to upset you, and it's not something way back in the corner of my subconscious somewhere either, that I've got to upset you for some perverse reason. That's not it. I think it's more that I can see very clearly now how tenuous life can be, and sometimes how short, and how it should not be wasted—"

"Big discovery!"

"You want me to go on or not?"

"Go on. I'll try not to interrupt again." She pressed her lips tight and recrossed her arms.

Carlson went on. "I really tried to shut my mind off

284

and do those fucking ads, and not think about writing anymore. If I was nothing, then I was nothing. Why mope about it or flap my wings against the cage, just go on. I guess I figured the children needed a daddy, I don't know. I love them and I guess I tried not to cop out on them. But I was only a walking zombie. I was just trying to get through each day, and I figured I had maybe forty more years to get through and I'd do it. But—" He spread his hands and made a face.

Margaret sat for a moment with her brows pinched, staring at her knees. Then she took a breath and spoke. "Do you know what I'd really like to do at this moment?" She looked at him. "I'd like to go to that phone and call the loony farm and tell them to come and get you and take you away. Cat, you are crazy, stark raving mad."

He grinned. "You think so, huh?"

"Go ahead, sit there with that shit-eating grin on your face. You are. Something's snapped in your head. I can see it in your eyes. You've lost all sense of reality. You're suddenly living in some kind of fantasy world and you don't know it."

"I told you I didn't think I could convince you, and I'm not going to try."

"You want to be a writer so bad that you think you are. But you're not. If you hadn't burned that manuscript, you could pull it out and read it again and see. If anything, you're only a failed writer, and not even that."

"Oh, I remember that manuscript very well. I don't have to have it here to read again. I know how bad it was. But I was faking when I wrote it. I was copying a thousand other lousy commercial books, and there wasn't one true expression of myself in it. Not one honest thought."

She shook her head. "If you had any talent, it would have come out."

She picked her coat from the closet and started out the door. "I'm going to Jarvis's to get the brochure approved. I'll be back before Luke and Jean wake up, but in case I'm not, he can't have the Hershey in the refrigerator, only an apple if he has to nibble anything."

"I'll tell him."

She went through the door and paused, looking back at him sadly. "Remember, not the Hershey. He's eating too much candy."

Carlson nodded and she departed with the long look still too much on her face.

When Luke awoke from his nap, smiling and rosy-cheeked, and immediately snatched the Hershey bar, Carlson didn't try to stop him or say anything. The boy's face shone happily with his forbidden delight.

Twenty–Eight

FOR THE NEXT few days, Margaret kept her distance, held her peace, and watched. Carlson was only momentarily contrary, she thought. Give him a little time and he would get over it. He was just trying to put her through some sort of stupid ordeal, and if she fought him he would keep it up like a child, but if she gave him room he'd come around and regain his senses. She had read a book about men feeling trapped as they neared forty and it was a phase they had to go through, or at least most of them did. So Carlson, in her mind, was in that kind of boat.

She continued working as if nothing had changed.

Carlson, on the other hand, set up his typewriter in the spare room and started writing as if he had been doing it all his life and everything in the world favored it. He accepted Margaret's hands-off truce at face value. That is, he knew what she was thinking, and it wouldn't be peaceful long, but he couldn't help that. He was going to do what he said and let the chips fall. It was understandable that she couldn't believe he was a writer, a real writer. Who could? He had never shown himself as such. And she might never accept the fact, but that wasn't something he needed to concern himself about right then. He was on the right track, that he was sure of, and things would work out somehow. They would. And he had to believe that, or else how could he possibly drop everything else and go ahead? Or how could he even begin?

Fortunately, the first few days of the new beginning for Carlson were good ones. He felt as if he had gained a new sense of perception. Some of the most ordinary things around him suddenly appeared slightly altered and oddly interesting. A simple shoe revealed to him an intrinsic worth far beyond its material and construction. Its shape in suiting its function also seemed to transcend it. A cereal bowl was a masterpiece of design and utility. A piece of toast was at once a wonderfully rich morsel and a gift of rare qualities. And, personally, each awakening in the morning was a form of rejuvenation. The hard gray dawn breaking through the winter buildings across the city was an everlasting pure light. Even a bath seemed a magical cleansing of sorts. The water washing his body was so simple and life-sustaining.

These were just a few of the things Carlson felt in his new frame of mind and with his changed, now accurate, attitude about himself. His senses were alive to the sights and smells and sounds about him. It was as if all this acute sensitivity of his had been a garden bulb buried in some frozen earth through a long winter that had now sprouted and flowered in a radiant spring. It was a wonderful thing. And for a good span of days, it was a whole new world.

Carlson's feelings, of course, were very similar to those of a man abruptly being healed and well again after being very sick a long time. He experienced the miracle of re-birth.

But only for those first few days at the beginning. After a while, the most extreme sensations of his sudden rebirth-ing faded. When he settled back into the day-to-day churn, he was not the same as before. He had found himself positively, and now he had gotten his feelers out and was using them.

He was writing with an enthusiasm he'd never before known, and in a very real way he was putting his heart down on paper.

"I just want to know one thing," Margaret said. Two weeks had passed and she was sitting at the kitchen table while Carlson was washing the dinner dishes.

"Yes, what?" he said.

"I just want to know what the hell you're doing. I want to read what you have written so far."

He shook his head gently.

"Why not?"

"It's only a beginning. It's not ready for anyone to read."

Margaret looked at him hard. "You're afraid."

"No, I'm not afraid."

"Then let me read it."

"When it's finished."

"You're afraid because it's no better than your first lousy book."

"It's not like my first lousy book at all." He smiled.

Margaret stood up. "Look, Mr. Sensitive *Arteest*, if I'm the one paying for this roof over your head to keep the rain off your precious typewriter, and if I'm the one bringing in the beans so you don't fall down faint from hunger and are able to write, then I have a right to know exactly what the bloody hell you're doing in there, whether you're doing anything or not. For all I know you could be in there working out crossword puzzles. Now, dammit, you show me!"

Carlson folded his arms. "Nope, sorry."

"Then I'm going to see for myself!" She shoved her chair back, pushing it over, and strode furiously into the spare room where he had been writing.

Carlson waited with his arms folded casually and listened to the sounds of her rummaging around and searching. He knew she wasn't finding anything to read, not even in his wastebasket. The only things she was finding on his table were a solitary typewriter and a stack of clean typing paper and a yellow pad and pencils, and an ashtray that was also clean.

She came back to the kitchen flustered. "You're not even writing!"

"What I write every day I put away."

"To keep me from seeing it."

"To keep it private."

"Where?"

"Oh, c'mon, Margaret, let's stop this."

"You better tell me. I'll find it."

"This is silly."

"I'll find it, don't think I won't."

"It's not where you can find it." He picked up her chair and put it back at the table, but where she could sit in it. "Sit down."

"I have a right to know what you're doing. If you're crazy and writing drivel, I want to know."

"Here, sit down, please." He held the chair for her.

She sat reluctantly in defeat. "I need to know, don't you see?"

"Trust me."

"Trust you?" She looked up at him almost wildly and then buried her face in her hands and cried, "Oh shit, I wish I could!" Then she started sobbing heavily.

He put his hand gently on the top of her head and stroked her hair in genuine sympathy. He knew it was tough on her and he didn't want to hurt her, but what could he do?

"I'm sorry," he said, and for her sake he was.

Carlson had never been completely trusted by his neighbors. He was from what they thought of as "Down South," meaning the Tex-Mex border. In their eyes, he was a mad radical, insisting Hubert Humphrey was a phony. No one ever believed he had done all the things he claimed to have done, and in some cases they were right. He did tend to lie a bit. He would get carried away with how things *could* have been, or dress up the tale to make it more interesting.

He was also the first "house-husband" in the neighborhood, the Carlsons' business being run now by his wife. Carlson did some artwork or writing from time to time, but mostly he worked on his novel. After the first few months of euphoria, he did volunteer to help out at Grafiks whenever Margaret needed him. But afternoons, he was always in the park with his kids, and in the summertime he would take off entirely—two, sometimes three days a week, he would load up the station wagon with young mothers and kids and take off for the beach at Riis Park. Naturally, husbands who went to work every day in the city—as Brooklynites tend to call Manhattan—were suspicious.

Nor did anyone actually believe he was writing a novel, or, if he was, that it could amount to anything. He did not talk like any writer *they* knew. His early schooling was not good, he often mispronounced words, had never been in analysis or any other therapy, liked to play touch football, and spent a lot of Sunday afternoons watching football on TV, drinking beer from a can and munching a bag of Cheese Curls. And having smoked grass on the Mexican border when he was a boy and it was cheaper than tobacco, he did not find it the kind of fantastic or even especially pleasant experience most people his age in the neighborhood lauded it to be. He thought a lot of smart people sitting around a fucking candle at some party passing a soggy joint was silly.

Objectively, Carlson and Margaret did not seem any less happy than any of their neighbors. They had two remarkable children, their little business was thriving, a woman came every day to take care of their apartment and the kids when Carlson was busy with his book. They had the first color TV in their immediate crowd, a washer and dryer and butcherblock tops in the kitchen, window air-conditioners in their apartment and another in the studio.

They agreed politically, on plays, books, the raising of children, restaurants, vacations. There was little quarreling over the things their friends quarreled about. They even liked the same people, agreeing in fine harmony on whom they wanted to see and whom they didn't. When Luke started kindergarten and found himself in the same class, and in immediate sympathy, with the towheaded little son of an official of the American Communist Party, Carlson and Margaret both felt it would be quite all right to invite this couple to their home.

The man looked exactly like a member of the Politburo. His skin did not look as if he had been outdoors in the daytime in his life. He went to Moscow for free medical and dental treatment. If he was any example, you couldn't say much for Soviet dental care. The only time Carlson actually talked with him about Communism was over dinner at the Carlsons' apartment, a debate that continued until three in the morning, and was concluded by Mr. Red saying with some spleen at the door:

"I have met every kind of Communist in my life, but *you* are the first *Utopian* Communist I've *ever* met."

Carlson was rather flattered.

Sometime later they met another active Communist, a Phi Beta Kappa out of NYU, who was traveling under an assumed name, eking out a living as a copy reader somewhere, running discussion groups around New York. He was the only brilliant Communist Carlson had ever met. He was finally kicked out of the Party for being a homosexual, they were told. Or perhaps he was an infiltrator for the other side. Who the hell knew or cared.

When Carlson went to a benefit for Woody Guthrie with this man, he was surprised to see him greet the FBI agent in attendance, calling the man by his first name. They shook hands. There was nothing secret about it. It was all out in the open. Everyone knew everyone else at such meetings, and they all knew the FBI man too.

Carlson would never forget this man's face when they spoke one evening of the possibility of revolution in America. Carlson got excited and told his Communist friend how you might be able to make a fully automatic weapon by fooling around with the sear of a Winchester Model-100 semi-automatic hunting rifle. The man had paled. He did not want to talk about actually taking a gun and shooting someone. He wanted to talk about *revolution.* Carlson felt like a barbarian. The last thing you wanted to talk to Communists about were guns and bombs. Then they would think *you* were a provocateur in the pay of the FBI or the CIA, Carlson thought. The Communists he met were the least bloodthirsty folk in New York.

They had other friends who may have been Communists or Socialists, or who might have been just the gentle, entirely well-meaning people they seemed.

One was a woman Margaret had met through Grafiks, who was generous, alive, essentially happy. Her husband, who had spent a lot of time in Greece, knew Theodorakis, and had been close friends with Lambrakis, whose experiences were dramatized in the film Z, had been one of the first men subpoenaed by the House Committee on Un-American Activities. The experience had cost him his job with a prominent firm and his health declined greatly from the stress. He was able to work for another company at greatly reduced income. Still, they harbored a South American refugee writer in their cellar, and held suppers in their backyard to which a lot of old and young radicals found their way and dipped happily into the chopped chicken livers.

This woman and her husband took Carlson and Margaret to a dance sponsored by the Greek Democracia Club, held in a church auditorium in Chelsea.

The dance was the most genuine fun Carlson had in New York.

He found himself dancing in a great line of people in whose faces both joy and tragedy lived in perfect harmony, simultaneously.

An animated little old man in a brown suit with a wilted small orchid on his lapel—a man at least seventy—was there with the bride whom he had married just that morning. She was a plump little lady in a blue dress, with an orchid corsage on her bosom, a shy possessive, apologetic look in her dark eyes when she looked at her husband. They all toasted the couple's happiness.

In honor of the occasion, the old man urged a large, shy girl, who might never catch a husband because of a cocked-eye set in an otherwise entirely ordinary face, to get up and dance for them. The band was playing Oriental–Greek music. Carlson had not seen the girl dance all evening, not even with the women. She had sat on the same chair near the refreshment table.

Reluctantly, she let herself be led by the old man out onto the edge of the gym floor. She wore a short hand-crocheted dress. She lifted her hands above her head, clapped them, and began to dance. It was a bellydance, more exciting for her being fully clothed. She became the most sensual woman moving to music Carlson had ever seen.

Her hips snapped like a fifty-pound metronome, her

belly rolled as if she had swallowed an anaconda, breasts slewed marvelously around.

Carlson caught the old man's eye and they smiled, both feeling something so joyous they embraced happily and babbled something at one another.

The girl climbed backward, plump arms like mating serpents above her head, and sank to her knees on the floor, leaning backward until her head touched the floor. Her eyes were closed, her lips parted somewhere between a smile and a kiss.

The old man began throwing dollars on her belly, which now heaved and rolled and twisted so that to think of having your cock in there while she did that was dizzying.

Everyone threw dollars at her.

Carlson could fantasize about glamorous women, but he knew intellectually that was not what he wanted at all. Here was the whole thing, a *real* woman, not glamorous, who could make any old night or noon exotic. And she was a *Democrat!*

When she finished dancing, she gathered the money and went to place it in the box to support the Greek Democratic Movement, every dime. Then she went back and sat the rest of the evening in the same chair, chatting with the older women and the young girls who came to sit beside her from time to time.

When Carlson had another couple of glasses of wine, he drifted near and asked her to dance. She declined with thanks. He told her she was beautiful. She fixed him with her good eye, smiled, and said gently, "You have a very nice wife."

He replied, almost shrieking, though he kept his voice low, "But she can never dance like *you*."

The girl was embarrassed and blushed. She said hopefully, "She could learn."

He knew she never would. Any more than she would ever learn to like making love with him.

Twenty-Nine

CARLSON LOOKED AT his wife as she sat on the couch, come from her bath to hear the President talk about Russian missiles in Cuba. She was wrapped in the expensive chiffon peignoir her mother had given her when she had gone to the hospital to give birth to Jean. One pale knee was crossed over the other in the opening of the rustling pink robe. Her sturdy long calves tapered to large feet—bare—one foot planted solidly on the parquet floor.

She was a tall young woman who might have stepped out of a Social Realist painting—though not in that peignoir. There was also a quality about her of one of Léger's nudes.

In the Brooklyn Museum, when their son was about three years old, they had stopped to look up at LaChaise sculpture "Standing Woman"—the enormous, gorgeously fleshy bronze balanced in daring vulnerability on tiptoe—and Luke had said very loud:

"She looks like you, Mommie!"

Everyone near turned to stare at Margaret, smiled, and tittered as she grew very red of face. Carlson had hauled the boy away quickly, even as he craned back to catch the rear elevation of the sculpture.

He had not been able to conceal his amusement or the smile that covered an impulse to laugh. Margaret did not like to be laughed at, however fondly.

She could be a strikingly beautiful woman, he thought once again, perhaps for the hundredth time. He always promised her that, whenever she seemed to be feeling particularly unattractive.

She glanced at him now and her lips tightened. She touched the opening of her robe as if to cover her bare knees, but then did not, looked up again to meet his gaze, the left corner of her lips turned down to almost imperceptibly mock him.

"What do you want to do?" she asked in the seemingly unconscious, double-meaning way she had after a couple of drinks. After a couple of drinks she seemed to leer from a gap in her otherwise rigid personality.

"We ought to do something," she insisted. "Are we just going to sit here and let the Russians drop bombs on us from Cuba?"

"What do you want to do . . . send a telegram?" he asked, unable to mask the sarcasm in his voice. "Dear Mr. President. We heartily resent the possibility we will be blown to atoms because of you testing your courage and manhood in bullshit games with the Russians . . . Peace . . . Jarl and Margaret."

She jumped up in a crackling swirl of chiffon and nylon and flew angrily down the hallway and into the bathroom, banging the door behind her.

Carlson continued to sit in the big bucket chair in front of the new color TV with a child on each knee. Luke sat on his father's right knee trying to be interested in what the President had to say. Jean, who was three, did not feign interest. She curled in the crook of her father's arm, sucking her left thumb, eyelids drooping, one lovely, chewable bare arm resting atop Carlson's own. Her fingers idly plucked at the hairs on the back of his hand.

"You look mad, Papa," Luke observed. "You mad?"

Jean peeked from behind the cascade of her pale hair to see if he was mad.

"Papa's mad," she echoed her brother wetly around her thumb.

Carlson hugged them tight and kissed their cheeks.

"It's all right," he assured them. "I'm not mad at you."

"Will we die?" Luke wondered, his eyes very serious, darker than his mother's, unblinking.

"We will try not to."

"How?"

"Well . . . if there is going to be a war there will be a little warning. We will take a picnic basket down to the basement and build us a nest in the corner."

"Jean won't go," the boy said.

"No? Why not?"

"She's afraid of spiders. There's spiders down there."

The girl nodded her head in vigorous affirmation, sucking her thumb greedily.

"Spiders won't hurt you," Carlson assured her.

"They will," she said, without removing her thumb from her mouth. She tightened her arm around her father's neck and burrowed her face into his neck.

"Come on, you two, let's get you to bed," Carlson said.

"Carry me," the girl begged around her thumb.

"All right."

Luke held his hand as they went down the hall, Jean's bare feet and legs hung trustingly limp from her flowered nightgown.

Carlson and Luke tucked the little girl into her bed and kissed her good night.

When they left the room, they heard her call, "Momma! Momma! Come kiss me 'night."

Luke slept in what had once been a maid's room off the kitchen of the new apartment. It had its own toilet, bathtub, and washbasin. A tiny turtle named Seymour had been left in a scant quarter-inch of water in the sink, which was also plastered with hard toothpaste droppings and cluttered with a fleet of plastic toy boats.

The boy scampered into his bed, snuggling down with a blind Pooh Bear he had loved since his first Christmas.

Carlson wiped a lick of light brown hair from his son's brow, bent and kissed him.

"Good night, boy."

"Good night, Papa. Tell Momma to come kiss me."

"I will."

"I sure hope we don't have no war."

"I hope so too."

"I love you, Papa."

"I love you too, son."

He closed the door behind him, heading straight for his manuscript.

He went to the large storage closet in the entrance hall and dug out an insulated box they used when they took motor trips. There was also a fitted wicker picnic hamper, very expensive, which Margaret had bought. He carried the two things into the kitchen, placing the two hundred pages of his novel carefully at the bottom of the hamper. Then he opened cupboards and studied their contents.

He was loading readily edible canned goods, crackers, cookies, and cereals into the wicker hamper when Margaret came into the kitchen. She had brushed her hair and tied it back with a black ribbon. It descended in a shiny mahogany fall to her broad buttocks.

She went to Luke to kiss him good night, then backed into the kitchen, quietly closing the door after her.

"What are you doing?" she asked Carlson.

"Well, if we have to go to the cellar, and should survive the blast, we ought to have something to eat while waiting to see how the radiation affects us."

"Cat . . ."

He looked at the stuff he was packing, then looked at her and grinned.

"Yeah . . . Isn't this something? It's really crazy. It just makes you feel so fucking hopeless. There is nothing a person can *do*. Man, they don't *care!*"

"Shouldn't we fill the bathtubs with water before we go to bed?" she suggested.

He laughed. "They're not going to be bombs you can put out with tap water."

She shrugged and brought him a drink.

He realized she was on her way to getting drunk. Taking the proffered glass he slipped his other arm around her waist and drew her to him against the everlasting, seemingly instinctive resistance in her body.

"What?" she asked. "What do you think you are doing?"

The taunting, turned-down corners of her lips returned. Her eyes were lit with wry, patronizingly superior knowledge.

He kissed her wide mouth. Her lips were pressed tightly together, cold, tasting of Scotch. He persisted, trying to work the tip of his tongue between her lips.

"Don't," she muttered. The movement of her lips gave him an opening.

He set down his drink and slid his hand up from her waist to try to cover her left breast, so soft and spreading beneath the rustling, lined gauze of her peignoir, and the silky nightgown she now wore beneath it. She had put on an expensive black nightie her mother had sent her. It had been her mother's and still smelled of Arpège.

During his mother-in-law's last visit, she and Carlson had gone to dinner together and she had asked what was wrong between him and Margaret. He had tried to tell her as best he could. When she returned to Ohio, Margaret's mother had sent her daughter a box of expensive lingerie. She had bought the things for herself shortly before her husband had died and had not wanted to wear them afterward. All the stuff was new or barely worn. Margaret had never worn the nightgown before.

He held her away from his body to look at her. He wanted to say, "I love you."

"Cat . . ."

"I want you, Margaret. To hell with this. Let's go to bed."

"What good would that do now?"

"Good? It would do *good*. I want you. I want to be in you. This may be our last night on earth."

"You don't care about *me*," she accused.

"Yes I do. I love you."

He had lifted up the back of her robe and gown and stroked her big cool buttocks with both hands. Her arms formed a barrier across her breasts, her hands were on his chest as she leaned back watching his face.

"Your last night on earth," she sneered. "You wouldn't care who you could get into. You don't care about me. You just want to fuck. I could be anyone."

There was truth in that, he recognized to himself. But he insisted: "I do care about you, dammit. I want *you*. Let's be good to each other tonight. Maybe if we can do that on the last night we might live, we can begin to make our life together really good, if there is a tomorrow. All the ideas, all the political crap we talk about and talk about, what good are they now? Let's just try to make each other happy."

"We've never made each other happy."

"We can try!"

"I'm afraid it's too late, Cat."

"That's bullshit. We can love each other, be close."

"You don't want to be close," she cut in. "You never want to just be close. You never have. You want to fuck."

"What's wrong with that?" he agonized. "What could be closer?"

"You will never know."

"Aw, shit . . ."

He forcibly drew her close and leaned over the barrier of arms to kiss her. Her lips were again unresponsive.

"You want me," she repeated resignedly. "Okay . . . little boy. Since this might be your last night on earth." She grinned, the corners of her mouth twitching uncontrollably.

She kicked back the squat tumbler of Scotch until the ice hit her teeth.

"I wish you wouldn't drink so much," he said.

"You wish a lot of things."

She eyed his glass and silently asked him for it.

"Go ahead."

She drank it all down.

In the hallway leading to their bedroom she said: "I'm not putting my diaphragm in. This may be *my* last night on earth as well."

"What if you get pregnant?"

"I like having babies. That is the one thing we do together that I do like. Not that you have a lot to do with it. Did you know I liked having babies? I do. You can wear a rubber or get me pregnant. Oh! I found your little cache in the back of your drawer under your goddamned Army pistol. Don't worry, I wasn't snooping. I needed a handkerchief for Luke when he had his cold. Who were you saving them for?"

"No one. Those are old. They are left over from when you wouldn't wear your diaphragm, from years ago."

"Um. Your lies are pretty old, too, lover."

"I'm not lying. I swear."

"You swear." She stopped suddenly and turned and clasped his face strongly between her large hands. She smiled evilly, drunkenly, showing the gums of her teeth. "I don't care, anymore, baby. I just don't care."

With her back toward him, she slid the pink peignoir off her shoulders and let it fall to the new wall-to-wall carpet.

They had decorated the room in grape, red, and white. The red matched the cut-velvet spread on the bed. Carlson called it "upper-class Victorian bordello."

In the full-length mirror on the closet door he saw that her face was expressionless, her chin resting on her chest, shadowed by the curtain of hair that fell down over her neck and breasts. Highlights on the shiny black nylon of her nightgown accentuated her belly, its large, deep navel, her hips and bottom. Her heavy breasts were cupped in the lace bodice of her mother's gown.

"You look very sexy in that gown," he offered softly. "You never looked more beautiful to me."

She whirled to face him, loosing an enormous bellow and moan so startling that he sat bolt upright, his hair lifted on his neck. She looked as if she might try to kill him.

Jesus Christ! he thought.

Her lips were drawn back from her teeth, fists clenched. She took a couple of steps toward him, then cried out again, clasped the bodice of her gown in both hands, and ripped it off her breasts. She clawed to get the slinky material off her flesh as if it were burning her skin, sobbing, cursing, making sounds like something only half-human. Her long hair flew about as she tore at the nightgown. It was ripped open to the base of her belly. The dark brown wealth of her pubes peeped from the tattered cloth.

With the gown now hanging in tatters, she got her feet in it and with both hands and feet she tore and stomped it until she fought free of it, wadded it in her hands, and threw it violently into the wastebasket beside her dressing table. It overfilled the basket. It seemed a living thing that had been viciously destroyed.

Naked, she screamed: "I WANT TO BE WANTED FOR ME, YOU GODDAMN SON OF A BITCH!"

Her face looked like a Noh mask of rage.

"I *do!*" Carlson insisted, staring at her.

Because he was not sure what she would do next, he got off the bed and took a cautious step toward her. He thought she might really be crazy. She was breathing like an animal, her belly heaving deeply in a strange way.

"I want you, not a nightgown," he told her. "But it did look good to me. Sexy. What is wrong with that, for chrissake? We wear clothes to look good, or why not all dress like Mao Tse-tung? Don't you understand, Margaret . . . ?"

"NO! . . . You don't understand! You never have understood about me—YOU BASTARD!"

She got rid of another moan from some infernal repository of despair, and Carlson thought he could virtually smell and feel it as a hellish presence in the room.

She collapsed on the carpet, her belly slack and distended, breasts slewing over flaccidly, one upon the other. Her shoulders and face were curtained by her fine dark hair. It fanned out around her on the carpet. She pounded the carpet weakly with both clenched fists.

He went to her and knelt on one knee and stroked her hair over her bare shoulder.

"Margaret . . . I'm sorry. I don't mean to hurt you. I really don't." He stroked her hair down to her waist. "I just want us to be happy. Don't you know that?"

She moaned again in a human range. "Oh, Cat, shut up. Just shut up, will you? Shut up."

He stroked her hair over her left breast. He liked to feel her naked skin through the fine scrim of her hair. The big nipple became erect beneath his palm.

"This is me," she said. "DAMN YOU, LOOK AT ME!"

He looked up at her face.

"I know I'm ugly. You can't bear to look at me. But

this is me, goddamn you. I'm not beautiful and never will be. I'm tired of your telling me I am beautiful. I'll never be beautiful. Not in the way *you* want me to be. *I* think I am beautiful. I have always thought I was beautiful. You don't want me the way I am. I hate you! This is me. Come on, you bastard, fuck me, if you're going to. Come on, make me happy. You can't. You never will."

He continued to stroke her body, smoothing her hair down over her belly until it led his hand to the coarser grove covering her sex. Her cunt was fleshy, firm, tight. But she kept her thighs clamped together. He tried to kiss her. She let him nibble her lips for a moment, then turned her face away from him. Her breath was peaty with the smell of Scotch. Her eyes were open, warily watching him.

"Come on, Margaret. I'll rub your back."

"You never just rub my back. You're always after something more."

"Hell, Margaret, if we had some kind of normal sex life I could just rub your back sometimes."

"Black nightgowns are normal? Oh shit, come on, do it and get it over with. I'm tired. I want to sleep."

On her last night on earth she would want to sleep.

She got up and he helped her to the bed. She lurched slightly. She sat heavily on the bed, then lay back as he sat beside her. One arm was flung over her eyes. Her nude body was there for him to use, if not enjoy. Her dark bush reflected points of light and he flashed curiously on her mother's expensive fur coat.

She said nothing.

He bent and kissed her unresponsive lips beneath the cool belly of her arm. Bending farther, he gently brushed her hair off one breast and kissed the soft, flattened globe for a long time, lipping and licking the nipple on which their children had fastened so eagerly as babies.

He freed her other breast from the weight of her body, turned her more toward him, gathered both tits in his hands, and loved them together.

Though she continued to cover her eyes with her arm, small spasms rippled over her belly, her thighs jerking involuntarily. He fastened on her far breast, bearing over her, and caressed her thighs, touched her sex.

Suddenly she wrapped both strong arms around his head and held him tight, her entire body quivering, rigid. There was a feeling that even as she experienced what should be pleasant sensations, something in her fought to resist them. He felt that she was afraid to let go for fear of somehow seeming a fool.

"Just do it, Cat."

He felt nervous, unready, yet wanting to be in her. He got between her legs. His cock was not fully erect. There was a painful congestion in his testicles, his loins felt clotted, but nervously so, confusingly so. His feelings were not together. He hardly ever had a full erection with her. That had begun to worry him.

From beneath his pillow he took the condom and rolled it on his less-than-hard penis. She was wet and the rubber was lubricated. He entered her easily. He caught his breath at the closeness and warmth of her in there.

On this, perhaps their last night on earth, he tried to go slowly, excite her with movement within her. Just as he felt himself growing more fully erect, she began to move—no more than three or four deep, slow moves. She clamped down on him and he could not hold back.

"Sorry," he apologized.

He rose to look at her.

"Sorry," he said again.

Her arm still covered the top half of her face.

As he withdrew from her, his cock came out of the condom, stripped from him by the grip of her vagina. The limp Latex skin hung disgustingly between her legs. He quickly plucked it free, palmed it, and rolled onto his side of the bed. He dropped the rubber containing the liquid bulb of his semen onto the carpet beside the bed. His head ached and he covered his eyes with his arm.

"Why don't you just *leave?*" she spit out. "Just get out and leave me alone? I don't need you. We don't need you. Take fifty or a hundred a week from the business, go write your fucking book, paint, find someone to fuck who'll parade around in black lingerie and do all the shit I won't do for you."

She rolled off the bed, her feet hitting the floor solidly, and brushed past him, one arm extended to fend him off if he made a move to stop her.

In the doorway, without looking back, she yelled: "I WANT A DIVORCE."

He followed her, was behind her when she turned into the library-dining room, and on through the swinging door into the kitchen.

"I'm not leaving the children," he vowed. "I'm not leaving a child of mine ever again. If you want a divorce, *you* take fifty or a hundred a week and leave."

"You couldn't run the shop without me," she snorted.

"That's probably true," he admitted, "even if I want to try."

She poured herself a drink, and began to smile wisely, though her eyes were sunken and dark, shiny with tears.

"I'm not leaving," he said again. "The children are as much mine as yours. I have done as much for them as you have. In many ways, maybe more. I figure it equal."

She looked at him, lifted her glass, and offered a bitter toast: "To equality."

"Shit," he said.

"Indeed, Jarl. Indeed."

Carrying the bottle, she moved again through the swinging door. He caught it on the backswing, flung it open and followed her.

She plopped on the corner of the couch and stared out the window, drinking Scotch.

The apartment was cold. The landlord had the heat set at the lowest legal degree. The ancient furnace had broken down half a dozen times since they moved in. By the time the heat worked its way up to the fourth floor it was criminally deficient.

Carlson took the bottle from her grasp, drank from it, and handed it back to her.

"Look, Margaret," he began levelly, hoping to initiate a rational discussion. "I am not leaving. You can if you want—Wait! Look, we both love the kids. We are finally starting to have enough money to live fairly well. We have time we never had before. Intellectually we agree on almost everything. What's wrong with us?"

"I just don't love you." She turned to smile bitterly at him.

"Aw . . . no. That's crap. It's just that we have come to the end of the romantic illusions. You aren't Sleeping Beauty and I am not Prince Charming, but we are pretty goddamned exceptional individuals. Now, why don't you like to make love with me?"

"You don't make love."

"I do. I try. I want to make love. You just want me to get it over with."

"Poor, poor baby."

"Margaret, come on. What's wrong with me?"

Slowly her face turned toward him, her smile spread maniacally until she looked like a character in a horror movie.

"Your penis is too small for me, I guess," she told him.

"Too small?" he heard himself ask through the subsiding ringing of blood in his ears. "What the hell do you know about penises?"

"You'd be surprised," she replied, and resumed her watch on the river.

He jerked her around to face him. She dropped her glass, spilling liquor on the couch. "Don't," she cried, now genuinely afraid.

"What the fuck do you mean?" he demanded.

"You aren't the only one who can have an affair!" she yelled back.

He had never admitted to her he'd had an affair, no matter how persistent her suspicions had been.

He grabbed her shoulders with both hands and shook her as the manic grin again spread across her face. She seemed to be laughing and crying and berating him all at once as he sought to shake her apart. Her breasts jumped and lobbed around.

"I'll shake your damned tits off!" he vowed.

Flecks of saliva flew from her lips, touched his face and body.

"KILL ME! GO AHEAD, KILL ME!" she screamed. "YOU'VE ALWAYS WANTED TO!"

"BULLSHIT!" he yelled back. "CAN'T FUCK ME! FUCK SOMEBODY ELSE! YOU GODDAMNED CRAZY BITCH!"

Her eyes started to go funny. He threw her back hard against the corner of the couch and heard her teeth clack as she recoiled off the springs.

"Who?" he wheezed.

She lay asprawl, her head tilted awkwardly onto her chest, saliva running slightly from the corner of her mouth.

"Don't pass out, damn you!" He shook her.

"Leave me alone . . ."

"Wake up!" He slapped her.

She screamed and curled to protect herself. "DON'T!"

He slapped her protecting arms. "Who?!" He tore her arms away from her face, caught her wrists.

"You're-hurting-me!"

"I'll smash your goddamned face, you pig. Who?!"

"Go ahead!" she challenged him.

"Tell me!"

"You are *hurting* me, damn you!"

He released her wrists.

"I want to know about this," he persisted.

"I'll *bet* you do."

He raised his arm to smack her again and she shrieked and coiled awkwardly to protect herself.

"I'm not going to hit you again," he said bitterly, suddenly disgusted with her and himself.

The bottle had been knocked over on the floor. The smell of alcohol filled the chilly room.

"He's big enough for you, huh?" he sneered.

She struggled to sit up. "Umm . . ."

She reached down and found the bottle and started to lift it to her lips. He saw her lips prepare to receive it, and slapped it spinning from her hand. He slapped her face repeatedly with both hands. She fell backward, her long brown hair swinging like curtains in a dream, back and forth across her clenched wet face.

"GO ON!" she encouraged him. "GO ON! HIT ME! HIT ME! HIT ME!"

When he stopped, she chattered: "You're so funny, Cat. You're really pathetic . . . Don't you want to hit me some more? Come on, hit me some more. Make you feel big and strong."

His lips were twitching. Amazingly, he had an erection. He saw her eyes fix on it.

"You stupid bitch. You and your kind don't know anything. You could get yourself killed and you don't care or know."

He pushed her down, roughly lifted her right leg onto the back of the couch, forcing her left to remain with its foot planted on the floor with his knee against her knee, and got between her widely spread legs and entered her.

They fucked wildly, cursing each other, shouting, weeping with anger and frustration.

He found her lips with his own. Her lips felt swollen, hot and wet. She kissed him back, wrapping her arms and legs around him, bit his lips, almost tore loose his tongue, let go with such ferocity that even as he came he felt overwhelmed by her passion.

"I HATE YOU!" she screamed.

"I LOVE YOU!" he yelled back, hating her.

She thrust beneath him so furiously she was lifting him. Something snapped deep in the Hide-a-Bed couch. She came with a loud sound like a man who has been stabbed. He was as shaken and disgusted with her in the full throes of her passion as he had been when she had been coldly passive.

If there is someone who can handle that, let him have her, he thought.

"Get off me," she said hollowly, sounding sober.

He raised himself above her upon the full extension of his muscular arms.

She yawned and stretched, extended both legs until her entire body was quiveringly rigid. Then she relaxed suddenly with a sigh. She tapped him on the back.

"Let me up."

He rolled off her and sat on the couch.

Margaret got up. Her wide, dark bush was at Carlson's eye level, their fluids slick on both of her pale thighs.

They became aware that Luke was standing in the open double doors between the dining room and the foyer. A wedge of his tummy was exposed between the tops and bottoms of his sleepers.

"Has the war started?" he asked sleepily.

Margaret swept a fringed throw from the back of the couch, wrapped it around herself, and went to the boy.

"You get back to bed," she said.

"I heard a lot of noise," he replied. "We going to the basement?"

"No. Your papa and I were just having an argument. It's all over. You get back to bed."

"I wish you and Papa wouldn't fight. It scares me."

"I know. I wish we didn't too. But we do. Come on, night-night."

"Night, Papa," he called from the kitchen door.

"Night, son," Carlson called back.

"If we have to go to the basement, you won't forget me?"

"We won't. I don't think we will have to go," Carlson called to the boy.

When Margaret did not return to the front room immediately, he went into the kitchen and found her warming up the glass pot of coffee.

"I'm not leaving," he told her.

"Okay."

"I mean it. I'm not going through that divorce shit. I think before I went into court and saw you get custody of the children just because you were their mother, I'd kill you. I really think I would. You know about my boy in Wichita. I'd kill you before I'd lose these children too."

She carried the coffee and her mug into the dining room-library. He got a cup and followed her.

The room was a good one. Shelves he had made were full of books that meant something to them both. Paintings

309

of the children on two natural wood plaques hung above a Mexican bureau.

Margaret stretched her arms over her head, the shawl opening over her breasts. Both nipples became erect as he watched. She stood up and yawned, the throw opening to reveal her body.

"You don't know how interesting this has all been." She patted him on the head. "Good night . . . Stud."

She turned and started toward the bedroom.

"Where are you going?" he demanded.

"To bed. It has been a very trying evening."

"To hell!" He leapt up. "What about your great goddamned lover?"

"Oh . . . Like I told you." She turned and smiled, and the throw she had around her opened again as she raised hands about a foot apart.

"*To hell with that!*" he bellowed and went after her when she turned down the hallway. "I want to know who the sonofabitch is."

"I'm not going to tell you," she flung back over her shoulder.

"You bitch! What the fuck?"

"What the fuck indeed," she echoed.

"*Goddamn you, Margaret,*" he roared as she turned into their bedroom.

"Yes, goddamn me."

"You lousy stinking piece of shit!"

"Sticks and stones, baby. . . . "

He caught her by the arm as she tried to go by and pulled her close to him.

"You suck his big cock too?"

"Let me go, Cat." She would have bruises where he held her.

"*Do you?!*"

"Cat!"

He had gone down on her but she would never go down on him.

"You scumbag."

He flung her against the doorjamb. She rolled on

around it into the bathroom and locked the door behind her.

He punched the door, splitting the panel and hurting his knuckles so much he yelled, turned, and punched the wall with the same hand, breaking a fist-sized hole in the plaster.

When she came from the bathroom his hand was already beginning to swell. She had put on her old tatty nightgown, stained and burst of seam. She swept past.

"Hurt yourself?"

She climbed into bed with her back toward Carlson, who stood in the doorway, torn between begging her to tell him who the guy was and putting ice on his throbbing hand. Others would have killed her. She was so god-damned careless about herself. *He* could have killed her.

"Tell me who he is," he demanded.

She took a deep breath, sighed. Looking out the window, she said: "There isn't anyone. There never has been. I lied."

"*What!*" The question ached in his throat. "*Why!*"

"I couldn't resist it. When I saw how you reacted when I told you your penis was too small for me, I just couldn't help myself."

"How do I know you aren't just saying this now to make me feel better?" he asked suspiciously.

She shrugged. "Why would I want to make *you* feel better?"

He considered that.

"For God's sake, Cat . . . *Look* at me. Who would want to have an affair with me?"

"Plenty would."

"No, they wouldn't. *You* wouldn't. If we weren't married, you wouldn't want me."

"You could be very beautiful if you wanted to," he insisted.

He touched her hair.

"I'll just hold you," he said.

"Promise?"

"Yeah. Promise."

311

His hand was really swelling. He was afraid there might be some bones broken in it. With his left hand he stroked her long hair, smoothing it down over her shoulders.

"You were really lying?" he asked.

It was harder to conceive of her lying than it was to imagine her having an affair.

"I was lying, Cat. Now, please, can I go to sleep?"

"Yeah. But why did you say my cock was too small for you?"

"I don't know. It just seems to be."

"Did it when we were on the couch?"

"Cat, *please!* I don't *know.* I can't even remember. I hated it."

"If we really made love, it could be good. I know it could."

"But we don't, do we? Please, Cat, I'm exhausted."

He stroked her hair until she fell asleep.

He felt curiously less secure about her confession that she had lied than he had been threatened by her lover with the big dick.

God!

He got up carefully from the bed and went into the bathroom and sat on the stool to smoke a cigarette. He lifted his cock in his puffed right hand and studied it. He played with it until it became hard and measured it with Margaret's big tortoiseshell comb. It was larger than average, he was certain, unless what he had read about such things was inaccurate.

The dongs on Greek and Roman statues were, if to scale, certainly of an average he had beaten considerably. But then there were those ancient pornographic drawings and carvings which told you men had been wanting gargantuan cocks since before Christ was a carpenter. The need had to stem from something.

He walked into the living room to turn on the radio. He wanted to find out if the decision to drop the bomb had been made while he and Margaret were screaming about big and little cocks.

It seemed from the news broadcast that Khrushchev

and Kennedy had resolved their differences better than he and his wife. For the time being, Carlson's children were going to be allowed to grow up.

The next morning before venturing out into the world Carlson looked at himself in the mirror. Margaret had just left, taking the children to school, and would go on to the office. He studied himself in the full-length mirror. Then he took a handful of handkerchiefs from the open bureau drawer that was within reach and stuffed them down into his shorts, forming the things into an impressive wad, thinking about Hemingway's bullfighters who padded themselves to look more manly in the skintight suits of lights. He studied himself in profile, moved a bit to "show a leg," as they used to put it in a foppish time not so dissimilar to the present. He decided to wear the handkerchiefs that day.

At the elevator he met the very pretty wife of an earnest young man who worked for a large New York insurance company. Her eyes strayed repeatedly to the bulge in the left leg of Carlson's trousers. She licked her lips nervously and her face seemed flushed slightly as they chatted and damned their landlord.

Olé! he thought.

That afternoon when he took the kids to the park some of the mothers began to look at him as if he were a new person they had never really looked at closely before. He was wearing a pair of the new tight chinos that were becoming fashionable even for men over thirty.

He wouldn't wear the handkerchiefs all the time, just now and then, just often enough to implant the idea that he was very well hung. It was a revelation to see the reaction in the faces of women when they would actually flash on it, or look quickly away. Women wore falsies, didn't they? he argued. There were ads in the paper for girdles with padded bottoms to give women fake *keisters,* to "reveal the natural lines of the body."

The wad was particularly effective on crowded subways

where a woman would look up and find this obviously big cock virtually in her face. Women with dates or their husbands began to take an interest in Carlson, often flirting even as they clung to their old man's arm. It was both heady and saddening. Heady for the open desire in their faces, the wonder, a clot of all the romantic conditioning which now had been turned wrongside out into pornographic romanticism. But it was personally sad because he knew they were turning on to a wad of Abraham & Straus's best linen.

How did those bullfighters handle it when it came time to skin out of their suits of lights? Carlson wondered. Certainly there had to be some disappointment in the *señoritas'* eyes.

Promenading along Fifth Avenue one day, he stepped off a curb at Fifty-second Street and one member of a three-piece buttoned-up duo was heard to say as they passed behind his back: "That's what you call walking softly and carrying a big stick."

A very attractive but entirely ordinary-looking young woman smiled with open joy at Carlson and clearly said, "Ummm-ummm!" as they passed. She stopped before an airline office window full of sunny, exotic temptations to which you could be transported at excursion rates. Honolulu! Carlson thought of the back streets and slums of Honolulu, and how the dreaming young woman would have felt when she found out what the *real* thing was like.

From Tiffany's popped a very well-dressed woman about fifty with a sweatered miniature something on a leash who took one look and sniffed as if she had been insulted.

Carlson thought he had begun to go a bit overboard on the quantity of handkerchiefs he was sporting. He was now up to five. One of the famous *matadors* Hemingway had written about had been an *eight* handkerchief man.

A gorgeous raven-haired showgirl type, six feet tall, with a black fur collar turned up to frame her perfectly made-up face, was walking by with an immaculately barbered, much older man. She fixed Carlson with her dramatically fringed dark eyes even before he spotted her. When he noticed her, she looked purposefully up from his trousers to his eyes, and pointedly, slowly, ran her enamel-pink tongue lasciviously all around her glistening open full lips.

My God! What if he had a cock equal to the phony he was flaunting in the face of the budding sexual revolution? He could be a fucking star! He hadn't known so many women really looked at men's cocks. A halfway decent looking chap with a big cock could form a harem during lunch hour on Fifth Avenue that would keep him busy for weeks.

He meditated on the injustice of the distribution of superficial physical traits and sexual apparatus that made him doubt again the existence of a wise and loving God. All those people tinkering with DNA toward cloning a healthier, happier, brainier, super individual had better be working out a fairer standard of sexual properties or they were just wasting their time.

Thirty

BY SEPTEMBER, 1966, Carlson had finished 1,200 pages of his novel.

He was anxious now to show it and have it recognized. After all, he had not written those words to conceal his thoughts, but to reveal them. And the only way to do that was to have them published, to find a publisher.

These 1,200 pages before him were good enough for any publisher, he felt. All one would have to do was take some time and read, and then, Carlson had no doubt, his talent would be confirmed. The promise he very realistically felt inside himself would be fulfilled. A moment in the sun, he hummed.

But how to go about it? He had no contacts in the literary world. No one who could advise him, or recommend his writing. And there was certainly no how-to-do-it kit to help him. Looking back later on his initial brush with the literary world, he could not believe how innocent and naive he had been at the beginning of his odyssey. These early efforts to be published accounted for much of his later bitterness.

He decided to simply deliver the manuscript himself. That way he could meet the editor personally, know that his work was in safe hands and going to be considered. Also, he could make a good impression, he thought. He could put his best foot forward when he had to, and if he made a good personal impression on the editor, well, what would that hurt?

He had a copy made of his material, picked the name of

the publisher of an author he admired, and looked up the address in the phone book.

When he entered the publisher's door he was a little taken aback. The furniture was shoddy, there was no decor, and the reception area was a small stingy space between the long, drab hallways. He had anticipated openness and opulence and a rich thick carpet. That's the way publishers' offices had been portrayed in the movies. But here was only a scruffy brown desk for the receptionist, a bare floor, and an old steam radiator against the wall. There were no windows, much less draperies, and only a posterboard onto which several book jackets had been carelessly tacked. The names of the books he recognized, of course. They were current best sellers, or books by well-known authors, but in such a poor setting and so artlessly displayed they seemed shoddily out of place. He should have had a premonition right then, but he didn't.

Instead, he consoled himself with the guess that the editors' offices down the hall had to look different, better, and more dignified. That the trappings of class and taste had been reserved for them.

He squared his shoulders and straightened his tie and stepped to the desk. The woman behind it was busy with the phone, transferring and holding calls, and making notes. She was no longer young and depressingly plain, with an old man's sweater draped around her shoulders, and her hair was a fright.

Carlson waited patiently with his manuscript under his arm and pretended to be easy.

The woman looked up with her finger still on a hold button. "Yes?"

"How do you do?" Carlson tried his most engaging smile. "My name's Carlson—"

"Just a minute." She went back to the phone.

After taking several calls she looked up again. "Oh, yes, your name is—?"

"Carlson. Jarl Carlson." He might have included his middle initial, but saying it was more pretentious than writing it, so he didn't.

She wrote down his name and asked at the same time, "You want to see who?"

He realized he didn't know and fumbled, "Well, the editor. Or editors. I mean, I've written a novel. That is, I've started writing one—" Then he added limply, "Here is the manuscript." He offered the thick envelope under his arm.

It made no impression on her face. She paused with her pencil. "If you'd care to leave your number—"

"I wanted to deliver the manuscript personally if I could. If you don't mind."

"The usual procedure is to submit your material through the mail along with a self-addressed stamped envelope. Excuse me." She went back to the phone.

Carlson stood foolishly and felt a peculiar ire rising along the back of his neck. But he forced himself to wait.

When the woman looked up from the phone again she seemed surprised to see him still there. "Yes?"

"Look, can I see the editors or not?"

"If you don't have an appointment—" She let it hang and shrugged.

"All right, let me make an appointment."

"To see who?"

"I don't know, to see one of your editors. Which one should I see?"

"I suppose that would depend. If you would care to leave your number, I'll pass it on. Perhaps an appointment can be arranged with one of our editors.

"Which one?"

"I'm sorry, I'm not allowed to give out names." She showed no emotion. She was being neither rude nor polite, merely impenetrable.

Carlson's patience slipped to the floor. "Look, why the hell can't you just buzz somebody on that damned phone of yours and ask if they'll see me. I've got my writing with me." This last as if it were the golden key to the palace.

She was not fazed. "I'm sorry, sir, everyone is busy at the present time. If you'd care to leave your number—" She poised her pencil to write thoughtlessly.

Carlson considered several obscene things he might

say to that woman's plain face to shatter it, but he knew the choicest he could utter would be useless. That face could look at the worst kind of human suffering and never blink an eye.

But he did say confidentially, leaning closer, "You know what? I bet your cunt is covered with cobwebs, isn't it?"

She didn't blink but mechanically went back to her phone as if Carlson had never spoken.

He was out on the street in another minute, feeling somehow locked out of someone else's garden, as if he had been an intruder they had seen coming and had hurriedly closed the gates before he could get there. A high, solid iron gate. He also felt like the kid he had once been from the wrong side of the tracks where the "better" people had shunned him.

But he wasn't really that same kid anymore and he knew it. Don't fall back and get hung up on that old psychology, he told himself; go on, you're going to run into shit here and there, go on.

He decided *that* particular publisher was an exception and others had to be different. After all, they were looking for good books, good talent, weren't they? They published crap, sure, but weren't they also in competition for the better stuff too? Sure they were.

You just had to get past the myopic sentinels at the front gate, that's all.

Carlson ducked into a phone booth and found the addresses of two more well-known publishers in the immediate area.

But these two publishers turned out to be almost a copy of the first. He was treated blandly but without interest by the receptionists and not allowed to see an editor, or even given an editor's name, as if that had to be kept a big secret, and nobody knew. He was instructed pointlessly each time to mail in his material, and to *be sure* and include a self-addressed stamped envelope, or they couldn't be responsible.

It was obvious publishers were falling all over themselves *not* fighting for the privilege to read anyone's first novel, and especially if it was only the beginning of a first novel the would-be writer had yet to finish. That sort of tidbit didn't cause them any excitement at all.

One receptionist did volunteer, "Well, you see, Mr. Carlson, we receive so many manuscripts each week, it does keep us all quite busy just processing them all."

Processing, the way she said it, had a bureaucratic businesslike sound to it that seemed to exclude art entirely. And *busy* sounded too coldly industrious.

And Carlson thought, *Busy, my ass. Don't hand me that shit. You're all jacking off like everybody else. You're all sitting on your editorial hemorrhoids picking lint out of your punctuated navels!*

"So what do I do?" Carlson asked the last receptionist. "I mean, besides going through the mail, how the hell does a writer get to an editor?"

"You might try an agent."

"An agent?"

"Yes, agents are generally who we work through."

"And how do I get an agent?"

"Well, I don't know, I guess that's up to you." She had tried to smile.

"Can you recommend one to me?"

"I'm sorry, sir, we're not allowed to do that."

It was absolutely amazing.

Carlson then tried two literary agents he found listed in a directory in the public library, selecting their names out of fifty others because of their Park Avenue addresses, and because they somehow sounded literarily impressive and vaguely familiar.

The first, when he called, said they weren't taking on any new clients at the present time, sorry. Very coolly.

The second consented to let him send them his partial manuscript and promised to respond within two weeks, maybe sooner.

Carlson was guarded but couldn't help feeling he had gotten his first break. And he waited in anticipation. He even circled the date on his calendar.

Then four weeks went by without a word.

When Carlson finally called, no one at the agency seemed to remember his name or his material exactly, but they were sure his manuscript was being *considered*, and that was surely the cause for the stupid delay. He needn't be too worried. When a manuscript was turned down, they said, that didn't take any time at all. It was when one had possibilities, or was being accepted, that careful considerations had to be made. Time was necessary in that case.

Carlson was hopeful again even as he suspected he was being given the runaround. All they had to do was read his damned stuff, just a few pages, that's all. They'd see.

Dammit, some sonofabitch could take two minutes and read twenty pages, couldn't he? That's all the hell he was asking really, just for the smallest slice of attention. You know: Hey, take a look, will ya, just a quick peek, if I've wasted your time, then I'll cut off my head.

After another four weeks, however, and still no word, he went to the agency.

They didn't remember him, but the agent's assistant searched another room and finally retrieved his massive manuscript which had never been opened, much less "considered." The assistant was sorry, of course. It had apparently been misplaced and somehow overlooked, but they were *so busy*, she said.

Carlson threw away his calendar.

And he started sending his manuscript to the publishers through the mail.

In the publishing trade this method is referred to as "over the transom," a term carried over from the old days when banks and businesses had windows with bars and transoms through which papers were passed. And for the most part, these unsolicited manuscripts mailed simply to the "Fiction Department" of a publisher, not to a specific editor, are stacked in an empty room and ignored. Perhaps once a month, or occasionally, some editor will wander in and thumb a few, scan a page or two, but never with much expectation or hope of even nominal consideration. It's a known fact that almost all the material sent in over the transom is pretty inept and awful and no publisher will ever find a thing he can use in all that junk if he looked for a thousand years. Consequently, they consider it a waste of time, although they don't usually let that out to the newspapers. It would make them appear too hard-hearted and insensitive. And too much what they are. Besides, they have enough offerings from reputable agents and already established authors to fool with the no-hopers and idiot aspirants and little old ladies trying to immortalize their cats and lap dogs.

This was the prospect Carlson faced, and he felt in his soul it was hopeless, but he wasn't aware of the reality. He didn't know the numbers involved. He simply resigned himself to sending his manuscript out, and when it was returned after several weeks with a reject slip, slipping it into another envelope and sending it out again. What else could he do?

The main thing was the writing itself, his need to write the best he could, and he had done that. When the rejects started coming in, he disregarded them. Whether anyone else knew it or not, he was a writer. And nothing could stop him from being what he was. "To thine own self be true," old Bill Shakespeare wrote, and Carlson was following that line in regard to his talent as close as he could.

Yet he could not start on his next book while he was waiting for the verdict on the first. He knew he was going to write, beginning with a scared fourteen-year-old who lied his way into enlistment in the Navy, but he could not bring himself to his typewriter.

He spent long stretches in front of the TV, staying up long into the night so he would sleep late and kill at least part of the day with unconsciousness. That way he wouldn't have to think until the mailman came each afternoon, either bearing nothing or still again his manuscript.

He sat now before the flickering screen in his dark living room. The children were curled in their beds. Margaret was snoring in the bedroom at the end of the hall—dreaming of what? He had no ideas at all of what she might dream. After all these years? God! Outside, along the park, the junkies and faggots idled beneath the lights, looking to score a fix or something like love.

Carlson sat, sipping a beer and smoking, staring at the color TV. The Late Late Movie was featuring some Roman nonsense with an Italian actress with big tits.

He walked to the kitchen, took a bottle of orange juice from the refrigerator and drank from the jar. There were three big cucumbers in there. He took the largest and held it for a moment at his fly. He imagined fucking Margaret with the thing. It was a crazy notion all the way. Maybe he was slowly going insane. He tossed it back quickly and closed the refrigerator door.

They had received some stuff in the mail after subscribing to *The Evergreen Review*, brochures offering many kinds or dildos and vibrators for the male and female called "Marital Aids." There were rubber cocks in "natural flesh tones," which looked to have been copied from Oriental pornographic prints, enormous, gnarled, and veined, which came with a suspender belt to attach the things to you, with or without a clitoral stimulator attachment. Obviously there could be no tactile sensation for the person who wore such a thing, male or female, only the satisfaction of artificially fucking someone out of their mind. Who the fuck would want that?

His eyes wandered to the butcherblock breakfast bar, which held a note from Margaret.

Jarl:
The kids and I are going to Mother's for a few days. She has gone into the hospital for another operation. We will leave early in the morning. I'm sure you can manage . . .
                                                          Margaret
P.S. You will have to take the newsletter proofs to Charlie. Be nice and invite him to lunch. You might also call on Sid and E.C.A. They like to know there is a man around for some reason.

He had been so preoccupied she had gotten into the habit of leaving him notes to make sure her messages got through.

He sniffed. He was getting a summer cold. Rather than disturb Margaret, he opened the studio couch in the living room. It was always made up.

Margaret had packed for herself and the kids the night before. In the morning Carlson helped her carry the bags down to the wagon. The kids were excited to be going to visit their cousins. There was a pad in the back of the wagon on which they could nap if they got tired, and an assortment of toys and games.

Standing on the curbing without socks, his ankles feeling quite cold, Carlson waved as they drove off. The kids' faces in the back window were happy. As the car receded along the park, he saw them all dead in the tangled wreckage of the blue wagon out on some turnpike and felt a wave of utter sadness, shock, and then a cheap thought that such a thing might be the end of his problems. But it was only Margaret he wished dead, not the kids—never.

As the day wore on, Carlson did as he had been told, delivered the proofs, took Charlie to lunch, called Sid. Then he went back home and waited for the mailman. Nothing this time. He turned on the TV.

Toward evening, still sniffling from his cold and with the television blaring behind him, he began to prowl the dark apartment like an animal in a cage. He had never before realized how comforting the sounds and sight of his family had been. Alone, he couldn't concentrate on the television.

He shut it off, locked the front door, and strode to the subway. He needed to do something, go someplace with people, lights, action. He sat impatiently inside the subway car, willing it to go faster, even though he had no particular destination in mind.

The train lurched to another stop. Forty-second Street/Times Square flashed before his eyes on the sign identifying the station. He got off, took the steps two at a time, stopping only when he got outside.

The All-American midway, Times Square, swirled, flashed, blurted out the final freak-show spiel of all before his eyes. All the geeks and gargoyles of the world seemed on the loose here.

A dark little man with a faint resemblance to Frank Sinatra ambled off the curb at Forty-second and Broadway sporting a straw snapbrim hat. He wore a tight fifteen-year-old three-button suit that fitted him like a fourth-form boarding school boy, a buttton-down shirt and skinny tie, and swinging proudly with studied obliviousness a length of cock in his tight trousers that reached nearly halfway to his knee. A tall black whore in a short aubergine-colored crepe dress flapped both arms like a bird and whooped loudly clear across the street at the sight of the little man. He ambled past Carlson, his face sublime, eyes far-seeing, cock of the world with a rubber dingus.

Okay, but *prove* it! the little man's capped heels rang out.

There were the giggles of two young girls behind Carlson. One laughed. "I don't believe it!"

He watched from the other corner and saw a blond secretary with marriage and Queens weighing heavily upon her, who'd had a couple of drinks somewhere and plainly was not on the way home, smile at the little man wantonly as if she was suddenly a citizen of ancient Sodom. She actually slowed her pace, then stopped entirely to stare into Herman's Sporting Goods Store, glancing after the small dude until it was clear he was not looking back. She studied the multicolored bowling balls in the window morosely for a moment, remembered she had never been a kegler, and moved on.

Up toward Forty-third, twenty yards from two blue-shirted patrolmen on the corner, a pride of fags urged on two male transvestites, one black and one white, who were within a word of going for each other's elaborate blond peruques. Purses swung wildly but with no contact and no more effect than a presidential public conference. The shrieks and whoops of those egging the two on jittered shrilly above the Square's constant low moan of traffic, gruff imperative horns honking without hope, adding an incongruous delightful fracture of joy to the tumult. The cops did not even glance in their direction. When the few curious passersby dwindled, the show stopped and the boys receded into the shadows of the buildings.

A prowling blood-colored Lincoln cabriolet pulled to the curb and two of the gentlemen sashayed over and leaned in the rolled-down window. When the Lincoln burned away from the curb, it nearly spilled the queen in packed brassiere and red-white-blue bellbottoms in the gutter. The others laughed, then gathered around the one who had nearly fallen to comfort him and ascertain the extent of his bruises.

Carlson was hungry. Were he in the Village he might have gotten an Italian sausage and pepper sandwich that would have been delicious, or any of a dozen other good things to eat. In Times Square all the food was plastic. In the window at his left was the orange imperative: BUCK-WHEATS! What could they do to a pancake? he asked himself and fell into the brightly lit, new, filthy place that was the chrome and orange Formica embodiment of the most unappetizing word in the language—eatery.

Kids from out-of-town in Army-Navy surplus sat over cold coffee cups in the booths along the enormous steamy panes looking more lost than they would have in London, Paris, Rome, or anywhere else. There is an "us" and "you" quality to every establishment in Times Square that cannot be breached by civility or any amount of money. If you weren't a sucker, then what were you doing there? A Calumet City strip joint might be more direct in its intention of separating a citizen from everything but his carfare, but the entrepreneurs at the crossroads of the world had streamlined the peddling of ersatz satisfaction to the ultimate portion-controlled point just this side of the total lack of human comfort.

The black whore in aubergine crepe sat on a stool noshing a cream cheese on bagel and chatting with a sister behind the counter. Neither was having a big night.

His short stack of buckwheats arrived on a cold off-white plastic plate flanked by two strips of tepid, under-done bacon. The maple-flavored syrup was served in an easy-opening little plastic sack in a quantity calculated by a computer, considering the absorbency of the pancake to the ultimate decimal, falling quite short of satisfaction, yet not so short as to inspire the recipient to insist on a second portion. The temperature of Carlson's short stack would not melt the single pat of margarine on its roof. He had to carve the stack with knife and fork.

A lemon Eldorado with green alligator roof pulled to the curb outside. Inside, the tan blade of a face beneath the wide brim of a shaggy dark fedora leaned into the light. The whore took a final gulp of weak coffee, tossed down a dollar, and trotted toward the door, her long skinny legs in elasticized white patent boots clipped beneath her like a thoroughbred's. The man in the car was not geared for explanations. He jerked his thumb imperatively—downtown. When he had pulled away, the whore stood a moment looking after the car, then hooked her purse more securely on her shoulder and flapped off in the indicated direction, head high, haughty but smiling to herself as at some incredible private joke.

Carlson ate half the stack before him, freed it from where it was lodged just behind his breastbone with the awful coffee, paid and left a twenty-five cent tip, which was scooped in by the sister behind the counter without comment.

One of the kids detached herself from a booth: a girl in overalls, with an American flag upside down on the sleeve of her shirt demanded without emotion of great expectation: "Can you let me have all your change, mister?"

Short on change, Carlson fumbled out a limpid dollar. She did not even check the denomination of the bill.

"Thanks," she said, already moving back toward the booth.

It had been quite the proper technique—don't get involved, avoid eye contact—yet there was a quality of superdetachment about the kid, as, say, compared to an old stewbum, that made Carlson feel old, sad.

Jaded, he told himself outside. *The whole fucking world is goddamned jaded.*

Knowing precisely what to expect, he tumbled through the small crowd of men gently jostling each other outside a topless bar for a better look through the peephole in the painted glass at a busy brunette in only a tiny G-string gyrating indolently beneath a blue light at the back of the joint. He moved on.

He was on Forty-ninth Street now, just east of Ninth Avenue, aware of a presence at his heels, thinking perhaps it was a silent dog or cat. Then both feet were jerked out from under him and his face hit the slush-covered pavement so hard he saw stars, yet was not aware of any pain. A knee with weight behind it was in the middle of his back. A knife was against his throat. A hot little sear burned just above his Adam's apple where the blade bit him.

"Make one move, sonofabitch, and I kill you!" a voice hissed in his ear. A rough black hand dug his wallet from inside his jacket pocket. It tore his wristwatch from his left wrist. Then it hit him on the left temple and he felt he was going out. He was flung over, hit in the face until he lost consciousness.

His first awareness was of the taste of vomit. Then he saw the sky. He rolled onto one elbow and cleared his nose. He put his hand over his face, discovering a lump on his jaw the size of a bantam egg. He worked his jaw carefully. He decided it probably was not broken. His bridgework felt intact. There was a burning place above his collar. He remembered all that had happened. It was a small cut done with a very sharp blade. There was a bit of blood on his shirt mixed with the vomit. He got up slowly. His clothes were filthy. His trouser pockets had been turned wrongside out. Then he realized he had pissed in his pants.

Through the hot, humid night a block away the electric neon blue cross of Christ hung out over the sidewalk, flashing a stuttering WELCOME across its arms. He got up and stumbled fixedly toward it.

It hung out from another ordinary brownstone in which no light burned. He made it up the steps and leaned on the bell until a light came on beyond the curtained old glass windows in the door beyond the tiny foyer. The foyer blazed brightly and a young man in khaki trousers and a faded Oregon University T-shirt opened the outside door to the extent of its heavy safety chain.

"Yes?" the young man asked cautiously. He had a short red beard framing a ruddy freckled face but no mustache. Around his eyes he had that pale lashless look of the especially sanctified, including the insane and corpses.

"Sorry to bother you. I saw your sign. I've just been mugged. I wonder if you could loan me cabfare to Brooklyn?"

Behind him, a plump, plain girl in a blue bathrobe appeared. She glanced at the door with distaste and went through the large old-fashioned parlor to a kitchen in the back where the brightness of fluorescence stuttered on.

The young man took in the condition of Carlson's clothes, smelled the alcohol-ripe odor of his vomit. "If we gave money to everyone who came to the door like you, we would be broke in a week," the young man said.

"A subway token then."

"Sorry, it's against policy. Do you want me to call the police?"

"No. I just want to get home. I swear, I'll pay you back. I'll pay you double."

"That's what they all say."

The young woman crossed again with a baby's bottle in her hand. She had long brown hair that fell to her hips. Her hips were strong and attractive. He envied the Christian and the careful logic of the policy under which he and the young woman lived.

The young man slipped him a handful of tracts from a convenient rack in the foyer.

"What the hell kind of Christian are you?" Carlson wondered. "Afraid to take down your goddamned night chain."

To prove he was not afraid, the young man slipped the chain and stood blocking the open door.

"What kind of love is this?" Carlson waved the tracts beneath the young man's nose.

"Without Christ there is no love," the young man assured him righteously. "You do not know love. You are without Christ."

"I'm without carfare home, mainly," Carlson explained. "Look, I'll leave you my jacket as security. It's a good jacket, custom-made. I love you, man. I love your wife. She's beautiful. I envy you your faith and happiness. I just want to get home."

"You should have thought of that before you got

drunk," was the young man's advice. "You don't love me. I don't love you. You are the Devil."

"*What!?*"

"The Devil. If you do not have Christ in your heart, then you have the Devil in your heart."

"Man, you know about religion the way my ass chews gum. Give me a fucking quarter, will you?"

The door was closing. "I do not bargain with the Devil."

"*I'd like to fuck your wife!*" he shouted and the door closed.

Asshole. Asshole! He went back down the stairs. Unbelievable. Christ. *Christ?* The human mind. Who gave them that house? How did they come to man that station? Call the police! Christ.

Yet the blue neon cross hung out its welcome.

In his hand was a tract on the evils of drink; one on the evils of smoking; one of the dangers of masturbation. He went back up the stairs. He punched the bell and stuck a tract in the door. "I haven't smoked in two years," he shouted up at the shade-drawn lighted window above.

Back in Times Square he spotted a middle-aged man with a plump woman in a sequined blond wig coming arm in arm out of Forty-ninth with a bead on the Hilton.

"Excuse me, can you let me have a subway token, I've just been mugged and I'm trying to get home."

The woman clutched the man's arm in real terror.

"Drunken bastard!" the man spat, yanking her away.

He tried a small fat man who called him "Scum." He slipped the little man the tracts on drinking and jerking-off.

At Forty-second and Broadway he found two cops standing in front of a cigar store.

"Excuse me, officers . . ." He told them his tale. They sized him up noncommittally. They were both over six feet. Big young cops.

"Shit," one said.

"Get moving," the other said.

He remembered the pancake house and the quarter tip he had left the sister behind the counter. A burly black man was now on duty. The minute he stepped inside the door the man started around the counter.

"Unh-uh! Nooo. Out! Out, man!"

Christ.

He stopped a hippie couple, traveling as if they were grafted at the hip. "No way, man. Sorry," the young man said.

"Peace," the stoned little chick grinned. They giggled away.

He just blew into a topless place and blurted his story to a blonde with rouged tits working behind the bar before the bouncer could spot him.

"Here." She slipped a quarter from her tip saucer down in front of him.

"Thanks," he said.

"Get lost."

On the subway he sat on the last car, which was shunned by most citizens as it was the car in which they were most likely to be mugged. Yet, a young couple dressed for a movie date chanced fate to hold hands in greater privacy. After initial distaste, they ignored him. A heavy woman who might have been a char ignored him completely, clasping a shopping bag over her fat raw knees as if the entire world lived to look up her dress.

He drew his stained jacket tightly around him. Local stops flashed past. The train braked sickeningly at the express stops. He stared at his reflection in the grimy glass and let it drift beyond. He wondered what it would be like to live on a cold northern lake in Sweden. He had never felt more like a foreigner in his life.

Thirty–One

FEBRUARY, 1968, MARKED a full year since Carlson started sending out his manuscript in the mail. He had an even dozen rejection slips to show for his efforts. He *knew* the book was good, dammit, how was it possible those myopic bastards couldn't see it?

If only he wasn't so goddamned helpless. His futility was strangling him. He was so despondent even Margaret was moved to words of comfort.

"It'll happen, Cat," she said, uncommonly tender in her voice and manner. "I told you how much I liked your book. You'll sell it."

But he didn't.

He supposed he heard Margaret leave one morning but he couldn't be sure. He seemed to remember the door closing, that's all. Anyway, when he finally looked around, neither she nor their children were in the apartment. If they had said something to him, he hadn't heard.

Before they could get to him, before she or the children could come back, he dashed to the door of his workroom and locked it. Then he collapsed to his knees and started to weep.

The lifelong feeling of worthlessness which had merely hounded him before, which had caused him to leave Caroline in Chicago, caught up with him, grabbed him in its slobbering jaws and was eating him alive. Jesus Christ, if he couldn't make it with this book, if after five goddamned stinking, sweating, mother years of producing a fucking masterpiece, he still couldn't get anywhere, he knew he never would.

It must have been hours later when he finally found

the strength to leave the room. He removed his sweat-stained clothes like a sleepwalker and stumbled into the shower. The water pouring over his body was life-giving, the gray light of the afternoon breaking through the slabs of high buildings seemed everlasting.

"I'm going," he told Margaret that night, after they put the children to sleep. "I don't know where or for how long, and"—he looked her in the eyes—"if you could let me have fifty dollars a week from the business, I'd appreciate it. But it's not necessary. Tell the kids . . ." He stopped. "Tell them Papa had to leave for a little while and will come back as soon as he's able."

"What are you going to do?" She sighed.

"I don't know. Wander, think, clear my head. I need to be alone. It doesn't have to be any particular place, a shack in the woods, maybe a room—I don't know. I can't stay here watching myself go to waste. I'm not even good for the children any more."

"Do you want a divorce?" She was busy with some artwork, her head down.

"No, I told you, I'm coming back. I love my kids and I want to be with them. But for a while, maybe even a year, I don't know how long exactly, I need to be away from everything."

He had not spoken to her so honestly, with such feeling, since before they were married. How odd that this great searing sorrow over his book should drive him to try to recapture the past. Where was the wall they had built between them for so many years? It was not there now, only a new awareness, a strange new closeness, and they both sensed it.

"You won't come back." The sudden fear struck her. "You're lying to me."

He was taken aback. She had told him to get out so often, her words now seemed oddly out of place. Why should she give a damn if she never saw him again?

Aware of her outburst, she tried to explain. "The children . . . they need you. And I . . . we fight a lot, Cat, but we *are* married. I think of me as married. I can't think of myself as a single woman."

"I told you, I'll be back. I promise." He knew how she felt about being left without a man.

"Yeah, sure," she said, turning away.

"Sure," he said. "Absolutely." He walked to her and gathered her in his arms. For once, she was not resisting. She let him kiss her, let him push his tongue inside her mouth, let his hand circle her breasts. He put his hand under her dress, and felt the quiver of her slick pussy. It was hot to the touch and opened to his long middle finger.

He got the beginning of a hard-on and wanted to fuck her. But when he started to take her clothes off, she pulled back.

"Can't we ever get close without you turning it into another sex scene? Just one goddamned time can't it be different?" she said.

"Jesus, Margaret, are you off on that again?"

She sulked for a moment. "Oh, all right. Here is your going-away present." She pulled off her dress, then her slip, bra, and panties.

"Oh, fuck you!" he said.

"That's what I told you," she said. "Fuck me."

He examined her nude body, those long breasts and hairy muff, and felt himself get hard again. He pushed her down on the floor, rolled down his pants, and plunged into her hot slit.

She moaned, and he began to fuck her slowly and thoroughly until she was breathing hard and writhing up against him, and then he was needing to come very badly himself. He could feel her hot cunt grabbing around his cock, suctioning it; his balls drawn up, but he wasn't going to come, he could tell. It was all up in him bursting to let go but somehow blocked. He fucked her harder and faster, slapping his thighs against her raised and churning ass. "Come, goddammit, come!" he yelled.

"I can't. I want to, but I can't—"

He thrust his gorged cock into her crack furiously again and again. She was biting her lip and clawing his back to shreds.

"Come, cunt! Come!"

"Oh, oh!"

"Come!!" He was thrusting with all his strength.

"Oh, oh! OH! OH!!" She screamed and held tight. Her body shuddered violently. The throbbing insides of her cunt convulsed into spasms.

At that moment his balls seemed to crack. An electric shock whipped his spine and straightened his body as he came inside her cunt in great heaving spurts.

Margaret began to cry.

Carlson took only a few clothes in an old Army dufflebag and rode the bus south and west. His destination was merely "someplace," like his driving when he left Caroline in Chicago with only a feeling that he still needed to find himself. He had been so sure he would come back to her one day, yet here he was, married to someone else, unfulfilled, goddamned unhappy. If he had only married Caroline . . .

He tried to rest in the narrow bus seats and watch the country go by, all that had been overrun and settled so densely in so few lifetimes, and all that had been built so indifferently and cheaply. More than half the people out there had no idea where they came from, much less where they were going. Most of the structures were already deteriorating and all the scenes were such passing things. It pleased Carlson to think of himself as only a whim in the passing scene, and that was the truth of the whole, wasn't it? And the secret was merely acceptance of the truth. Ashes to ashes, dust to dust. You were here today and gone tomorrow. You could flap your wings against the cage and butt your head against the invisible prison wall and flail about blindly until you were bloody and your weapons were all broken, or you could fight your battle calmly and steadily—you could choose your way. That's what he hoped to find—his way.

When the bus pulled up for a rest stop at a little town in southern Arizona, Carlson looked around at the scene. There were only a few stores and adobe houses, a desolate street with a broken caution light swaying in the dusty air and tumbleweeds lodged against the side of a lone service station. A little café, featuring tamales and enchiladas, had a torn screen on the front door and beyond was only a flat desert dotted with gray sage and yucca, and a wide horizon where a blue sky dropped behind the brown world.

The Interstate had bypassed this town and after the bus motor was shut off, the place was filled with a huge amount of quiet. It seemed the end of the earth where a hawk might circle for hours and never find prey. It was a solitary and singular place, so plainly what it was that it was strangely beautiful.

Carlson stepped down from the bus and filled his lungs with the dry air that bleached the forgotten bones of men and cattle alike with complete impartiality. The sand beneath his feet seemed to buoy him up and give a new springiness to his legs.

He carried his bag into the café and sat on a wooden stool at the counter. A plain young girl, who could have been Mexican except for the freckles and red hair, finally approached within a few feet behind the counter and waited, but without actually offering service.

Carlson at first wasn't sure she was the waitress. Then a woman's voice from the kitchen said something gruffly in Spanish, and the young girl moved closer, but with her head down and her eyes averted. *"Si?"* she mumbled. "You want something?"

Carlson said, "Just a Coke, please."

A large fat woman came from the kitchen, rattling Spanish at the girl, and turned to Carlson. "Hey, you miss your bus, you know that? It went off without you."

"No, I got off. I let it go."

The woman eyed him suspiciously and wiped her pudgy hands on her apron. "What, you get off the bus here?"

Carlson nodded.

"There won't be no more buses for three days, you know that? You know somebody here?"

"No."

"No?" She had a guileless manner and a really pleasant face, but she was bewildered. "Then what you get off here for?"

"It seemed like a good spot."

The woman's eyes widened. "A good spot? Here, in this dump? There's nothing here. Just this café, that old service station, and look how they're sleeping over there right now sitting against the walls. And Jimmy's store, they got canned goods in there so old they're sprouting leaves. Look, Jimmy's old dog sleeps right in the doorway and nobody bothers him. A good spot? Mister, you must be crazy or you don't want nothing."

Carlson smiled. "You're right. I'm probably crazy, and I don't want anything."

"Then you come to the right spot. But what you gonna do? Ain't no jobs here."

"Well, I'm not looking for a job—" He hesitated saying he was a writer. "I only want to live in a quiet place for a while."

"Then you come to the right place. It sure is quiet here." She laughed broadly, full of good humor. "Anyway, my name is Maria."

"Glad to meet you, Maria. My name's Carlson."

She extended her round little hand and they shook. Then she spewed Spanish at the girl, who immediately sped into the kitchen.

He asked about a place to stay for a while. Maria thought a moment, then led him around the corner of the café, down a few dusty blocks that disappeared into a dirt trail leading outside of town. They came to a shack sitting alone in a bare field, a one-room thing half adobe and half weathered boards. The roof was old pieces of rusted tin and the floor was packed clay. Surprisingly, the door was still hinged and there were two good windows on two sides, but the room was little more than a shell and there was no plumbing or electricity.

"I don't know." Carlson scratched his head. "Not even a bathroom?"

"Sure. Wherever you like—" Inez indicated the whole of the barren desert outside. "You got the biggest bathroom ever built."

Carlson had expected a little more, and for a moment he was about to shake his head, but something told him, no, this was perfect. This utterly plain little room was all he needed.

"How much?" he asked.

"Fifty dollars. We got a deal?"

"Yes, a deal."

They walked back to the café and Maria made Carlson a huge breakfast of tortillas and ham and eggs rancheros while several boys—some her sons—carried a table and chair, a kerosene lamp, an old bedstead, and a big rain barrel as well as a supply of firewood to Carlson's new home.

After breakfast Carlson gave Maria a hundred dollars for two month's rent in advance.

He developed a routine quickly. A big breakfast at the café, followed by a leisurely exchange of news with the regulars.

About noon he would leave the shack and start across the desert, alternately jogging and walking, swinging his arms and breathing in the clean dry air. For a couple of hours every day he would exercise his body leisurely but thoroughly until he was tired, and then he would go back to his shack, eat some raw fruit and cheese, and take a nap.

After that he would make notes of what had come to him in his sleep, perhaps read some light paperback left at the café, and do sketches of the little town and the yucca in the desert. Sometimes he only sat and whittled. And he let his mind rest from writing.

At night he ate again at the café and listened to the local talk.

To the casual observer it would appear Carlson was living an easy and restful life. He was fortunate to have the monthly check Margaret sent him to pay for the basic necessities of food and shelter, but life was far from restful and easy. Rather, it required enormous amounts of psychic energy and an act of sheer willpower that exacted its own payments in personal sacrifice. He had to retrain his mind, had to force himself not to think of his failure, to purge himself of all the misery he had left behind. He missed his children; strangely, he missed

Margaret too. But he wouldn't permit himself to call them, and he had told Margaret not to call when he first wrote her his address.

He was beginning to lose the flab from his waist, and his body was tan from the sun, from jogging and walking in shorts every afternoon. His muscles had toned and there were no cricks or jams in his joints. He had returned to an athletic form and moved almost catlike on his feet. He even looked younger and almost boyish again. His eyes were clear and bright.

And his mind was sharper than it had been for a long, long time. The brightness of a crisp spring morning was in his head, and ideas and images pattered about in his imagination like sprinkling summer rain. There was no smog or pollution mixing with the gray matter anymore. No traffic jams or loud noises.

Once a month, he wrote a note to Margaret, telling her nothing except that he was getting better and was still there and to give the kids a hug and a kiss for him. In the corner in a small heap, Margaret's letters to him over the past months were lying unopened. He hadn't read them, and wouldn't. If she had problems, he couldn't do anything about them, and if she was encouraging him to return as soon as he could, he didn't want that foreign urgency on his mind.

He didn't want anything on his mind except what was before him, and he knew that was entirely selfish but at this point in his life, it was the only thing he could do.

He finished this month's note and walked outside to look at the stars. His ancestors had challenged the unknown following those same stars, and whenever he looked up at night he felt some of that old blood boiling in his veins. They had put to sea and crossed the unknown in small boats. He too was crossing a sea in a small boat.

Then it was over. He couldn't remember exactly when he had come to Arizona. Must have been spring, he decided, for the air had been so balmy. And then it was summer when the heat was stifling and sweat had drizzled through his body. Now it was fall, with a sweet coolness. And he was going home.

He called Margaret to tell her. He spoke to Luke and Jean, telling them over and over how much he loved them and longed to see them. He would be home in a few days, he promised.

In New York, Margaret was uncertain of him again. He seemed distant to her and somehow a stranger.

They made love the first night as if they wanted to, or should, and it was not very satisfactory.

His children were excited to see him again, and he them, but they were almost a year older, there was a gap in their lives he'd missed, and they had changed. Sometimes he looked at them and hardly recognized them at all.

"You didn't answer my letters," Margaret said.

"I wrote every month."

"But you didn't answer any of my questions. You didn't comment on any of the things I told you."

"I didn't read your letters. I received them, but I never opened them."

"Why?"

"I didn't want to have them on my mind."

"When I wrote you about Luke being sick, you didn't read that?"

"No." How could he explain it? When he left, she had seemed to understand his need, his pain, so completely.

"No?" she asked now, incredulously. "You just couldn't be bothered, could you? Not even about your own son being sick?"

"Look, I couldn't handle it."

"And you didn't want to be bothered."

"No, I couldn't help myself. My God, don't you think I care about Luke, love him?"

"Do you? You're just as selfish as you ever were." She bared her teeth. Their moment together before he left was forgotten. She had been neglected with her letters. He had gone away and shut off any concern for his children.

They were back to the same old situation, in the same fix again, and it made him feel weary. They had never pleased each other, never loved each other, except that one time when he had broken in front of her. But now he was back and she didn't care that he felt well again, whole. She only cared about the way he had done it, the way her letters had been ignored.

"Selfish bastard!" She whirled from the room.

Carlson sighed. The war on the home front goes on, he thought, and the sun also rises.

Thirty–Two

CARLSON LINED UP in the slot to the right. He drove straight ahead toward the corner back, gave his man a head fake, then accelerated on an angle that just brushed the kid's A&S copy of a Giant's jersey, turned behind him, and took the ball high over his left shoulder, both feet off the ground. The middle was open for twenty yards, and only the former starting end for Bishop Ford High School, playing in a hinged elastic knee brace, stood between him and the goal. Jimmy the Pole's pass had been right-on. Carlson heard his son, Luke, who was running one of the yardage sticks—ten yards of clothesline between two broomsticks—yelling, "Beautiful, Papa! Beautiful!"

Then Matloff, a city engineer with minor political pretensions, was coming from the left on a collision route with the tall young safety whose total concentration was on tagging Carlson. He could see the kid's wide, unblinking eyes focusing on the center of his own tensed body. It was a totally impersonal occasion. He liked the kid. The kid liked him. The kid owned a Ford Galaxie hot-rod— perhaps the only one in Brooklyn of true California quality. He and the kid often talked cars.

The kid did not see Matloff. The man took him from the right side, in a vicious shoulder block between the kid's hip and knee. Carlson saw him fold sidewise, his mouth open in a silent cry, his eyes still riveted on Carlson. Six points.

The kid lay curled on the ground in a half fetus position, moaning, his hands outstretched like a faith-healer's toward the pain, enclosing the dynamics of it without actually touching the place.

The President Street gang huddled around him. Matloff, Carlson, Jimmy the Pole from across Prospect Park who had never gone to college but who could throw a ball forty yards, kneeling to ask, "It is bad, son?"

The kid nodded that he thought it was.

"Think you better go to the hospital, Donny?" Matloff asked.

The kid shook his head that he did not.

"Can you get up?" Jimmy the Pole asked.

"Yeah, I think so."

Jimmy slipped his arms underneath the kid. Matloff got on the other side. The kid groaned when hoisted upright. The knee would bear no weight. Between the two men, one short, the other as tall as himself, he was helped to the sidelines where his girlfriend wrapped a ski jacket over his shoulders. He lay on the blanket she and some of the other girls had brought to sit with his bad leg extended.

"He'll be all right," Matloff assured everyone.

It was Jim Matloff who had organized the Saturday morning game in Brooklyn's giant Prospect Park as a way of bridging the distance between the adult community and the kids. The boys were all in their teens, mostly sons of men like Matloff—middle and lower middle-class kids with little or no dreams of ever getting out of the neighborhood. Most of the men, however, with the exception of Matloff and Jimmy the Pole, were college-educated and not of the neighborhood, men whose fortunes had forced them to seek permanence in the ranks of Park Slope brownstones or the commodious old apartments ringing the city's second great park.

The games had started while Carlson was in Arizona. Luke had been invited to come by one of the neighborhood fathers, particularly in view of his own father's absence, and joining in had been one of the ways Carlson used to once more get close to his son. Besides, he enjoyed the roughhousing.

There were sweatshirts from Fordham, Notre Dame, Virginia, Harvard, Yale, Columbia, Dartmouth, Penn, and Brown. Carlson was the furthest *auslander* in a faded gold midwestern state university jersey from which both sleeves had long since been torn and the black satin 33 on the front and back within a few stitches of anonymity. Under the jersey he wore a heavy gray sweatshirt. Below, a pair of Levi's, sweatsocks, and a pair of tired low-cut kangaroo cleats into which he'd had to slip foam-cushioned insoles. It had been years since his feet wore a tough natural brown sole cultured by being painted daily with a trainer's mixture of tannic acid, formaldehyde, and God-only-knew-what-else. His belt pinched his belly when he got down in a three-point stance. He wore glasses. Yet, he consoled himself, there was no one forty years old on the field who could come within a mile of him. Except for Kelly, the beer salesman, who was just meat, he was the oldest man out there.

Carlson watched the nose of the ball out of the corner of his eye. When it moved, he broke to the right. Jimmy faked a straight-ahead dive to Matloff, who threw a good block on the coming linebacker as Jimmy stuck the ball in Carlson's belly. Carlson ducked one shoulder toward the hole inside the tackle, then took one more full stride as if going around the end, giving some ground to the kid pouring in on him. It was going to be good.

He never saw the end of the play. There was the kid in front of him, arms upraised, face contorted for collision, then a fat Irish kid in a kelly green jersey put a shoulder into his ribs, and the next thing Carlson knew he was looking at the clear, high winter sky between the faces of Jimmy, the Irish kid, and his own son.

"You okay, Papa?" Luke asked.

Carlson rubbed his ribs. "Yeah. Knocked the wind out of me."

The Irish kid grinned.

"Was it good?" Carlson asked.

"He came down with one foot out of bounds."

"Twenty-all!" the Italian quarterback captain of the other side cheered.

"Playoffs next week!" one of the kids announced.

"Super Bowl!"

"This game is gettin' too rough," Matloff said thoughtfully. "We oughta figure somethin' out."

"Naw, good game," Referee Kelly pronounced. "Do 'em good to get knocked on their ass a little."

Carlson didn't see Kelly risking his own. His ribs really hurt.

"You have a head like a billiard ball," he told the Irish kid who helped him up.

"They ain't broken, are they?" the kid asked rather too hopefully.

Carlson shook his head. Taking his son's hand in his own, he started slowly for home.

He was sending out his manuscript regularly again. He was getting rejection slips just as regularly, but, strangely, they did not bother him as they had before he went off to the desert.

He had written his novel the best he could and no one could take that away from him. The fact no publisher was beating down his door to put him in print seemed almost beside the point, a vague sort of abstraction. He would go on sending his manuscript out into that land of never-never and go on with his life believing deep down that some day someone would recognize his worth and he would get it published. No fantasies paraded his mind about being rich and famous.

He and Margaret worked on their accounts and struck a kind of truce. She didn't criticize him, and he quit trying to have sex with her. The children were healthy and happy enough, he thought.

After his solitary months in the desert he liked now being alone with his thoughts. He had even started the other novel, and it was beginning to occupy him a little more each day. It was not going too well but he kept at it anyway. He wasn't able to apply to it that same continuous concentration serious writing demanded, not with the business and the family and all the other distractions of city living, but the sporadically good writing he was able to do helped balance his mind and moods. Besides he was a writer. Whether he was ever published, whether he ever received recognition for his talent, that's what he was.

His ordinary life could have frustrated him again except now he had a new self-esteem and strength, he could hold the pieces together and keep the hounds of hostilities and resentments at bay. Perhaps he had matured some too. Whatever, he was a contained force and lived his usually uneventful life now one day at a time. If he preferred the results of a sudden battle, he was also prepared to endure a long haul. Since he knew who he was, he could wait. And he could go on after fourteen rejections and no encouragement.

He was not normally a politically active person, but the "new" Carlson was becoming involved with the war in Vietnam. Margaret joined the Women's Strike for Peace and he helped to write and publish the organization's tracts. He stayed home with the children when she went off to hawk petitions against the war in front of their supermarket on Saturdays or was parading through Brooklyn to support draft resisters.

If Jean had not come down with measles, the entire family would have gone on the historic 1969 March on Washington to protest the war. Margaret stayed home with the little girl while an excited Luke got up at five A.M. to go to the capital with his father.

By seven o'clock they were in front of the library at Grand Army Plaza, where they had been told a chartered bus would pick up their set of Brooklyn marchers. It was still dark and only a small group was milling about, stamping their hands and feet and trying to keep warm.

"Cat! *You* joining the revolution?" Carlson turned to see Paige Fasano, a Park Slope neighbor, striding toward them in her greatcoat, her head encased in a warm wool turban.

"Hey, Paige, you look very smart in that coat and hat," he said.

"Well, I must say, I am surprised to see you here. Margaret, I would have expected. But *you* don't demonstrate . . . Do you?"

"First time for me," he said.

"Me *too!* But why *are* you here?"

"I don't know. I just decided a couple of days ago I

would go on this one and have a see. I got up this morning to get on a bus to Washington, even though I know nothing we do today is going to change a thing."

"You don't think it might? I mean if just *everybody* shows up, won't they *have* to do something? I'm not as cynical as you."

"Then you better stay close to my little black bag. You might get cynical all of a sudden if you're tear-gassed."

"You don't think that will happen—*really?*"

"Yeah, I think it can happen. They are very scared down there."

"And yet, you're taking Luke?"

"He'll be all right."

"Think I *will* stick with you . . . if you don't mind?"

"Our pleasure."

"Okay with you, Luke, if I tag along with you and your"—she hesitated calling Carlson by the name she knew his children used—"your papa?"

"Sure," Luke said brightly.

"You're really a brave boy to be going along on something like this."

The boy did not reply. He knew that in the bag his father carried there was Vaseline and a canteen of the kind of water his mother used in her steam iron, to wash out their eyes if they got gassed. Also bandages, their sandwiches, fruit, Pepsi, and a bottle of whiskey. He was excited and looking forward to Washington. Brave seemed an inappropriate and embarrassing word to use for what they were doing.

The bus arrived an hour late, an old Greyhound bus that hadn't been in regular service for years, with CHARTERED in the little window above the sullen driver.

Paige squeaked, "Here we go!" and clutched Carlson's arm. He handed her up in the bus and guided her into a window seat. Adelle Richards, who was a friend of Margaret's and the group's leader, sat across the aisle also near a window; Luke took the aisle seat next to her.

It was almost nine when they pulled up on Flatbush near Windsor Terrace to take on another party, which filled the bus.

Paige felt good snuggled in her greatcoat—as much as a woman who is almost five eight and has to do everything for herself can feel snuggled next to the bulk of a man beside her. It was impossible for two people their size to sit in such seats without touching. Soon she was aware of how they fit together, hip, shoulder, and thigh. She relaxed, dropped her head back into the big collar of her coat, and closed her eyes. A little smile made her face look very beautiful in profile. She turned her head to face Carlson and opened her eyes. He watched her hair loose around her face and under her cheek, and thought that's how she would look if they were in bed. She smiled and let her right hand fall open against his thigh where his hand captured it, engulfing fingers and hiding it tightly between them from his son's and everyone else's eyes. She scooted down and let her head fall on his shoulder where he breathed the perfume of her hair. Perhaps she slept a little. He was not sure.

Smug, pretty, self-assured Paige Fasano was married to a sculptor who spent most of his time at his studio some- where in downtown New York City. They lived mainly on Paige's income from inherited stocks.

Paige and a younger brother were the last heirs of a dying midwestern family who had made a fortune in flour and then diversified. Her mother had recently died and an aunt was an almost permanent resident of a health farm for wealthy alcoholics. There was an uncle who shepherded the last of the family fortune.

Her mother had been a great international beauty and had had many celebrated friends. A life-sized full-length portrait of the woman dominated Paige's Brooklyn apart- ment.

On her fifteenth birthday her mother took tall, lanky Paige on her first trip to Europe. As it happened, they sailed on the same ship as Ali Khan, whom her mother had known years before. The first morning out they met the prince seated at a bar on deck. He was very gallant with Paige, and was the first man in the world to tell her she was "beautiful."

After college, Paige had come to New York to become

an actress, and found work as a model. She met her husband through a girlfriend, a fellow actress. He was working as a bartender in the Village. They had a romance that could have been a 1930s film about New York, meeting in borrowed apartments, renting rooms in side-street hotels, with spontaneous picnics in the park, certain they would become fine actors, if not great popular stars. Neither found a real job in the New York theater.

They got married on Paige's money and moved to Brooklyn when the children came. She never joined anything as daring as a protest march in her entire life.

They missed the great march entirely. The bus arrived adjacent to the Jefferson Memorial a bit past noon. Adelle Richards, the group captain, was livid. She warned the bus driver she was definitely writing a letter of protest to the bus company.

"I'll demand our money back," she assured the man.

"Good luck," he told her.

A lake of people surrounded the Washington Monument. Lines of people queued for fifty yards before the portable toilets set up at the edge of the parade. Their faces were stoic masks of singular determination that transcended blood or filial ties.

"I've got to go," Paige whispered.

"Then you better get in line," Carlson told her. "Luke and I will take a walk around the crowd and catch you back here."

"All right," she said, the look on the faces of those waiting before the blue Fiberglas facilities beginning to settle over her own.

"Under that greatcoat, if you can manage it, no one would be the wiser," he suggested, envisioning her walking away from the puddle with superior aplomb, like a lady with a tarrying toy schnauzer on Fifth Avenue.

"It isn't funny," she assured him.

It was a hell of a crowd. Carlson and the boy had been to Indianapolis on race day, and at Daytona and Atlanta for the big stock cars. This crowd was larger than all of them. Rebels had climbed the flagpoles around the monument and hung their own banners. The peace flag was much in evidence, American flags with the peace symbol in the blue field where the stars usually were. They stood out boldly in the cold breeze beside the huge crimson banner of Harvard and the blue of Yale. A crewcut kid from Michigan was struggling up a pole to hang their flag. From his buddy at the foot of the pole Carlson learned that Michigan had filled four hundred buses. On the next pole, a long-haired, skinny pot freak in tattered jeans and old Army field jacket was shinnying up to fly the flag of North Vietnam.

An old black man, his eyes glazed with beatific purpose, wandered slowly, alone, through the crowd with a hand-lettered sign that hung around his neck on twine:

DEAR PRESIDENT NIXON
I COME HERE TO PROTEST
IN THE NAME OF GOD TO
ASK YOU TO END THIS WAR
BEFORE ANY MORE OF OUR SONS
IS KILLED. I AM HERE TO
TESTIFY FOR MY ONLY BE-
GOTTEN SON SPEC. 2 LEROY
JAMES MURDOCK JR. WHO
WAS KILLED IN VIETNAM.
AND I JUST HEARD YESTER-
DAY.
            Harvey Clay Jackson Sr.

Affixed to the top of the sign were two tiny American flags of the kind one could buy at the local candy store. In his hands the man carried the matte portrait of a smiling black paratrooper. Hanging from the dime-store gilt frame were still-glistening medals: a Purple Heart, the Good Conduct Medal, and a Bronze Star for Valor. The old man walked alone in the security of his son's credentials.

A well-dressed senator and his attractive wife, hung with expensively cased binoculars and camera, stopped to address some words of sympathy and assurance to the black man. His face never changed. His gaze never wavered from the purpose he saw somewhere in the distance. The woman's eyes were misty. The senator put his arm around her waist. They went on, somehow smaller than they had been.

Two young men, hair cut short in the back and sides, popped up in front of Carlson and his son, armed with strobe units on their camera, and snapped their picture.

"What paper are you with?" Carlson asked.

They did not reply, clicking half a dozen shots. They wore the kind of inexpensive oxfords, highly shined, an off-duty corporal might wear.

"Tell Ron Connelly that I still think he is a fink," Carlson instructed them. "Jarl Carlson's the name. This is my son, Luke, the best ten-year-old quarterback in the country. We are both very dangerous men." As the duo turned to shoot the senator and his wife, Carlson shouted to the two photographers, "What are going to do when you get out? Go to work for the Philadelphia police department?"

Luke did not understand his father's anger.

"They are soldiers of a sort," he explained, "sent to take pictures of the crowd, shooting people who don't look like the ordinary run of hippies who always show up at these things. They call us 'persons of interest.' Somewhere over there in those buildings," he indicated the Capitol complex, "they will print the pictures and spend hours trying to match them with any other information they have on us. Perhaps they will find out that we are friends of the Manheims, who are Communists, that Mama gave your baby buggy to that girl married to the Quaker who showed up for induction at Fort Hamilton chained to her and refused to go into the Army. Maybe they will find out we like Rube, who is an old Socialist. They will put our name on a list. And when you grow up they will watch you. You will try to get a job in an aircraft factory or join the ROTC in college and it will pop up. Suddenly, without explanation, there will simply be no place for you."

"I ain't joining ROTC," the boy said.

Carlson smiled and hugged Luke's ski-capped head.

351

"Why do they do it, Papa?"

"Because they are fucking nuts. Because they are stupid."

Official helicopters, like giant dragonflies, constantly monitored the crowd in the parade around the monument. Yet, Carlson noted, there were no news or TV copters around.

Completing the circle of the main body of the throng, stepping through the sleeping bags where several hundred young people slept or huddled to keep warm, Carlson asked the boy: "How many do you reckon are here?"

"More than at Indianapolis last year." The boy was certain.

"I would say so too."

They met Paige near the portable johns where she was talking with a woman, the female writing half of a husband-and-wife children's-book-producing team from their neighborhood, who was there with her twelve-year-old daughter. Mother and daughter wore astrakhan coats.

"We were just discussing how large the crowd is," Paige said.

"I'm a little disappointed," the other woman added. "Of course we didn't arrive until after the main body had begun breaking up."

Carlson said, "Well, I think if you count all those milling around in the city now, there must be at least a million. There's an awful lot of people here. You would have to say there has never been such a crowd in one place in the history of this country."

"Oh, do you really think so?" They seemed buoyed by the news.

"Yes. I'm sure of it," Carlson said.

When Paige took Carlson's arm, there was a puzzled look on the neighbor's face. As they moved off, Paige said, "Now there's the beginning of a scandal."

They walked well together, her long booted strides matching his own. Her soft breast through the heavy coat rested warmly against him. In a woman less tall, she would have appeared quite busty.

Around the portable stage the crowd was singing "We

352

Shall Overcome," led by Peter, Paul, and Mary. Mary, in tie-dyed jeans, boots, and jacket, her straight blond hair flying around her face, stepped forward, clutched the mike, and cried: "Let them hear you! Let them know we don't want any more of their fucking war!" The crowd loosed a great yell.

A group from the Street Protest Theater passed by, smeared of face, clothing and bandages caked with blood, bearing the bloody entrails and hearts of some beast. They snaked easily through the crowd that understandably parted for them, their way marked when the crowd had closed behind them by the huge North Vietnamese flag borne by their tall leader.

"I think that is going too far." Paige shuddered against Carlson.

"Why?"

"Well, I think you can protest without something like that. It's gruesome."

"So would it be if they bore the bodies of real Vietnamese or a GI."

"But why do they carry that flag?" There were dozens of other similar flags grouped before the stage.

"Because they want the underdog to win. Haven't you ever wanted an underdog, SMU say, to knock off Notre Dame?"

"Never."

"Forgot your Catholic upbringing. The St. Louis Browns, then, to beat the Yankees?"

"It hardly seems the same thing."

"You're right. This is more serious. Those kids don't give a damn who is playing football. Nixon is over in Maryland at a game today. It was in the paper. He isn't even here. Yet up there somewhere on those buildings is a little bastard named Ron Connelly, who was head of the Student Government Association at my university when I was there. Like Nixon, a perennial third-rater. He went through ROTC as a distinguished military graduate, then into Air Force Intelligence, a dodo, a bird that doesn't fly, the lowest form of humanity in the Air Force. Eighteen months of that and he goes to work as personal secretary to Raymond Black, that dandy little anti-Communist senator.

"What kind of man takes shorthand for a living? I never knew a good reporter who didn't invent his own speedwriting and could type with more than four fingers. So anyway, Black comes to Washington and Ron turns up as his 'military advisor,' for chrissake! *For what kind of war?* Then Nixon gets elected and Ron is one of the first assistant secretaries of defense. He's the official liar for the Pentagon. Master of the bland facts: 'Yes, we are conducting interdiction raids on North Vietnam.' Every time someone catches us with our pants down, catches us in an outright lie, up pops Ron to admit it with all the righteousness of a good Calvinist taking rents from first-ward cribs on Friday night. He's up there now. Still wears a crew cut and white socks. A more self-righteous sonofabitch never drew a breath. Up there now behind the goddamned forty millimeter ack-ack guns trained down on us, behind the hidden mortars and big machine guns."

"I don't believe that," Paige protested. "They don't have guns up there."

Carlson spotted a young man in a fringed leather jacket with a pair of Navy 7X50 binoculars around his neck. He towed Paige over and asked the man for the loan of his binoculars. He scanned the buildings. On the roofs at each vantage point were armed lookouts. He let Paige look through the glasses.

"Behind those cats, out of sight, are regiments of paratroopers, with all their heavy supporting weapons. If this crowd moves beyond some secretly agreed-upon line of control, it will be sprayed like fish in a barrel."

She shuddered. "I still find it hard to believe."

"I find guys like Ron Connelly *impossible* to believe. How does a man become a fink? They said in the papers he was conducting part of 'the defense of Washington' in case the crowd should be precipitated to violence. They have been *expecting* violence. I know that fuck secretly hopes there *is* violence. As long as it isn't head-to-head and hand-to-hand when it's his hand and head."

They avoided being engulfed in the main body of the

crowd before the stage. They drifted through the looser fringe. Abbie Hoffman, his head shorn from his stay in the Chicago jail, made a speech. It did not carry well over the P.A. system. Only those up front could hear. Then he led the crowd in the chant: *"One, two, three, four, we don't want your fucking war!"* Paige started off daintily, then let go, matching Luke in screaming the refrain.

But as at all such things, when the crowd has risen to an emotional peak, and there is no way for it to proceed to direct action, the chant died of its own frustration, first in the fringe, then rapidly receding toward center until only Abbie and the group with the flags before the stage were still yelling. At the end, the voice of a single young woman shrieked a ghostly final: *"One, two, three, four, we don't want your fucking warrrrrr . . ."* Abbie urged the crowd to gather at three o'clock in front of the Justice Building to protest the infamy against the "Chicago Seven."

Abbie was replaced by Joan Baez, who made a speech, then led the crowd in another version of "We Shall Overcome." She said some more words lost in the post-singing hubbub. When the crowd had stilled, she said, "Now I would like to ask you all to join hands and sing 'The Battle Hymn of the Republic' with me." It was a beautiful and poignant moment.

Carlson let his voice swell and grow in the song he loved as well as any other this side of Woody Guthrie's "This Land Is Your Land, This Land Is My Land," which he thought ought to be made the official national anthem.

Such a fine, bright, crisp afternoon.

The song left Carlson shivering. He unpacked his flat quart of Irish whiskey and offered it to Paige, who took a small nip. He handed it to Luke, who had a taste. Then he poured a lot down his own throat. It tasted like syrup. It radiated quickly to all his parts.

Near the steps of the Smithsonian they ran into a reporter Carlson knew, from the *St. Louis Post-Dispatch.* Carlson asked, "Anyone getting any aerial photos of this crowd?"

"No. The government won't permit any overflights.

Time-Life had a camera up in the monument. UPI and AP did too, I think. We'll get something over the wire. They closed the monument right after the march. Officially the police are saying two hundred and fifty thousand. Multiply the goddamned buses by sixty and you get over three hundred thousand. I'm calling it 'well over half a million.' "

Carlson offered the man a drink. He took it gratefully. "There were only sandwiches for breakfast at my hotel this morning. Most of the staff didn't turn up. They took all the furniture out of the lobby, so people who got gassed could be brought in for treatment."

"Are you serious?" Paige asked.

"Yeah. There was some trouble just after the march this morning. Brought some kids in and treated their eyes."

They had seen the white-coated volunteer corpsmen with Red Cross armbands in the crowd from time to time.

"Most of them are young doctors, med students, ex-corpsmen," the reporter explained. "It's really quite something to see them work. They're beautiful."

"Last time I saw you," Carlson recalled, "we were covering the Democratic Convention in Chicago when Adlai had Steinbeck holed up out at Northwestern trying to give his speeches more grassroots appeal. Remember Kennedy making his run for the vice-presidency from the balcony?"

"Right. You should have been at the *last* one." He showed Carlson a still-pink stitch along his left jaw.

"Jesus, politics are really getting rough," Carlson said.

"Crazy! What did you think about McCarthy?"

"Even less than I thought about Adlai. You know, a stiff dick has no conscience."

"Poor bastard."

"Nixon isn't troubled that way. A real drudging, seat-of-pants *schlepp*."

"Well, good seeing you again."

"You bet. Keep in touch."

They had only time to see a bit of the first floor of the museum before the guards began rousting the thousands of hippies who had come inside to get out of the cold. Two were hauling a stoned freak and his chick from Henry

Ford's little WWI tank. They stopped to watch. The older men were not being rough with the kids. They wore expressions of disbelief, the exasperation of those shoveling sand against the tide. One told Carlson, "No sooner do we get a pair out of something than another pair has gotten into something else. There were people *sleeping* in here last night. Found a couple in the backseat of that old Stanley Steamer we got back there. We're closing the place up. Can't keep up with them."

Carlson offered the harried old custodian a nip. But he refused it, dashing off toward where another freak was preparing to bed down under the "Spirit of St. Louis" exhibit.

Outside Carlson said, "They'll be findng kids in there for a week. They'll have to search every damn exhibit twice."

They took a wrong turn and found themselves at the edge of Abbie Hoffman's demonstration in front of the Justice Department. A phalanx of the Progressive Labor Party was offering to join forces if Abbie's group would in turn march with them against the Department of Labor. A deal was struck. But when those in the forefront of the protest against Justice began trying to smash in the enormous bronze doors the Progressive Labor people decided they had been caught on the wrong side of the uprising and tried to make amends by directing their monitors against the Chicago group. Minor jostling ensued.

The first shove on the door brought the government's flying squad from some subterranean holding point, advancing behind yard-long nightsticks, white helmets atop gas masks. From behind them came high-lofted tear gas canisters, breaking with soft pops and seeping ground-hugging white smoke. A Progressive Labor Party member in his forties, in mackinaw and Lenin cap, raised his hands to stay their advance, to explain *his* point of view, cop a plea. He caught the tip of a stick right in the teeth, thrust like a bayonet by a black cop. The man went down and disappeared in the onrushing crowd. The cops split the group in two.

Carlson, hurrying with Paige and Luke on each arm, ran

toward the adjacent open parade. He saw a stocky girl, her long hair tied back with a bandana, stop and pick up a gas canister and throw it back over the front line of cops. Her braless big breasts leapt with the effort, hauling her sweater up over a fine round belly. A cop knocked her flat with a stroke alongside her head. Others in the rear scooped her up, spreadeagled, one holding her head, two others at each leg, and rushed her to the rear. Yippies, freaks, Progressive Labor people, middle-aged women in galoshes, scattered in all directions. The cops cleared the street and formed a cordon around the outer curbs, leaving the Justice Department building awash on a low, foggy sea of tear gas. As after any battle, the area inside their perimeter was strewn with bits of clothing, the ever-present odd shoe, and an incredible amount of paper.

Carlson stopped in the lee of a building. He bent Luke's head over his arm, held his eyelids open, and washed the boy's eyes lavishly with the sterile water in his canteen. Paige stood by, gallantly trying to help, tears streaming down her cheeks from behind her glasses, running with a touch of mascara into her wet mouth. He washed out Paige's eyes next, then tilted back his head and doused his own.

His stepfather used to beat the shit out of Carlson when he was a boy. He hadn't actually wept over anything since he was twelve. He thought perhaps something had dried up his tear ducts. In any case, he did not produce much moisture to counteract the burning of his eyes. He laved a thin coating of Vaseline on all their faces. The faint odor of alfalfa, skunk, and exhaust fumes hung over the area.

"Let's find our bus," Paige asked. "Please."

"Right. You okay, son?"

"I'm okay, Pop."

"Good boy."

They started looking for their bus by walking miles in the wrong direction. Buses were double-parked on both sides of the streets at the rear of the monument. They tried to find bus number 743. It was growing dark. Carlson began to wonder if they hadn't made a mistake about the number when they spotted bus number 741. He popped inside to find the black driver and a white girl, who looked no more than fifteen, balling on the long backseat. Paige was behind him. He said, "Excuse me," and almost bowled over both Paige and Luke getting off the steps.

They trudged on for an hour more, following the lines of buses. Paige had a blister. Luke could hardly walk. Carlson supported the boy with his hand, talking to him. "You can make it, son. If we don't find our bus soon, we'll just hop on any one and take it where it goes and get a room. You can make it, can't you?"

"I'll try, Pop. It just feels like my feet and legs are dead. It hurts all the way up to my butt."

"Why can't we stop and rest?" Paige begged.

"Only for a minute," he said.

"Why? Why are you so tough? Poor Luke is about to fall over."

"Because in this cold, you will tighten up. It will be worse than just keeping going, slow but steady."

"Oh, you and your goddamn theories!" She took the boy's other arm. "Go on, darling," she encouraged the child. "Let go, cry if you want to. It's all right. Go on. Let it all come out."

Luke shook his head that he would not do that. "I can make it," he croaked.

"He can make it. Tough it out. Take long easy strides. We'll get there," Carlson said.

"*Damn you!*" Paige stopped. "You think you can simply carry everyone on the strength of your goddamned will." She shouted as man and boy continued on, not breaking their pace. Soon she came at a crippled lope to catch up.

Carlson put his hand under her arm, high up under her armpit, and lifted just that much burden from her feet.

A gentle, tired traffic sergeant at the intersection where the street ran onto Hunt's Point advised them: "Your bus could be there or it could be back down Maryland if you didn't find it in town. There are buses backed up all the way into Virginia. Sorry."

They elected to try Hunt's Point. It was another three

miles out to the tip. People in the same plight as their own were scrambling aboard any bus that was leaving, regardless of destination.

"If it isn't out here, we'll catch one and get us a room," Carlson promised.

At the farthest tip of the point they found their bus. Someone told them Adelle had been seen at dusk getting onto another bus. Luke had to leak. So, suddenly, did Carlson and Paige. She went to squat under a bush. Carlson and Luke stood at the railing above the inlet that separated the Point from the airport across the water. The lights of the airport winked on the water. Luke pissed a stream halfway to Virginia. Carlson laughed and loved that boy as he had never loved another human being in his life. He was a far braver boy than Carlson had been, far less frightened. How long had he trudged with blisters on his feet and his bladder about to burst? He was going to be a hell of a man, no matter how he turned out.

Mark. His other, older son's name popped into his mind. Often when he was with Luke, watching the boy grow up, he thought of Mark and worried again if he had made the right decision to stay out of this son's life. Sharon had remarried again, Carlson's grandmother had written, soon after he left Wichita, and so he had let reunion with Mark remain a memory. But, God, he missed that kid, felt so fucking guilty each time he thought of the boy.

He bent and kissed Luke. "I love you very much," he said.

"I love you too, Papa."

"Well, we're on our way home. You ought to be able to write a hell of a report for school. Been tear-gassed and everything."

"Yeah!" The boy brightened.

Roll call produced only half their original number, though the bus was completely filled in a matter of half an hour.

"Let's go to New York!" a young man from the seat behind Carlson, who looked as if he could be an actor, with a very stunning brunette who could have been a model, shouted happily. They hadn't been on the bus originally.

Carlson and Paige took a drink from the bottle he had, toasting each other, then Luke. Luke took a snort, toasting them. The young man and woman behind them thought it was the greatest thing they had ever seen. Carlson gave them the bottle and told them to pass it on.

As Carlson's bottle made its way around the bus, he produced his sandwiches and distributed them by halves to Paige, Luke, and the couple behind. They had some good rosé and French bread and cheese. Soon everyone was offering and sharing groceries as if at a picnic. The driver was given a sandwich, whiskey, wine, coffee.

"It's just *beautiful*." Paige welled up and kissed Carlson on the mouth.

Luke turned away from what was none of his business and was soon asleep across the aisle.

With the lights inside the bus extinguished, they again passed an area where the streets had been cleared with tear gas. The still lingering essence seeped inside the bus, making their noses and eyes smart.

Paige snuggled down on Carlson's shoulder. He kissed her passionately several times, put his hands inside her coat, and covered her breasts.

"I can get out for the Andy Warhol Show in a couple of weeks. We can go to my aunt's apartment," she breathed.

"Okay," he agreed.

"I love you," she said.

"Love you too," he replied, wondering what in hell he meant. Lots of times when he said "love" to a woman, his mind flashed to Caroline. He had loved her truly. He wasn't substituting "love" for "fuck." But now with Paige, he only knew, all things being equal, he wanted to get between her long legs. Somehow it was all tied with the obvious happiness of the couple in the seat behind them. He would have liked to have lived like that.

When his bottle came back to him, there was still a drink left in it. Everyone had thoughtfully left something for the next one.

Perhaps that was how it would work with Paige.

He killed the bottle.

Thirty-Three

AFTER THE MARCH on Washington, Paige and Carlson began to find excuses to walk away from the others at the playground, taking their children to the zoo and other wondrous places in the park. They met for drinks in out-of-the-way bars when both were going to be in town at the same time. They held hands and kissed a lot and spoke of being alone together soon.

About two weeks after Washington, Carlson was sitting on a bench in the playground while Luke terrorized mothers with toddlers by zooming around on his skateboard in a pair of cut-off jeans, his knees and elbows red with Mercurochrome and plastered with the largest Band-Aids; Jean dinged about on her pink tricycle with her Sasha doll clinging on behind. Paige came into the playground on long purposeful strides, trailing her daughter, Zandra. She carried a battered old doll in her arms. As soon as she entered the playground, she broke into a beaming smile, eyes glistening as if she had drops in them.

Carlson felt they were closing toward something. He felt more than love and desire for this leggy, slender woman with such soft breasts and thighs. She was an American princess, but one who had been an ugly duckling and therefore was real.

She stopped directly in front of Carlson, smiling, and extended a closed fist like a little girl offering a surprise. He put his opened hand under her fist, his fingers touching the pulse of her wrist. She put a key in his hand and wrapped his fingers around it.

"I can get out all evening tomorrow and I don't have to be back until late."

"What's this?" He grinned.

She dropped down next to him, close enough for their hips and thighs to touch.

"The key to my brother's apartment. He isn't there. He hardly ever uses the apartment."

"Tomorrow?"

"Yes . . . You *can*, can't you?" A frown wrinkled her brow.

"Yes."

"Good!" She sat back and smiled.

He took her hand and squeezed it tight. Over by the sandbox the eyes of many mothers were on them. They assumed the mothers supposed they were having an affair. Still . . . Paige had already confided in Lynn Paterson, her best friend, and probably had said something to Anne, another friend about whose affairs she had been told and was supportive to the extent of her ability. Anne was married to a musician, more into drugs, sexual circuses, and whatever was going down at the moment than either Paige or Lynn. Carlson didn't like Anne much at first. She was out of Barnard, one of those pretty, aristocratic-looking women with a snobbish ability to absolutely erase from the landscape anyone or anything she did not care to deal with. He considered Anne somehow threatening, though he hadn't figured out why she should be.

Leaning forward to help her daughter, an excruciatingly shy little girl, put on a pair of plastic roller skates, Paige bent far over her knees. Carlson let the back of his hand brush the length of bare flesh between her skirt and waist. When she had finished, she touch the back of his hand with her nails, and mouthed "Tomorrow," like a kiss.

They held hands tightly for as long as they dared.

They left the playground together with their three children. Jean liked Paige and was chatting with her. She touched Jean's hair and laughed at something the child said. Luke was walking ahead. Zandra held onto one of Carlson's fingers. For a moment, in the richness of Paige's laughter, he really felt they were a family, the family neither she nor he had ever properly had. It felt good. A quiet feeling of possessiveness came over him. He put his free hand around her waist and it felt totally natural. It felt right.

They met in Manhattan at La Fonda del Sol.

It was still a good bar then. The restaurant had never been much, but the bartender was from Guadalajara and made the best Margaritas this side of Mexico City. Carlson was working his way around the frosty, salted top of his first one, nibbling the fat Spanish peanuts from the big bowl before him, leaning on the bar rather than perching on a stool, when Paige blew in—literally: it was not only her way, but the result of a persistent, chilly, blowing rain that had been sweeping the city since before dawn. He knew when it had begun because he hadn't slept well. He had gotten up several times during the night, debated taking one of Margaret's Doridon tablets, then decided against them for fear of being logy for the next twenty-four hours afterward. He had stood sipping orange juice in the living room watching the last lonely queers and junkies trying to score at the corner of the park when it began to rain. The lonely men fled for the subway up at Grand Army Plaza.

He felt good about Paige. She had become everything he ever thought a woman should be. Staring at the rain falling like minnows through the high-intensity lights along the park, which were supposed to make the night safer for citizens, he prayed that Paige and he would be beautiful together, dreamed of the two of them in Paris in the spring and up at a lodge in Michigan with their kids at Christmas time.

He didn't know how they had reconciled it with their spouses, but he dreamed they were married to each other and watching their children play at shaking great falls of snow upon each other from the lower branches of trees. Deer came for handouts. The kids fed the deer from their hands after being shown they needn't be afraid. There was a Christmas tree in the lodge's main room only slightly smaller than the one they put up in Rockefeller Center. There were gifts wrapped prettily beneath it. When the children were tucked into their beds, Paige stood by the fireplace in the sleek, black, bias-cut gown her mother was wearing in the portrait. It fit every plane and curve of her model's body. There were delicately strapped party sandals on her feet. Under the gown she wore nothing but a musky perfume that mingled nicely with the smell of the tree and the fire. Shadows of antlers and horns reached toward the lofty beams above. They made love on a bearskin rug before the fire, and it was all good.

There was time and money enough to do everything they really wanted to do. Sail the seas, explore, write, create a life that was full of love, which neither of them needed to find a word to express.

Sometimes Paige went shopping with Truman Capote and they would have ice cream sundaes and gossip, after which she would arrive home horny as hell, and act like a tall slut, wanting to be fucked on the floor or atop a billiard table or against a wall. He had never thought of Truman as an aphrodisiac either way, but that is how the waking-dream ran.

Before she even took off her new trenchcoat, Carlson kissed Paige soundly, possessively. Men in business suits who had been watching her turned back to their drinks. The bartender smiled approval and made her a Margarita and topped up the peanuts.

"I love you," Carlson whispered in her hair.

She laughed and squeezed his hand.

"How many of those have you had?"

"This is the first."

"That should be all right then."

They smiled at each other.

They sipped their Margaritas and looked at each other over the salted rims. He wanted to tell her about his dream but when he mentioned it she frowned and said abruptly,

"No more dreams."

He assumed she meant this was the real thing.

He had never felt so anxious about making love to a woman he truly wanted. To reassure himself, he told her again, "I love you, Paige."

She said she had just been to her broker, ordering the man to sell all her stock in companies known to be supplying chemicals and war materiel for the government's effort in Vietnam. She wanted her money in something she could live with, even though it meant a loss in dividends. She said he had advised against the move and she'd had to be tough about it. She was still acting a bit tough.

In the car, a big blue Ford station wagon, Carlson put his hand between her knees as they crept through the rain up Sixth Avenue. He threaded the wagon between a battered yellow taxi and a moving van with two inches to spare on either side, made the light at Fifty-seventh, and accelerated through the fire lane past central Park. Paige finally relaxed, closed her eyes behind her tinted glasses, then opened them and smiled at him. He reached over and patted her leg between her knee and short skirt. She opened her bag and slipped the list she had been clutching inside. She slid across the seat and his right hand squeezed the inside of her thigh. She wrapped her long fingers around his wrist in answering pressure.

"I love to drive with someone who can really handle a car," she said as if it was something she had not done in years. She slid over next to him in the seat like a midwestern high school girl out with her steady, dropping her left hand along his thigh, raked it gently with her short nails. Her right hand slipped up to grasp his bicep tightly.

She wore pantyhose over bikini panties. He felt the warmth emanating from her soft sex.

"I hate pantyhose," he said, a smile crinkling the corners of his eyes.

"They are God's gift to women—maybe not to men, but certainly to women," she replied.

"Eschew all gifts of God," he advised her. "They always cost you more than the convenience is worth."

"Next time, for you, I'll wear stockings," she promised.

A Puerto Rican truck driver alongside stared from the high cab of his battered truck, honked, and shouted something in Spanish. His partner leaned across the driver for a look. Carlson shouted back in the same cadence as the driver's obscenity, *"Chinga tu mano, compadre!"* And sped easily ahead.

Paige closed her eyes happily and pushed herself against his hand, gripping his arm and thigh tightly.

Driving up Central Park West, he cut over on Sixty-fifth Street, finding that the parking lot where Paige had left her car had a FULL sign blocking the entrance. He whipped a left turn and found a metered parking place in front of a small delicatessen.

"You will get a ticket here," she warned.

He reached for a bottle of wine in a brown paper bag from the backseat, got out, and walked around to let her out, but she had not waited. She never waited for a man to open doors for her. He locked up the car, then stepped around and turned on the siren burglar alarm that had a key-switch on the left front fender.

"You'll get a ticket." She was certain.

He put his arm around her waist reassuringly, and they moved along the rest of the block together, her long strides matching his own, yet totally female in their leggy swing. He didn't give a damn if he got a dozen tickets.

Nearing the apartment building entrance she again became haughty, purposeful. The uniformed doorman touched his hat and smiled. "Miss."

She nodded and called his name: "Joe." She swung directly through the marble foyer to the elevator. A distinguished, gray-haired man, slim and neat in blazer and ascot, nodded a greeting in exiting the elevator. She smiled and said, "Good afternoon."

Going up she said, "He's a television executive. Has the penthouse." She had pushed the button for the eleventh floor, only one floor below the penthouse.

At the door of the apartment she fished a key from her bag and opened the door into a large room that smelled as if it had been closed a long time. Most of the furniture was under white dustcovers. She turned when he stepped inside, the door closing against his back, and slid both her arms around his neck, pressing against him so he stumbled slightly backward, the door supporting him. She offered her mouth in a ravenous, passionate kiss, all haughtiness and assurance flowing out of her. Clutching the wine bottle behind her back, he gripped her soft yet furiously tight ass with his right hand as she moved to find his cock with her sex. Her tongue drew his tongue into her mouth. Their teeth clashed in the intensity of their embrace. He began to become erect against her seeking body. She found him, shuddered all the way to her toes. She broke off the kiss and gasped for breath. Then she sighed completely, smiled such a sad, tearful smile there was nothing he could do but tell her, "I love you, pretty lady."

He kissed her gently, sweetly, deeply, trying to love her as he had never loved anyone in his life; trying to live only and fully in the moment; trying to become truly connected with this sad, beautiful woman who had needs he felt he could never fulfill. He pushed her gently away, holding up the bottle. "Let's find some ice for this. And get some air in here."

All capability again, she took the bottle and flitted away toward the small kitchen off the large L-shaped room.

He ran the draperies back, then the net curtains, found the cord for the venetian blinds, and ran them up to reveal Manhattan framed like a picture postcard. Below, dumpy women in raincoats were walking their little dogs. A wino was already on the nod on one of the benches, oblivious of the weather. A citizen stepped automatically around the leavings of the women's dogs.

"Oh! Champagne!" Paige exclaimed from the kitchen. "Good champagne!"

She carried the wine in a sweating silver bucket to a low table in front of the covered divan. She sat it down and busily stripped the dustcover from the divan to reveal plush green velvet. Next she stripped the cover from the great winged chair by the table.

"Can't find a way to get these windows open," Carlson said.

"They don't open. You have to do something with the air-conditioner."

Beneath the window was a room-length heating-cooling system. He opened the little control door and fiddled with the knobs until stale, dusty air began filtering through. In a few minutes the system had cleared itself and fresh air began pumping gently into the room.

Streetlights glowed on the pavement, cutting through the rain, as he stood at the window. In the street below, the women with their little dogs had fled for the security of double-locked doors to tune in the outside world via stereo and TV. Carlson had never been with a woman surrounded by so much luxury. He turned from the window.

She was curled on the divan, her feet tucked under her, the sheen of fine nylon sweeping in luxurious length back into the down-filled brocade from which peeped the patent toes of her pumps. She was smoking, the cigarette held in her left hand before her smiling, expectant face, her right arm extended along the curved back of the couch. Two crystal champagne glasses stood ready beside the silver bucket.

"This is really great," he said, though more with wonder than enthusiasm.

She smiled in the dim light. She was pleased, but there was still no joy in her eyes.

She was so much a part of it all to him—the furniture, the expensive books, the silver, crystal, brocade, and down —the expensive view. He wanted to embrace it all, feel a part of it. Yet knew the only key to it hung between his legs. She wanted *him*. For his part, he wanted something more than her, something that had very little to do with the trappings within which he found himself. He felt nearer to the soaking wino on the bench than he did to the beautiful woman on the divan. He felt like a burglar. He was about to be caught in some kind of ridiculous lie for which he felt only minimally responsible. He twirled the wine gently in the bucket without a sense of guilt, only a misplaced sadness.

He removed the cork without fanfare, saw the smoky effervescence from the bottle's mouth. She lifted her glass. They touched glasses.

Her face over the rim was so like a sad child's on her birthday; he wanted to warn her against high expectations. He was awed, fragmented, his mind in no way connected with his sex. He knew everything he was supposed to do. He kissed her. Her mouth was soft now, yielding, her right arm curled around his neck.

He sat in the chair facing her. She extended her legs, her ankles across his knees. He removed her shoes. She set down her glass and arched herself, reaching under her short skirt to peel off her panties and sheer tights to where he could skin them the rest of the way from her tan legs. He placed her right foot on his cock and relaxed back in the great chair, taking up his wine. She fondled him gently with her pedicured toes.

"You're beautiful," he said.

She laughed. "Oh, God, Carlson! I used to be the ugliest, most awkward, awful thing you ever saw. I hated myself when I was a girl. The only person who ever called me beautiful in my whole life until I was in college was Mama's friend Ali Khan."

"Yeah, you told me. But I find it so hard to believe. I mean, you *are* beautiful. You always had to be beautiful. I know! I *know!*" He waved away her protest. "I've read all about poor little rich girls. Margaret's mother was a beauty like your mother—one class down, but the same thing. Kept her daughter plain at all expense."

Paige said, "You don't know how often I saw kids, poor like you were, who could ride their old bikes and seemed to be doing all the things I could never do—having real fun, you know? Darling, I was so fucked up."

Her toes were giving him an erection. Her long legs running straight and prettily back to her crumpled short suit skirt, her pubic hair just peeping from the nubby hem. He stood and pulled her up from the divan against him.

They kissed. He could feel her warm tears on his face. They ran into their mouths. He swept up the back of her skirt with his right hand and felt her soft smooth, high posterior. With his left hand he unzipped himself and let his cock begin to rise against her already wet sex, finding its way through the hair.

She gently broke off the kiss. "Let's go to the bedroom." She led him quickly into the other room. She stripped the dustcover from the bed, leaving it covered with a dark velvet spread which, in the dim light, he could not define as blue or maroon. It was tasseled in gold around the edge like the curtain at Radio City Music Hall. She undressed quickly, yet with grace, letting her clothes fall carelessly about her, arms raised and head bent to unpin her hair. She moved onto the velvet bed in an utterly feminine series of movements—left knee raised, arms out, right leg at full extension, buttocks white and soft in the dimness, long pale breasts swinging loose. Then she was on her back, flicking her long blond hair out from underneath her in a single motion, smiling wanly, arms upraised toward him, left knee cocked a bit over her right, her dark-nippled breasts squeezed together beautifully by her slender arms as in offering.

"So beautiful, lady," he said.

As he moved to her, her arms opened to slip around his neck, her breasts lolled to either side of her chest. He went into her easily. He felt the rolled rubber ridge and greased membrane of her diaphragm covering the hard neck of her uterus. Like his wife, she was afraid of getting cancer from taking the pill.

"I have polyps," she said as if she sensed some need in him for an explanation. "I'm going to have them removed. But I hate doctors." She kissed him wetly, smearily, and began to fuck. "Oh, um, yes," she crooned. She moved nicely.

But he began to lose it. She increased the tempo of her passion to revitalize him. He too began to try and pour it to her. She drew back her legs, locking them high across his back to get more of him. He gripped her by the ass with both hands, moving her by body and hand with his entire strength. The bed sounded as if they were in Persian heaven. But he was flaccid within her. He stiffened slightly just before he came, but only slightly. Her need was so great. Yet his need was greater, and far less explicit. He was coated thinly with cold perspiration in the stale room. Her perfume and his smell were good. His heart pounded furiously against her breast. Her hands soothingly stroked the length of his back, his buttocks and thighs.

"It's all right," she crooned. "It's all right, darling."

"I'm sorry," he panted.

"It's all *right*. Really."

"I love you," he promised her.

"I want you so much . . ." the last swallowed in her hiss, her slender arms again painfully tight bands around his heaving body. He slipped from her, kissed her breasts, her belly, would have gone down on her, but she stopped him because of the jelly and the diaphragm and drew him up beside her. He drove her to wild shaking with his hand, massaging her erect little clit, then thrust his middle fingers deep within her, bouncing her rubber-covered uterus, ringing it until she approached climax, but could not quite make it, falling off in a long, low, agonized moan of frustration. He went back to her clitoris. Then, when she trembled uncontrollably, wet, dilated, wanting, he entered her with his thumb, stroking her slick, clean rectum with his forefinger, entering it slightly in concert with the movement of his thumb in her cunt.

She yanked furiously on his dead penis, moaning, "*You!* I want you. I want *you*."

"I want you too," he breathed beside her wet cheek. "But death wouldn't raise the sonofabitch."

"I don't care. I want *you*," tugging him on top of her by his limp member.

Lost within, grinding pubic hair against pubic hair in an insane charade of intercourse, more furious for their frustration, he again managed to ejaculate without ever achieving an erection. Exhausted, she fell back limply from the brink to which she had so willingly aspired and had not achieved.

Again he apologized, angry at his impotence. "Jesus Christ! Paige, here I am in a better place than I have ever been with a beautiful, beautiful lady whom I want to be good for more than anything at this moment than I have ever wanted, and can't get it up. SHIT!"

"Shhh. It's going to be all right. I love you. Forget about it. I'm content. Maybe if I kissed it . . . ?"

"No!"

"No?"

"No. It wouldn't work. I'd hate myself more."

"Don't. Really, I'm fine. You know, maybe if you didn't think about me as beautiful *lady*. I don't want you to think of me as a lady. I just want you to take me. You're a big, strong, beautiful man. You fuck like a bull. I'm no lady. I just want *us* to be together. Do you know?"

"I don't know. I want you too much, perhaps. Perhaps you are right. Still . . ."

"Well, just don't worry about it. I'm not."

He bounded off for the champagne. When he returned, she had covered herself with her short chemise. She hadn't put it on, only laid it over her as she sat with her back against the headboard of the bed.

He stopped with bottle in one hand, glasses in the other. He was not ashamed of his body, only his performance. He felt fine being naked before her. "You're very beautiful to me," he told her. Her light hair flowed over her shoulders and arms. She looked like a Käthe Kollwitz drawing. But she nodded her head in refusal of his compliment.

"Hey!" She smiled.

"What?"

"I love you, Cat."

"I love you too, pretty"—he caught himself—"baby."

"You know something?"

"What?"

"It's going to be just fine."

"Isn't it nice to think so?"

"Oh, baby, come *here*." She extended a hand. When he was beside her, she took his face between her hands as if he were an errant child. "Listen. Don't let it get you down. Really. I am very happy. Just love me. Forget that 'pretty lady' crap and we'll be just fine. Okay?"

"Yeah."

So they drank the champagne, talked, and cuddled for the better part of an hour. When he asked, "Do you want me to make you come?" she said, "I really don't think I can. Sometimes I have a very hard time. Besides, it's getting late. I've got to be getting back. What did you tell Margaret?"

"That I was going out. Going for a walk or something."

"Doesn't she ever suspect?"

"What?"

"That you are screwing around."

"This hardly qualifies as screwing." He sensed he had bum-rapped himself to the limit of her patience. "Sure, she always *suspects*."

"What do you do?"

"Lie outrageously."

"Why?"

"Because a lie is easier for her to believe, even when she's certain it is a lie, than the truth—whatever *that* is."

"Do you and she . . . ?"

"Fuck? Sometimes. When my need is greater than my distaste for how it is with us, or her need or responsibility buoyed by Scotch overcomes her frigidity. Do you think frigidity is infectious?"

"Definitely, darling."

They were dressing quickly now. She could get herself together in about five minutes flat. She was re-covering the bed.

"Perhaps that is what I've caught. I feel like I ought to give you back your key."

"*Stop it!*" She faced him. "If I ever want it back, I'll ask you for it."

"Right. Good enough. You are all right, Paige." He sat on the bed to put on his socks and shoes.

She came over and laid the side of his head against her flat belly, tousled his hair. "It's going to be all right. Just have faith in me."

He ran his hand up under the back of her skirt and caressed her now cool, smooth bottom. He kissed the mound of her sex through the nubby cloth. "Okay." He slapped her ass and bounded up. "No more 'lady.' Just a tall broad who fucks like a snake."

"That's it!" Her face was beaming beneath those goddamned sad eyes, so full of need.

They kissed.

He walked her to her car. It sat, now alone and cold-looking, in the empty lot. He kissed her again and put her in the vehicle.

"Thank you," he said.

"Don't *thank* me," she insisted.

"Oh, I always thank the girls," he said.

"Okay, then. Whatever."

He closed the door. She passed him, headed down Seventh Avenue, her chin high, hair wadded into its soft bun, her face already set for walking in her door.

Carlson walked to his own car and drove toward the Brooklyn Bridge, the key to Paige's younger brother's apartment in the overburdened case that hung from the car's ignition switch.

Off Atlantic Avenue in Brooklyn, he turned onto Fourth Avenue, hitting all the lights to Carroll Street. Driving past their business, he glanced up at the big plate-glass windows in which lights burned brightly all night and saw that all was well.

He had to park two blocks away from his apartment. He was suddenly hungry. He was anxious to see his kids. There was a night football game on the new color TV. He would make salami sandwiches on French bread and have a bottle of Heineken's beer and watch the game with Luke.

At Paige's apartment the lights were all on. He saw her head, then her husband Al's head, following her across the window toward the part of their apartment where the bedrooms were.

He felt he could fuck her now. Then he forgot about it, looking forward to the game on TV and the company of his son. Jets and Patriots? Jets and somebody. He was already anticipating the certain strikes of Joe Namath's clean, crapshooter passes.

He supposed it was his newfound serenity that made him certain he would be able to fuck Paige the next time. He had no doubts. Two days later, when he was again in the park with Luke and Jean and Paige came with her little girl, he could watch her walk over to him with an almost lazy enjoyment.

She looked cool and more elegantly beautiful than he remembered. There was a promise of luxuriant sex between her thighs and a hint of wildness in her sleek hips that was immediately provocative, and he felt his scrotum tingle in arousal. Right there in public he wanted to open her blouse and put his mouth to her sweet breast and suck on it, and he wanted to grab her ass in both hands and pull her sex hard against his. Right there in the park in broad daylight. He wanted to rip her expensive clothes off and fuck her on the park bench, or up against a tree. But he kept his hands in his pockets and smiled when she sat next to him.

"Cat," she said.

"Hi." He looked to make sure Luke was still on the swings and Jean at a safe distance by the sand pile.

"I want you," he said.

"I want you too."

"I want to fuck you. I want my stiff cock in your beautiful cunt. I want my hands full of your pretty ass and my mouth full of your breasts."

"Cat," she said again, and blushed.

"When can I see you?" he said.

"Tomorrow, okay? I'll say I'm going to a movie with Anne. I can't wait to be with you."

"Baby," he said, "you don't know what anxious is."

They met in front of Paige's brother's apartment, conscious of each other's every move going up in the elevator with a small boy and his dog.

He barely had an erection, they had barely kissed, when

she shed her clothes in a pile and pulled him down on top of her. She was almost desperate to have him inside her. He tried to kiss her but she was pulling at his soft cock frantically and trying to stuff it through her thick muff.

"Wait a minute," he said, laughing.

But she couldn't. Her wet cunt was gobbling ravenously at his cock and she was moaning and scratching his back.

She excited him terrifically. His cock became engorged and he rammed it into her. She grunted and grabbed the cheeks of his ass to pull him further in.

"Fuck me, Cat, fuck me!"

He raised her ass off the bed and fucked her furiously. Her legs jerked and quivered spasmodically until she came, and came again, and he kept fucking her until she was sobbing and limp and then he exploded inside her. And stiffened. It was like an electric shock through his body, and there were brilliant splinters of light, and then he collapsed on top of her exhausted as she hugged and caressed him to her breasts and moaned warmly, "Oh, that was so good, Cat, so wonderful, never like that before."

Then they slept.

"He is so good." Paige was trying to explain the other man in her life, the one she had been having an affair with before she and Carlson got involved. "I never knew anyone like him," she went on. "He's incredibly bright, he's been everywhere, he's knowledgeable on practically everything. He's so different from my husband. I always felt I entered another world when I was with him. You know, the best restaurants, the latest books, knowing *everybody*.

"We were together for four years," she continued, her hand playing lightly with the hairs on Carlson's chest. "He would talk sometimes of leaving his wife, but I never felt he meant it. I couldn't tell you when it began to be over. Oh, I still enjoyed being with him, and I knew he always found me desirable. But months ago I sensed something and he did too, I'm sure. It was just that we really like each other, and we had loved each other for all those years; it didn't seem right to walk away. But when I met you . . ." She stopped.

"Are you still seeing him?" Carlson asked, a sharp stab of jealousy in his belly.

"I'm not going to," she said. "Not that way at least. I'm going to tell him about you."

"You don't have to do it like that."

"Yes, I have to. We've always been totally honest with each other. He'll understand. I told you, it hasn't been the same for a while."

"Even so," Carlson said, "it won't be easy."

Then he added, "I don't want to lose you."

She smiled. "Don't worry about that."

They met nearly every afternoon in her aunt's apartment and made love beautifully each time. It seemed almost too good to be true. And they talked. At first about Paul, Paige's former lover, and Margaret and Carlson.

Then Carlson talked about his writing in general terms, the first time he had talked at all about it to anyone, and that was all right too. He even let Paige read parts of the finished manuscript, and she was very moved. She said it was the most beautiful thing she had ever read, and cried.

But when Carlson told her about his futile experiences trying to reach a publisher, the long months of frustrations and rejection slips, she became strangely quiet. She appeared to almost recoil.

Carlson asked her what was wrong, but she said nothing.

Finally Paige came out with it. "If you want me to, I think I can help you with your writing."

"How?" Carlson was surprised.

"I know an editor who'll read it, if I ask him to."

Carlson almost said: And who's that? But from the look in Paige's eyes, it was obvious and he said instead, "Paul?"

She nodded.

Carlson shook his head as if in wonderment, but actually more at the fickle finger of fate and the corniness of the coincidence. Then he had to smile. It was a break.

"If you want me to," Paige said again.

"If *I* want you to? Does that mean *you* don't want to?"

"No, I want to do it, if it'll help you."

Carlson read her feelings. "But you'll have to tell him the manuscript is from your lover, isn't that it?"

"I guess."

"Then don't."

"But you need to find a publisher. You have great talent, Cat. You need it recognized, and I have no doubt it will be some day, but why not now instead of later?"

"That's sort of what I've been asking myself."

"Then give me your manuscript and I'll take it to him."

"But if he knows it's from your lover—do you see what I mean? He's going to be delighted to tear it to pieces. If it was the Twenty-third Psalm, he would still tell you, and me, it was a piece of shit."

"No, you don't know Paul. He'll be fair, and professional, I know. He's very honest."

"You think he can keep his personal feelings out of it?"

"Yes."

Carlson shrugged. He had nothing to lose. "Okay, let the bastard read my stuff, see what he thinks."

"Don't call him a bastard."

"Well, he's your friend, not mine."

Thirty-Four

PAIGE HAD INTRODUCED them awkwardly and excused herself. "I would only be in the way while you two talk."

She left them sitting at a little table in a corner where the service should have been bad, but Paul was known and catered to. Their drinks were brought promptly and refilled thereafter as if by magic.

They sat facing each other silently for a moment.

Carlson immediately took a dislike to Paul, who was apparently completely at ease. The man had an air about him that Carlson viewed as "superior." His face was pleasant and to most women probably handsome. He was graying around the temples, expensively dressed, and well manicured. His voice was cultivated in a manner that suggested a wealthy upbringing. Carlson could picture him as a snotty little rich kid who grew up on an estate and attended private schools, and had gotten everything money could buy.

"So—" Paul smiled through their silence.

"So," Carlson answered and waited.

"After reading your material, Mr. Carlson—"

"Call me Jarl."

"All right, Jarl—Well, I can't tell you how much I've been looking forward to meeting you."

"So?" Carlson wanted to be surly, felt like it.

Paul seemed to know exactly what was facing him and changed the subject effortlessly. "How's your drink?"

"All right. Not bad." Actually it was damned fine Scotch, much better than bars usually pour.

"How about some lunch now? They make a wonderful quiche."

"Is that what we came for, to eat?"

"And to talk about your writing, but—"

"Then let's get on with it. Say what's on your mind and let's get it over with. I don't have time for fencing, okay?" The guy could stay with the rapier if he wanted to, Carlson preferred using the ax.

Paul leaned back and sampled his drink and then spoke forthrightly. "You're a sour sonofabitch, aren't you?"

"You want to discuss personalities?"

"I'd rather discuss your writing, but you don't seem quite in the mood."

"Look, I know what you're here for, so let's cut the cutesy banter. Let's level. Paige's told you about me, and she's told me about you. You're not making it with her and I am, and that sticks in your craw, doesn't it?"

The blood drained a little from Paul's face but he kept his composure. "It was over between Paige and me before she met you."

"Sure, sure. But I am the one making it with Paige now, and you're going to try and put the knife in with my writing. That's the way it is, isn't it?"

"I'll have to admit, I considered it."

"All right." Carlson spread his hands in an open gesture. "Now that we've gotten past the footsies, let's hear it. You need to vent your spleen, have at it. I'll trade you lick for lick. What I can't stand is all the fucking subterfuge." He downed a stiff drink.

Paul considered a moment before speaking. "I appreciate honesty and candor. It's a rare thing these days, and sometimes surprising when you find it. You haven't made it easy."

"Come on, Paul, out with it. I promise I won't punch you in the mouth."

"Your writing, well, honesty was one of the first things that struck me about it." He paused.

"But?"

"But nothing. It's very honest, very fine writing." He stopped.

Carlson sat for a moment before it registered, what he

knew he heard. Still he was suspicious and kept his guard up. "Yeah, very honest, very fine, but what?"

"Well, it's not finished. You would need to cut parts of it, for example."

"Hell, I'm prepared to work."

"It's a truly fine piece of writing, and if you do the revisions, it will be a remarkable first novel. Maybe even a great one."

Carlson took another drink. "You're joking with me. Don't do that, Paul, I warn you."

"I'm not joking, Jarl. You have real talent. What you've written proves that beyond all doubt. But you don't have a finished book yet, and a finished book is difficult to do well."

Carlson smiled. "You sonofabitch, you almost had me going. But I know what you're doing now. Trying to put doubt in my mind, aren't you? That I can't do the final stuff."

"No, that's not it. I was trying to lead to something else."

"Well, I'm going to sell this novel, that I know. So whatever you say now doesn't matter. I know I'm going to do it, I don't give a shit what happens. And fuck you."

Paul shook his head slowly. "You're a defensive sonofabitch too, you know that? You've got your guard up before you even enter the ring."

"And you're a patronizing bastard. Who the hell do you think you are anyway?"

"We don't like each other, do we?" Paul sighed.

Carlson laughed. "That's the first straight thing you've said."

"And since we don't like each other, we may not make it."

"You're already married, honey, and so am I." Carlson was being sarcastic.

"I'm talking about working together."

Carlson had a glimmer then of what was coming and couldn't believe it. He held his breath.

Paul leaned forward. "Look, Jarl, I came here to meet

you because I wanted to make an offer on your book. I think you've got the makings of what could turn out to be a very fine novel."

"Now wait a minute." Carlson wanted to get it straight. "You mean you're making an offer."

"No, I said I came here wanting to, but now I don't know. We obviously don't like each other, so it's going to depend—"

"On what?"

"On you, I suppose. If I make the offer and you accept, then I become your editor, and you'll be working with me. Now, I don't really care about personalities. You can be a sonofabitch, which you obviously are, for all I care, and I can separate a sonofabitch from his work, if it's good enough, but you may not want to work with me. I think that's what it comes down to. If you can't keep me and my editorializing separate in regard to your writing, then it's no go."

Carlson felt a little stunned. Somebody, a real editor, had wanted to make an offer, but hadn't made it yet. And maybe wouldn't. There was a clinker in the works apart from his writing, a sort of catch, and it appeared to be simply Carlson himself.

He thought hard for a minute, and finally said, "I think I've got it straight, but you seem to be holding out a carrot. Now what kind of shit is that?"

"To tell you the truth, I've never found myself in this particular situation before. I've probably spoken my mind more than I should have."

"The thing is, you don't like me, right?"

"That's right, and you don't like me either, right?"

"Right."

"Then, you see, that's sort of the problem, isn't it?"

"Yeah, I don't know that I'd want you messing with my book. I don't like your 'airs.' " Carlson realized the strong Scotch had gone to his head and he was a little high.

Paul doodled with his finger on the table. "Look, here's the way it is. I can separate my dislike for you from your writing. So I'm going to make the offer and you can think about it. I'm going to take a chance that the book you've started will be what I think it could be in the end. You decide whether it's in you to be professional and put aside personalities too, okay?"

"What's the fucking offer?"

"A two-thousand-dollar advance against royalties. A third on signing the contract, a third when the first-draft revisions are in, and a final third upon completion and acceptance."

"*And* acceptance?"

"*And* acceptance. That means you can't fake it and write shit and expect to get paid. It has to be publishable and more. Anyway," Paul left his card and stood up to leave, "that's my offer. You think about it, and especially about having me as your editor. Then you can either accept the offer or stick it up your ass." He turned away and took a step before stopping and adding, "I mean it about your writing Carlson, it's really very fine—very fine indeed." He left.

"Indeed," Carlson said as he looked at the card and read: Paul Chapman, Senior Editor, Fischer and Franklin, Publishers.

Fischer and Franklin, Publishers, was one of the largest and most prestigious publishing houses in the world.

Carlson whistled silently and ordered another Scotch.

He tried to get drunk that night and couldn't. The liquor didn't seem to affect him at all, and when he tried to sleep, he couldn't do that either. Anyway he knew what his decision was.

He called Fischer and Franklin the next morning and asked for Paul Chapman, got his secretary, and finally Paul.

"This is Carlson."

"Yes?"

"I accept your offer."

"I'll have a contract drawn up and sent to you then."

"When?"

"You'll get it next week."

"Okay—thanks."

"Yeah. Congratulations to you and we're looking forward to a long and happy association between publisher and author, and all that stuff." It was what a publisher usually says to a new author, only more nicely and sincerely.

They both hung up without further comment.

It wasn't quite the way Carlson had imagined placing his novel. He had perhaps dreamed of an exciting reception, a few drum rolls at least, an embrace, a ticker tape welcome into the golden realm, the red carpet treatment, something for chrissake to herald his debut. But that wasn't the way it was. He wasn't even euphoric. There was a bad taste in his mouth and the whole thing seemed mean.

His first impulse had been to simply ignore the offer. There was no way, he thought, he was going to form a working relationship involving his writing with some bastard he flat didn't like. That would be no good at all.

But when he tried to get drunk and couldn't, one thing kept coming back to him: The guy *recognizes* my talent. He *likes* my writing. He must. Or, otherwise, because he hates my guts, he damned sure wouldn't say so.

Then it occurred to him because there was no friendship, no feelings to be concerned about, Paul might be the very best kind of editor to have. He would concern himself only with the work and not the writer's ego. He would say exactly what he thought and couldn't care less if it hurt Carlson's feelings. He would be absolutely honest. No pussy-footing. No bullshit.

And that's what I want, Carlson realized. I want the most honest and direct appraisal I can get. If I'm going to get the truth out, I've got to be able to receive it, and with no bullshit attached—Paul, you sonofabitch, you're my man.

Margaret cautiously didn't believe him. "You sold your book?"

"Yeah, Fischer and Franklin, Publishers. They made an offer yesterday and I just called them and accepted."

"You have a contract?"

"Coming next week."

Margaret had to see the contract before she was convinced and then she didn't know what to think, but she started looking at Carlson a little differently. And she was going to wait. When the book was truly finished and in print, well, maybe then she could credit him. Maybe then she'd believe he was a writer, but it seemed so unlikely.

They had remained strangers during the long journey of their life together. Only occasionally had he glimpsed her fears, insecurities, vulnerability—all the things he suspected had made her stay married to him. She shared the fears of most women of her generation. Where would she go if she didn't have the rock of her marriage, crumbling as that foundation was? Her sense of identity, like that of so many other women, came not from her business success, which was extraordinary, but from her identification as wife and mother, greater signs of achievement than any she could have outside her home.

With her considerable intelligence, Carlson was sure Margaret understood this. But there was a wide, insurmountable gap between understanding and acting on that understanding. She would stay with him. She would be *Mrs.* Jarl Carlson. And in its blind way, the world would smile when she passed.

As for himself, he suspected he needed hostility from his wife, he had to have that separateness that kept him to himself. It was probably why he could not have married Caroline. It was not in him to stay close to anyone for any length of time. He could not bear the emotional dependence. He could not face the possibility of its loss.

So, strangely suiting each other, he and Margaret stayed together.

Paige was thrilled. "Oh, Cat, I'm so happy for you!" She attended to his body with special effects and rewarding new warmth. She started calling his one good ball her "little Balzac." And his cock his "real protagonist."

But when Carlson seemed distracted, as he soon started

to be—the fact he was going to be published acted to spur him and was increasingly more lost in his writing thoughts—she became suddenly suspicious of only having been used.

"You knew," she accused him. "You knew about Paul and me before I told you, didn't you?"

"What are you talking about?"

"You knew I was going with him, and that he was an editor, and you planned it, didn't you?"

"Planned what?"

"To get your manuscript to him through me."

"Don't be silly."

"You were only using me."

"If I only wanted to use you, why are we still together now?"

"It doesn't seem like we're really together anymore. Sometimes I don't feel you even know I'm with you."

He tried to caress her and soothe her. "Hey, come on, you know better."

They held each other and tried to make love but neither could really enter into the spirit and the more they tried, the more impossible it became.

Finally Paige eased away. "Well, something's happened. It's not there now, is it?"

Carlson felt rotten. "I'm sorry. You're right, sometimes I am miles away. I don't know, I guess now that I know my book's going to be published I'm too wrapped up in it."

"And you knew I was going with an editor before I said so, didn't you?"

"No, I didn't. I wanted you, just you."

"Yeah, sure."

"I did."

"But you don't now."

"No, I do. I still want you, just you, but—I don't know. My writing, I guess, takes over. I can't help it."

"And I can't help feeling like a second fiddle either. Because that's exactly what I am now, isn't it?"

Carlson covered his eyes with his arms and sighed deeply. Sheer wonderful sex was so complicated. The body and mind were so godawfully intertwined. One little signal could slip off the track and the whole tangly system would go haywire. The more you had going on above the belt, the less chance you had of anything great happening below. Sex was so simple if you could concentrate on it without actually concentrating on it at all, if some other more compelling interest didn't take over.

Paige and Carlson began seeing each other less often, and once again Carlson was aware of how he became involved with fine women and how they never lasted with him, but this time it wasn't something he dwelled on.

Something else had become acutely more important to him.

At Paul's request, he had cut the manuscript to nine hundred pages; he called his editor, who merely said to send it to him, which he did.

Then, after he had read the pages, Paul called back and suggested they meet to discuss the matter. The phone calls were short and to the point, and Carlson arrived at Fischer and Franklin, Publishers, at the appointed time. He was promptly ushered down the hall to Paul's office. The receptionist had known he was expected and acted as if he always had a standing welcome. In a way it was disconcerting that he was allowed past her this time when, before, all the gates had been so closed against him. I'm the same person, he wanted to tell her, the same talent, you should have let me in then too. You should give all writers a better chance, dammit, you damn sure should. What the hell are you afraid of?

Paul was matter-of-fact in their discussion, and Carlson was tense. It was his baby they were about to dissect.

"This character you're building here," Paul held up some pages to show the subject, "does he know where he's going?"

"Some things happen to him further on, in the next chapter. That's explicit, I think."

"But does he know where he's going?"

Carlson felt caught and finally said, "No."

"Then you should make that plain. It's important." Paul put that section aside and went on to another while Carlson held his temper. Dammit, he had created that character, knew him like he knew the palm of his hand, what the hell did the damn editor know about him?

"Now this whole business on the aunt—" Paul showed more pages. "Where does this lead?"

"You don't think that's interesting?" To Carlson that was a very nice series of incidents.

"Yes, I think it's interesting. Very. I like it. But where does it lead?"

"Nowhere, that's it. I wanted to put it in."

"I think you should leave it out entirely. It doesn't add to the story, in fact, it detracts and slows the story line to nearly a halt at that point."

Carlson held his tongue.

Paul went on, "And here, the scene goes on too long."

"That's good dialogue. They're saying a lot of interesting things."

"But it goes on too long. The confrontation is resolved but you go on then too long and bore the hell out of the reader. I would suggest you cut it here." He marked a place.

Now Carlson came back. "Bore what reader? You're the only reader so far."

"In my judgment, if I'm bored, most readers would be too."

Carlson gritted his teeth. Paul was an arrogant bastard. "Okay, what else is wrong, in your judgment?"

"That's it, so far."

"Good." Carlson stood up and gathered the pages. "Just those matters, not much at all, was it?"

"A helluva lot. You just criticized the best parts, the real guts of the whole thing."

"Overall, I think it's coming along very well. Just those points you might think about."

Carlson left without another word. The bastard had challenged parts of his work and stung him. The parts, too, that Carlson had liked the most.

But when Carlson collected his feelings and calmed down and considered his writing again, more objectively, he knew Paul was right. And he made the changes accordingly.

He started making other changes at a faster pace as he began to see the light at the end of the tunnel, and the knowledge that his book was going to be published and people were definitely going to read it lent him greater energy. He would finish the final draft in six months. Every day didn't pass without a stumble, of course. A great deal of his writing was plain work and sweat, a mental struggle, and sometimes emotional turmoil, but his soul was driven, and nothing stopped him for very long.

He submitted about every hundred of his revised pages to Paul and each meeting he had with the editor was cool and conducted with an air of detachment, but also less disturbing as he grew to respect the man's judgment. Paul was invariably astute and had an ability to instantly separate the husk from the kernel. They had their arguments and sometimes Carlson won, but Paul always made a valuable contribution. And as their relationship went on, Paul curiously became a kind of inspiration. Carlson found himself eager for his approval, and his dislike for the man personally began to wane. He no longer thought about liking him or not.

Once he found out something about Paul accidentally, in an overheard conversation in a bar frequented by a literary crowd. Two men were discussing an editor named Chapman. And Carlson couldn't help listening closer when he heard the name. They were saying something about Chapman's drinking, that he had been on the skids, but for some reason he had taken hold of himself and was working hard again, not drinking any more at all. He had not done well with the last several books that he had edited, but now he seemed to have found something— Carlson didn't hear what—that he was very interested in. Something that might even give his sagging career a new boost.

At their next meeting, Carlson pointedly asked Paul, "By the way, what are some of the books you've edited in the last couple of years?"

"You wouldn't be interested."

"Some dogs, huh?"

"Worse than that."

"How come?"

Paul hesitated. "I don't know, they say athletes go through a slump, maybe editors do too."

"You had sort of a slump."

"You might call it that." He wasn't going to describe it.

For a moment Carlson felt a little sorry for him, that the man had been saddled with impotency, that it must have thrown him for a loop, but he asked, "You need a good book to your credit right about now, don't you?"

Paul didn't flinch. "An editor can always use a good book any time. And writers too, don't you think?"

The man had his pride, you had to hand him that, and beyond that, he knew his job.

Paige seemed to have slipped from the picture without mention.

As Carlson knew he was nearing completion of his novel, he became anxious. He felt a little like a mad scientist who had worked meticulously to put together a body, and it was almost all intact, the whole torso, but in the end would it actually come to life and live and breathe? To the scientist, it was a beautiful creation, but would others perceive it as a perverse monstrosity? Would the thing be loved, or hated? But the main worry now was: would it come to life, or be stillborn?

Carlson searched his work for the vital signs. He went over it again and again like a master sleuth to make sure no detail had been overlooked, to be certain he had enough evidence for proof that where there was smoke there was fire.

He agonized.

Finally he had six hundred pages stacked neatly in front of him on the table, but for some time the end of his work didn't quite sink in. He kept thinking there needed to be something more, another paragraph, another sentence, something. He read through the final chapter again slowly and critically. When he came upon a misspelled word or typing error he felt almost grateful. A small correction was something he could still do to the thing, and there were sentences he still might rearrange, ideas he might rephrase, words he could replace possibly, or even a conjunction here and there he could switch—but he knew: there was nothing really important now he could do to all those pages. He could sit till doomsday and worry a few words around but it wouldn't make any difference.

The story was all there. The book was finished.

A great weight seemed to lift from his mind. "I'm finished," he said to the empty room. "I've done it."

He curled on the sofa and slept soundly for fourteen straight hours and didn't dream.

Paul was cautious about the finished manuscript. "I like it, Carlson. It's solid. But now, you know, we have to wait and see."

Carlson had hoped for more enthusiasm. He hadn't expected the reserved editor to exactly jump up and down and shout, "Hooray!" but he had expected a little more praise, a little more light in the man's eye. Hell, the editor didn't even shake his hand or pat him on the back! And worse, he had another damned year to wait for the finished book. Not until the middle of 1971 would he feel like a real author.

The manuscript came back to him copy-edited; it looked like it had been severely graded by some fussy high school English teacher. There were red marks all over the place, and he was a little shocked. His first fear, that they had totally rewritten his story, however, proved false. It was mostly grammatical corrections, and not much else.

Then the first galleys came and for the first time he saw his story in "print."

It read like a real story and somehow seemed infinitely more interesting than in manuscript form. It also *looked* like a real story. He could begin to imagine it bound between hard covers. The galley's title page announced the author: Jarl Catlin Carlson. A helluva name for an author, a damned fine great-looking name! It had been printed in Gothic Bold.

Carlson savored his first impressions of the galley for a day and a night before it began to appear to him alternately wonderful and puny. In the library there were thousands and thousands of stories in the same kind of print. There were title pages with other authors' names printed on them in row after row. There were so many books in the library that were never read, and their authors never known or heard of again. His could very well join the hordes of the unread and undiscovered and neglected.

The fact that it was in print was no assurance of fame or immortality. No assurance at all.

Margaret read the galleys and commented, "Well, I'm surprised. It's very well written, Cat. A lot of it is very beautifully written, in fact. I cried at the end—but—"

"But what?"

"It didn't seem like you. I mean, I never got the feeling you wrote it."

That obviously perplexed Margaret, but it pleased Carlson no end.

Carlson didn't know his prospects or the situation he faced, and if he had known, he might not have cared. The important thing with him was: He had written the best he could. That's what counted. He was a writer. And he would continue to write no matter what happened. If he never became famous or wealthy, or even recognized, so what? He had done his best with what he needed to do, with what he was, and no man could cut the mustard any better than that. He knew he still had worlds inside him he'd never be able to get out completely, and that he'd never be able to write as well as he wished, but it was the journey that mattered, not the pot of gold at the end of the rainbow.

Before the galleys went to press he finished the opening scene of another book. It was about a boy dreaming of being a soldier, and he would become a soldier, then a man.

Some time before publication of his book, one day when it was raining and dismal and Carlson was in a somber mood, Paul called.

"I've got some good news," he said. "We've just received word"—he paused purposely for effect—"you're a book club selection. Congratulations."

Carlson didn't respond immediately.

Paul spoke again. "Did you hear what I said?"

"Yeah, book club selection—what does it mean?"

Paul laughed in the phone. "It means you've just been passed through a secret door, a very narrow opening."

"Is that right?" Carlson didn't feel anything yet.

"That's right. You've just been separated from the herd."

"And now what?"

"We still wait and see a bit. But I believe you can rest assured you're better off."

"Better off, huh?" Carlson was beginning to smile.

"Definitely. But as I said, we still wait and see."

"About what?"

"I don't want to tell you. I don't want to get your hopes up too much. I know how sensitive writers are."

Carlson noted a touch of warmth in Paul's voice. "Well, it's the first time you ever sounded like my sensitivity was something you had to be concerned about."

"That's because you're hardheaded, Carlson. Kid gloves wouldn't have worked with you."

"I might have appreciated a kind word now and then."

"Yes, you might have appreciated that, but you didn't need it, did you?"

"I guess not."

"Anyway, the book club is a very good thing. You have been singled out. Let's wait and see what happens next."

What happened next was a lot of softcover houses bidding on the paperback rights to his book, with one of them finally offering an astounding one hundred thousand dollars. Half of that sum, of course, would go to the hardback publisher, but the other half still made Carlson delirious. He would be able to live and write wherever he wanted. There were articles in the papers and magazines about his sudden success and about him as a new literary light on the horizon.

He had made it! Glory hallelujah!

In May, 1971, his book came out. Carlson had thought the appearance of the book itself would be an anticlimax, but it wasn't. It was a thrill to finally see it, to hold it, and to open its covers. He placed it on a shelf and stood back to look at it from a distance as a customer might in a store. The title on the spine leaped to the eye boldly and the book itself was a wondrous sight.

Life is a miracle, he thought. And I am very, very lucky.

Thirty–Five

IN THE HEART of New York where the dirty yellow taxis prowled in grimy streets in prides like so many gut-shot beasts, Jarl Carlson experienced a shivering déjà vu of the Tiger Balm Gardens of Hong Kong.

"*Come in! Come inside!* It's more than a gallery. More than a show. We have Billy the Kid in here. And Jean Harlow. It's all inside. Alive, alive-o!" The barker howled from the yawning jaws of a papier-mâché tiger's head, gesturing for all to step through the fangs toward yet another Andy Warhol Retrospective Show. The barker was a small, balding man with tufts of wiry orange hair. He was dressed in a caricature of a 1930s double-breasted, pin-striped suit, standing in tiny boxed-toed brown and white oxfords, looking like nothing so much as a tout from a road company production of *Guys and Dolls*.

Inside, there were Andy's Campbell's Soup cans, Brillo boxes, the magenta, lime, and yellow Marilyn Monroes and Elvis Presleys glimpsed between the costumed bit players. In one corner people were drinking champagne from the navels of some pretty girls who looked like off-duty stewardesses—perhaps supplied by the caterer.

It *was* all very inside. Carlson was there by virtue of his reviews. They had made him a small celebrity in the world of the arts.

There was Viva showing her tits through chiffon, and Ultra-Violet, who resembled a young Hedy Lamarr with raspberry jam in her hair. There was Andy's own left- and right-hand man, who might indeed have been Billy the Kid in a former life, although this Billy was a wide-eyed, totally American urchin who had never pulled a knife on anyone.

He was earnestly confessing to Mary Devlin, who now was in New York writing on show business, that he was fifteen before he ever learned to catch a ball and had yet to learn how to properly throw one. He had never wanted to be anything but an actor, he explained, a revelation that had just come to him three months before when he was offered the part of Billy in an Off-Broadway revival of *The Beard*.

"What did you do before?" the young woman asked.

"Uh, I went to high school, you know. Then I hitched to the coast. You know. Nothin', uh . . ."

Jean Harlow was a mere imitation of Carol Baker's Jean, her small eyes burning through her ignorance solely with the arrogance born of her bias-cut silver satin gown beneath which she wore no underwear. Under her white makeup, around her mouth and chin, she was breaking out with pimples.

It was all a show. To Carlson, it had the quality of a drag queen ball. Everyone, indeed, was there—except Andy, of course. Andy would not have been caught inside —dead or alive-o.

Carlson stood off to one side until Mary finished talking with the kid. Carlson had worked on the Waukegan newspaper with Mary. What had it been? Fifteen years? About that. Christ! She had not changed. Still the kid just off the train from Nebraska, with all the bounce of a new rubber ball. She hadn't gained or lost an ounce of weight. Absolutely titless, tiny, black hair flowing to her waist, she stood in a pair of wedgies, out of which purple tights grew up to a pair of cerise satin hotpants which she topped with a sleeveless yellow pullover emblazoned fore and aft with magnificent appliquéd butterflies. There was a lot of premature gray in her hair. Her skin was yet unlined, like good vellum. She did not take the sun. Ingenuous, never on the make, she was a source of gossip sans malice that delighted Carlson. She knew the whole story of Eugene McCarthy in Chicago, and had a better theory on what really happened at Chappaquiddick than any Carlson had heard. She knew who all the famous homosexuals were and who were not—John Wayne, in spite of all wishful thinking to the contrary, was straight as a right to the jaw. When asked frankly, "Are all the beautiful people truly that beautiful?" she replied in total honesty, "Yes, they really *are!*"

She had the upper two floors of a house in Chelsea where she lived above a stone-deaf landlady, with an old-auntie beagle, Winifred, and two cats. She had an ex-boyfriend, Arnold, who had turned fag on her, living in the basement with his lover. She suffered heartbreak with an equanimity that surpassed saintliness. For Carlson could not recall any record of a saint who laughed, nor any graphic saintly representation in which joy shown in the beatific forgiving countenance. She never expected the world to be any different and never enlisted in any formal campaign to change it. But across her office windows on the twenty-fifth floor of the great literary magazine where she worked she had spray-canned in red the word PEACE in letters four feet high. It was a personal command that had begun when she was but a little girl searching the long prairie grasses for signs of the long-gone Sioux. She had sprayed it on with love and slight hope and no more rancor than she had felt when she had arranged for Arnold to move to the cellar.

Mary turned, clenched both hands into fists until her knuckles shone white. Then hands and face flew open as if she had flung open French doors upon herself.

"Cat! You *really* did it! Oh, sweetheart, what a great, *great* book!" There were tears of joy in her eyes that made Carlson shiver, his scalp crawl with delight, and yet humbled him with a curious sadness, as if her happiness for him was too pure for what he had achieved in his novel.

"Jesus Christ, Cat, you make me feel like I should never presume again to try and write a line." She kissed him on the mouth. "I'm really so glad for you. I got the book the minute it came out. I started reading it. I read all night. Didn't eat dinner. Didn't take Winifred out. She shat all over the hall. You really did it, baby!" She hugged him again. "I hope you make a million dollars. Just like I told you in my note."

He was nodding his head happily, unable any longer to look in her eyes. "I hoped you would like it."

"Like it?! Man, it's all the things I have always known but never really knew until I read it by you . . . You know?"

"I don't know." He put his arm around her waist and they sidled through the throng toward the champagne. They clicked plastic glasses and smiled at each other over the rims.

"You are going to be very rich," she said.

"Maybe a little rich." They toasted the book club and paperback money.

"How is Margaret?" she asked.

"Fine. You know."

"Is she happy about the book?"

"Well, she has read it. Came out of the bedroom and said very seriously: 'Good job, Cat.' With that total sincerity—you know—just short of shaking my hand."

"Are you two staying together?"

"I guess. She asked me, 'Will you give me a year?' What was I going to say, no? I owe her a lot. Yet, in a way, I feel she has collected it all."

He laughed. "Since that guy in *Esquire* compared me to Hemingway, I've been talking like him. *What I want, honey, is a queen fuck*," he said out of the corner of his mouth.

They both laughed.

"Here's to Ernest." She giggled.

"Seriously, Mary, I've become a family man. All I want is a woman who *tries* to look like Sophia Loren and thinks I'm God. Margaret won't try and knows better."

"Funny."

"Oh yeah. I laugh a lot about it."

"Man, when we were in Chicago, I wanted you so damn bad. And you were only making it with that beautiful doctor."

"Yeah." Carlson's throat tightened, thinking of Caroline. Damn, he missed her, still. His cock missed her, but his mind and heart did too. So many years and he could remember her laugh as if he'd heard it five minutes before. Shouldn't have left her, shouldn't have, shouldn't have . . .

"Hey, how was Rio?" he asked, eager to change the subject.

"Venereal."

"You got VD?"

"Listen, there is VD and there is VD, my friend. I went to my friendly gynecologist. He is sort of a putterer. I'm up in the stirrups and he is probing my exquisite vagina— I swear that is what he called it—and going on about air pollution. And he says, 'And now they are talking about putting in a new airport!' I shriek, 'In my vagina?' He says, 'No, in Queens.' God help us all. What I have is called Herpes Virus Type Three. It's as epidemic now as American hamburger joints in London."

"If you had told me, my guess would have been it was a great truffle growing," he said.

"Would that it were, man. Painful mother that penicillin can't touch. Think he swabbed me out with tannic acid and caustic soda. Don't even mention Rio and Mardi Gras to me. I hope the polluted bastards down there all kiss each other. Particularly one very smooth taxi driver with five kids."

They drank to the demise of all cabbies.

"What are you doing here in your sincere blue shirt and sincere stripedy tie, anyway?" she suddenly wondered.

"Sincerely waiting for a misguided child of midwestern wealth with very long legs who thinks I am going to ball her and save her soul, or at least make her life better. I think what she really wants is for some nine-foot-tall Black Panther to drag her into a doorway and rip the cashmere off her Mary Poppins, and I'm the nearest thing to that fantasy in our neighborhood. You can see, it is a very limited neighborhood."

"Anyone I know?"

"I don't think so. She's a photographer."

"But you said you were becoming a family man."

"Well, we must keep trying, mustn't we?"

The people moved around the gallery, rarely glancing at the pictures on walls. A tall woman, fingers nicotine-stained to the second knuckle on both hands, resembling

401

a basketball forward in drag doing Rosalind Russell, kept shrieking to the Harry the Horse she had in tow: "But do you think he is *serious?*" Serious coming out "*Sear*-ee-us!" The word being dragged alive and kicking through a length of tiny tubing.

Carlson and Mary moved into and through an enormous pipe in which most of Andy's movies were being shown on the continuous surface simultaneously, as well as upon the moving bodies and faces of patrons making the passage.

In an alcove beyond, her back to all of Andy's Marilyn Monroes, stood Gloria Steinem, who contrived to be one of the world's most beautiful women in spite of a slight Seven Sisters' school tendency to speak as if her jaws were wired. She stood head high and at full stretch, her honey-colored hair clipped back by the bows of slightly lavender-tinted Air Corps sunglasses. She did not blink as frequently as lesser mortals. Yet she was not afflicted by the forced necessity of maintaining sincere, boring eye contact with her audience. Her magnetism reached to the tips of fingers on the most eloquent, exquisitely feminine, capable hands Carlson had ever seen, long white fingers with nails like blanched almonds on each hand. Her left hand brandishing a Pall Mall waved wreaths of smoke around the purple, perennially floppy hat brim of Bella Abzug. Bella carried a raffia bag the size of a weekend valise crammed with God knows what legislation for the greater glory of mankind, and weighty enough to pole-ax a phalanx of decathalon champs. Norman Mailer in a vested Saville Row suit was doing his drunken Irishman number, having been convinced some years past by Jimmy Baldwin that there was no way he could be a spade. The former light-heavyweight champion, José Torres, stood closely by, listening intently. Every man in the room—that is, every man like Carlson who shared Mailer's pretensions to some essence left in the spoor of Hemingway, whether they were writers, poets, artists, ad-men, or what —was in love with Gloria.

Carlson smiled. From behind her tinted glasses their

eyes met across the gallery for the space of a single heart-beat. Did she think he was smiling at her? There was no electrical exchange in the fleet glance. Perhaps a wisp of wonder as light and common as the autumnal spray of cottonwood trees in the Great American Midwest from which they both had sprung. No more than that.

"She is what we all want to be," Mary said, shaking her blue-black hair.

"I'll drink to that." They clicked glasses. "Hey," he said, the thought suddenly occurring to him, "do you have a beautiful belly button?"

"I don't know."

"Well, there you are. How do you expect to be a perfect feminist when you don't even know your own body? You think you have an exquisite vagina because your gynecologist told you. If no one examines your belly button and tells you about it, you don't know."

She dragged her shirt out of her hotpants and thumbed down her waistband. In the center of alabaster flesh as flat and hard as a prepubescent girl's was a long, deep navel that, surrounded by forty pounds of additional flesh, would have been the glory of all Turkmen.

"It's a *very* good belly button," she said after examining it. "Come, look, enjoy a work of art."

While he was bent in inspection, a voice rasped behind him, "Now, what in hell is all of this?"

He straightened and turned to face a young woman as tall as himself who was not smiling.

"Belly-button inspection, Mary, Paige. Paige, Mary. Mary is an old friend from Chicago," he explained.

"I certainly hope so," she said dryly. The women shook hands without smiling.

She had walked over with the long strides of a pacer, always moving with the style of one who had complete assurance in fulfilling a very specific errand, peering myopically through silver-rimmed octagonal glasses tinted the same shade of lavender as Gloria's, which tended to slide down her rather small nose. She had spotted Carlson bending over the exposed stomach of a slender, modish dark-haired woman and felt for a moment all the terror she had known as a gangling girl absolutely convinced she was the ugliest duckling ever hatched by one of the most elegant swans that ever set sail on international social seas.

"Very nice to have met you," Paige said in her flat, husky, sorority, almost jocklike way, linking her arm possessively in Carlson's.

"Right," Mary replied, tucking in her shirt. As Carlson and Paige edged away, she said again, "Great book, Cat. What are you going to do for an encore?"

"Go after the Great White Whale. What else?"

"Good fishing, baby."

"See you, Mary."

Paige had the printed list of the show in the hand of the arm that was linked in his.

She said, "I have hated my navel since I had the children. I hope you haven't been disappointed."

"I have a bottle of champagne in the car which I will be delighed to drink from your belly button," he assured her.

She squeezed his arm. It was imperative that he meet her eyes in a long soulful stare in which she smiled like a virgin bride. Then glancing quickly from side to side, she kissed him fast and fully on the mouth. It was reaffirmation of the promise they had struck on the bus back from the Great Peace March on Washington a long time ago.

Paige's hand on his forearm was like a talon. Looking into her sad save-my-soul eyes in the beautiful, vulnerable face framed with soft blond hair, he felt as if he had already cheated on her.

She thought it was so simple. He wanted to explain to her there was really no way they could just do it—conditions being what they were. There was only the sad charade of love to be played out.

It hadn't been that way with Caroline. But that was a lifetime ago, never to come back. Now he had Paige.

"What did you say?" she asked.

"Nothing."

On the way out he looked back over his shoulder and

decided the scene looked less like a drag queen ball than a waystation for pilgrims on their way to Canterbury . . . with Bella Abzug as the Wife of Bath. Mary had edged over to the group and was rapping a mile a minute.

Still clutching her program to prove to her husband where she had been, Paige looked back not at all.